Review: Davis steeps her fictive world in evocative imagery—"He watched her eat daintily, the long thin fingers picking at her food like knitting needles"—and a vibrant, lyrical prose... While her characters weather hard lives and capricious fates, they still see loveliness and divinity in everyday life. Harshly beautiful stories, shot through with spiritual exaltation.

- Kirkus

ISBN-10: 0972838643
EAN-13: 9780972838641
LCCN: 2011903171

Author's website: www.AnnRDavis.com

LOOKING OUT THE BACK DOOR:

Visions of Past Lives

Ann Richardson Davis

Dedication

To all those noble, struggling ones
who need their stories told.

Contents

Author's Note

At first, I thought I should merely record these things that I "saw" and somehow just "knew." Later, when I decided to make a book out of them, my son told me it was missing something. He said I should also insert myself. I hadn't thought of that, but I realized he was right. I needed a biographical vehicle so that the reader could understand my feelings about this "happening," its extraordinary impact on my thinking and the path of spiritual growth on which it led me. I devised the "Dear Richard" letters to fill that need. I ask the reader to understand that although the editor named Richard is a fictional person, the account of how this happened and the steps of truth-seeking, God-yearning and spirit climbing that I experienced and express in the "letters" is quite true. Also, although I can't say for certain their origin, in my deep self I don't really believe the stories are "fiction," at least, no more than our waking present lives are. But, (although I know many people have had similar experiences) I can't expect others to believe the same. Therefore, I have decided to label them as "fiction" (a painful decision) because none of it can be proven and because I don't want conflict with anyone.

In this age, something exciting is evolving in the human consciousness. It is up to you, dear reader, to decide what you want to believe – and perhaps even to make it happen.

Just try to make it GOOD.

Dear Richard,

Thanks again for taking my call and consenting to read this manuscript. It's such a relief to have an editor among our friends. I don't feel so uncomfortable disclosing this experience to you; especially since you say you have been told of such things before.

As I told you, the first event happened when my husband and I were driving along on a trip to North Carolina. I call it a vision. I don't know what else to call it. As an artist, you can understand I have an active imagination but when I daydream I am always conscious of being in control of it, guiding it along, rejecting and accepting parts of it. This was different. It was just like watching a movie in my mind. I was not consciously controlling it. Actually, I was just an observer. Anyway, we were driving along on a rural road, no buildings on either side, just fields and trees flowing by, the highway coming toward me. When we came to an intersection, I had just told my husband that my ancestors had lived not far from that intersection. My thoughts turned to pioneers of the past; wondering how they lived. I know I was feeling unusually peaceful and this feeling expanded. I felt so good, so filled with love, when it happened. I saw this man: I saw him plowing his field; I saw his house, his wife. And I guess you could say that I communicated with him, in that if I wondered about something, he seemed to answer it, and in his own dialect. Richard, I didn't actually *hear* it, but I *knew* it.

Explaining this is the hardest thing I have ever tried to do. I don't think it really can be explained in words. It has to be experienced to be understood. It was delightful, though – such love and warmth that I have not experienced before. When it faded away, I turned to my husband and started to tell him about it, "I have just had the most remarkable..." And then I hesitated. Because only when I tried to explain it to him, did a sense of weirdness come upon it. I could see it then as it would seem to anyone else. Until then, it had seemed so wonderful, so *normal*, such a blessing. I plunged ahead, though, because he encouraged me to do so, this man of my life. Then he told me I should write down what I had seen. I made notes in the car and wrote it down when I got back home. I added to it later when I found that I could return to this place, these people, by lying down and relaxing. I had to be peaceful and uninterrupted. It was more vivid the first time it happened. I don't understand it, but I think the movement of the road coming toward me had somehow facilitated it.

I couldn't write the entire thing as I saw it (in present tense), but decided to put most of it in a story narrative that would not be tiresome for the reader.

It's strange, but I got this first story as a serial of three, each complete of itself, yet about the same family. When their story ended, I was stunned to find another one beginning – a new one with different people. As soon as I got all those notes down, another scene, another story began. Tell me what you think. Should I go forward with this? I will tell you the truth, it scares me a bit. What is this thing that is happening to me?

Heart's Home

There is a dark log house in the middle of fields, which are all tilled now. It is not a small pioneer cabin, but of substantial size, with a porch on the front. I see a tall, thin, raw-boned country man. Earthy himself, he loves earthy things, taking great satisfaction in growing his crops and tilling his soil. I feel great love for this man, whose name is Elliott, (pronounced "Ell-yut"). When I wonder what field crops he grows, he seems to say in a country drawl, "A little of this, and a dab of that"…a "right smart" amount of corn…and some carrots. (Carrots? I question.) Then his answer comes to me; "They're for my mules. They like a re-ward, same as anybody." He plows with a mule. He enjoys this work in the field, plowing. "Myrd" he seems to say, will "fix him up" in the middle of the day with food. When he has this mid-day meal in the field, he saves the bread — biscuit or corn pone — and taking off the wide-brimmed hat he wears, he puts the bread on top of his head. Then, shoving the hat back down over his brow, he continues plowing. Later, at the end of a row, he takes a break and stands there, chewing the bread, washing it down with a dipper-full of water from the wooden bucket placed in the shade of the tree for his thirst and that of the mule. When he is finished, he brings the bucket to the mule. He appreciates this animal that works so hard for him, and treats it kindly.

Sometimes he calls his wife, "Myrd-Bird"…and suddenly I can see her. A small woman comes out of the dark house in the background and makes her way down the front steps with a queer but appealing gait…She bobbles along, her head

nodding rhythmically with her little steps ("See?…like a bird," he seems to say).
Then I understand the nickname. Her real name is Myrtle, but it's his pet name for
this woman he loves. She is a neat, trim, little person…She always gets right to the
point, sparing words. "Big Bible reader" he seems to say. She is the one who tends
the chickens, ducks, geese, and guinea fowl. She is, he thinks, "afraid of nothing 'cept
death." Elliott is not afraid of death. He is in awe of his wife.

Later, I find that whenever I relax and allow myself to do so, I can "drift" back to
these people, of that place. Little flashes of scenes appear in my mind. If I question some-
thing, the answer just comes. Sometimes it seems I can feel and even smell things there.

One evening as I lie in bed, I can see the woman more clearly…Her scent is
clean – that of soap and starch. The stiff cloth of her dress feels scratchy against her
baby's soft cheek – but a more tender mother could not be found.

Her waist is trim and she has small, slim hands and feet, yet she does not ap-
pear dainty for there is a sense of wiry strength in the way she carries herself. Im-
maculate in her appearance, her dark hair is worn up off the neck – every hair in
place. Her dress has long, tapered sleeves – puffed at the shoulders – and is made
of good quality black broadcloth. She wears black often, which accents her neat
appearance. Her Sunday dress is embellished with lace. Against the background
of black a gold brooch glimmers where it nestles in the lace on her breast. She has
few articles of jewelry but those are fine heirlooms. She has a habit of tucking a
handkerchief up her left sleeve. When she points her finger with that sharp jabbing
gesture she often uses when speaking, the lacy top of the handkerchief flutters beneath.
When she scolds her infant son, he is distracted from her pointing, admonishing fin-
ger, his eyes following this enticing, waving handkerchief. It seems she is always in
the kitchen…I have a very distinct flash of a scene in full color, like a still life, yet
crackling with reality: A potted plant sits on the dark unpainted wood of the kitchen
windowsill. It is bathed in strong, warm sunlight. It vines across the thick ledge; the
whole of it – with its tiny round scarlet fruits, like miniature tomatoes – sharply
outlined in the light. For a split second my heart leaps – enthralled as I am by the

sight of it. Then, I am taken aback…for my mind asks why I should see this scene so vividly when it seems so trivial?

Myrd cuffs her sleeves and then puts on white over-sleeves, or cuffs, that cover her arms from elbow to wrist. Thus protecting her dress, she sets to work peeling potatoes in a basin of water. When she is finished, she fishes out the peeled potatoes and throws the peels and water out into the yard. All the fowl run forward expectantly, even though they do not eat potato peels, while the child sits in the doorway watching. It seems to him, as it does to the fowl, that only good things could come from this woman's hands.

Myrd was from a "fine" family – the Jacobs. They felt she had married beneath her, but she was very satisfied with her choice of marriage. In fact, she wore a satisfied – perhaps even smug – expression most of the time and hummed as she did her work in the kitchen. Her strength was sufficient for the work she did, so that she did not need a hired person to help in the house, such as her parents had had. Elliott was a good man and a tireless worker, so – unlike some women hereabouts – she didn't have to do much work outside. She was fastidious about her person and her house. Her everyday skirt was hemmed above her black button shoes to keep it from dabbling in the dirt outside. Her husband removed his boots at the door, and if any soil should trespass where it was not wanted it was not allowed to remain beyond the moment of her discovery but soon banished by her ever-handy broom.

It was evening. Dusk was drawing in around the dark unpainted house. It was time to go in. Elliott dusted off his hands on his pants legs and stomped his feet on the porch, then went inside to wash up. His slow footsteps sounded on the wooden floor as he stirred around the great room, occupied with their daily ritual; lighting a lamp, putting on his spectacles. The lamplight was warm and misty; casting a comfortable glow in the darkened room. Then he opened the deep Bible box and took out that "Blessed Book." He sat down in his chair – a rocker with a pillow headrest on the back.

(Myrd had made this ornamental pillow, ornately embroidered and fringed, but Elliott hated it because as the chair gently rocked, the fringe on the bottom of the pillow would flap back and forth, tickling his neck. He didn't say a word aloud, but she could tell. He would slap at it and his mouth drew down. At first, Myrtle was impatient with him – that he couldn't adapt to this work of her own hands, made for his comfort. Then she was amused at herself. Here was a man who made her proud, who pleased her heart. This pillow, beautiful though it might be and a symbol of her affection and good wifery, nevertheless made him uncomfortable. Her heart turned over for love of him and she got out her sewing scissors and whacked off the annoying fringe. She left the ugly stubble intentionally as a constant reminder to herself that such things were unimportant – that Love should always prevail.)

Now, as he leaned forward in his rocker, Elliott held the Bible on the corner of the table, tilting it to catch the lamplight. He read aloud as Myrd sat in her chair, a footstool under her little feet (for without the stool, her feet would dangle from the height of the chair). Her shoes were neat but snug. She never took them off until she was ready for bed, because her feet would promptly swell when released from them and she wouldn't be able to put them on again until the next day. But this was the happiest time of her day, no matter how tired she was. In years past, while she listened, she would sew – pausing now and then to dwell on the thoughts in her head that the scripture had evoked. Now, as she listened to her husband read, she had a child on her lap, his sleepy head resting against the ruffles on her breast. She was blessed by God and very content. There was comfort for them all in this daily ritual, and love was so strong at these times, that it permeated the house like a fragrance.

Elliott, calm and gentle, loved the earth and all that sprang from it. The essence of it had become his God. It hadn't begun that way. When he was young, he had seen things with shallow vision. You might say he inspected things; livestock and crops, how they fared and what they would supply. He had even assessed the girls of his acquaintance for wifehood. The times hunting, fishing, dances and socials, the taste of his mama's food, were fun and all but somehow it was all shallow dipping compared to what he came to realize later. After he and Myrtle had got their farm and built their house, while he was tending his land and growing his crops and livestock, he began to see what was not there, or what he had been blind to before. He began to sense things. They were what other people would call "small" things, he supposed. Stopping his plowing to hear the song of a bird, watching the magic of it, the ruffling, pulsing feathers of its throat, the bright eye, the pure, thrilling music rising to a pitch – he realized there was something more to it than what he saw. He had once seen a bird fall to the ground and, picking it up – the still dead thing it then was, he knew for certain that that disappointing dead thing was not the bird – that it had never been. That whatever was "bird" had flown and had been gathered up somewhere into all that was, that symphonic energy he detected all around him, in all living things, in the wind, the air, the sunlight – even rocks seemed imbued with it. All farmers knew that, he supposed, though none ever talked about it. But he learned to look for it, that unseen reality that dwelled within the shell. He marveled at the shell, how that which was not substance, could seem so real, while that which was unseen, which activated it, must be the ultimate reality.

Suddenly, I can smell that distinct odor of green corn stalks baking in the heat of the summer sun – The scent drifts through the house window. Corn seems to be everywhere, green, sharp-edged and fragrant. It makes a jungle of tall green spikes, marching right up to the front porch, and surrounding the house, except for the barnyard and back yard area.

This boy – the one child Elliott and Myrtle had been allowed to keep – was their "all and all." Myrd often called him her "dear one," "There's my dear one" she would coo, and the child would look up from where he would be sitting on the floor and his body trembling with excitement, he would hold out his arms and lean toward her like a plant to the sun. Those were his first words – he would call them both "dear one" before he learned "Mama" and "Papa."

He had got lost in the corn patch when he was a baby and had cut his soft mouth and hands on the razor-sharp edges of the corn leaves. At first, when he had wandered into the fringe of that wonderful, sweet-smelling growth, it had seemed delightful (for he loved the cornfields which surrounded their house). But then he had cut himself trying to taste those lovely leaves, and soon after, he was lost. All around him the dark green corn stalks towered above his head. Seeking escape, the only opening he could find was a small blue patch of sky above his head. When he looked up at it, he staggered and fell. The corn no longer seemed so warmly familiar. It was now a horrible jungle that cut his hands and made him bleed – a strange place with no way out. Panic rose in his infant breast...He wanted his "dear ones" to come save him from his trouble – as they always had in his short experience of life.

When they found him, he had finally given up blundering about and was sitting there among the white rooted stalks, staring upward toward that one open patch of blue sky and wailing his heart out (a pitiful sight). This experience had frightened them badly, for he was the only child they had succeeded in raising beyond infancy and their love centered on and surrounded him.

There was a dog on the farm, a mongrel but sort of setter-like, black, shaggy and lean. He jangled slightly as he loped along, from the metal doo-dads on a string that the child had made him a necklace of. The child called him "Moosey" and loved him. They would roll together in the dirt, the little boy laughing, the dog grinning, as neat little Myrd would watch despairingly but dotingly, from the kitchen window. It was a very happy home since the child had come. Her hopes had risen with the days that had followed his birth. He had shown no signs of sickness. It seemed she would be allowed to keep this one.

I have this picture of a back yard with four paved and covered walkways. At the intersection of these walkways is a covered well. It is centered there rather like the hub in the spokes of a wheel. There are stables somewhere nearby. This is a favorite place of the child, and he is very attracted to it. This vision of the well seems to draw me with a sense of importance, or looming, unwelcome knowledge…Danger? I wonder…But I notice it has a wooden cover over it, so that the child can not fall in.

* * *

Now, whenever I relax and allow the vision to come, I just see the well and feel uneasy…Nothing further.

* * *

Another day: Once again, I am drawn to the well. I have a feeling of dread and reluctance, then:

This chubby-legged little boy, trying to outrun his dog, races to the well and jumps up onto the lid with a thump, turning his head to laugh at the dog. But instead of it being safe (as I had thought) the lid snaps in two in the middle and the child, along with half of the lid, falls down into the well.

Screams echoed upward from the depths as he fell, his stubby fingers scrabbling frantically at the mossy sides on his way down. The well lid pressed down on him and the moss flew into his face...then the water came – so cold – it came over his face like an unforgiving hand, suffocating him. Where were the "dear ones"?

His mother had heard his scream and rushed from the house. Intuitively she ran to the well, shrieking when she saw the gap – knowing what had happened. Elliott heard her screaming and was there within minutes. Distraught, he tried desperately to think clearly how to save the child. He knew he couldn't lower himself into the well, because he was too large, too heavy for the rope and pulley to pull them both back up to the top and Myrtle was not strong enough to hoist both his weight and the child's back up again...There was no one else to help within miles....It would take too long to fetch help and come back...and all the while Myrtle was panicking – screaming to hurry, hurry, before the boy drowned. He explained that he was too large to go down the well. Well, then she would go down..."Hurry, hurry," she kept saying...for it was taking so long – too long.... Then she was practically over the rim before he caught her. He could see no other choice – time was flying by. His mind racing, hands shaking, he cast the bucket aside, wrapped the rope around her lower legs, securing the hem of her dress to keep it from falling over her head so that she wouldn't be able to see. Using the pulley he lowered the little woman, headfirst, down the well. The crank groaned and squeaked but she made it. He could hear her thrashing around in the water (she who had always been afraid of deep water). Myrtle held her breath and reached out...stretching her arms fair to breaking.... frantically searching in the dark wet for her child...the heart of her heart.

The child's fall down the well makes me nervous and upset, and I am glad to return to the present time.

Some days later, though, I need to know what happened....

They had got the child out and into the house, but there was no sign of life in the little body.

They had listened at the small chest for a heartbeat, and heard none...had felt for breath – even with a feather beneath his nose – with no success. Myrd, holding the child outward in her arms like an offering, stalked around the room keening and babbling. Elliott knew her reason was gone. He stared at her. Her face was white, her eyes straining from her head as she paced back and forth. She was no longer his familiar, beloved wife but a shocking stranger – and the shrill long-drawn out cries coming from this stranger raked up his spine unbearably. As she thrashed around the room, she would look upward to her blind God and down to her child...

Then an eerie change came over her that was worse than the wailing. She stopped stone still and silent, as she looked into that little face, for she had accepted the verdict of an unmerciful, unfeeling God. Her mouth was bitter, her voice rasping and the cold words she said sliced her husband's heart, for he could not believe she would say such a thing, nor would he believe it was true. She would lay him out, she said, before the little body became too stiff.

Her capitulating thought had been about how the boy had never had the chance to wear the fine baptismal clothing she had made with such careful, meticulous stitches, and had laid away for him...She wanted to dress him in it, now.

(The other children she had borne had died early or stillborn and never had she been able to dress one for baptism. Normally, the boy would have been baptized as an infant, but they had not been willing to risk tempting fate…Baptism would have been a sign of their high hopes and expectations that this child would live to grace their table and their hearts their whole lives- it seemed like it would be raising a flag for the enemy to fire upon. So – although they had not discussed why – they both agreed not to baptize him until they could be sure he would outlive his sisters who had been born before him. Then, when he had passed his babyhood and they had allowed themselves to hope, to dream of a future with their living son, their circuit preacher had been called away for some time to start another church, and so the baptism had been delayed awhile longer.)

Now, as she laid the white-faced child upon the bed, Elliott staggered away, shocked, by the scene in the room with the weeping – and it seemed to him – *lying, traitorous* woman.

He could not believe it – refused to believe it. He was numb. That grief, still waiting on the edge of his consciousness to consume him, could not be allowed to enter his mind yet, for it was too much for him. He drifted (unaware that his feet carried him there) into the front room. There, his glance hesitated on the Bible enthroned in the grand box that he had made for it – carved with grapevines – "for life." That cruel thought flickered through his shattered mind as he stood in front of the cabin window looking outward. No longer vigorous, loving and earthy, he seemed withered and struck by the harsh light of the day. Framed within that casement, this trembling white-faced man stared out and saw – not his beloved land bathed in sunlight – but a great, black void that stretched out forever.

His mind clamored in desperation. He was an honest man and normally humble, but there is no meekness in those who are truly desperate. Inside him was a scream was against God, but he snatched at it, tempered it so that it emerged instead as a prayer, "You say you will not give us more than we can bear," he whispered, "This is more than I can bear, and *you know it.*" Elliott wrestled against "reality" like Jacob with the angel, for he would not believe this terrible thing, it was a vicious dream. Yet there was also a traitor in him and much against the divine within him a sliver of thought tried to slide through the crack of the door he had shut on it – a glimpse of the future without the child. "Our only child, the last one, the only one that we can ever have"…"Oh, God, Myrd will never be the same, it will break her spirit and ruin her mind." But he steeled himself, rejecting it still – his whole soul revolting against it. "No! It can't be real! Oh, no, God please don't let this be real. It's an evil dream; madness!" he insisted, and clinging to this, he began to bargain," Oh, God, don't let it be – Don't let it be, and I'm your man, for the rest of my life, I'm your man." And although his mind was in shock, his spirit knew what he meant.

He was already a good man, a believer, but this was far more – this was deep commitment. He was offering himself into the hand of God, to always be subservient to his will – sincerely, totally his. Then suddenly everything slowed down and he moved into a place of precious stillness and absolute quietness. With it a presence came and calmed his laboring heart, filling him with powerful love. (Later he was tempted to think this strange, but it wasn't strange then. It was familiar – like an old and very dear friend, enclosing him within a warm promise.) While in this time-stall his stricken mind suddenly became clear as light; his thought, joined with this mysterious presence, became quite organized. Something was given him, yet words were insufficient for what was conveyed. "Always and forever you *are* mine" was the sense of it that he made, the translation he gave it. So sure was he that this entity was there that he opened his eyes to see him, but the vision was beyond his ability to see; his mortal eyes were blind to the presence that was both with him and inside him, yet it was there, sure as anything on earth. And so it was for he was one with it then, filled up with it, this overwhelming love;

this kind and gentle joy. Grief was forgotten. Somehow his peaceful heart knew that everything would be all right.

Meanwhile, in the bedroom, Myrtle was bending over the little body on the bed. She crooned lovingly to the child and wept at the same time while she performed the ritual. This had been the normal routine for generations of women before her – "laying out" the body of their loved one, before stiffness set in. She had done it before – her mother, an uncle, her two little girl babies. Ah, but none had been as hard as this! She could hardly see for the tears streaming down her face.

Bathing and dressing the lifeless doll in his fine clothes, she repeatedly raised and lowered the chubby little arms and legs, leaning the little body forward to button the many buttons of the blouse. Then, as the child was heaved upward once again, suddenly two plugs of matted stuff popped out of the child's nostrils. She heard – though it was barely audible – a gasping for breath…saw him shudder and stared in shock as the little face screwed itself up. His tongue was working against the roof of his mouth, trying to push out the stringy, mossy green and brown stuff that was clinging there. Then his blue eyes flicked open, the soft little lips quivered, he whimpered like a kitten…and he sneezed. Myrd's mouth hung open, her whole little body vibrating like a lightening rod as her wits struggled to believe what her eyes were seeing.

Her screams (not of horror this time but trilling with joy) brought Elliott instantly to the bedside as though whisked there by ecstatic and conspiring angels, for he hadn't realized that he had moved.

Elliott touched his son, looked into his living, bright eyes (Yes! There he was!). But hadn't he known it beforehand? Yet, when they had had their fill of rejoicing, Elliott began to notice a feeling of loss. That phenomenal awareness, that lovely possession, had eased away from him. Ashamed of being ungrateful, yet wanting to hold onto that which he had experienced, it was somehow no longer enough that his world was as it had been before – or was it the same? He tested for it – feeling around within himself for some glowing remains of that which had filled him up moments before, within that timeless space. He looked around him, hoping to detect the presence standing by in some invisible dimension... There was, he sensed, a lingering energy. This reassured him. That glorious powerful love was now banked down, peaceful, subsiding but constant, as though it only waited in attendance upon his will. Love and gratitude, so powerful that he was shaken by it, gushed from him toward that unseen but still felt presence.

Their boy had been returned to them! But then, he had never really died. It had been, in truth, a lie.

He would never forget this pivotal point in his life. The memory of it returned again and again and at those times he would stand stock-still and wonder about it. How such a thing could have been and how foreign to the world it was, for it could not, could never be, aptly described in words. Sometimes his mind would reach for one hopefully, one that would nearly fit, and would give it up yet again and shake his head. He was a simple man with little education, but he was sure no words that man had invented were sufficient for such an experience. They fell far short for they were meant for things of shallow depths, for worldly experience. His had been communion with God or Christ and They did not care about language. Any attempt by a man, be he a wondrous poet or mystic, to capture the voice and way of God would, even at best, be but a poor translation. He was humbled by it, then quickly upon this feeling would come the thought that how could such a simple, country man as he was, how could he have had such blessed-ness bestowed on him? But, whenever such doubt raised its head, his heart rose up and victoriously grasped the reality of the miracle and held it to itself, precious as it was. He would not allow such a wonder to escape him, to be taken away by doubt and false humility. He had been blessed. That was enough.

He thought about this recurrently. As he plowed his fields and shucked his corn, he struggled with man's perception of reality and truth. Which was which? How could one know? It gave him new ideas about the books contained in the Old Testament, about those violent words that seemed to conflict with a loving God. Maybe those prophets hadn't seen it quite right. But maybe it was the best they could do with the words they had. Yet, he asked himself, even though we do not see clearly at the time, even though we do not see the whole truth, shouldn't we try to share all we receive, even in its imperfect translation? (He didn't have an answer to this, for he was a gut-honest man and would not care to mislead his brother.) But surely, he thought, a man's way of living along with his words would be a testament to his union with his maker. Surely that was true.

So, Elliott, hard-struck by this miracle, became a flame by which many souls warmed themselves when chilled by the evils of mankind's making. For he remembered well the lesson – his temptation to deny the love of God and to accept suffering and death instead. His battle had been with the devil of man, the one who whispered that God willed suffering; that He stood upon the neck of His beloved creation and cared nothing for his pain. Elliott had proof that this was not so. Although he was, as promised, "God's man" he did not become a preacher, but he was a gentle shepherd to his flock of neighbors. Whenever he stood up in church, everyone fell silent and listened. His voice was quiet, but full of truth and conviction. Sometimes his fellow parishioners wept at his simple words. The flame within him never burned out during his lifetime (although during hard times, it may have flickered a little). He tried to pass it on, in the hearts of his beloved son and the converts he left behind. These were converts, not to a religion, but to Love and a forgiving heart.

He had illustrated to them that there actually was (in spite of all they had seen with their eyes) great good within a man.

* * *

Continuation: The Life perception of the boy:

Sitting in my chair months later, this came to me. Two little boys in bed. I don't see one very clearly, but I am conscious that he is there and that he has straw-light hair. The other one has dark hair. He is wiggly, his gangly legs and arms are all angles, sticking out of his too-big, borrowed nightshirt. This is cousin Leroy who has come to visit. He may be a bit silly, but his cousin is fond of him. The oil lamp casts big, lurid shadows on the white-washed boards of the ceiling and walls. They giggle and snicker and make shadow pictures on the ceiling, twisting their thin arms and fingers into grotesque shapes, then collapse giggling when they try to make pictures with their feet and legs. Can't make too much ruckus, though, or Mama will come in.

There is a built in cupboard and clothes closet on one wall. This little low cupboard holds the chamber pot. If one of them must do so, they can use it in the night. In the morning they take it out to the outhouse, empty it, and then rinse it out at the pump. They toss the rinse water into the bushes, return the pot to the cupboard and replace the metal lid. Once a week they put wood ashes and water into it, let it soak, rinse, wash it with lye soap and return it to its place. The privy is at the edge of a gully. Rain washes downhill, carrying residue with it to settle in a low area which was now green and rank with fertilized growth.

The boy, during all his growing-up years, loved to come late to evening prayer, so that he could stand some distance outside the house and look toward it. When the lamp was lit and the light spilled out into the darkening yard, his heart would leap with pleasure and he would stand for a few moments, savoring the scene.... tantalizing himself with the knowledge of warmth and love that awaited him inside. Then, when he had had enough, he would fly across the yard and into the house. Later, when he was grown with a home of his own, he sometimes passed the old house at twilight and he would stand outside in the growing gloom and look toward the window, yearning -- but no light glowed there anymore and the house lay dark and lifeless, an empty shell.

The "dear ones" were gone.

* * *

Note: The preceding story was followed by two others about the same people and place and those were published as "The Husking" and "The Stopping Place" in the book, "Heaven in a Hole in the Ground and Other Earthy Stories," Black-berry Books, Sea Griffin Publishing, 2003.

Dear Richard,

Yes, I think you must be right. My fear, however mild, does inhibit these experiences. Perhaps as you say, I am questioning it too much. Thank you for your reassurances. Your suggestion of self-hypnosis may be the correct one, given the highway coming toward me, the peaceful frame of mind, etc. But it doesn't settle the question of what *it is*, does it?

Yes, the first story does seem to hint at reincarnation – the boy in the story never actually being seen. I couldn't see further than his legs as an image – whereas the mother and father were seen and experienced in detail. The boy's fall down the well made me very anxious. It was as though I were looking through his eyes and feeling his anxiety. Over the years, I have come to believe in the continuation of life, before and after the present one, so I can accept that, if it is indeed the case.

There are some parallels in the story with my life and preferences in the present time, such as my strong attraction for old abandoned houses. I have always looked for one to buy and live in. It doesn't seem like home to me if it isn't old. When I was in first grade I painted a rustic little brown house and titled it "the old, old, old house in which I lived." I had to have help with the title, and asked the teacher how I would say that I had lived there. She asked me if that was my house, and (after some reluctance and confusion) I said no, I just liked it. Later, my mother, looking at the painting, asked me about the rather adult phrase and was appalled that my teacher would think I lived in such a house. By then I couldn't understand, myself, why I had drawn and titled it that way – why I had felt so at home there.

But I well remember the drawing of it and the warm, loving feeling that accompanied it. I was happy. I felt "right" about having lived there. I guess it must have been similar to the feeling that accompanied that part of the first story that I saw while riding along the highway. Other coincidences: I have a fear of drowning and suffocation. I cannot stand on a precipice and look over without anxiety. When the past life possibility hit me, I was a bit unnerved that this character was male, whereas I am female. But I have moved past that now.

In this second story, a rustic house, or cabin, also appears as the home of the central character, Thusey. Here, there are also parallels in my present life or personality. I have always been interested in wild plants and when I was a child, I spent time in our yard stirring up concoctions of weeds and water in an old pot, holding up a plant, examining it and saying to myself "and this is good for......." I really don't know where this could have come from, since my family was not into such things. Yet, I was somehow sure I knew about that plant, if only I could bring it to mind.

As you know, I am southern white and come from generations of the same, but as a child I thought little brown babies were so beautiful, more beautiful than plain white ones. I yearned to know black people better and made a nuisance of myself to those interesting brown women who came to help my mother when she was sick. I remember standing on tiptoes by one such woman at the sink while she washed dishes, longing to touch her black skin that looked so like velvet. I wouldn't have done such a rude thing. I was a polite child. To my frustration and sorrow, they never let me into their private feelings.

I can't think of any other clues to a possible past life experience in the following story. Not of my own, anyway. But when he was little, my son had nightmares about "the Gim-balls" who were "going to get him."

Thusey

Thusey, the old herb woman, lives in a hut surrounded by the garden she has planted. She is very old, hunched and thin, with big feet thrust into vintage shoes with slits in them to provide relief for her bunions. She has few teeth and her hands are gnarly with arthritis. She is free, though, as free as any human ever is, while chained to the earth and the deeds done on it. This is her story.

When Thusey was born, her mother died. The doctor who had attended the slave was Doc Alderson. He was offered the baby as payment for his services, since the owner of Thusey's mother had no wet nurse and no one who could be spared to attend to the child. Thusey got her name from Doc Alderson's daughter, Amanda, her new owner. At age three, the lisping Amanda could not say "Susie" the right way, so her black slave was always called Thusey. Doc brought home the thin, puling babe, swaddled in a soft blanket and presented her to Amanda. To give credit to Amanda, she was duly impressed, not just with the gift, but with her responsibility to the baby. As her father held her out for her to see, he told her how the baby was now alone in the world except for the Aldersons and that it would now be Amanda's responsibility to see to her needs, as it would be to the child to help Amanda, later on, when she grew older.

Amanda, of course, could not care for the infant, so a young woman was provided for that, but she spent time with "her baby" every day, crooning over the cradle, and reporting the progress of the child as Thusey grew "fat and sassy," as Amanda said. Amanda was a "born little mother," as her father said and Thusey was, in her mind, her child.

This was how Thusey grew up in "the big house," and knew no other life before. She was oddly privileged for a slave, since the family had the habit of forgetting that she was one. She was schooled with Amanda and the neighbors' children, by a tutor who came to live with the Aldersons for less than a year. Then the neighbors took turns and he lived with them for a year apiece, at which times Amanda went over to their house for lessons. At first, Thusey was not invited, of course, but Amanda carried on so, that they let it go, and allowed them both to come. After several years, school was over for the girls. Girls were not expected to know much besides the baking of bread, how to make a tasty and filling meal three times a day, needlework - fine and everyday sewing, housework, food-preserving, jelly-making, gardening, nursing, church work, and having babies. Boys continued their schooling a few more years, with gaps in between when no teacher could be had. Most of them would grow up to be farmers like their fathers and grandfathers before them, and would learn the various skills thereof, and of their families needs, such as leather tanning and shoe making, how to make a wagon wheel or build a barn and other outbuildings, castrating hogs and dehorning cattle, and keeping their women nurtured, content and in line. The Aldersons lived in a community of comfortably well-off farmers.

When she was a child, Thusey sometimes grieved because of the difference in her's and Amanda's stations in life, and for the things she could not have. She sometimes muttered sullenly about this to Auntie, who worked in the kitchen. Auntie was the cook, and a free Negro (there were several free Negro families in this community). She was not at all sympathetic to Thusey's grousing, since Thusey's position in the household was a marvel to her. Even though Doc Alderson was not a planter-slave owner, to Auntie it was still a wonder to behold, and not at all a proper upbringing for a slave-child. It encouraged the girl to think herself above her kind of people.

Auntie was not paid in money, but in food, medical care and odds and ends. She was glad to get the Christmas ham, and other things, but never knew what she was going to be paid in next. Sometimes it was clothes that she would never wear because they were too fine and would attract attention, but she could not afford to quit this job, because the Aldersons more than made up for those occasional mistakes in judgment. She lived a hand-to-mouth existence, but still considered herself far better than a lowly slave, so she resented the little brown girl, without knowing why. She finally lost patience with Thusey's upstart ways, which were "jest crazy," to Auntie's mind, and stormed at the child. . . "That's because Missy (Amanda) is white folk, you crazy little heathen. You jest a nigger, you see that?" and she bent down - face-to-face with the little girl, so that she could look her right in the eye, and snarled, "Jest a nigger!" Then her eyes veered away from Thusey, for she had seen Amanda standing in the doorway. The room was silent as Auntie's face resumed its habitual mask.

Amanda and was both hurt (for Thusey's sake) and puzzled by what she had heard. "What is wrong with being a nigger, Auntie? Ain't you good? You go to church and you are a good woman, Auntie . . . and Thusey's been baptized, too. What's wrong about being that?" Auntie, who normally would have remained silent, was goaded to defend her outburst, and said, "She's a slave. No white folks are slaves, only niggers."

Amanda didn't know what to say to this. In her mind, Thusey was something between her baby-doll and her friend. She had never thought of her as a slave, and wasn't sure what being a slave meant. Amanda's nature was as placid as still water, but not usually as deep, so she let it go. Thusey, on the other hand, was intense and passionate, and when she was worked up over something, it was very hard for her to let it go. Their friendship was a good thing for both of them, because they learned from each other.

Once, when the Aldersons had gone out to visit friends, Thusey, once more left behind, was grieving that she didn't have a hat, like Amanda was wearing when she had gone off. Amanda had lots of hats, as did Mrs. Alderson, she pointed out, whereas she, Thusey, had none. Auntie, with a weary sigh, went over to the trunk against the wall. It was trimmed in silvery, embossed metal, and was used to catch all the odds and ends that had no place elsewhere in the house. With a groan, she eased herself down onto arthritic knees and with her bountiful butt raised over the rim, she scrabbled around in its depths until she brought out a wide strip of faded red cloth. Then she lumbered back to her seat at the kitchen table and with her needle and thread, she gathered the cloth along one long side, ruffling and turning it so that it became, first a spiral, then a coil which formed a rose shape. Tacking it into shape and adding cords to the sides, she clapped it onto Thusey's head and tied the strings under her chin. Finally, she fetched the hand-mirror to show Thusey how she looked in her new finery. The reflection of the little girl beneath the "rose" hat, showed a little mouth shaped in an "O" of surprise. Then she turned a sweet smile and glowing eyes up at Auntie, who in that moment of sympathy, was finally reconciled to the girl. After all, she mused to herself as she returned to her work, she was only a child - she wasn't responsible for her strange upbringing.

The Aldersons returned, clattering through the kitchen door (there was nothing formal about the Aldersons). Thusey was excited to show her new hat and ran forward, to stand poised on tip-toe in her excitement, twisting her hands together, the nervous smile showing all her white teeth in a pearly row. Doc, surprised in the act of shedding his topcoat and hat, was highly amused and laughed outright, which shocked Thusey and embarrassed Auntie. Tactful Mrs. Alderson and Amanda hastened to reassure

Thusey and to make over her, saying it was a "lovely" hat. Still, Thusey stood shifting from one foot to the other, as unsure as a bird about to take flight.

Actually, she was a charming sight - a little dark girl in a dress of bleached domestic, above her large, liquid eyes, a faded red "rose" of a hat perched atop her funny braids. It was the eyes that Doc noticed then, for he saw in them alternating flickers of shame and confusion. His laughter died away . . . for Doc was a good man.

Amanda clasped Thusey by the hand and insisted, "It's a superior hat, Thusey." Everything was "superior" to Amanda these days since she had learned the word. New words, to Amanda, were new food, to be relished, savored over the tongue, and brought out grandly, with a flourish, in her everyday speech - like dessert was served at their table.

One day, when she was ten, Amanda seemed weary and "lack-luster," as her mother said. They soon found out why. She was sick with the influenza, and of course, Thusey soon caught it, too. Up until this time, Thusey had slept on a cot to one side of the kitchen, near the warmth of the stove. Now, the ailing Amanda begged so for her to come to her room, that they put the cot in there, where the girls could talk to one another during their sickness and recovery. Mrs. Alderson was a little disturbed about this impropriety. Not just that it was unusual, but that it would set the tone for something that would continue. It wasn't done. Doc said it was easier for him to tend both girls, when they were in the same room. Since Mrs. Alderson was soon too sick herself to argue, this arrangement was settled and continued for years afterward- although eventually, Thusey's small cot was replaced with a straight, narrow bed.

Mrs. Alderson was a mild, pleasant woman, with no meanness in her. She shunned, or ignored, the complexities in life, desiring that things be kept as simple as possible. If her family was content, so was she. Her daughter was like her in nature. As for Doc, he had seen enough misery without ever wanting to contribute to any, himself. They didn't fit into any particular social set, and didn't care about it. If they were snubbed, they probably didn't notice it, for Mrs. Alderson's focus was on her home - Doc's; on his work. All three of the Aldersons (they never had any more children) wished everyone well, and most of all, desired peace and harmony in their own household.

It seemed to be at the time of the influenza that Thusey became interested in medicine. Doc Alderson had a room on the side of the house, which could be entered from a long window of the verandah. This was where he kept his instruments, surgery table and the many herbs that he gathered and used in his decoctions and infusions. She and Amanda had crept in there before, but they were never much interested then. Now, when the Doc came into their bedroom each day and administered to them the bitter syrup, and tapped their chests, it became an enlightenment for Thusey. Never just a dabbler, medicine and herbs now became a part of her life. Her interest infected Amanda - although in a smaller, less passionate, degree. When they were well again, they went for buggy rides and walks with Doc, into the hills and by stream sides, to find the herbs for his work. Doc was pleased with this turn of events, since he enjoyed the companionship of the chattering girls and was a willing teacher. However, he often puzzled over Thusey, looking at her a little sadly, and wondering how she could ever put this knowledge to use. The idea of selling Thusey had never occurred to him. He just assumed, if he thought of it at all, that Thusey would go on living with Amanda after his death.

There was an incident about which Doc never knew. There was a place in the yard behind the washhouse where there stood an iron kettle and other discards from the kitchen. The girls often played there. Thusey, "the doctor," stirred up a "decoction" of black alder, cohosh and rusty water from the kettle and dosed her "patient." Amanda, who cooperated like a nestling bird, gurgled down the medicine quite willingly. All that afternoon and evening, Thusey covered up for Amanda's absence while she spent hours either in the outhouse or on the pot, green-faced and chattering. The Negro girl was terrified, but dared not let on. One good thing came out of it; it had taught her the valuable lesson that the weeds of the woods were powerful, and not to be administered lightly.

Thusey prattled on too much in what she thought of as "doctor talk," for Amanda's liking. Amanda didn't care very much for learning all the names of the herbs and their uses, finding it tedious. But Thusey had a vast collection of them under her bed, in jars all carefully labeled. She kept them until they turned brown, brittle, and fell into dust.

I can see them lying on the shed roof under the hickory limbs that formed a tent over the roof. If they lay with heads downward, following the slant of the roof pitch, Amanda's face would turn red. "How red is it now?" she asks, sitting up. Thusey admires the deep rosy hue. "How red is mine?" she asks. But Amanda can't tell. They feel each other's skin. "See, Thusey, yours is kind of velvet-like. Mine is soft, but it's different". . and they compare, stroking each other's forearms, marveling at the difference. Yet, "Sister," thinks Thusey as she touches Amanda's cheek, "You're my true sister."

There were more social events for Amanda as she grew to be a woman. This was a critical time when there would have been more concern about her friendship with Thusey, but the girls had learned the ways of the people outside their home and were careful to keep up the image of mistress and maid in the presence of guests and relatives. It was like a game of pretend with them, and could be funny sometimes. When they were together in her room, they could be, as they said, "natural" again. Amanda told Thusey everything, and Thusey, who had grown in wisdom and patience, listened with her heart. She knew, by this time in her life that "Missy" (as she always called Amanda) had given her a rare, choice opportunity far beyond a slave's normal experience.

During Amanda's courting days, there came a distraction for Thusey. When she was fifteen, Doc Alderson took Thusey with him to deliver babies. He had decided that Thusey, since she was interested, might make a living as a midwife. Mrs. Alderson was scandalized. She thought the girl should not be exposed to that area of life at so young an age. But Doc scoffed at her. So, Thusey continued to learn from Doc and recorded all his remedies in her stiff but well-formed handwriting.

Later, when Amanda was married to Joseph Beckwith and Thusey lived with them, Amanda gave her the greatest gift she had ever bestowed upon her (and she had always been generous) - her freedom. Her new husband mildly questioned this, saying nothing would change since Thusey had an exceptional life for a Negro. Amanda's answer was that she knew Thusey would remain with her, and life would go on as before, but that Thusey needed to know that she was remaining *of her own free will*, not because she *had* to - just because it was the law. Secretly though, Amanda was a little nervous about it. She was not always sure about Thusey. Since they had grown up, there was a side to Thusey that was private, even from Amanda, a side that Amanda thought of as "dark," like Thusey herself, which she - as a white woman - could not intrude upon. She didn't understand it, but she respected it.

She was exactly right in her judgment of the affect that being free would have on Thusey. As Thusey herself often said in later years, Missy was almost always right, when she looked back on it.

Thusey out-grew Amanda in physical stature. She was tall, slim, and straight; a meticulous woman, speckless in her turban and long, straight dress with the long, white, bibbed apron that she wore. Amanda, the full-blown woman, was soft, round and easy-going, and wore fluffy, fussy clothes. A happy person herself, she wanted everyone around her in the same frame of mind. Her husband, Joe, was also portly and deeply satisfied with his choice of a mate. Once, Thusey - seeing them perched on the porch swing, laughing and content - was reminded of two plump partridges. She loved Amanda as ever, and was fond of Joe, but their relationship had, of course, changed. Joe Beckwith had a mercantile store in town, so Amanda still had the material comforts she had formerly had in her father's household.

Doc Alderson caught a chill coming home from treating a patient on a cold and rainy winter's night, and never recovered. Her tranquility finally destroyed, his wife soon followed him.

Thusey didn't fit in anywhere - not in the white community, where they simply regarded her as an upstart servant, nor in the Negro community, where she was seen as a white-talking, white-acting upstart trying to be white. She had first ventured into the Negro community as a child attending church, sitting in the slave balcony with Auntie; looking down to where Missy and the white folk sat nearer to the preacher. She had consoled herself by thinking that they, up in the balcony, being higher, were closer to heaven. There had been social occasions among the Negroes. Corn shuckings, the honey taking, and such, were well attended by both Negroes and whites. This is where the division had become most apparent. Amanda, of course, had remained with the white folk and played with their children, and later, when they were all grown, had danced with the young men. Thusey had been expected, by those less simple-minded than the Aldersons, to mingle with the Negroes of their neighbors. Auntie's presence had made it easier while she lived, but she died while Thusey was in the throes of budding womanhood.

There was a family who claimed kinship to Thusey through her natural father, and these she visited sometimes, sitting out on the porch of their cabin with them on Sunday afternoons, seeking tenuous roots and some sense of belonging. But she never fit in, to her way of thinking, nor to theirs. They couldn't understand why she didn't just lay down her white-acting ways and be herself - in other words - like them. They didn't realize she was herself, and trying to be like them was too hard. So she was not comfortable with her kin, even though they were kind. She thought they seemed a little coarse, and too ignorant. Then, too, she was shocked and repelled by the ordeal of the slave life. They all worked hard, both white and slave, at the homesteads in their grange, but the Negroes of the fields were beasts of burden. No one wanted field work. House slaves were much elevated in their own esteem and that of their peers. There were not many slaves in the community in which Thusey and Amanda lived.

Finally, Thusey was courted by, and married in the church, a free black man who was smitten by her unusual relationship to her white folk from the "big house." He was no match for Thusey. Even though he had a little education, which was much more than any of his peers in the shanties, he found, to his disappointment, that he was not accepted by her white family in the same way that Thusey was. Amanda and her husband provided a home for them, but did not approve of the man. Thusey was always at him to improve his manners, and corrected him in front of the white people. He couldn't understand it; couldn't take it, and eventually he took off. Not long after, he married, in bigamy, a simple-headed, face-pretty wench, which shamed Thusey so that it was years before she could hold up her head again. After that, she was through with men.

She returned to the big house and attended to Amanda, who bore four children. Two of these - sons - had died as children, the last son, Abram, (named for her father, Abram Alderson) was killed at Shiloh. This "like to have killed her" said Thusey. Only the last child, Lily, the daughter, (as sweet and pure as her name implied) remained. She was "the baby" of the family - the pet. She alone remained to be hovered over and doted on. How did Thusey feel about these children who must have been dear to her? At first, she was hard; bitter because she wanted children of her own and was jealous, in spite of herself, of Amanda's - but her jealousy died somewhere along the line while she and Amanda were grieving together over all those lost sons.

After the war was over, Amanda died. There was nothing anyone could have done for her, although Thusey tried. There was no remedy for a weak heart. Amanda was the last of the Aldersons. She had made her husband promise that Thusey would be taken care of after her demise. Therefore, Thusey was given the deed to the lot and cabin to which she and her husband had moved when they first married. It was better than most of its kind, on the edge of a wood, with plenty of room for a garden. Thusey withdrew to this place after Amanda's death and stayed there until her own demise.

Thusey's and Joe's grief was great but they grieved alone, each in isolation. Once, when Joe went to the cemetery to sorrow over Amanda's grave, he found Thusey already there, curled up like a grub worm on the still-raw dirt bank - she who usually was so meticulously clean. It shocked him to the quick to come up suddenly and see her like that. It seemed so unnatural. Wallowing and wailing, her hair (which he could not remember ever seeing before) had escaped from the turban; her clothes and face encrusted with the dirt of the grave. She was retching, and seemed to heave up her misery in great painful gasps. She had not yet seen him there, and he continued to watch her for awhile as he considered, for the first time, what her pain must be. When he compared it to his own he was suddenly enlightened. He could see that with her death, Amanda had taken away Thusey's whole life as she had known it. Amanda had been Thusey's everything - mother, sister, and friend. She had no one else - had never, really, had anyone. She had no real friends because she wasn't like the other Negroes. Now that he thought about it, he realized that Thusey wasn't like anyone he had ever known.

"Get up, Thusey, aw, Thusey, girl, get up now. . . aw now, don't worry Thusey, it'll be all right," and so encouraging her, he patted her shoulder soothingly and she, shocked when she saw him there, brushed the dirt off herself and arose in a similitude of the dignity she normally possessed. She would have skittered away then, hiding her face from him, but he detained her for awhile. So, they sat there on that mound above the creature who had made the earth a real home for the two of them, softly talking, as autumn leaves fluttered and skidded dryly across the marble slabs. He spoke of her freedom and that she was free, in that sense, to go if that was what she wanted, but that Amanda still needed her, for she had left behind Lily, the girl-child of Amanda's middle age, who would need Thusey's guardianship. Actually, Joe wasn't sure this was really true, but he knew Amanda would want it so, and right then he could feel Amanda's presence weighing heavily upon him, as though she were with them, pushing him hard to take care of her Thusey.

He had said the right thing, for then Thusey, shot through her intense, feverish body with that new knowledge - that Missy's child needed her — came up from that mound of earth and took on her new calling with the determination of a convert rising from the altar of redemption.

* * *

The child was a love, "a sweet breeze in summer," said Thusey. She was her child, as much as could be. But sadly for all of them, it only lasted a couple of years, because that was when Joe Beckwith's sister from Beaufort came to live with them . . "to raise the motherless child," she had said, but really to escape the grinding poverty and horrors of reconstruction in South Carolina. Of course, it was unthinkable that she would allow the familiarity which had existed, up until then, between Lily and Thusey. The Negro woman was so unlike any she had known, that she was very uncomfortable in her presence. So, eventually, Thusey went back to the cabin, bereft once more. Lily, now twelve, also grieved, for she loved Thusey. She ran after her when she left the house - with more hugs and promises to visit often.

Thusey's cabin was quite pleasant, trimmed in blue, with real shutters. But it had no echo of little feet. In the mornings, she sipped her coffee (faithful Joe kept her supplied from his store) at the window that overlooked the front yard and some of old Mrs. Alderson's peonies, taken from the masses that still grew at the homeplace. She should have been happy - she was fortunate beyond measure. She had a place of her own, and little to do. She was still supposed to do day work at the homeplace, but the Beckwith sister was too jealous, ("too eaten up with meanness," thought Thusey) to allow the easy conversations, the loving words, to pass between Lily and the Negro, and so the work hours became shorter and shorter. Her mind dwelled on these things as she sipped her coffee and whiled away the lonely days in what was most unusual leisure for one of her station.

* * *

A few years later: Thusey's cabin is ensconced in a bed of herbs and vegetables, fruits and flowers. She spends her hours gathering the medicinal herbs and making "decoctions" after the ways of Doc Alderson. The main part of the cabin is raised with a wooden floor, but the back of it steps down onto another room with a brick floor. There, a stove stands in the left corner, shelves along the right; in the middle is a long table on which to work and eat or work. The shelves are filled with shining glass jars containing curious things . . . many sprigs and roots hang drying from the rafters.

The place took on a scent, inside and out, which Lily always connected with Thusey. She came to visit still, and more often after her sixteenth birthday. Their soft, peaceful voices could be heard within the cabin as they worked together with the herbs, laughing and sighing over remembrances, and idly gossiping. Lily, stringing up the herbs with slim white fingers, watched Thusey's wrinkled brown ones as they deftly mixed and poured. She loved those dark hands and often reached out to place her hand on that of Thusey's. Thusey was still handsome though weathered somewhat by her constant treks through the countryside, but her real beauty sprung from within to light her eyes and countenance. Now that Lily had come back to her she was revived with love and spiritually strong. She had also become a force to be reckoned with in the community.

Negroes often came for medicine and treatment, for she charged little - a chicken, fish, a trap for small game and the like were enough payment. White people came occasionally too, for her reputation as a healer had spread. Mr. Beckwith would come by for Rheumatism balm, and to chat with Thusey, for old times' sake. Walking home on the dirt path, he would think how he had always been fond of her. His aged and ailing sister was difficult to live with, small-minded and petty. It was not like the days when the two women in his home, Amanda and Thusey, were like two content and busy hens, making that pleasant nest he had so loved.

Some of the poorer whites who came to see Thusey, came because they couldn't afford a doctor. Some of these came humbly and went away grateful. Others came stiff-necked, unwilling to admit they needed the care of a

Negro woman. The worst of the latter kind were the Gimballs, white trash who never paid, but were so threatening in manner, that Thusey was afraid to turn them away.

In this way Thusey's life continued, and was placid enough, until Lily tore it apart with the news that she was pregnant.

The only one who knew besides Lily, was Thusey, and the full realization of what this would do to an upper-class white family was an explosion in the calm of her existence. That great shame and life-long humiliation would be visited upon her Missy's child was unbearable. Lost in her worrying thoughts, she wandered about the cabin and woods like a specter. Guilt weighed down her days as she considered whether she had done right by the girl who had been left in her care. Had she let Missy down? She had warned Lily always about the pitfalls of life, but this particular one had remained somewhat ambiguous, since she had never told the girl what happened between men and women, exactly. Somehow, she had thought the family would do that - that the Aunt, now dead a year, would have taken care of that.

Lily had conceived in the secluded pasture behind Winn's old abandoned house. The irony was, it wasn't really for her own satisfaction. In her feelings, she was still an unawakened virgin. Like her mother, she always sought to please and nurture those she loved. Her lover then went off to the West to find cheap land and a new future for them, away from the South, on its deathbed of reconstruction. She had not heard from him since.

Lily had to do something soon, but how soon, she didn't tell, and due to ignorance, didn't really exactly. Thusey made excuses to delay this awful chore. "It's not time yet for dodder to be found, not late enough in the summer." She needed dodder as one of the ingredients of the potion to produce abortion. She had never used this potion to destroy a human child. She had used it for animals whose lives were in danger, but she had promised her-

self and God that she would never use it on a woman. She had been promised much in the past to break that vow, but she had not been tempted. She
thought it would work the same on a woman, Doc's books said so. Days
went by as she fretted and dallied. One day, she had stopped to pray in the
woods and had seen the answer. When Lily came again with her pathetic
appeal for the herbs that would bring on an abortion, she confronted her
with that vision. "Give me your baby!" she said and her face was so intense
it bordered on madness.

The girl was appalled by this entreaty and Thusey's wild face. It was so
unexpected, that she reeled. She didn't understand that Thusey's whole soul
revolted against killing a baby (she who had always wanted one so badly)
that now she was having dreams of the child living there in her cottage
with her - her own child. They would live an isolated life, all to themselves
(because even she realized that negro folk would never understand where
she'd got a white child. They would gawk and stare, at the very least. At
worst, they would fear she had conjured up the child with hoodoo). But Lily
had a vision in her mind, too, of angry white folk descending upon Thusey's
cabin, especially the white trash, for they surely would never let a white
child live with an old Negro woman. How could she explain its presence in
her house? Lily trusted Thusey not to divulge who its mother was, yet they
would have to be idiots not to easily guess. She knew it was impossible and
she tried, in the days following, to make Thusey see that, but poor Thusey
could not let go of that sweet dream: She and the boy (Thusey was sure it
would be a boy) having their little meals together, growing the garden, her
teaching him the ways of herbs, the way of nature.

Why shouldn't she be a mother? Thusey would think. She had given
her whole life to a family not hers. She was finished with that now. Lily
was going to have a child she didn't want, and couldn't have without great
shame to her. Why shouldn't she take the child? It all seemed so reasonable –

oh, it was such a peaceful, love-filled dream. . . They would fish, and she would teach him to read and write, too. All the books Missy had given her were on her shelves, waiting for him. He wouldn't need the white school, nor the one for the Negro children that the Yankee schoolteacher ran. He wouldn't need anything or anyone but her. He would fill her life, and she would fill his . . with everything good, everything she had been saving and had not had a chance to give to any one of her very own. He would be Missy's grandson and her own, too. It all seemed so *right*. So, the Negro burned with intense desire for this white child.

How could it be arranged? How could Lily go through her pregnancy and actually give birth without notice? Thusey had an answer for that. Lily would stay with her in her cabin. It was remote, wooded all around. She wouldn't be able to go out during the day, unless to the woods behind the house, and then she would have to be very careful. Lily could cover her absence by telling her father and friends that she was going to visit one of those school friends of hers, maybe the one in Alabama. Those friends would cover up for her if necessary. There was only her father at home now, and he was not really conscious of much that went on around him, for he was ill and yearning to join his Amanda.

It didn't work out, of course. It had only delayed things further. Thusey was broken-hearted and bitter, but Lily finally made her see it wouldn't do. So she finally gave in to Missy's daughter's pleas, and administered several doses at timed intervals. Lily stayed on in the cabin. During the days it took to work, Thusey was greatly distressed and wandered about muttering and not as careful with her appearance as she normally was. She had broken a vow never to give a potion to abort a human child . . . but it was for Missy's daughter Lily - what else could she do? What she didn't know was how far along the pregnancy really was. Finally, Lily was really sick, and in the refuge of Thusey's cabin, the cause of all this anguish was aborted. . . Yet it was not a fetus, after all, but an infant, with fingers and toes and everything in place even though it was as yet too tender and small to breathe on its own. It lay in Thusey's arms, cold and white. She had given Lily a sedative, so she had not yet seen the baby. Thusey, so shocked to see an almost full-term child, was in a quandary - should she try to revive the child and keep it alive? Although suffering greatly in her soul, when she found no pulse she did not try to revive it, nor did she massage life into it or breathe into its little lungs. She stood in the light from the cabin window, gazing into his little face, a face which bore a great resemblance to Missy. With all her heart she yearned to wrap him warm in a blanket and try to make him breathe. But, then, for Lily's sake, she hardened her heart and laid it aside in the cold - naked, unwashed, and unloved.

The cabin is stone cold quiet. The girl still sleeps, unknowing. Her prolonged sleep and innocent face begin to irritate Thusey, whose anger has risen while she waits. . . She thrashes around the room, staring at Lily who lies there so peacefully sleeping, cursing her and yes, even cursing Missy for having brought her to this evil. Finally, she can wait no longer. She shakes the girl awake; then drags her by the arm from the bed and into the back yard. Lily, confused and still half-asleep, stumbles along behind her. Thusey, looking like an angel of vengeance, grabs the shovel on the way and heads toward the fresh little mound near the walnut tree.

Though she feels suddenly so old, she starts digging with the determined energy that the flame of her anger has provided. The girl, fully awake now and filled with foreboding, protests hysterically. Her large eyes are dilated with fear, and she keeps snatching, snatching at the other's arm to stop her from doing this terrible thing. Thusey thrusts her away and continues to dig until she exposes the hat box, which contains the infant. Lily is moaning, her face in her hands. Thusey yanks the girl's hands away from her face, and rips off the lid to the box, thrusting its contents under the girl's nose. For she is determined that she must see it too.

She must suffer as she did. "There, see? This is your Sin!" Having pronounced that word with intensity, she pauses and moans,". . and it's mine, now, too. No, Look," she commands, as Lily shrinks away, "Look at it. . . This was a babe without sin." As the girl shudders and turns away, Thusey pushes her face into her's. Lily is shocked by that face, the ugly grimace of that face she loved. Merciless, though, she will not be ignored."This sin is ours, girl, this sin in ours." Then they both stare into the box as though hypnotized, tears running down both faces, then Lily, as white as the flower she was named for and forever wounded in her heart, falls to the ground screaming.

While she wailed in misery, she knew that Thusey was right. She had not thought of that before, when she should have. It hurt especially that she had brought a sin onto Thusey, whom she loved. Meanwhile, Thusey reburied the box, much slower this time, as she felt all the years of her age and more. Then she bent over the girl to pull her to her feet. Lily stared into her face as if into the face of truth. She had been so anxious that her sin not be exposed, but to be covered up, like that hat box, deep in the ground. But it was still there, would always be there - in her's and Thusey's hearts —the heavy weight of it to be shared for the last of their days. As they trudged back to the cabin she realized they were truly yoked together with this terrible secret and its misery for all their years on earth and, perhaps, beyond.

* * *

It is January and there is a crust of old snow, capped with ice, all over the ground. It is unusually cold for that part of the country. I hear heavy, booted footsteps crunching through this layer, making their way to Thusey's cabin door. The sky is dark, although it is still daytime. The man, well wrapped up in a homemade coat with a half-cured fur collar, pulls the cord which activates the wooden knocker on the inside of the house. He hates to call on the herb woman . . . hates her and her strangeness, but it is necessary, tonight.

Thusey hears and sees the contraption, the knocker, moving, which alerts her to a visitor. Straightening up from her work at the fire, she comes with her usual dignity to the door. I see her, in color, and her figure is still fine - tall, slim, small-waisted. One cannot tell she is old without a closer look at the face beneath the turban. Although her clothes were handed down to her years ago, they have been meticulously cared for, and are extremely neat and new looking. I see flashes of red pattern in the long skirt she wears, her shirt-waist, white and crisp, reflects the lantern's light as she strides elegantly to the door. Then she stops and hesitates in front of the door, a little uneasy. She calls out, "Who is it?" and receives the answer she most dreads: "Gimball," he says, and clears his throat. "My girl's real sick and we can't get a doctor." Thusey leans her head against the doorsill as she thinks for a minute. Reluctantly, she unlatches the door to let the man in. The warmth of the cabin melts the frost from his clothing and beard and he drips on Thusey's clean, bare-board floor. He waits, resentfully, but humbly, as she gathers her things and wraps herself against the weather. While she does so, she asks side-long questions: "Does she have a fever?" "Has she been sick long?" The vague, evasive responses she receives discourage any more questions. Her uneasiness increases; her thoughts are in a turmoil, because she suspects what the errand might be.

Finally, as they are leaving, she turns to the man, saying, "Where is your wagon?" but he shakes his bear-like head and tersely indicates that the crust of ice made it impossible to come by that means. "You mean you walked?" she asks, "All that way from Bog Hill?" He nods. Impatient to be off, he has walked ahead of her, following his own footsteps back. He has not considered that she might not be willing, or even able, to tramp the five miles of rough, icy terrain over which he has just come. She is just a nigger. He turns to go, expecting her to follow. She stops him with the words; "Miss Lily, at the house, she expects me to come with a potion for her. I have to stop there to give it to her. If I do not, she will wonder what has happened *to me and will send someone over. I'll have to stop by there first."* He gapes at her *as he considers this. Then he nods and trudges forward, she following, toward the* *"Alderson house," as it is still known.*

When they arrived, she hurried forward to see Lily, leaving Gimball in the hall under the wavering eye of the current live-in help. This was a mulatto girl who bragged to anyone who would listen, that her father had been a Union soldier (as though that were a badge of honor), and who, to Thusey's mind, was sloppy in her housework.

In the back bedroom, she explained to Lily what had happened. She wanted to borrow the wagon, and to let Lily know where she had gone, as insurance against her disappearance (for Thusey did not trust the Gimballs not to do away with her, if they thought it necessary or desirable, as in this case, they might).

Lily, who was worried about contagion, wanted to keep Thusey from going. "Girl, I'm worried," Thusey said, "but not for that reason, for I fear I know what the trouble is." Then Lily, after a searching look at Thusey's face, knew what it was, too. She threw heavy clothing over her house gown, and not listening to the startled protests of the other woman, thrust her feet into boots and led the way down the hall. There she sized up Gimball and pinned him down with her eye, like a butterfly to the wall. (Thusey had always admired this ability of the gentry white to humble the trash, and would have liked to emulate it but had not found it safe to do so.) "I will accompany you," Lily spoke loftily, "I have a wagon and the trip will be easier and faster." Then, leaving the man to think what he would, she led the way to the barn, ordered him to help her equip a small farm cart with pegged wheels (a safeguard for just such icy days as this), and to harness the overgrown, furry beast that passed for the family horse to it. This he did, stumbling, red-faced and obviously troubled over something. Finally he approached her, as she jumped up into the wagon, making the mistake of placing his hand over hers on the reins. As she stared icily at him, he hastily removed his hand and plunged into a sputtering speech, "Miss Beckwith, it ain't necessary that you come. Your nigger can do the thing. My girl is sick . . but not that sick," he paused, stumbling over the words, he seized hopefully upon, "but she might have somethin' catchin'."

Thusey watched from her seat beside Lily, who did not answer but instead, whipped the reins into position and seemed prepared to leave the yard - with or without Mr. Gimball. He, seeing as things stood, decided to heave himself into the vehicle. "Mr. Gimball," she said as they rolled out of the yard, "Thusey is not 'mine', she belongs to herself. She is, however, my friend, and I value her safety." Then, after casting a side-long glance at that whiskered, steaming face, she had second thoughts, (their being alone with the man) and tried to make amends, "It is a long trip and you both could be very sick indeed if you traverse it on foot." (A rule of the gentry: always sprinkle into your conversation with the riff-raff, long words they won't understand - it puts you in the driver's seat.)

Thusey smiled secretly and felt better. Her thoughts scanned the past as they scrunched through the snow. Missy's girl was turning out all right. She had never married, and that worried Thusey, who saw marriage as the proper environment for Missy's daughter. But, "Whom am I to marry?" was Lily's answer. All the young men of quality in their neighborhood had been killed at Shiloh. There was a gap between them and the mere boys coming along to replenish their ranks, and these youths were mostly illiterate and poor, having suffered through reconstruction and lacking the advantages of the previous generation. They had never again mentioned the birth of the dead child, but Thusey's mind was brought back to it tonight.

When they arrived at Bog Hill, even Lily was unnerved. They entered the cabin, and it was small, dirty and rough-wood plain, partitioned half-way up and down the middle to divide the row of beds in the back from the cooking and living area in the front. On a cot in the front room, seeking warmth from the stove, sat old man Gimball, the grandfather. He had a strangely infantile face, and his large, round blue eyes stared blankly at them as they stared back. He now had only remnants of the long, straight, blond hair he used to have, this forming a fringe encircling the head from ear to ear, with a few lank strands lying greasily across his pate. He gaped, toothlessly, silently. His mirror image (except in age and abundance of hair), his grandson, sat nearby, whittling chips onto the floor from twigs he had gathered. There seemed no purpose in this; no form took place under the horny fingers as the pile on the floor grew. After the first startled stare he gave Lily, he hid his curiosity but glanced up warily, from time to time, the corners of his eyes showing flashes of brilliant blue. The lank, blond hair which lay so smooth that it appeared painted on his head, had been rubbed into this arrangement by nervous habit and greasy hands, a gesture he often repeated throughout his waking hours.

These two did not move, nor did they rise when the women entered, although Thusey had the impression the youth had stared out at them on their arrival and had only just returned to his slat-backed chair. It was too damp in the room, and the stove barely kept the cold at bay. She asked for more wood for the fire, but was given to understand that they are saving what little they had and that it was green, uncured and slow-burning, any-way. Apparently, the storm had caught them in their lazy ways.

The women were led behind the rough partition to the bed area behind. There in a corner, the girl lay, wallowed up in a cot barely large enough for her frame, on a hollowed out corn-shuck mattress. Dirty bed clothes were rumpled and tangled about her, and she had scrunched her heavy body down to the foot of the frame, her knees raised and akimbo. She seemed dead, or unconscious.

Thusey hurried over to the hump in the bed and raveling the sheet from round the lower part of the girl's form, gasped and stepped back. Revealed by the lamp Lily carried into the room, was a horrible sight. Between the white limbs was a grossly extended bulge, a broad expanse of flesh caught in the trap of the vagina, pushing that inadequate passage beyond extreme, and unhinging the birth canal of bone and membrane. The abdominal swelling above, which represented the bulk of the infant, lay low just above the pelvis, like a heavy object in a cloth sack, unable to escape from the hole in the bottom.

"How long has she been like this?" she demanded of Mr. Gimball, who simply shrugged, and turned away in repressed fury. The women looked at each other with mutual understanding. Up until this time, Gimball had been able to pretend that his daughter was just sick, not with child. The presence of Lily, of the gentry, at this scene galled him. He was humiliated by that and he feared that now she knew, the entire community would know of this shame.

He sat down heavily on the foot of the iron bed, the only decent bed, a little way over from the girl's cot, and Lily, made suddenly gentle by her own secret shame, made her way over to him. Fleetingly, she wondered about the family's intimate life, the couple (the wife had died years ago) who had shared the double bed, their children on each side. There could not have been much privacy. Soothingly she talked with the bowed-over man.

Thusey, frantic with the need for haste, had placed her ear to the girl's chest and receiving reassurance of a faint, fluttering pulse, rushed from the room to find water and rags. When she asked the boy, he gestured to a pan on the plank table in the middle of the room. What she saw when she got there both disgusted and alarmed her - a few inches of water, aswim with dirt and trash. "Is this all you have?" she cried out, disbelieving. He rose, dislodging a shower of wood chips from his dirty pants, and came over to look, also, into the pan. "Wadn't time to get no more," he said as he stared short-sightedly into her face. Thusey, taking this to mean that they were caught without any water in the house before the stream froze over, despaired, relented and looking around, seized a pail and shoved it at him. "Take this out and find some clean ice and snow. Not dirty stuff, now, get it off the bushes, or something, not off the ground . . . and bring it in a hurry, you hear?" (She had shed the patronizing manner she normally used with the poor and bitter whites; no time for that in this crisis) and he, after a glance toward the partition, went obediently the door, letting in a cold gust of air as he went out.

Thusey could see, through the crack of the door as the man left, that it was getting dark. She donned a clean, long and white bibbed apron, and rummaged through the satchel she had brought with her. Thank God she had guessed right about what she might need. She hurried back to Gimball and Lily, and bluntly asked the man for a sharp knife. He looked up, she could swear, with relief in his eyes . . . and then she understood. He knew, and she knew, that the only way to save a farm animal in this condition, was to dismember the issue and bring it out piece by piece . . . and this is what he *wanted* done. A shiver rushed up her spine. Then she asked him, trying to keep the sarcasm out of her voice, "If you have to choose the babe or your daughter, which would you rather I save - that is," she amended, "if I can save either one?" After a glance around the dirty house, he hung his head and said simply, "We need her." And Thusey, turning away from him, wondered if that were wise, if it would not be better for the girl to go on to her maker, for at that time, she suspected the child might have been sired by incest. (She was wrong in that, though. The old man would never have touched his daughter.)

The son loved his sister, she soon discovered. He rushed back into the house and put the pail of slush on the stovetop to heat. He understood what was needed once she pointed it out, and was willing to help. She examined the knife and was relieved to find it razor sharp, for she was acutely aware of time racing by along with the life draining out of the girl in the cot. Although it had been only a matter of minutes, it seemed like hours. Telling Lily to try to find clean rags or sheets in the house, she went over to have another look. Everything was the same. Further contraction was not possible, although she saw a tremor run over the lower belly as the muscles tensed uselessly. The girl moaned - only a whimper really - and this spurred Thusey on to see what could be done. She ordered Gimball to stoke the stove, to do whatever he had to do to make it warmer, no matter what he burned. He lumbered across the room to take up a dark wood cradle, and smashing it against the edge of the stove, he stuffed the pieces inside. Then, crossing over to his son's chair, he swept up those shavings with his hands that were like shovels, and scooped them into the rising flames.

Thusey didn't wait to see what he did, but after dropping an herb from her bag into the water melting on the stove, she washed her hands, passed the knife through the flames and hurried back. She didn't have time to wait for the water to boil, thinking, " It will be a miracle if the girl lives anyway, long enough to get infection." She had learned about infection from the stories of the soldiers in the war - those who limped home without legs and arms. Lily had found some half-way decent rags, but Thusey, squatting on the floor, thought she saw something move in the bedding and required the men to move the girl to the iron bedstead, which was higher up.

It was hard, so very hard. Thusey worked and gently maneuvered the baby slowly but with such difficulty that sweat poured from her. Lily watched with amazement and helplessness, wiping the sweat from Thusey's eyes, keeping the knife at the ready. The knife was used only once, to enlarge the aperture, already torn, enough to allow the shifted infant to make a better appearance. First an arm, then the head, appeared. The girl on the bed had regained some consciousness. Bloodshot eyes rolling in her head, she gazed at them wonder-ingly, and then she heaved a great sigh as the babe gushed from her womb to lie inert upon the sheet.

The shock of the sight immobilized the two women for a moment, then Thusey snatched up the child, cleaned the flared nostrils, reached into the mouth with nimble fingers, searching for obstructions; finally, massaged the darkening skin. A feeble cry, so soft to be barely heard by the women, emerged from a mouth much like Thusey's own, lips finely sculpted, but broad, too broad . . . but the hair was red, and damply straight. They puzzled over this manifestation for awhile, as Thusey gave her attention to the afterbirth, and the winding strand connecting this strange, dark infant to the blonde, white-fleshed girl in the bed. She was rousing a little now, but Lily pushed her down into the pillow, urging her gently to sleep, sleep, give herself up and be healed. When she'd finished, she and Lily looked at each other and the child, wondering what to do.

The father, stationed in the front of the house was waiting for his daughter to be relieved of this burden. It was against his wishes, though unspoken, that the child was alive. What would he do when he found out this child was of mixed blood? They knew there was only one answer to that. Silently, their eyes made a vow to each other that the death of this child would not be on their hands. In harmony, they cleaned the baby and swaddled him up to his red hair, in a woolly remnant of something that had been worked on, but never completed, by some female of the family.

The stirring in the other part of the house warned them that the men were restless. The absence of noise had roused them, and they were aware of some change in the movements of the women.

When Gimball appeared at the end of the partition, Lily was hold-ing the infant tight against her, its face to her shoulder, only the red hair showing. Thusey drew herself up to her regal height and faced him.

Her unease was great, but she was determined to brazen this out. She decided to address him politely. "Mr. Gimball, the babe lived, after all, and your daughter, well . . . She is very weak and tired, but I believe she will live. She shouldn't do any work for at least two weeks." He didn't seem to hear her. He was staring fixedly at the tiny red head. Then he glanced away, staring into nothingness, a puzzled expression on his face. His lips moved, mumbling, but "Red" was all they made out. "Mr. Gimball," Thusey called out, interrupting his reverie so that he stared at her once more. His face was becoming inflamed and he was trembling, because he had hoped the baby would die, and was now sick about the future once more.

"Let me have the babe," Thusey said.

His face changed as he took in her words; his mouth fell open, the expression on his face changed from fury to amazement. Lily, also staring at Thusey during this interval of tense silence, and realizing Thusey's mistake, spoke urgently to the gaping man. "Mr. Gimball, no one will ever know. These things happen . . . happen to lots of folk," here she cleared her throat and paused, then went on hurriedly, with all the persuasion she could muster, "We would take care of the child and find it a home. No one would know where he came from. We promise, Mr. Gimball. We swear to you here and now that he will have a good home" (She paused, remembering that Mr. Gimball didn't care if the child had a good home, he preferred him dead) "and, if anyone asks, she added, Thusey will say your daughter had influenza, and she treated her for that." She looked at Thusey for support, and saw that her face, sculpted by lantern light, was turned to the man with utmost sincerity. He looked intently at her and Lily, and could not doubt that they meant what they said, but he was most puzzled as to why they would do this.

His son had come in without them knowing, and stood in the gloom where his sister lay. "Pa," he said gently, "Let 'em do it, Pa. What harm's

in it? We will tell Sissy the baby died, and everything will go on as usual."
Gimball considered this fantastic idea, and as he thought it quickly began
to lose its strangeness and became a lifeline in his mind. As he wavered, his
son continued to reassure him. "It'll be all right, Pa." he said, as he looked
down at his sister, who was deeply sleeping, but breathing normally. His
face softened as he stood there a moment, then he looked up again, "We
didn't have anything to pay 'em, anyway, Pa." Gimball, grim again, looked
sharply at Thusey, who hastened to say "Nothing is necessary, under the
circumstances."

Taking it for granted that the deal was settled, they scattered before things
could change. Thusey made stitches in the girl's torn flesh and Lily cleaned
up, as fast as they could. They were not giving the father a chance to change
his mind, nor to have a good look at the child, which they bundled up like
a cocoon. Lily carried the child out to the cart, with Thusey following, after
giving the brother instructions. She promised to be back if the girl took a turn
for the worse.

She never went back. They did not call for her, and she, cowardly,
would not venture over without being called.

Some time, perhaps a year later, the girl disappeared. She was seen
taking a train at the depot, but no one knew in which direction she went.
They never knew who the baby's father was. Lily heard that the girl had
been working for a boarding house, cleaning rooms for Yankees who had
come down years ago to plunder and had stayed on with jobs in various
departments of government in town. The shanties out back of the boarding
house were rented to freed slaves of no account. Some worked odd jobs for
the railroad, but others just lived off the land and what they could steal.
They were the scourge of the land, and people of both races hid from them,
and carried knives to protect themselves, should they be caught alone with
them. The Yankees had seen some of these Negroes taunting the girl and

had cheered them on. Lily and Thusey never knew if the child was a product of rape, or of misplaced love.

No matter. If the child was conceived in violence and hatred, he soon
became a child of love. Thusey had what she wanted, at last. The red hair
of the child fell out, and new hair came in, frizzy and dark as Thusey's, but
still with a red cast in the sunlight when he played in the yard. He grew
"prodigiously" as Thusey told Lily, after the first months of tediously nursing him along with no breast milk. Goat milk and sweetening was the best
they could do. He was weaned early to the cup, and seemed not to mind.
He was a really good child - "good as gold," she'd say.

Thusey told visitors who came for herbals that he was her sister's grandchild, now orphaned. Since most of the older people who could remember
Thusey's origins were dead, this was accepted. Anyway, no one cared, and
life went along placidly and happily for Thusey and the boy. Her only
worry was that somehow the Gimballs would hear of the brown child with
the red glint in his hair and, putting two and two together, would realize the truth and their "shame" would return. (What irony! That such as
they would feel they were demeaned by such a thing.) Therefore, she would
caution the boy to stay close to the house, and if he saw a man come to
the house, to hide himself away until he was gone. When the boy asked,
"Why?" Thusey would say, "Because the Gimballs will get you, that's why,"
she'd say, like it was a joke.

But nevertheless she foretold the truth.

* * *

Dear Richard,

Okay, so I will try to obtain some peace. Your encouragement has meant a good deal to me. I've grown tired of the scared little me. Also, I have discovered spiritual writings and great teachings that have brought me comfort and led me to enlightenment. I spend a lot of time in my garden and have had some great blessings. I guess you would say I am on a spiritual journey. I've decided I like it. What's more, I have discovered that I am *not alone*. I can see it all around me now. A lot of people are waking up.

This next story was just a bit about a little girl. I never saw her grow up and I don't know if she did.

Dancin' with God

I am daydreaming in the garden - and a vision starts coming in a rather nebulous form. It begins with the sense of a person. I relax and let it come, this picture. . It seems to be a little woman - a miniature person in Victorian dress. I wonder, "Perhaps she is a dwarf?" Though she is so small, her presence is very strong, because she is a forceful person.

Then the picture unfolds and, as I see her prating childishly to herself - weaving a tale about the imaginary beau with whom she is dancing - I realize that she is merely a little girl, after all. It was only that she is quite convinced she is a woman grown. I have a glimpse of bouncing blonde curls; blue eyes. She likes and admires her own plump arms, her creamy skin - no blue veins mark her. Love, love — she is filled up with love - love for life, love for herself, love for the countryside - the "downs" . . . What are downs? Meadows . . . There are sheep in them with bells on. The lead sheep wear bells. The lead sheep being the faithful ones who can be counted on to always be with the flock.

She prattles on to herself in a soft voice. She is enamored of shepherds. When she is of age, she will marry a pretty, red-cheeked shepherd boy, no matter what her sister says. The thought of her sister, and how she treats her like a child, makes her sullen. This day she would not go out at all, since she was required to wear her boots. She sits by the window, looking out. It is a lovely day. Her attention is soon caught by a dray delivering to the stables, then something — (what is it?) — moving in the meadow… She soon forgets her pique and flits out the door. But it is true the boots hamper her agility. "A curse I must bear, I suppose," she says aloud — just for the pleasure of hearing those deliciously melodramatic words laden with injury. She hums to herself, "Johnny will go for a sailor." She falls to musing about what it must be like to be a sailor. And then — A sailor would be her future husband! A sailor with eyes as blue as the sea and the sky above his ship. He would somehow find his way to their land-locked town (many miles from the sea) and would propose for her and carry her off with him on his fine white horse (sometimes it was a carriage). She is unsure of the proper equipage for someone whose usual mode of transportation is a ship, and thus this dream is curtailed.

The child has very little converse with other children. Her sister, slim, soft low voice, patient but terse to her silly little sister . . her hair worn up. She is a good deal older than her little sister, is married and now lives elsewhere. When she is in the house, she "squinches up" her eyes and glares at her little sister from narrowed lids. The child "knows" her sister does not want her to be happy. "Spoiled monster!" She has overheard her say to their father, after the child had carried a tale of woe to their mother.

* * *

She had this notion of adult-ness partly because she had no friends except grownups - her parents, servants and neighbors. She was a plump little thing, but as light on her feet as a fairy. Only anger, grief and her outdoor boots made her heavy. She was a child of nature and loved to go out onto the moors and hillsides, returning home with damp, straggling hair; her sash untied and dragged in the mud and slippers ruined past wearing to church or visiting. Slippers were for house-wear only, but she would balk at wearing her boots, because (as she said) she could not "dance in those things." (One must be *light*! It was *necessary*!) Sometimes, though, she was caught and forced to wear them. Although she wiggled and wailed pitifully, the servant girl, Pauline, knew she would eventually give in, for she was obedient in spite of her passionate nature. Of all the emotions that energized the little girl, love was predominant, so she would always capitulate in the end. Therefore, Pauline would wait patiently through the usual storm of crying, until the fire and lightning had gone out of the child, when she would collapse upon herself. A damp little bundle she would be, swathed in her outdoor clothes, wet with tears and perspiration. One could almost see her misery rising up, along with the steam evaporating from her overheated little body.

When things had reached this point, Pauline would harden her heart and - with the help of the shoehorn - would force those ungainly but remarkably durable boots upon the little feet. As she did, she hated them fiercely - hated them more, perhaps, than the child did. The thought had come to her once that it was like some cruel thing that bad boys did to little animals. - like catching a bird and weighting its feet so that it could no longer fly but must flutter about helplessly. (Now why should she think that? She had admonished herself. It was only a matter of *shoes*, for goodness sake! Other children wore boots quite happily without all the fuss this child made! But when she tried to look at it logically, it never succeeded.) So, Pauline despised this task, and the girl - catching sight of her sad face - would feel sorry, once more regretting that she had caused her to be miserable... She would reach out with loving little fingers to smooth the stern expression from that well-loved face (and, of course, that only made it worse for Pauline).

After some time of this struggle over shoes, Pauline wouldn't stand it anymore. She had taken to being elsewhere when the child was given permission to go outdoors. After that, the child ran out unhindered to play outdoors, joyfully forgetting that she was supposed to change her shoes, or perhaps hoping with childish naiveté that "the rule" had somehow elapsed.

The girl's mother, an invalid who could not walk - cherished her and understood that she was a wild child who needed to be out in nature . . . was one with it. She understood that her child needed to dance upon the moors and as she lay upon her couch she looked forward to her daughter's return. She would always rush in with the smell of the country air in her clothes, bits of grass and twigs caught in her hair and clothing; her nature calmed and sweetened for having been freed from her cage.

One day she came to her mother bursting with her day's adventures . . . the flowers abloom, the turtle, the hare, the skink on the rocks, and finally how - surrounded by all that beauty and wonder – she had thought of her mother there on the couch . . . thought of how *she* could not be there. *She* could not see all the lovely things under the sky, and so she had grieved. But then, she said, while she had wept, a little breeze had come and softly fanned her hot face and tickled her hair . . had circled and returned to caress her cheek; to dry her tears. (As the child struggled with words to explain, her eyes were bright and burning with revelation.) It had been a "knowing" thing, she said, this breeze that had comforted her so lovingly. First, it had calmed her and succeeding in that, it then beguiled her as it danced away over the moor. Brushing the tips of the grasses in its passage, it had started them waving so happily, that she knew it said "Come dance with me!"

Following the path it made, she had run out to join with it – carefully trying to stay within its current, so that she could be a part of this joyous thing. She had often danced with the wind - but this time it was different . . now she knew that the breeze was more than she had formerly believed. It was really *somebody*. She gushed, "It, it . . *loved* me, the little breeze, Mama! It loved me!" Then she floundered for want of better words to explain to her mother the sheer immensity of her discovery.

As she leaned toward her mother with her hair standing out from her face like an energized halo - her eyes sparking with such intensity and strength of will, Carla was a little alarmed - not for the first time doubting her capacity to rear such a daughter. She remembered what her aunt had said so harshly - that her girl was "filled with foolishness" and "should be bridled." But this moment of weakness was fleeting, for she and her daughter were kindred spirits and her heart warmed to her notion of the breeze. She could understand it, for she too - in the days when she had been well - had "danced" joyfully with skittering leaves caught by a playful zephyr.

Choosing her words carefully she said, "Well, God made the wind, and he manifests himself in all that he created" ("even in you, my little daughter." she thought). Then she had to explain what "manifest" meant - that all things which were felt, heard, smelled, all those things, and more - even unheard, unseen things - were conceived by God and his spirit moved and dwelt within them. The girl - grateful for her mother's understanding - listened with her mouth agape and her eyes clouded over with introspection. She was silent for a while, then — still in the grip of her daydream - she wandered away to further examine this thought and its complexities in a quiet spot of her own.

On the next clear day, the child sat quietly on a high rock overlooking a sweeping landscape. As she sat, she thought about God. All around her was GOD - the trees, the sky, the flowers, the squirrel in the tree, the birds flying over - all this was what He had created, all that He WAS. The delight which stirred within her warmed and grew into love for this being, for God - for didn't she love all that He had made? Didn't she rejoice with the rapturous birds' song? Didn't she breathe deep when the air was full of the scent of wild roses and crushed herbs? Didn't she dream with the floating clouds in the blue sky, and dance in the waving grasses? Didn't her heart love the sweet breeze which raised her curls and cooled the hot dew from the nape of her neck . . that encircling spirit that had dried the tears from her cheeks and mesmerized her so that she had forgotten her sorrows? So . . . . *All this was God*!

As she sat there surveying it all, she became overwhelmed and her little body shivered, for Love had turned to awe. But, since awe is short-lived in all human beings, soon her child-mind wandered. Some swallows circling overhead captivated her and she got up from the rock to mimic their flight. Soon she was racing across the field with her arms outstretched. As she went sailing, sailing, she was thinking, "So, this is how it feels to be a swallow!" But, in trying to trace their flight, she gazed upward too long, tripped on a stone and, when she fell, a briar scratched her face so that it burned. From rapture to pain! Such a rude awakening! She sat on the lush grass and contemplated this. The world was so beautiful! Why did pain exist? Why sorrow? Her thoughts went to her mother at home.

Then, a breeze gently stirred her attention, cooling her burning, stinging cheek. Once more, she was filled with gratitude. Quick as a flash, she leaped up and - holding her arms out wide - she embraced the breeze and swept into a dance. Yet, this time her dance partner, her invisible lover, was not mere mortal man – a shepherd or a sailor- nor was the dance so wild. But so lovely, she thought - surely she danced as she had never danced before! Was she not most graceful, the steps she took so beautiful? She wished fleetingly that she could see herself as she danced, but then - because she could not then BE her at that moment - she rejected the idea. So she danced on, bowing, circling, hovering (it seemed) above the ground - only just skimming its surface as she bent and swayed like a tender-stemmed flower in the breath of spring. . . And all the while her heart was full to bursting with joy and delight.

* * *

When her mother died, the house was yet more unbearable for the girl and she would escape to the hills at every opportunity, to return in the usual deplorable condition of disarray.

Her father - staid and constrained always - was now insensible to all around him and lived within himself, accompanied only by grief. One day, he sat at his escritoire to the unwelcome (but expected and thus necessary) duty of responding to condolences. Often as his pen scratched across the paper, his mind strayed to scenes of the past and what he perceived to be the unfair tragedy of his wife's illness - the infirmity of one who had so loved to dance and to mingle with people. He had never cared for such. He had always been quite satisfied with a dull and quiet life but she had always been the bright one, and he had learned - albeit reluctantly - to bless her joy in those things. So, on this day his memories alternately pleased and tortured him. He forced these thoughts aside and turned to the task of paying bills, but he had hardly started on this business, when he became dismayed over the number of pairs of shoes he had been required to buy in a year's time, for only one little girl. He called to Pauline.

Soon, the servant stood before him, twisting her apron anxiously, trying to find the words to do justice to the situation - for his face was severe and she wished to protect the girl. He had never been involved with his daughter's upbringing. So, how could she explain to him "how she was?"

The child would not wear boots, she told him, because they were heavy and ungainly for dancing, and her heart was for dancing on the moor. She had seen her out there, she said wistfully, and she had been a beautiful little thing, so graceful - a butterfly flitting among the flowers. When she had been required to wear boots, it was as though she wore anchors on her feet - so dampened were her spirits, so leadenly she walked about . . . (Her eyes slid to his dour face and she tried to interpret the flicker of expression she detected there. It was not going well. She put starch in her spine and drew herself up defensively) "It's more to her than just playing. She says . . (Here she faltered, her faith slipping out from under her.) She says she dances with GOD. . . ." Her voice trailed away. It was silent in the room. She looked to him appealingly, hoping that he might grasp what she could not express.

He stared at her as though he could not have heard her right.

Finally he said, "She does *what*?" Again she said it, lifting her chin defiantly now, for she refused to be ashamed of such a thing, though a shiver went up her spine as she said the word. "She says she dances with God!" Her voice sounded queer within the quiet room — her words gilded with awe. They stared at each other and there was nothing but the clock ticking for a few moments as each was lost in his own thoughts.

He was thinking of the empty ballroom, where he had danced with his wife a time or two (feeling stilted and foolish) but where they had never had guests for dancing, for he had never liked that idea. He had deplored the expense of such a thing . . . had not wanted to be bothered with it — that among other things. But she had never complained, so he had thought it hadn't really mattered to her. Had it mattered? Had she pined for want of a dance? Had she needed to express her joyful spirit in this physical exercise that he abhorred? She had been such a lively, bright spirit when he had married her. Had he — in his heavy way — smothered her joy? And later, of course, she'd had no choice! No more walks in the countryside, no dancing then, for Carla!

He turned his back to Pauline and scraped his chair closer to the desk, sighing as he bowed his head over his pen and paper.

She had turned to leave when she heard him speak — his voice abrupt, harsh, rising into anger — "Let her wear slippers if she wants. Buy her a dozen pair! . . Let her wear them all out with dancing!"

She'd thought he was finished and was going out the door when he spoke again. His voice was gentle now, so that she barely heard it. She turned. He was staring off into nowhere – a queer, sad look upon his face. "For God's sake," he said, "*it's only shoes. . .*"

* * *

Dear Richard,

Here's the fourth story. This one was emotional for me. I was sitting there at my computer in this modern time but I felt I had lost my protective skin, alternately whipped and gentled by each sensation this story from the past evoked. I don't know how it will come across to an uninvolved reader. As far as a tie to reincarnation, the only parallel to my present self is that I have a rear horror of rats, and as a child, I remember hearing of rabid animals and being terrified. My father didn't have to tell me twice to run into the house when there was a strange-acting dog on our property.

I could see the scene with the oxen coming through the wood's edge so very clearly. I could hear the noises they made; the crunching of the underbrush, snuffling, even their wet noses were in close-up view. Other scenes were also quite clear, while some things were not - they just came in narrative. Why is this? I can only think that since I am writing from another viewpoint, I have to bow to the realization that, to the people involved, some details were important and others were not, even if I think they should be. I believe this is a story of guilt and the importance of forgiveness.

Oh, you asked about names. I was so sure about the name Susie/Thusey in one of the previous stories but I am very dim with names. I made up the names in this third story. I don't know what they really were.

That sentence I just wrote makes me feel very anxious. Yet, deep down I feel that these experiences are factual - real, actual events in time. Am I living in insanity? Sometimes I think I am. Part of me (the frightened realist) says I am and it tortures me daily. But the dancing, creative spirit comforts me, gently telling me *everything is okay*, giving me peace.

Needless to say, I am torn.

The Settlers

It is dusk, the air is soft and there is a peach glow on the horizon. I can see a man standing at a rail fence, looking out toward the fringe of trees beyond the tilled pasture. He is calling something. (It is a strange call, not like "sooey" for pigs.) His in-laws, the Camerons, say it must be Episcopalian - not Presbyterian, this call - because they've never heard anything like it. The dogs come running up to him, jostling for his attention, and he glances down, but he is not calling for them. There is a movement - a shuddering in the leafy branches at the edge of the woods, and long horns, wet nose, shining coat …. an ox appears. Oxen are valuable in this country. These tended to stray into the woods behind the pasture late in the day, and the man can't take a chance that the wolves might hurt them, so he calls them in to the shelter of the homestead. The sun is going down quickly. The man, now joined by his wife, stands out in the yard to watch it set over the treetops. It dyes the sky hot and orange, but there is a chill in the air - for fall is coming on. The woman shivers a little, and wraps her arms around herself for warmth. I can see from her silhouette against the sunset that she is tall, almost as tall as her husband. The setting sun highlights sparks of red in her smoothly-bound hair.

* * *

Some days later, I have a vision of this man again. He is working in the open area around their cabin, burning little piles of trash, twigs, grass; forming a sort of circle around the house. It is twilight at this time, too, (morning or evening I cannot tell) and he is waiting for the birth of his child. He rakes and burns, glancing up uneasily toward the cabin from time to time, until he suddenly runs for the house. Why the burning of the trash? Something to do with insects? I don't know, but I feel there is some protective motivation behind it, connected with the impending birth. Perhaps it is a superstition, to guard against something. There are two women in the house, besides his wife. His child is fine, the women say, both smiling. His wife is tousled and red-faced, and complains of being too hot. They have covered her in a quilt, and she is sweating.

I will call this couple James and Jean Richardson.

Her sisters said that James and Jean should move back where her family was; where the couple had come from. Where they lived now, they said, was too isolated from others - but this fell on deaf ears. He was determined, and she was equally determined to be supportive of her husband, as a good wife should.

The child was bathed and dressed in clothes made ready for him, including a little cap since it was turning cool, and placed in a cradle by his mother's bed. The cradle had been fashioned of dark wood by a grandfather Richardson and had been passed down through James's line. Hardly had one infant finished with it, until another had need of it. It was well-worn by the hands of many mothers rocking many children, but it was still beautiful.

In the front part of the one room cabin the women sat at a table, eating and drinking, idly talking, in the pale light from the open cabin door. These sisters, Mary and Caroline, were pleasant, amiable young women. They glanced back toward their sister now and then, to see that she was sleeping peacefully. Before she could rest, Jean, leaning from her bed over the cradle beside her, had lifted the swaddling and inspected her son. As her sister held the crude lamp, its light bathed the rosy face of the child and the polished wood of the cradle but revealed no deformities. Then she had sighed and gave herself up to deep sleep in the bed at the back, where it was normally dark and gloomy - there being no windows in the cabin as yet. A quilt had been draped from a rope strung in front of the exposed side of bed during the birth, but it was pulled back now.

It must have been dawn, rather than dusk. It seems the light is increasing. The women continue their vigil, washing some things in a tub on a plain wood table. Someone comes for them in a wagon, later (it is afternoon by then, I think) - a young man whom they are glad to see. He hears the news, says something, grins, takes off his hat and enters over the narrow threshold. He talks to Jean, and admires the baby. This man, (I think his name is Virgil) is a good, lovable and loving person. He is quick to anger, though, if he perceives himself or his clan threatened from out-side, and then he can be fierce. At first, I thought this was a husband of one of the sisters, but then I realized he is a brother - a Cameron.

James Richardson and Virgil Cameron had grown up together, as close as brothers. Hunting rabbits and squirrels together, they had shared, and later often told, adventures filled with close escapes and blood-seeking Indians. There was a time when James had felt overpowered by the Cam-eron Clan. Now their numbers had been reduced by a general migration into Georgia which had included among its ranks, his own younger Rich-ardson brothers. The remaining Cameron branch, however, was still strong, demanding their due and accepting no insults.

* * *

One day, when the child was old enough to walk, James had gone to town to sell a wagon load of corn: "He will not be back until late," Jean thought, because he was a man well-thought of and liked, and as such was sure to be waylaid by those friends he met with in the town, for convivial discussions of crops and politics. She knew how it was. She was used to it by now, but it was lonely for her sometimes.

She was stringing up corn to dry and later to feed her black and white-spotted fowl. She tied each ear with twine, wrapping twine around base of ear, going on to the next ear, in succession. The length of twine in between each ear was looped over a peg on the rafters under the barn roof. Unlike the cabin, there is a raised wood floor in the building. Things ran around under there. She was afraid of rats, and was nervous, warily looking into corners, and jumping with a start every time she heard a rustle of shucks. She had pleaded with James, her husband, to trap the rats, but he had always been busy with something else. He didn't think she had to worry about it, but she had a recurring dream and it scared her to death.

She bent over to pick up another ear, and was about to pull the shucks back from the kernels, to hang it, when she saw her worst fear - a large rat, red-eyed and crouching to spring. She screamed, flinging the ear of corn aside where it hit a metal pan hanging on the side of the barn wall. The clanging echoed the alarm in her mind - a sickening sense of horrible fate — Oh, God! It had happened; it was *real*. Her mind said, "Run" but it was too late. The rat leapt for her sleeve, and even before she could raise herself entirely, he had plunged his yellow teeth into her white throat. Slobbering, he then leapt to the pile of packing cases, where he performed a wild, seemingly rejoicing dance, back and forth, back and forth, staggering, raising himself on hind legs, frothing at the mouth, squeaking loudly. Then he clumsily lay down, panting, in a corner made by the piles of crates, still watching her from red-lit eyes, while she continued that long scream that seemed to have started hours ago and hung in the air for an eternity. She clutched her neck as she bolted from the loft, her scream rising up a scale as she realized it was covered with the slime of rat saliva. She slapped at the drool, furiously, trying to rid herself of it, then staring at it in horror as it dripped from her fingers, desperately scrubbing her hand on the side of her skirt and apron as she ran out of the loft.

Completely hysterical by then, she missed her footing on the ladder and fell into the dirty hay below. She raised herself up again, gurgling as tears streamed down her face along with her long hair which had escaped its knot, making it difficult for her to see. Through a haze she fled through the barn door and across the yard to the well at the rear of the cabin, where a drawn bucket of still-cool water awaited, beckoning her. No oasis had ever seemed more vital, more pure - "Please, God, Please God" she moaned as she ran.

By this time, the child, who had been peacefully playing in the dirt yard near the cabin door, had heard her screaming and was terror-struck. He stood stock-still and rooted to the ground, bawling loudly as she ran toward him on her way to the well. The air about them seemed electrified with a rare horror, of guardian angels in disarray. Her mother-heart wanted to hush, to calm her child, yet she knew she must cleanse the filth from her now, now! So she ran around him to the well. Still shaking violently, she looked toward her child and tried making soothing noises, saying words she did not recognize, as she doused herself with pure, clean water from the bucket. Forcing aside the immense aversion she felt toward touching that disgusting saliva, she bathed her neck with her apron - sopping it with water. The cool cleansing water sluiced the stuff from her. She was careful not to let it drip on her dress, but leaned forward to let it drip on the ground in front of her. As it splattered to the ground, there was yellow froth and dirt mixed into the blood. She stared at it and the shock started her moaning again and made her feel faint, but she did not scream anymore, because of the child. There was a lot of blood, now. She could see it and feel the warm trickle from the punctures. The child, not fooled by her caressing words, was still bawling. Jerking himself loose from the spot where his little legs had frozen, he stretched out his arms and stumbled toward her. Hurrying, she stripped the filthy apron from her and washed her hands again, not wanting to touch her child, for she was foul, yet she yearned to comfort him.

She would not let him into her arms when he came, although it tore her heart. Holding his hand she walked him back into the house. There, she lifted him onto his cot and stroked his hair, soothing him with gentle words. He was somewhat better then, but troubled, for he wanted her arms around him, and wondered why she didn't gather him to her . . . then he noticed the blood oozing from his mother's throat. He was shocked by this odd thing and began to sob anew. She gave him a biscuit, which he could not eat, but crumbled onto the cot, sobbing pitifully. He was still reaching out for her when she turned away to find clean clothes and something to bandage and stop the flow of blood.

* * *

Later in the day, James returned. The place was so quiet he thought, at first, that there was no one there. Then he saw his little boy - hiccupping and white-faced - sitting on the slab floor beside his mother's bed. The child was exhausted and leaned his head weakly against the bed frame where his mother's hand lay upon his silken head. Jean was weak from the loss of blood, but had managed to staunch the flow and had saved her strength the best she could, for the comforting of the child. James's heart turned over and fear filled his eyes and made his voice shake as he drew the story from her.

It was too far and too late in the evening for all of them to make the trip in the wagon to the only doctor in these parts. He could go on horse-back to fetch him, but he was filled with dread and great misgivings about leaving the two alone in the house. ("*Too late,*" some demon chided him,

"You're *too late*.") Jean wanted to send the child to her family, and to wait alone, but the child would not leave his mother willingly. In the darkening, dusky room, Jean reached out to touch his small, cold hand and whispered for him to go with his father. "Do it for Mama," she said, and surprisingly then, he went. He was taken up on the saddle horn to ride against his father's chest, where he fell asleep to the mingled rhythms of James's heavy, rapid heartbeat and the horse's great hoofs striking the clay road. At the "Aunts' house," as the boy thought of it - the Cameron homestead - he was taken up, fed and put to sleep. He could hardly think anymore about what had happened, and fell asleep in his grandfather's featherbed.

(Jean's ordeal during all this time can hardly be imagined by a person of sanity. Since the child left her and she was no longer responsible for him, she lapsed into a state which allowed no thought at all, as though she were part of the quilt which covered her, and not human - not *mortal* - for death loomed at the closed door of her mind, and she could not bear with it now.)

I see her sisters and her brother, Virgil, riding the rattling wagon out of their yard and into the night as fast as it had ever gone. Those three grim profiles are chiseled against the moonlight, like a triple cameo, linked both by blood and purpose.

The jolting of the wagon jarred their bones, but not the vision which all three shared: Their well-loved sister - Jean, the awful rat at her throat . . an unbearable vision. Jean, weak with loss of blood and dying, perhaps even as they rode . . . *so slow, so slow*. . . . and looking into the future, they saw the worst possible nightmare - Jean in the grip of the hydrophobia, in which she suffered the extremities of which they had heard . . . hellish tales embroidered upon by grizzled pioneers who had witnessed these and other horrors of their raw country. By the time they neared the homestead, their bones were nearly jolted from their sockets, but they scarcely knew, because their foreboding was so great. Virgil, whose great strength welled up in him as a natural spring, was rendered impotent now, a most unwelcome feeling for him. As he had driven the horses at that unaccustomed pace through that moonlit night, unmanly tears had rolled down his cheeks and into whiskers bleached red by the sun - but no one saw or cared.

The doctor and James were late coming. The doctor was in the middle of a joyous, life-giving occasion - the birth of Sutton's twins. He was reluctant to leave a difficult birth for what was surely a lost life at that homestead in the upper pastures. James could not bring himself to force the doctor to come (which is what he desperately wanted to do) while he was a guest in the Sutton house. He could hear the Mrs. Sutton's cries mingled with the admonitions of the doctor. Mr. Sutton, sitting hunched over in a slat-back chair, would look up at James occasionally when he paced by, but said nothing. Finally, James removed himself to the yard where the Sutton children waited - quiet, for a change. They were all tow-headed and stared at him without speaking from haunting, identical blue eyes. When the doctor tossed the last of the bloody water from the basin into the yard, he saw James hunched over and heaving, by the pines. His heart turned over and once again he cursed that organ's tenderness. He gave instructions to the oldest daughter and Mr. Sutton, now the father of nine. He felt unbearably tired and abused. His anger made him abuse James, in turn, on the ride out. He should have taken better care of his wife, he said coldly.

Although his mare kept pace with the doctor's graying roan, inwardly, James rode alone through the pit of Hell. Yet, at the same time, he was strangely conscious of the beauty of the night - the stars were particularly brilliant and the moon rode high through blue-edged, drifting clouds.

As they rode, the doctor was ranting. He was tired of people expecting miracles from him - miracles he could not give them - while they looked at him with pathetic eyes. He glared at James and told him baldly, that, judging from what he had been told, the rat probably had hydrophobia and if it were so, there was no hope for his wife. James heard him but his thoughts slid away and hid. The doctor had never met Jean, or he couldn't talk that way, James knew. He couldn't be so hard and cold if he had ever looked into Jean's eyes - those eyes as blue as fall asters. Moonlight bleached the doctor's face into a craggy skull, but it was not his face James saw as he stared toward him, but rather Jean's. James' own eyes were black holes of bottomless misery and the doctor became uncomfortable and turned away, so that they continued their ride in silence.

Inside his hell, James was thinking, over and over, how Jean had always been afraid of the rats in the barn. She was a bit afraid of the bugs and the lizards which came after the bugs, but when those little things would get in the house, she would shoo them out, or kill them. He hadn't thought much about it. There were always rats in barns where corn and hay were kept. It had seemed useless to trap them eternally, when there were always others to take their place, scurrying in from the woods behind the homestead. He should have gotten cats, but cats, they said, could suck the breath from a new-born child, and he had never liked them. Now she was dying, and it was his fault. She might even be gone by the time they got there. At this last thought, his face blanched even whiter and he urged his mare to even greater speed.

He was wrong. It took a long time for Jean to die.

At first, they pretended it might not even happen. For a while, she seemed well enough, physically. The wound healed over except for a glassy scar. However, it became clear that Jean would never be the same again, even if she lived. Mary stayed with her, but Jean didn't seem to notice that her sister was there most of the time. She sat in the rocker, shrouded up in an old quilt that Mary had bundled around her that first day she was able to sit up, and she stayed there - day in and day out, sunrise to sundown - taking no interest in anything. The silence was interrupted from time to time when her nervous rocking, rocking, rocking, took on momentum, and the tension in her built up to stifled moans and sometimes sudden shrieks while she picked at the bandages on her throat. Mary would drop what she was doing and try to soothe her, but her eyes would be wild - like she was having a waking nightmare.

James spent the first couple of days at the barn with his gun, purging himself of his guilt with unleashed fury and noise, until finally, on the third day, screams echoed from the cabin and Mary showed up in the doorway, flapping her arms and apron at him to stop. After that, he just set traps and crushed their heads with his booted heel afterward. There was little comfort in it. He didn't tell anyone when he had found the dead rat. He just picked up the strangely stiffened, rotting carcass and carried it off to the woods edge to bury it deep. Mary, watching from the cabin door, saw what he carried, noticed how very long it took him to bury it and return, and tears ran freely down her face. Their worst fear was now confirmed.

Virgil, determined to raise Jean's spirits, (for that could only be good, he said) brought to her her favorite flowers from the higher pastures. Joe Pye weed, trumpet vine, blue and gold asters. Sitting beside his vacant-eyed sister, he patiently wove them into a wreath, reminding her how they used to sit on the roots of the old oak doing just this, when they were children together (surely a long time ago). How they had loved the land, its crystal streams winding about rolling hills - the deer which had stood still and stared at them as they played in the meadow.

As he draped the wreath about her neck, tenderly, and careful to avoid the bandage, she finally seemed to become really aware. He was thrilled and remained as motionless as the deer while she stared steadily into his face - the face of the brother she loved so much. Tears welled up into her eyes, reflecting the blue of the asters lying on her breast. She reached out a thin hand to cover his, and big, courageous Virgil, touched to the quick of his being, broke down and bawled into her lap, great wrenching sobs. Jean laid her hand on his head, stroking it as she did her child. She already knew, and told him softly, that there was no going back to that beautiful land of their remembrance.

Although she had lost that former unawareness of her surroundings, she went back to dreaming out the window. But now, at least sometimes, she had a new vision - one which eased her soul and mind. She and Virgil were in another place, and this place was clean and pure, all unspoiled by vermin and disease, with virgin forests and perfect flowers. They walked through pastures strewn with these flowers of rich, jewel-like colors, brighter and purer than any she had ever seen. They could pick them as they chose, to make beautiful crowns and wreaths, yet there was never an empty space from where they gathered them . . . and all around, there was a great light which seemed to bathe the trees, flowers and themselves with its warm and comforting glow. It was bright, but not blinding, soothing, but not severe. She shivered with delight of it. Then as she and Virgil looked into the distance, they could see James, beloved James, moving through the flowers toward them, his dark hair ruffled in that wonderfully refreshing breeze which seemed to revive and renew with its every breath. Hurrying toward him, they were supremely happy. (Mary happened by as Jean sat in this dream, and saw the unearthly smile which had transformed her face. She was shaken and alarmed. Not wanting to touch her, nevertheless, she watched to see if she were still with them, or if she had already escaped to the beyond.)

They had been warned what to expect, unless a miracle occurred. They often prayed, but no intercession came this time. When she became truly sick, they all moved back to Cameron's. The boy was no longer allowed to see her. It was hard, for when he heard her scream, he would flail at them and bawl that they were hurting his mother.

The waiting was misery and hard work. Grandfather Cameron, an invalid himself, required care also. The other Cameron sister, Caro, the wife of Jamie McBride, and their near neighbor, came over daily. The old man, although born in Scotland had come over from Ireland. Thinking he would distract the pitiful little boy, he told him tales, mumbled through toothless gums, that the child couldn't understand - tales of war and clans, and a bitter Irish sojourn.

At first, Mary angrily protested against tying Jean down to the bed. "She's my *sister*!" she said, and then tried to make Jean as comfortable as possible - placing a soft pillow under her head as she thrashed about in her sweat, cooling her skin with damp cloths, which seemed to drive Jean more mad. Later, when they had to tie her down on the floor, even Mary began to hope the end was near. Jean was not pretty Jean anymore, but a clawing, slobbering, pitiful wretch. Her hair hadn't been combed for days, and they couldn't restrain her enough to do it. Mary just couldn't stand it, sometimes. She was a tough country girl, and had delivered several babies and foals, with ease, but this was different. She couldn't bear to watch this extraordinary degeneration and the supreme pain which, she was sure, accompanied it. Her sister was a lovely creature, kind and good. It wasn't right, and inwardly she fought an angry battle with the death-angel, swearing when he finally came she would spit in his eye.

Finally, the crisis they had at first dreaded and then begun to long for, came. After a few minutes of retching and straining at the tethers which held her earthbound, Jean floated away, and the body she left behind was finally still. Those who watched that earthly face saw that it eased and became pretty again. Then suddenly, an expression of unutterable delight,

(so quick that, later, they doubted they'd really seen it) flashed across it. . .
Finally, the features were still, composed in perfect peace at last.

No one else, not one of them still in that earthly household, had peace
for a long time. They were bone-weary and dried up. All they were left with
was bitterness and the ashes of a once-hopeful life. The boy was dressed in
a new black suit and taken to the cemetery with his father. Both of them
seemed oblivious of anything done for, or to them - obeying as directed,
but staring at nothing. The settler's cemetery, still raw in its newness, nevertheless held several graves, most of them small. Caro's two infants lay
there - one still-born, the other, Dudley, had died at "2 years, 2 months,
1 day"; of a mysterious fever. Infant mortality was a reality, braced for by
young parents. Each time the community attended the funeral of one of
these temporary gifts from heaven, each mother, shaken and chastened,
went home with renewed determination to hover over her children and
keep the angel of death at bay. At this burial, the Camerons, Virgil especially, were too sunk in their own grief to notice very much the stillness
of James and the boy. Unlike those two, the Camerons were different; they
grieved greatly, loudly and openly - as mighty people did.

Afterward, Virgil, with a stony heart, walked out over the pastures and
came back alone in the evening to place a wreath over the cypress marker
on the grave. Mary wore a lock of Jean's hair in her mother's old locket.
During those days when her grief stabbed her heart, she would clasp the
locket on her bosom, until it eased. But, the Camerons all shared their
anguish. The other two - James and his son, were a different breed and
could not expel the poison so easily. Thankfully, Jean's son was but a child,
and safe in the Cameron arms once more, he was loved into forgetfulness
at last.

Eventually, James left Cameron's and returned to his homestead, alone.
After a few days of wandering about and staring into emptiness, he went

out with his gun, and as the sun set over the fringe of the trees behind the pastures, he walked into those woods and was never seen again.

Virgil, who set out to look for him, returned, burning up with swamp fever. He died at Cameron's, in the same year - 1823. Those wounded hearts who were left behind would sometimes say, "Ah, well, they're with pretty Jean, now."

* * *

Dear Richard,

"Soup" is much longer than the others. Yet the character has so many adventures that I haven't been able to shorten it. I wish I knew what group or nation the ship's captain and owner represented and what their mission was. The strongest scenes or sensations for me were the grandma's face in the kitchen scenes, the loving feelings in that room, the smell of yeasty bread, the absolutely gorgeous colors of that panoramic expanse of sky over scrubby low land that they could see from their house; the feeling he had when he faced murder, and the gratitude he felt for other people and the turtle. That sense of warmth and gentleness he had with his own children at his own kitchen table was due to his ability to glean through his past experiences - keeping the good and discarding the negative.

As we are still on the question of whether or not these are past life experiences, I will say I have a great love for yeast bread and I'm always weak with hunger whenever I smell it baking. My favorite, most satisfying meal in childhood was my mother's soup and I love it today, but it must be thick with vegetables and meat, not thin broth.

I couldn't learn to swim when I was a child because I would be overcome with fear when my father or sisters held me in the water. I just couldn't let them touch me. I knew I should trust them; that they wouldn't really let me drown, but I was always overwhelmed with a *threatening* feeling. I like the water and live near the sea. I am attracted to ships and sailing vessels, but haven't been indulged in that in this life. I was on a ship only once. I will say I wasn't seasick and enjoyed the sensation. I have always especially loved turtles, and I'm attracted to things Dutch, including wooden shoes and the blond Dutch boy and girl quilt my mother made. I have always wanted to live on a tropical island, but doesn't everyone? However, I have a fear of heights, or rather of being on a precipice, which doesn't correlate with this boy's exhilaration on his mast high above the sea.

Was there such a term for a sailor called "sail monkey?" I haven't a clue. This is only one of many things I can't verify and don't fully understand.

But you know what has really come to my attention? These are stories within a story. My life is a story; your life is a story. If we "reincarnate" then each of us has a whole string of stories that we are not presently conscious of. In that case, we are all actors, each living a role that we have, previous to birth, picked out for ourselves for this particular time. Perhaps actors are very fortunate. They can live out their evolution in the fast track, experiencing "pretend" lives within their present one. Maybe that is why some of them seem to be living at a break-neck pace.

Anyway, I think we crave particular adventures, experiences and challenges and manifest them in our lives. We confront our bogey men, our fears, and hopefully, we banish them. My stories show a spiritual nobility in man. "The shallows, wherein the body dwells, gives little evidence of it, but it is there. When this nobility reveals itself, the story is certainly worth the telling." Don't ask me where I got this, I don't know.

Perhaps, even if we don't always act wisely, we should live richly and nobly – with that inner love that reveals us as we really are.

When I see someone this day, even if I sense what he really is, I am seeing only the tiniest bit of his essence. Don't you think it is ironic that all we see is the superficial action figure when the real action is going on inside? Inside is something awesome struggling to manifest itself beyond its pitiful prison. This realization has changed and embarrassed me. My shortcomings are coming to light. How can I criticize others? I don't know where they've been before in their travels, their experiences. They are trying to work out the tangles and smooth the hard places in their being, just as I am. Their experience here, where (we think) we know them, is only a single page, tomorrow's fleeting memory.

Soup

As far as the eye can see the landscape is flat and rather muddy — a great expanse of open fields scattered with twiggy growth. Bushy windbreaks angle across the fields, and only an occasional tree or windmill breaks the flattened skyline. It would seem this view should be extremely monotonous, yet it has a sweet, wild beauty, especially at this time of day . . . There is the most startlingly beautiful sunset beyond the fields - brilliant shades of orange fill the entire horizon and the twisted limbs of the thorn trees and wiry scrub which are laid against it look like lace - no tame, disciplined embroidery done by a lady, but wild and eerie lace - adorning the scarlet petticoat of a heathen goddess.

Within this landscape there is a small cottage, and inside are a little boy and his grandmother. This is his story. I don't know his name, but in order to tell it properly, I will call him Jan. I see them together at their small rustic table having their supper. Their faces are lit by the warm glow from the fireplace. Its light settles in the wrinkles around his grandmother's scrunched mouth, illuminating the finer lines around her eyes, the high rounded cheeks. She looks up at her grandson. Her eyes are a lovely cornflower blue. Her face is very dear to her grandson and as he reaches out to touch it tenderly with his fingertips, his heart turns over with the great love he has for her. She is a gentle, loving soul. (His mother had also been blessed with pretty blue eyes and nice round apple cheeks. She had lived here with them but now she is dead.) This scene is very vivid. I can sense his intense happiness, his adoration of his grandmother; even the steam and aroma of the soup.

(All their evening meals are soup, because she has no teeth to chew more solid food.)

This cottage means warmth and love to the boy. His love is centered on his grandmother - spilling over to include the cottage, their daily life, and the bit of earth they live upon. It is a greatly satisfying life to him, for they are ignorant of anything else. They do not even know who rules their country now. Their life consists of the day to day struggle for food, warmth and the repair of their shelter. They are so far beneath that struggle for power and gain that it is of no consequence here. It flows above and past them where they dwell in this still spot. If armed soldiers were to come here, why would they come to their door? There is nothing for them here. And grandma and grandson would only be told there was a change in their rulership, about which they care nothing, for it meant nothing. There would be no extra turnips, no gifts of pigs or chickens, flooding would not cease and fertility of the soil would not return.

They are more keenly aware of sensations than people in busy cities - of love, beauty, the delight of satisfied hunger, the pangs of hunger not yet satisfied, the thrill of sunsets and the misery of struggling through the mire; these sensations are magnified because only these simple things fill their days. Ignorant and isolated, they lead a mere mite's existence in a tiny corner of a busy world about which they know nothing.

They wear wooden shoes out of doors, but when they come indoors, they change to soft woolen slippers. It is often damp and cold here, but they prefer the weather a bit cold, since after the freeze, they are able to walk more easily than when it is muddy. Summers are short in this country and there are great swarms of flies, then. Their garden is extremely important to them. They grow, among other things, a sort of root plant, which looks like a large turnip or beet. Jan feeds these to the hogs which bite into them lustily, dreaming away into space as they chew each large root down into smaller and smaller pieces. As he watches them eat, he wonders what they have to dream about. They will never kill these hogs that they have saved for breeding, for then they would surely starve, but there has been no litter of pigs from the sow this year and this makes the grandmother and boy fearful.

They used to have a cow and calf, (that was when life was good - "the time of the cow" they still thought of it). The cow had been a good milk cow. They had sold the extra milk, butter and, sometimes, a cheese. Later, when she did not give as much milk and his grandmother was ailing, they would sell all the cream and butter, keeping only the skimmed milk for themselves. After that, the cow had died and everything was worse than ever. Sometimes, the only vegetables in their soup were green onions, the tops of the root that they feed to the pigs, and a wild herb. A few times, she has even used a kind of grass, boiling it, then straining it out of the liquid and throwing it away. She insists the broth of such is at least nourishing and better than no herbage at all.

The grandmother's teeth have almost all needed pulling, and she has pulled them herself with a metal tool that has a claw on one end. It wasn't easy to wrench some of them out, but she would not ask her grandson to do it, for she knows how it would upset him. Her bed is made onto the wall - like a shelf. I see her lying there, turned to the wall, her legs drawn up because of the pain in her mouth. She has many pains, because she is old and ill. She never complains to him, but just goes to bed. She does not go outdoors much, for in these latter years the wooden shoes make her suffer so. Her toes are all knotted and skewed out of their natural position - piti-ful, twisted things. It is impossible to cram them into the wooden shoes, even though her grandson has hollowed them out more to accommodate her toes. If she must go out, she stays away from the mud, wearing the soft, splayed leather shoes she has fashioned for herself.

The gown she wears is a rough woven material. This common material for peasant garb does not bother the young, but her skin - so thin and transparent, so shockingly delicate in her old age - is red and sore in places from the scraping of that harsh fiber. She makes an unguent of melted beeswax and grease and applies this to her skin. In this, her final year on earth, she often goes about the house without *her gown, clothed only in her softer underskirts and bodice, her shame of being half-dressed before her grandson overridden by her discomfort.*

Although he barely remembered his mother, he remembered his father quite well, with, if not as great a love as he held for his grandmother, as least with fondness and gratitude. His father had been a steward for the farmer on whose bounty they lived, on whose land they dwelled. Unlike some peasants, he was skilled in mathematics and could read and write enough to keep accounts of the farm. This rudimentary knowledge he had passed down to Jan, who had strained his eyes by candlelight for enough precious hours to have absorbed a little of his father's teaching. This was his only inheritance from his sire. For after the death of his mother, his father had taken to staying at the farm. A room in the stables was warm enough for him; the kitchen where he was well fed was nearby and there was a milkmaid who came and crept into his cot to ease the loss of his pretty blue-eyed wife.

Jan knew about all this. It caused him no ill feeling – this was the way of life. His father would return to their cottage at intervals, bringing whatever he could that would feed them awhile or make their lives easier in some way. Then in the evening, Jan would have his father with him, by the stove, or if it were in summer, outside where they would sit in their stick chairs under the eaves. His father would rock backward so that his chair bore his weight on its rear legs, the backrest leaning against the cottage wall. In this way he eased his aching back. Jan copied this eagerly, as he did most things his father did. But his father was not one to fill a quiet void with idle words, so they sat on in silence, Jan basking in the nearness of this man, wondering about him, but not asking. Sometimes they worked, doing repairs on the cottage, or his father would ask Jan to show him his sums he had worked since the last time they met thus.

One day Jan had gone out into the yard with a knife and basin, to cut cabbages. He stopped, struck still by a distant figure flapping toward him like a scarecrow in the wind. The knife and basin fell from his hands. He could not tell what the man was shrieking about, yet he froze in fear from the sound of him. It was Pieter, a stable hand at the farm. The news he brought was fearful indeed. Jan's father had been killed at the farm. Standing in a lot where cattle had been brought to be examined, he had been crushed against the fence, and then gored, by the farmer's new bull.

The thing that bothered Jan the most was that the farmer would not kill the bull afterward. The farmer showed Jan the receipt for the bull. He held it out, pointing to the large sum he had paid for the animal. Nodding, he seemed to think that this explained all – that any logical person would understand why he had not put the animal down for the killing of his servant. But Jan's heart broke. His hands fumbled for his pockets as he thought of it. He had nothing to show to the farmer. He had no receipt for his father, yet wasn't he more than equal to the price of a bull? Not to the farmer, he wasn't. Only Jan and his grandmother felt his loss. The farmer had allowed them to stay on in the cottage, promising the use of it for the lifetime of the grandmother, but times were very hard after the death of his father.

As he was growing into a youth, Jan's hunger was never quite satisfied. It seemed to him that his grandmother was always quite content with their meals (her appetite was small) and he was ashamed to tell her that he was still hungry, because he knew they had very little food. They had to forage for whatever they could find, for now they were very poor. Sometimes he would find berries and bird's eggs, if it was the season. He began to go to the village to find work every day. Seldom did anyone hire him, for nearly all of the villagers had plenty of children to do such chores as he was able to do. Sometimes he was hired to run errands, or to deliver merchandise in a hand cart to those who had bought it, and although this earned only the smallest coin, he was grateful, and he always spent his earnings upon flour, seed or such things that would bring them sustenance a little longer.

He was a good lad, but one day while he was in the village, sin overtook him. He smelled it on the air, and it was too potent, too wonderful, and he was too hungry, to resist. Indeed, he had never smelled anything like it before. His mouth watering, he was drawn toward the house from which this delightful smell emanated. There, he spied a round, fragrant loaf within reach of a low window of the cottage and he reached in and snatched it with shaking hands.

The woman who had baked the bread glimpsed the disappearance of her loaf, and whisked out of her door, to see who had stolen it. "Ho there," she cried, and the honest boy - instead of running away - stopped and stood looking down at the loaf and his tears fell on the crust as he waited for her to come and club him, or worse, for stealing it. The woman strode across the yard, her arms rolled up in her apron as she surveyed the bread and the boy. His hands were none too clean and the bread was slightly soiled. She was fastidious, and too, her heart was touched by his thin frame and shamed expression. Since she was both kind and wise, she could see he was not a common thief. So, she told him to keep it, or eat it, but to come to her house when he was finished and she would give him work to do in return for the bread.

Relief washed over him, gratitude expanding his inside so that the words flew out of him in a stream. He would eat the bread *after* he had done his work, and if he had pleased her with it, he said as they went back to her cottage, he loping along like a half-grown pup by her side. She laughed, because she was a bit startled by this burst of boyish eagerness, but almost immediately her heart was seized by him. Seen close-up, he was too thin. Here was a starving boy who put off assuaging his hunger until he had done the honorable thing.

Jan naturally loved old women, because of the love he bore for his grandmother. This woman, a widow, was a little younger than his grandmother, he thought, and she was much better off than they were, for she had a nice cottage, a large stove and pantry, a milk cow and fowl - all of which were real riches in this boy's eyes. He was weak with hunger and nervousness, but he swept the cobbled walk and yard, fetched water, milked the cow and fed the fire. Then he scoured the hillsides for kindling and bringing it, filled the box by the stove. The widow was well pleased with his work, for he had done more than she had expected, or had asked him to do. Warmed by her concern for him, his heart opened up like a flower and he explained the situation to her of his grandmother, who was good and kind, but of small appetite and small means. This was when their friendship began and their bargain was struck. She would give him bread whenever he was hungry, and he would work for her in return for that and a bit of money now and then.

On his way home, he stopped just outside the village and sitting on a rock by the stream he devoured the whole of the loaf, rinsing it down with the fresh cold water. He did not spare a crumb, for he could not think of a way to explain part of a loaf of bread to his grandmother, and he was truly starving. Nothing had ever tasted as good to the boy as that loaf, and for all his lifetime thereafter, he relished the kind of bread that the widow had made.

The bargain turned out to be an excellent one for both parties. The widow needed some help with her property (for her sons were all grown and living elsewhere) and the boy filled out with the good food she gave him. Sometimes she would open one side of a half-loaf of bread with her knife and poke a wedge of meat or slices of boiled egg into it before she gave it to him - for, she reasoned, a growing boy must have nourishment. When there was enough in her garden, she sent little gifts to his grandmother - a nice large turnip or little cabbages - and she helped them by breeding their sow with her boar, so that soon there were more pigs in their lot.

His grandmother had been surprised when he said that he now worked for Bess, the widow, but she was pleased - not just because of the food - but because the widow had some standing in the village and was respected for her wisdom. She was proud of her grandson, and thinking he was becoming a man, it occurred to her to give him more solid food, not minced or stewed to the softness that she had herself. Jan was grateful and truly happy now that he was free of that constant, nagging hunger.

The widow Bess's grown sons were good to her and brought her money and gifts. Two of them worked for a great man, and earned a good living. Griff, the younger, had gone to sea, and came to see his mother less often, but once Jan met him when he came to visit her. Griff liked being a sailor, for he was adventurous and liked the sea. It was hard work, he told Jan, but if the Captain was a good man, then it was a good life and exciting. The tales Griff told about his and other mariner's adventures at sea amazed the ignorant boy, and if Griff had not been the honest widow's son, Jan would have thought him a liar.

Bess loved her sons, and as her affection for Jan grew, he became like another son to her. With a mother's care comes worry, so the widow turned her thoughts to what future the boy might have. Jan was unskilled in any trade and she knew that when his grandmother died, he would have to leave the cottage, since the landlord had allowed them to remain there as a charity for the rest of his grandmother's lifetime, in return for the service that their family had rendered in the years past. The village held no promise for him. Since her son was a sailor and her brother was a sea Captain, she thought a sea-going life was a good one, so she began to turn over in her mind whether that occupation might be the salvation of the boy. She had seen how his eyes lit up while he listened to Griff's tales.

At the same time that Jan started to flourish, his grandmother began to decline. She got up from her bed less and less, and her pain became so much worse that eventually, in her last days, she cried out in agony - no longer conscious that she was scaring her beloved grandchild. Clutching her chest and throat, she thrashed about as he leaned over to catch her gasping words - something about "the worm," "the worm" that was "eating her from within." These words - and the vision of such a thing - filled the boy with horror. Finally, the widow had come to stay and watch over the grandmother, and when he told her, she tried to reassure him that there was not really a worm there in his grandmother's heart, only a gnawing pain. But that didn't soothe him very much when she would shriek and moan upon her narrow cot. In the light from the one window, her out-flung arms, so thin and bloodless they seemed translucent - would violently shake and he would tremble with her - his eyes wide and staring as he bent over her - for his vision of the worm eating its way through her heart like an apple still lingered.

During those last days, his grandmother was mostly unaware of anything outside her inward suffering, but suddenly at the end, she became as lucid as he could ever remember her. She lay there still and calm and softly said his name. He stirred from the verge of sleep and looking down at her, he was amazed, for there was no pain on her face then - on the contrary - it was beautiful with the glory of age and appeared as though it were lit from inside by a candle. She seemed to glow - the great love she had for him beaming from her eyes. . . . His heart leapt out to her as he reached out to hold her hand - but then, abruptly, that candle was snuffed out.

Suddenly, the room was still and empty of life and love. A chill breath of air feathered the nape of his neck. Her bony hand turned cold and fell from his as he shuddered and jumped to his feet. He stared in shock at the lifeless husk that now lay on the bed. What was this thing? This was not his grandmother lying there! It was an ugly thing - an old, distorted, wrinkled carcass. This was a stranger!

As soon as his grandmother had gone, it was as though he had awakened in a strange place where nothing was familiar. The little house which was so beloved by him before, now seemed odd. There were things about it - cold and shabby things - that he had never noticed before, and it frightened him that everything seemed so strange. Every little thing brought fresh terror to his mind and soul. Finally, he could not stand the place any longer. When the landowner's agent came and pressed him to leave he was poised like a nervous, chittering sparrow teetering upon the sill - ready to dart up and fly away.

But what was he to do?

Although he was only thirteen, when the widow encouraged him to go to the seaport and find work upon a ship, he seized the idea. She worried over it, and hoped she had done the right thing - but, she reasoned, what else was there for him to do? His fate at sea could hardly be worse. So, the few shabby things his grandmother had owned were sold. At that time, the farmer came and set firmly into Jan's palm, some silver coins that he said was pay he owed Jan's father. Jan observed him as he cleared his throat and spoke out decisively. He knew his father had no more pay coming to him, but the farmer needed to give him something, so he took it. And that, together with some money that the widow gave him, furnished enough coins for his subsistence for a short time at Amsterdam, until he could find work.

Oh, that great sea-city of Amsterdam! The port and its many tall buildings were talked about in their village as though it were a foreign country - even though it was only a little over forty miles away. The families in their sparsely inhabited area of the Netherlands had lived for generations on

that spot and few had roamed beyond it. It required a good deal of courage, they thought, to contemplate tearing oneself away from the only bit of
earth one had ever known and going to such an alien place as Amsterdam.
So, the villagers talked and speculated about this adventure of Jan's and
how the widow's son was to help him get work aboard a ship at that city.

He set out on foot and walked a good part of the way. He could not
travel in the dark and found a hut for sheep where there was dry hay. There
the grateful boy made a nest, because, although it was infested with vermin
at least it was dry, but it was not to last. Before daybreak, the shepherd
found him there and demanded money for his stay there among the owls,
feral cats and rats. Indignant, Jan left and walked slowly down the moonlit
path until daylight afforded him better traveling.

He was lucky, a few times, when he was taken aboard the carts of farmers who were taking their produce to market. He slept in the sun aboard
a cart full of rolling cabbages, dreaming of the sea. These country folk
offered him food - apples, grapes, a bit of bread - and he ate turnips from a
field he passed by. Because he was saving every coin, he did not buy food in
any village he passed through, so when he finally arrived in that great city,
he was already weak with hunger.

There, the sight that greeted him made him weak indeed. He could
not take it in, for he had never seen such tall buildings and so many people.
The noise was overpowering to ears attuned to hear a lone lark's song across
empty fields. Although his heart raced, he told himself he was not afraid,
for he would do what he had to do. Jan was only a small person in a big city
- but he was fortunate. Since he had no idea what the future would hold for
him and was ignorant of the ways of the great world, he had no qualms but
rushed hopefully toward the tumult at the docks.

It was the first sight of the sea that took his breath away and drew
him up short. He stood riveted to the quay - overwhelmed by its hugeness.

It was not just the breadth of it (he could see nothing but water all the way to the horizon) but its *fullness* - It seemed to billow up and forward, as though it were full to overflowing, and would, at any moment, flow over the barely-confining restraint of the wall and flood the city. As he stared at it, there was a sinking sensation in his spine and his breath began to come in little gasps . . . . He tore his eyes away from it to look at all the people around him and could scarcely believe that they were just coming and going - seemingly oblivious to any danger at all. Slowly, his gaze returned to the water, for he was drawn to it and afraid at the same time. The sight of it - so vast and swollen - hypnotized him. He stared as his mind struggled to accept it . . . . The continuous motion of its mounds of liquid surging upward and then sinking alarmingly as though their bottoms had fallen out . . . . Ugh! It sickened him and made him dizzy, so that he stumbled a little way to a bench, fell on it and sat there, light-headed, his teeth chattering; his mind awhirl. So this was the sea! . . . . That great sea that he was supposed to sail upon! He was alarmed and filled with misgiving that he had come all this way for this!

Still, he had no choice. In an effort to accustom himself to it, he continued to sit on the bench and stare at the water as it swelled and sank . . . pushing upward out of the depths, and sinking away . . . heaving and swelling like a fat man's chest. His hands held tightly to the bench and he forced himself to look out over the whole expanse of it that could be seen. Everywhere the water was spiked with masts of sea-going ships sailing in and out, and small boats with fishermen aboard them. All were going about their business with no fear. His weaving eyes focused on a fisherman, balanced precariously on the bow of his boat, throwing a rope to a man on the pier. As he sat and watched the people working, his anxiety faded somewhat and he became aware of his hunger. Ah! That, he told himself, was why he was feeling ill. Thinking he would find a food vendor, he got up and walked on, but he averted his eyes from the heaving sea so that he could walk steadily.

There were vendors selling food cooked over braziers and open fires and the smells made his stomach shrivel; his mouth to salivate. He shopped carefully for the best buy and settled for a scorched leg of hare and a pie. Those things were cheap, and familiar. He did not know what some of the victuals were, and was leery of them. The hare was tough and stringy, but tasty and comforting and the pie's crust was rich and filled with spiced meat. As he ate, his eyes were busy with the scene before him. There was so much color, for the clothes of the people there were dyed in colors he had never before seen and their dress was unusual and ornate - some even adorned with feathers and beads. That alone took some getting used to. After he had eaten, and was feeling himself again, he thrust away his anxiety about the sea, and decided on the next step in his plan to find work. He thought he must find someone who worked on the ships and could advise him, so he returned to the docks.

Still averting his eyes from that great, too-full water, he marked a man whom he judged by his dress to be a master of a ship, but when he engaged him with questions as to how he must go about preparing himself to obtain work at sea, he found the man was not a Captain at all, but only worked on a fishing boat. The fisherman was curious about Jan, looking him up and down. He saw a twig of a boy, pale-faced, dressed in barbaric fashion, carrying a sack, and with wooden shoes on his feet. This last he pointed his horny finger at and, with laughing ridicule, told the boy that his shoes would never do to go to sea. Seamen, he said, showing him his own shod feet, always wore leather shoes, or canvas, made especially for them and with the soles treated against slipping. Well, where could he get such, Jan wanted to know? When the man directed him to the cobbler's shop on the quay, Jan made his way there forthwith, for he was in a hurry to find work on a ship as soon as possible - before his money ran out.

The cobbler had a pair of these boots of the right size, ready-made - the fitting of the actual form of the foot being of no great consequence. Jan watched as the cobbler heated a pot of a dark mess, and loading a brush with this, he slathered it on the sole of each boot, applying it liberally on the sole and up the sides of the boot for about an inch. It cooled quickly. Jan paid the man and put them on, giving him his wooden shoes as part payment. As the clogs left his hand, though, he felt a pang, for they connected him with the old, familiar life. In his mind he saw his grandmother, the wrinkled face so dear to him. He smelled the aroma of soup, and saw the light of day as it dawned over the distant scrubby fields. Now, the old life was slipping away, and the new one was unfamiliar and frightening.

He had to turn away from the cobbler quickly because there was a knot in his throat and his stinging eyes were threatening tears. New-shod and determined, this little fellow made his way out to the busy quay again.

Back in the bustle, he sought out those men who were shod in sailor's boots and asked questions. Some of these men turned away from him without answering and he did not at first know why, but when one of them - a swarthy man with dark hair and whiskers - responded with a spate of words he did not understand, he realized they did not speak his language. He remembered then, that the widow and her son had told him there would be foreigners at the seaside.

He had been told by the widow Bess to see the Port Master, the agent who supplied the ships' owners and Captains with sailors and trade merchandise. Finally, he engaged some sailors in conversation, who told him that the Master was always out and about, but could easily be seen above the crowd because he was a tall man and wore a tall black hat. Jan wandered through the crowd, jumping up now and then to see above the heads.

In this way he finally spied the man, whose tall black hat could easily be seen above the other heads in the crowd. He pressed through the mass of workers and idlers, until he reached him. The Master was indeed tall - his length emphasized by the top hat and long black frock-coat he wore. Jan tugged upon this garment to get his attention, then walking fast to keep up with the long-legged man, he asked for work.

The Master slowed his pace and scanned the boy manfully keeping in step beside him - noting that he wore the new boots of a sailor, but the rough garb of a country yokel. He was thin and small - too small. The top of the lad's head barely crested his breast pocket, but in manner and speech he was direct and hopeful, not hanging his head or ducking his eyes. This impressed the Master. He humphed, and muttered a word under his breath, but instead of sending him on his way, he allowed him to walk on with him. Slowing his pace a bit so the boy could catch his breath, he plied him with questions to learn his history. Immediately, he showed he was honest, since he confessed he had never been to sea. But he had a friend, he said, (naive hope shining in his eyes) who was a ship's mate, ("on his way to being Captain," he bragged) and this friend's uncle was a Captain (when he gave his name, the Master recognized it). It appeared the boy hoped to find him eventually and join his ship. He was silent while he thought about what could be done for the lad.

He had turned onto the quay and Jan - talking all the while - hurried along in his wake as the Master easily parted the throng of people coming and going. Their steps clattered down the board walk, then the master, who was too tall for his own doorway, ducked his head and, entering his office he went behind a high counter. Flipping out his coattails, he sat on a tall stool and bent his attention to sharpening a quill. As his last words trailed away, Jan began to lose confidence, for the master seemed not to be listening any longer. Looking down at his maps and tools he was making some kind of computations. Jan was still and waited, earnestly hoping all would yet be well.

In the silence, the master's quill scratched over the account book for awhile then he glanced up again at Jan, who was studying the face before him, to see if he could tell what kind of man he was. It was a long face - thin and clean-shaven, the eyes were those of a wise man, and not unkind. Jan did not think he looked like a Dutchman. One of the sailors had told Jan that the Port Master was a foreigner to the Netherlands. No one knew the country of his origin, he had said, for he had made the whole world his habitation. Now, Jan stared at this man in awe, as he thought about what it could possibly be like, to know about the whole great world.

The Master leaned to one side, studying the boy and deliberating what he could do for him. He was willing to do something, since he knew the widow Bess' brother and respected the man as a good Captain. Besides, the lad was forthright with none of the subterfuge and sly ways of the city dweller, and he liked that. It had been a long time since he had seen it.

The buildings in that part of the docks were cheap-built and the boards of the floor gave way to sway underfoot like the sea. When one of his clerks came in, the squawking floor boards awoke the master from his reverie. Jan still waited while the two men discussed their business, but by now he was beginning to be uneasy. Finally, his restlessness caught the eye of the master, who called him to come nearer. The boy was startled when the Master's long arms reached out to grab him by the shoulders, but he stood still while the man's bony fingers probed his chest and shoulders, though he stood staring into the master's face in wonderment at what this was all about.

The Master drew back and shook his head, for he knew this thin lad was not ready for the sea. In his present condition, he would not live long enough to see the ship dock at its destination. So, he began to reason with

Jan. His voice gentle, he persuaded him that he must stay yet awhile before he tried to get work as a sailor. "The Captain of a ship will not take on a raw, puny boy," he told him, "Why should he? He needs all his crew to be fit, or he would never complete his voyage. Working on the docks will build up your body so that you will be fit and strong enough to handle such hard work before you take your first sea voyage. "Look at you," he said, once more poking his hard fingers into the boy's ribs, "You are too thin! You will need to eat well and work hard. That is the way to build the body for strength." He nodded his head - pleased that he had made the right decision. Then he leaned back to see what Jan would say or do. But he knew the boy would do as he was told if it made sense. He was that kind of lad.

Even though he knew the master was right, Jan was so disappointed that he was awash inside with unshed tears and could not speak at first, for fear he would shame himself before the two men. Then, to his surprise, the master did not send him on his way but turned and gave his servant instructions regarding him. "When next this lad comes here, take him to the man, Sheim, and tell him he should use him for boy's work only, at boy's pay." Then, he clapped one hand on Jan' shoulder and led him to a woman he knew, who was, he said, "the keeper of an inn for sailors." She would take care of him for awhile.

This building - the inn - proved to be a loosely woven affair, a strange nest of wooden boards nailed up in a hurry with additions added on so that the front and rear of the house were joined by an extremely narrow hall and the rooms of the ground floor were at different levels - a hazard for boarders to navigate in the dark. There the Master left him, promising him work on the docks until the time came for him to go aboard a sailing ship. "All in time," he said and as he turned away he called back to him, "There is all the time in the world, boy, your whole life lies before you. Make wise decisions and you will not look back with regret." Jan watched the tall man walk away, and as the high black hat and frock coat disappeared into the crowd, he was a little lonely, for he sensed the Master was a friend.

The woman into whose care the Master left him chilled Jan to his bones. He thought she looked old, but not nice. Her hair was skinned back into a knot and her eyes were pale - one of them having a white film over it. He disliked her immediately, and his impression did not change with the months he stayed in her house. She had a chronic cough, and whenever she spat, she curled her tongue like a blow tube and shot the phlegm out of her mouth. Outdoors, this was not so noticeable, but inside, her target was the base of any of the walls in the house. This was his first experience with an old woman who was not a precious, comfortable body like his grandmother, nor good like the widow, and his disgust for her grew with each passing day.

The ramshackle inn had a constantly shifting patronage of dockers and seafarers. Among them was the burly man named Sheim, who worked for the Port Master - the one to whom Jan now looked for his subsistence. He had a wry sense of humor and Jan was relieved to meet him. Work on the docks was very hard, he found, but Sheim was not a bad man.

Sheim would work on the docks for awhile, sleeping at the inn each night, and then he would collect his wages and go home for a few days to his wife and children who lived in the country. When Jan asked him about this, he explained that he would not have his family living in those ramshackle dwellings near the docks. When the boy asked why, Sheim was bewildered. He was amazed that the boy was so ignorant in the ways of the world. For a while he was silent on the matter, but as days went on and they were more comfortable together, he decided to tell the boy about all the wickedness he might find there in the city, for, he reasoned in his mind, wouldn't he want someone to warn his own son, if he were cast upon the streets of the city as this boy was?

Eventually, his education on the docks about the various pitfalls of life began to weary Jan. The tales Sheim told him made his spirits low. He knew Sheim was teaching him about the ways of depravity that he might be on guard against it, but the enthusiasm in the man's face and voice made him suspect that Sheim relished those tales of misery and sin, so after a while, he tried to hear only those things he thought might be wise to know. He filled mind and arms with work. Looking out to sea which had become familiar now, he welcomed the fresh wind which came in from it, to blow away the sickness which such tales of "life" made him feel.

In a short time, Jan's work on the docks had made him immune to the throes of the sea and the fullness of it no longer frightened him. He had become so accustomed to its ways that he felt secure even while carrying a heavy load up the most precarious gangplank. His body suffered, though, and he could find no ease on the pallet which was his bed in the inn, but the work was so exhausting, that he slept in spite of it. For a while, when he awoke at dawn, it was all he could do to rise from the floor-bed and walk, but it became easier with time - after his frame filled out with muscle.

He had seen some men swimming in the sea, and that caught his interest. Not many men possessed this skill, but it seemed to him it would be a good thing for a sailor to learn, in case he should fall overboard in a storm. So, one day, after his work was done, he found a quiet cove, and went in. Hanging on to the bulwark, he learned the feel of it, for he had never been submerged in water before. Each day he worked at it a little more, and found - to his delight - that it also eased his sore body. Concentrating on keeping his nose out of the water enough to breathe, he learned to paddle and move himself forward on the surface. The quiet water was best for this but eventually, he taught himself to maneuver in the rougher water, too, for that, he reasoned, was how it would be if anything should happen to "his" ship.

One day, his maneuvers and splashing about were noticed by a cocky young sailor who asked him what he was doing. When Jan explained, the sailor, (who could not swim, himself) laughed at him, and said, "Don't you know if the ship goes down, it would do you no good to keep afloat? You would just be in misery the longer. Better to accept your death like a man." Jan thought about that, but decided there was always the possibility that he might make it to land. It was a sobering thought, for although he had made peace with the heaving sea, he hated with all his heart the thought of dying in it.

At first, his evenings at the inn were just lonely. The landlady paid little mind to him, but cuffed him with the back of her hand if she was coming down the narrow corridor and he stood there, unable to back out fast enough to allow her to pass. There was no anger against him in it - it was just her way, for she was a bitter woman. When it was time to eat, she would bang a ladle in a bailed tin pan and that familiar clatter signaled her boarders that food was on the table. Indoors and outside she would go, clanging, and they would come in a hurry. They would fall on the joint, or the stew, tearing the bread to sop it up and gobbling it all down quickly. . . "Like animals," Jan thought, for they did not take the time to savor the food. There was usually fruit such as the boy had never seen, for it came on the boats from other lands, provided by the sea Captains. Sometimes there were stalks like little trees of dried fruit - so sweet it made his mouth draw up. Until he had received his first pay, he was not allowed to eat with the others, but ate from the leftovers in the kitchen. Still, he had plenty, even for his increased appetite from working on the docks, and the food was savory with herbs and spices. Yet a simple soup was what he yearned for -

soup and good crusty bread - his grandmother and the good widow Bess, who had looked after him.

As he ate in the kitchen he could hear the tales they told in the dining chamber. He was glad he ate alone, for some stories made him blush when he understood what they meant. Later, when he had been paid his first wage, he was allowed to eat with the other men at the long table. He learned to turn a deaf ear to the obscenities, and to hark when the conversation turned to adventures on the sea. What he heard at the sailors' table were sometimes fearful things that made a morsel difficult to swallow, yet more often it made him yearn to be asailing on the breast of that great sea.

* * *

There is a woman who frequents the inn. To Jan's still-innocent eyes, she appears no longer young, but not old exactly. The lines and sagging curves of her face are not the pleasant kind attained by conquering life, those which could make one more beautiful, but rather, stamped into it in an ugly way he does not understand. She comes flagrantly to the all-male house to find a man there, or more than one. To be allowed to do this, she must pay a certain amount of her earnings in this filthy trade to the innkeeper. The hall leading to the back of the inn is very narrow, wide enough for only one person to traverse it comfortably - a really stout person could get stuck. This woman enjoys catching the boy coming down the hall at the same time she comes from the other end, so that he will have to pass her. She leans back against the wall and waits for him to come by, her pelvis pushed outward, grinning . . . This is disgusting to him, although he does not understand the first time or two why she is doing this strange thing. He despises her and avoids her like the plague. Although he is innocent, he is embarrassed, and rushes to his hole of a room, which he is thankful is all his (It is merely a sort of closet space, just room enough for his pallet and to maneuver around it. His clothes, such as they are, hang from pegs on the wall). The foul woman stinks, and her smell seems to linger on his clothes from her touch. Back in his room, he gags at the memory and strips off his clothes, shaking the smell out of them. Just the thought of her makes him want to wash himself . . . . And this is what leads him to a regular routine of bathing. Although he has to take a basin to the community well and carry it back to his room, strip, and bathe a little of himself at a time, still he feels better for it. And it is a regular thing with him, unlike the other sailors and dock workers who stink - and not only of salt, tar, and bacon grease.

Some months later, Jan was impatient to be gone from the inn and the city, especially now that he understood some of the wickedness within that house. So, he returned to the Master and appealed to him for work on a ship. He had filled out, he said, as he showed him the tightness of his clothing and his muscular arms.

The master was amused as he watched the boy stretching himself upward and out as far as he could - expanding his torso and height by sheer will. He noticed, though, that he had indeed grown a little taller and had developed a tough, sinewy frame. He wondered why the boy seemed so anxious, but then he remembered what he had heard about the goings-on at the inn. It was just the usual thing in such places and he had not thought about it when he had taken the boy there to live. He looked closely into Jan's face and could see his eyes were not as open as before. Exposure to the dark side of life made the eyes of even the most innocent turn wary. It seemed an invisible shield covered those orbs to guard against any unwanted penetration into the mind - a guard against the filth of the world, he thought. It was invisible, yet it left a certain cast to the eye that was detectable. What would life at sea with rough sailors and foreign shores do to this boy who was so anxious to plunge ahead into that career?

The master was always forthright and he knew the boy was the same, so he launched into the subject, as plain-speaking as possible, so that Jan would understand. He never avoided the boy's eye as he drilled his words into his mind, for what he said was too important, "Lad, you must always guard yourself against those who would use you, or your body. Even at sea, where all are men, you must be able to defend yourself against those men whose natures are wanton, and would use a boy's body as they would a woman's - when they have been out to sea for a long time." He paused to let the boy absorb the meaning there, and when he saw, from the flicker that passed across his eyes, that he understood, he continued, "You must always look after yourself, but it would be wise to have a friend by your side, also. You will need to be - not only wise" - he said with emphasis, "but cunning." He leaned forward, his instructions clear and terse; "As soon as you are aboard your ship, watch the crew. Learn what kind of men they are. Then ally yourself with the biggest and the strongest at the outset. If the biggest and strongest man is an evil man, then ally yourself with several other good men who would take on the bully man. But you must make friends among those of power, for you are still small and young, and will need protection against those who would harm you." The boy stood stiffly - his expression most serious, so the Master was satisfied that he had been understood. "You'll be all right," he said as he patted his shoulder. "You are a wise lad and you will watch and learn. You will survive."

When Jan went out the door, he was a little shaken and full of troubling thoughts, but he had the agent's promise that he would send for him at the first opportunity.

During the next few days, those same sobering thoughts gave Jan misgivings about life at sea, but to his great relief, a new ship came into port and suddenly he had a friend at the inn. It was Griff, the widow's son, and Jan relished the sight of him, though Bess's boy had a rather startling appearance since this voyage. Where his pigtail showed beneath his hat, his hair was bleached nearly white, but when he removed his hat, the hair above that line was much darker. It looked, Jan thought, as though he

still wore a hat beneath the other. Set into a face that had been burnt dark
brown by the sun, his eyebrows and lashes were also bleached white; his
eyes pale blue. . . It made him look odd. He smelt like a sailor - salty and
with the reek of tobacco smoke in his clothes, for he had taken to smok-
ing a "rope" - a twist of tobacco leaf lit and inhaled, he told Jan. But Jan
decided he was still a pleasant-looking young man and it was good to see
his friendly smile again. He had sailed to many exotic ports and had tales
to tell Jan that amazed and excited him. He was especially enthralled with
Griff's story of the Orient, where all the people had slit-eyes and black hair
in braids, where the clothes of the rich were spun by worms and dyed in
glorious, shining colors - the material so light, it would float on the air, so
that they looked like butterflies in the sunlight.

Griff had been surprised to see Jan in port, but when he understood
his situation, he took on the job of teaching the boy. He was alarmed that
Jan knew so little about ships, so he quickly put him to work learning the
rigging and components of the ships at port. He was a hard task-master, for
they had little time for Jan to learn all he needed to know in order to be a
good sailor. When Jan wasn't busy loading and unloading, he was climbing
the masts and running up and down the deck, reciting all he knew about
the parts of the ship. There was still time for laughter though, for they were
young and strong and they were liked by the sailors and those who lived
and worked at the docks.

It was lucky for Jan that Griff had come when he had, for within a
fortnight of his arrival, the Master sent for Jan.

A tall ship had entered the harbor - its masts the tallest trees among
the forest of masts at port. There, it rested its great hulk while it was refit-
ted and a new crew was hired. The city was buzzing with talk of the tall
ship and the unusual venture connected with it. Jan listened to all the talk
about the ship, but it was confusing, and he never really understood what

all of it meant. The owner was a foreigner, it seemed, who had great faith in the ship carpenters in the Netherlands, and the ship needed some repairs. The tale told in the harbor was that the ship was to sail for the Spice Islands and beyond. The venture was bold, the route of the voyage long and risky, and it would require good weather, or their supplies would not hold out.

The Port Master was a very busy man, but he had an unusual feeling of responsibility for that rustic country boy who had so boldly asked him for work months ago, so he had given the matter considerable thought. The lad had never been upon the open sea, yet the sailor, Griff, had come home and taken the boy under his wing, teaching him the ropes. He had even watched the boys as they hung from the rigging and Jan learned the working of the sails. Jan would do for this crew, the agent decided, since there would be more than one sailor to work the sails, and he would soon learn to keep up his end of the job. He was agile and light, and unafraid of the height, so that was an advantage he had over some of the experienced sailors who were leery of the tall ships.

So, he sought out the sailor, Griff, and asked him what he thought of sending his friend Jan as "sail-monkey" and deck hand on this unusual venture - for it would be a risky voyage and a long one. Griff was an experienced sailor and understood the risk, but he was young and adventurous. There was a gleam in his eyes while he thought about what such a voyage on that marvelous ship might contain. When he spoke, it was to say not only that the boy should go, but that he himself should go also, to look after him. Both the Master and Griff knew if the venture was a success, the boy would benefit greatly - more than he would in many years at sea as a sailor - for they would all share in the profit.

There seemed to be a lot of confusion among the people in Amsterdam about the destination and objective of the tall ship's owner and it's Captain. Most of it did not make sense to poor Jan, for he knew nothing of the exotic places they spoke of. He knew that the ship's destination was not familiar to most of the sailors, but it had been told about - so some adventurers had been there. There would be many stops along the way. "Jungle," they said, and harvesting something from trees there - something good for ropes. They needed lots of ropes for seagoing vessels, so he could see the need for that. There was another reason for going, but he didn't know what it was - spices, perhaps. "Stormy seas" between, they said, for it was possible at that time of the year. The Captain had a new, previously unknown instrument and had studied maps - old maps - which had excited him.

The rigging out of the ship had received special care and many people clustered at the docks and watched as it went through the refurbishing. All new materials were used and extra materials were brought aboard, to keep the sails in excellent repair. Griff and Jan were among those loading the vessel with food (tons of food, it seemed to Jan), secured against rats and insects. This wisdom on the part of the Captain set their minds at ease, because such a man was not fool-hardy, so they reasoned, the venture, too - although it sounded very daring and even foolish - must be a good thing after all.

For the time that it took to fit up the ship, the talk among some of the dock hands and passers-by grew more extravagant. Their tales grew steadily until some said that the ship would go to a great pit in the sea and would be swallowed up. This talk scared Jan at first, but he knew the boys who said it and knew they were stupid. Griff laughed at it and said that there was no pit in the sea. There were some strange things that had happened to sailors, but no pit, he said. "Pay no attention to those fools. They have never been beyond this point. Never have they been on the water, Jan. What do you think they know?" Jan had never been on the water, either, but he had confidence in Griff.

Griff went home to see his mother for a few days and brought back with him knitted neck-warmers for the both of them and a loaf of bread for Jan. It was a misty day when he returned and there was a crowd at the dock. Jan stood on the planks and tore off pieces of Bess's loaf, sharing it with Griff who sat beside him as they watched the traffic to and from the ship. The bread tasted familiar, yet different at the same time, for it seemed the mist and salt sea air had soaked into the loaf so that it took on the new flavor of this place. People had come from far away to the docks to see this ship take sail, to speak to the Captain, or to bring others to sail with it. Some of these sailors were foreign-dressed men but their clothes of dark woolen were good quality and they wore caps on their heads. Griff was silent as he chewed bread and studied these new recruits. Then he murmured, "No poor sailors, these."

Jan was quiet, for he was confused by the strangeness of it all and the language. Tongues were mingled there at the port city and although some words were familiar to him, others were not. The sailors and merchants spoke more than one language, and most often some of each. He could not grasp the sense of what he overheard that day.

When the great ship finally weighed anchor, a minister came to bless their venture. Praying hatless in the pale sunlight, the few strands of hair he possessed stirring in the breeze, the words he said were lost to those, like Jan, who were aboard ship. As they left the harbor, a chorus of song from some in the crowd, also meant as a blessing, followed them out over the water. Jan, as sail-monkey, was very busy as they left the port, adjusting when necessary; untangling the rigging.

He had thought getting used to the height and tilt of the tall ship as the sails filled and the wind swept them out the sea would be the worst part, but instead, it thrilled him because he could see for such a great distance. He was enthralled and amazed as he sat perched in the crow's nest, feeling as though he were a great flying bird. At the bow lay the great ocean, but when he turned aft, he could see the whole country laid out for miles and miles, behind him. For a moment, he thought he could even see home. . . . His eyes followed the road from town as it trailed and wound away into the distance, and he fancied he saw a familiar speck there . . . . But surely, he couldn't see that far. Just the same, he pretended he did, and that his grandmother was still alive and waiting there. He waved toward home and called out, "Wish me good voyage, grandmother, for I am off into life . . . breaking away. . . sailing off for . . . ." and he paused, then said, "Well, I don't know exactly where - but I'm going! I'm going!" His excitement mounted so that he could hardly stand it.

Onlookers from the port saw only a little fellow - a mere speck - perched in the highest mast of that great, tall ship, but Jan felt as big as the world as they sailed away over the great swell of water that had so frightened him when he had first seen it, nearly a year ago.

* * *

Soon, Jan has great blisters on his hands, and Griff, saying he must toughen them up, gives him some balm for them and coats them with a bit of tar, to make a crust upon them, so that the flesh beneath it could heal yet he could continue to climb the masts and work the ropes. Fortunately, in the days following their embarkation, the wind is constant and there is not so much to do, so that his hands toughen as he gains strength and skill as a sailor.

Jan has not forgotten the advice of the Master. His life-long habit of being an observer begins on this voyage. There is a man on board who is in charge of the venture; he is slender, with straight light brown hair and beard. They had left port in a mist, and this man had wrapped himself in a long cloak which came down to his ankles, above fine leather boots. Jan has never seen such clothes, and he stares at the cloaked man, thinking he must be wealthy, indeed. ("Sir Knight" is how he

thinks of him) This man and the Captain have some debates about their expedition,
and sometimes these discussions are noisy, reaching members of the crew. Jan can see
that the Captain is not always pleased with the decisions, for although he has had
some say in matters, the other man has the last word on this. "Sir Knight," how-
ever, is careful that he and everyone else acknowledge that the Captain is in total
charge aboard the ship and everyone on it. However, Jan, who has had opportunity
to observe the two in their conversations, thinks the Captain is in charge of the ship,
but the other man is in charge of the Captain.

The Captain is a burly man, with short, black grizzled whiskers. Although his
expression is always severe, his eyes piercing, and he is short of speech, Jan discovers
he is not really a fearsome man but is merely impatient with stupidity. Apparently,
he has seen enough of that in his lifetime, and has run out of patience with it.

The ship they are on has a banner, or flag, with a single red cross emblazoned
on it. After some days sailing, they dock at another land, at another city with tall
buildings. Here they are joined by three other ships - (two of them are already there
when they arrive) one having a banner with a rampant lion on it. There seems to
be some secrecy about this voyage. Jan would like to see this town, but they are not
allowed to alight there.

I think they are going to Africa and around the cape.

The Captain called all sailors on deck when they were well underway
and told them the rules of his ship. He threatened to draw and quarter any
of them caught in sodomy. Of course, the Captain could not be everywhere,
but this had a considerably dampening effect on those who would have
dared such a thing. Jan had to ask Griff what this punishment was, for he
had not heard of it yet. When it was explained to him, it was hard for him
to believe that their Captain could cut a man into pieces and leave him on
deck for the others to see. Yet, he was relieved, too, that he would not be
molested in the way that the Master had warned him of.

Those who wore coats with fur discard them because they are soon out of cold seas and into warmth. "Sun is a blessed thing," Jan thinks, as he raises his face to it. It penetrates his clothes and flesh - all the way to his chilled bones. He is sleepy all the time, because of the warmth and the balmy breeze, and is reprimanded several times for this.

Up in the masts he makes gestures which can be seen by those below, as well as shouts, because a shout may be carried away by the wind, but broad gestures can be seen and understood. The forearm held out with hand upward in a fist, means a large ship - like theirs - is in view. If more than one ship is seen, the gesture is repeated. The forearm held out and up with fingers spread, like a tree, means land can be seen on that side. If he sees a man overboard, he hangs over backward by his knees from the bar, dangling, waves his arms and shouts, "Man overboard!" He enjoys the wind and his work in the rigging. His perch above the great blue expanse makes him feel euphoric - the ship and mates below dwindle away and he is alone in this glory. He can spy creatures swimming below - great light shapes beneath the surface. Just above him, are great white clouds stretching as far as the eye can see, puffy on top, flat on bottom; they seem to scud along with the ship, - a cloud armada. For the first time since his grandmother died, he is truly happy.

He has a horn to blow to signal his first sight of the land they seek, and he looks forward to using it.

Sir Knight, since he had little to do on the voyage (not having any work to do like the common sailors), idled on deck and enjoyed watching the boy whose work took him high up in the sails. He could see the lad was clever, and was flourishing at sea. "Rather like a dancer," he thought as he watched him hang from the masts - for he was graceful and full of life - his cheeks blooming with youth and sea breeze. Sir Knight took an interest in him and saw to it that he was treated fairly by the other, rougher, sailors. Being an intelligent man, he was curious about the boy's history, and liked to speak to him when they came together on deck. He knew the boy was ignorant, but he was not stupid. In fact, he thought the boy had the seeds of wisdom in him. Therefore, while Jan was within hearing, he would sometimes ask the Captain questions - purposely engaging him in conversation about sailing and the sea, so that the boy would overhear them and learn. In this way, he secretly furthered Jan's education.

When Jan was not so busy, Sir Knight would motion for him to stand beside him on deck and he would tell him about life in the cities of Europe, and the life at court. He had expected the boy to be impressed, so he was startled when Jan laughed . . . and when he asked the lad why he laughed, then it was Jan's turn to be surprised - for, he thought, surely the gentleman shared the joke - he who was telling the tale. He replied that he laughed at "the silliness of it all." Sir Knight, at his age, was well acquainted with the foolishness of man, but he was surprised the boy saw this so well. He encouraged the lad to explain what he meant. Jan, who had few words to express himself, tried to explain his impression of the world of Sir Knight. "Those people make living so difficult, when a simple life is so much better. To have such great riches, one must maintain them, one must work harder and harder, and those who wished to rule are always striving to keep their power, to gain standing in other people's eyes - playing silly games . . . and fighting one another in secret. Why do that," he wondered aloud, "when a simple life could be so much easier - so simple and beautiful, so peaceful . . . Why make it so difficult?"

After this conversation, Sir Knight remained engrossed in his thoughts as Jan went about his work. He had told stories of the glittering world to an ignorant country boy who, instead of being impressed, had laughed, who could not see sense in pomp and strutting ostentation and why the flaunting of money, or indeed, of having more money than one truly needed, was so important to those strange citizens of the great cities. As Sir Knight gazed into the dark sea he saw the world with the boy's eyes. He examined the depth of folly of those who were rich and vain and thought so well of themselves because they lived in rich houses in big cities. They went about with artificial manners and elaborate customs . . . and striving, always striving for more of those trappings which ensnared them further. The boy was right. Better to leave it all and live as simple and unencumbered life as was possible, so that one could be free to enjoy the natural things which fed the spirit of man. Jan, he had learned, thought true happiness was rising from a bed of straw in a snug cottage and beholding the peaceful beauty of sunrise, or sharing a dish of soup with his grandmother. A shiver went down his spine. "God forgive us all," he murmured.

When they had been out on the sea for some weeks, Sir Knight became quite ill. Then the crew found that the gentleman was not such a quiet fellow when he was feeling sick. As the Captain said, "He suffers, so all else shall suffer." Yet, he was not unmoved by his friend's misery and came to see how he fared.

Sir Knight complained loudly to the Captain about his "fouled ship," and said that the pain in his stomach must be due to a worm that was gnawing his insides (the biscuits were always wormy, no matter how tight the barrels in which they were kept). His emotion mounted with his misery, until he bellowed that the worm had eaten his insides and he felt it was growing, that indeed it would soon be up his throat. The Captain's patience snapped at this and he roared back at him, "And I hope when it does arrive, it will bite off your tongue, so you will cease complaining."

This last volley of speech froze Jan, the eaves-dropper beyond the open door of Sir Knight and the Captain's quarters, who wondered what the great man would do then. But, even in his misery, Sir Knight could see the humor of this.

Jan was amazed at the sound of weak laughter from the writhing form on the bed. The boy had heard the talk of his shipmates and was worried. One sailor had said to another that Sir Knight had a weak stomach for the sea - "was not a good sailor." But the other man replied, "but why now, since the sea is calm?" And it was so - there was not as much for him to do now, because the sea was quite placid. Sir Knight's ravings about the "worm" that Jan had overheard upset him; for it brought back the memory of his grandmother and her complaint that a worm was gnawing her from within.

Jan went furtively to the galley while the cook was busy elsewhere and from the dark cool cupboard where such things were kept, he found a withered carrot which still had the green top on it. He collected this, with a potato and a few green onions. The carrot top he chopped into small pieces and took to Sir Knight.

That gentleman was lying in the darkened room, trying to lie still so that his misery would not start up again, when he detected a rustle beside his bed and an odd smell. He stared into the gloom and recognized the boy with something in his hands. "What have you, little man?" he asked weakly. Jan was a little timid but explained, "We out yon have heard of your belly ache and I have here a remedy to try."

"What?" said Sir Knight as he raised himself upon his elbow and stared at what the boy carried, "Is it a cure? Do you vouch for its success?" But the boy said, "No, I cannot say it will or that it won't but sometimes in the village at home, I think that it was tried and worked."

"Ah," sighed Sir Knight, "an honest fellow." He sat up and rested his weary head upon the panel behind him. "Never change, boy, but you must learn to trumpet your skills about a bit more - never lie, but it does not hurt to present yourself at your best." Then he willingly did as the boy bade him, since he did not think it could harm him, and might even help a little. He chewed the carrot top, a little at a time, making sure it was thoroughly ground between his teeth before swallowing. After, he was to have no liquid and no food for a day. Then, Jan said, he was to have only water, and a lot of it. But, "Sir" pointed out, the Captain had rationed fresh water to all on board until they docked at the place where they expected to get more. "We must obey the Captain's rules, for he is the master of the ship," he said.

Late on the second day, Jan went to the galley and stewed a little pot of water, potato, onions and the carrot. When they were stewed, he mashed them all in the water and added salt only. This soup he took to Sir and bade him sip it till it was all gone, which, to his own surprise, Sir was able to do. His stomach had been better behaved since the carrot top affair two days ago, and he was ready for some food. "It was amazing - such a simple thing as carrot leaves!" he exclaimed to the Captain, "and that simple soup! That was what I needed," he told him — "not that wormy biscuit and dried beef that the crew eats."

* * *

Most of the crew are Dutch and a few are French. They speak both languages. It seems that the four ships split up along the way. Their sister ships have merchandise to trade, and are ahead of them. Also, they do not wish to be seen in a group. Jan knows they are following the coast of Africa down, to make some stops along it, and plan to meet the other ships at the cape. Then they will go around the tip and eastward. I think they want to avoid the Spanish, and the waters near Spain. Jan has been told that they may see the "black swans" and that they will trade in the Spice Islands. One day, he is sent climbing up into the rigging to look out for storms - the Captain has not liked the gusts they have been having - says such peculiar little gusts signal a large storm coming. The boy sees, far out on the horizon, a storm of dark clouds and lightning. He signals "lightning" with a "yo, yo" and clapping his hands together. The Captain himself comes up part way into the rigging with his spyglass, curses and comes down again. He hurries away to study his map in order to chart a new course for the nearest land.

They were all glad, even for the shelter of this small island on the west side of Africa, for the storm was breathing down their necks. The sea was rough, so that they had only time enough to make anchor on the leeward side of the island, and could not get to the island with the rowboats. Jan, Griff and the wiry mate who used to be sail monkey, all worked like the devil to get the sails down and lashed securely in the wind which was already a nuisance. Jan was nervous, for he had never been in such a storm before and the fear of the old-timers alarmed him. He fumbled with his work and the Captain yelled at him from below. It was the first time he has been so harsh with him, and that made him more upset than ever - yet he no longer fumbled. When they were done, they were all exhausted from the hard work done at such speed and their hands hurt from haste and rope burn.

All of the men were huddled down below deck. The crashing and roaring of the storm outside made all of them afraid. The Captain and Sir were with them, but even they were not entirely calm. The crew's sleeping places - cots built against the wall, and hammocks in the middle - were uncomfortable perches in this storm. The hammocks swung crazily, and it was impossible for a man to stay on his cot, so they were clumped together in one swaying mass, braced against each other and the ship's side. The lantern held by the gimbals on the wall jerked as it swung, spewing hot oil outward on the mass huddled together below.

Then those hardened sailors began to pray. One, being Catholic, took out his crucifix and muttered his plea. The sight of the crucifix caught the attention of the others and a few whispered together. The Captain was a religious man and a staunch Protestant, and when he caught sight of the thing, he cursed the man for a heretic. This was only because of his anxiety - he normally did not care what religion his men were, just as long as they were good sailors. Then, Sir Knight called for calm and said, quietly, "It is no matter how they pray, only that they pray," for they were all afraid, even the Captain and Sir Knight.

The wind settled down somewhat, but lightning and thunder continued unabated. The lightning was a thing many feared, for the tall masts could attract it, some said. The men were murmuring about this, when one of the mates told a story about how he had seen lightning strike the main mast of a ship at sea. He had seen blue lightning illuminating the entire ship and the water around it, and claimed that when he and his mates had boarded her the next day, they had found that some iron pins had popped out of the wood of the ship and were lying around on the planking. The ship had been partially burned and was littered with dead men. This sailor spoke with a speech defect, so the story might have been tedious, but it wasn't. His words fell in the silences between the crash and roar of thunder and his stuttering only heightened the tension of the story. At its end, the men groaned with fresh fear.

Just at that time, lightning tore its way down the fabric of the atmosphere with an unbearable screech which was immediately throttled by heart-shaking thunder - then, only the wind, once more. The first mate, loudly expressing his anxiety for their tall masts, was cut short when Sir Knight's voice rang out, "Well, then, Pours, since you are so afraid for the masts . . . Go out and fetch them in!" In the silence that followed, Jan chuckled in spite of his fear. He enjoyed the wit of Sir Knight. This kind of badinage was new to him.

As the men tried to sit tightly in their places, their eyes strained at the visions in their minds of what horrible damage might be happening to the ship; what might happen to them there in that God-forsaken place. They were fortunate in one thing, though - they were not far from land. If they did not drown in the turbulent sea, they might make it to land even if their ship broke up.

Every man had his own troubling thoughts. Griff yearned for his mother, and was afraid that he had taken Jan on his first and last voyage - to his death. Then, Sir Knight spoke into the void, saying a strange thing, Jan thought; that they were on a mission for God and therefore, God would spare them. This was the first the men had heard of such a thing, and their thoughts turned away from their worries as they wondered what that mission could be. Soon, there was a lull in the storm, but the Captain and some of the older sailors cautioned them all to stay where they were, for it might be only the eye of the storm, with the worst yet to come.

Throughout the storm, the Captain had made his way out the door and back again, trying to see beyond the light of the lantern he held into the blackness outside. He was anxious to see what damage had been done to the ship. Only when there was another streak of lightning could he see anything and that only for the seconds that it lasted. During the lull he and two mates walked the deck with lanterns, trying to see the damage. Then, he returned and battened the door behind him. "It could have been worse - I have been in worse," he said, and began to hope they would all survive. They sat through another bout of the storm lashing their ship. They could hear crashing noises all around and above, as it tore at the timbers - yet they were still afloat, though roughly thrown about in the ship's belly. When it was over, they rose to their feet and stretched their weary limbs. They were all a little shaken and weak-hearted about going out to see the damage.

They were relieved, for they could see that it could have been worse, as the Captain had said. Only the foresail mast was entirely gone, one of the other ones broken, but the mainmast was still undamaged. The cabin roof had lost some lumber. They still could not find a mooring (an inlet into the island) and had to continue at anchor. They made trips to the island in the small boats to find timber that would suffice for the mast so that they could make it to another port where they hoped to find a proper, seasoned timber to replace it.

The interior of that island was very steep and wooded, blocking any view of the windward side. While they repaired their ship, some of the sailors explored that leeward part of the island near the water. Jan was allowed to accompany them sometimes. One day, as they were rowing to the island, bringing tools for working the tree they had cut for the mast, they saw two men walk out of the fringe of trees onto the beach. One of them waved to the sailors in the boat; then they waited for the sailors to approach. As the boat neared the island, Jan could see that one of the men was very blond with light skin; his clothing torn and shabby. The other was a shocking sight, for he was a very black man - shining black, and tall. "Look!" said one of the sailors in awe, as they all stared at the strange twosome - "It is the devil and an angel with him!" Jan thought it was not so, for as they beached their boat, he could see that the black man, though black, did not look truly evil, nor did the blond man look anything more than human. They were a strange sight, however, and they had a strange tale to tell.

The blond man did all the talking, for he could speak English and a little French. The black man they could not converse with, since he seemed not to know their language, although he listened to them as they talked and watched their gestures. Whether he understood or not, Jan could not tell, but he did not like the man's appearance. He did not quite trust the fellow's face. His eyes rolled - the whites of them showing against the black skin in such a way that it made Jan shiver. The blond man explained that they were survivors of a shipwreck, and had sought the elevated shelter of the rocky hills in the center of the island during the storm, within a cairn-house they had built there.

The crew was pleased that they had knowledge of the island, and asked where they might find fresh water, but the blond man told them there was only catch-pool water on the island - no spring. (They were to question whether they had been told the truth of that, later on.)

Jan, who only knew one language and bits of English, did not under-stand all of the conversation between his mates and the strangers. Although he had always been an observant lad, he had taken to heart the wise advice of the Master and had sharpened his powers of observation since he had been at sea. Now, he decided he did not like the men before them - the one so "pretty" and speaking so glibly, yet seeming to force them to his will. The other, too, seemed to know more than he let on. Jan had seen, now and then, a flash of understanding in the black man's eyes as he listened to his mate speak for the two of them. They both seemed so glad they had found "rescuers" and the white man seemed to be so sure that they would be taken aboard the tall ship. Jan watched their first mate's face as he replied to the blond man and didn't see any distrust written there. He knew not, the first mate said, what the Captain would do - whether he would take them aboard or send someone back for them. But the blond man urgently pressed him, saying he would talk to the Captain himself, if they would carry them aboard the ship. The first mate shrugged. He was agreeable to let the Captain take control of the situation.

There was not room in the skiff for all of them, so Jan was left on the island with the other man until the boat came back. The boy was uneasy with the black man. Instead of looking Jan in the face, he rolled his eyes to look at him from the corners of them. "Shifty – he is a shifty man," Jan thought to himself - and he walked down to the beach to wait alone, well within sight of their ship.

It was very bad luck that the Captain was feeling like a good Christian that day. He felt blessed that they had been spared by the storm and in his benevolence; he decided the two men (since they were agile sailors) could come with them - at least to the next port. So, the two men came aboard the ship and were set to work helping with repairs. Early the next morning he was to regret that decision . . . but not for long.

* * *

"Death Angel"

Jan and a few men are still sleeping in their quarters. They were late abed, for they had been the night watch. He had been sleeping heavily, for he had been very tired, but now, he is conscious of a sense of foreboding - although sleep and that same, growing uneasiness seem to bind him to the bed . . . His eyelids part unwillingly, slowly . . . and the first thing he beholds is a pale glimmering light. Vaguely, he realizes it is the azure glow of early morning coming through the porthole. Then, he is listening . . . . strange noises above, on deck - frantic and angry sounds. . . Then, a dark shadow moves over him as something passes across the porthole, blocking the light from outside. His eyes try to identify the silhouette, but it is black against the light - surrounded by a nimbus - then it moves nearer. It is the blond man - and lo! (Sudden, cold terror strikes Jan like a beast leaping upon his chest.) He has a knife in his hand and he is spattered all over with blood! The boy's heart is pounding, but he is afraid to stir, remaining frozen to his cot. His eyes follow the man as he moves about . . That's when he sees that there are bodies lying around - not asleep. . . His shipmate is half-hanging from his hammock, blood trickling down one dangling arm and the other sailor with whom Jan had stood watch lies dead on the planking nearby.

The boy jerks himself erect and starts to leap from his cot - his shout making a queer, vibrating sound in the quarters . . But the blond man is instantly above him,

holding the knife to his throat. "No! Be still and behave or I will kill you, sure."
Beneath the growl, Jan is aware of something like a plea in his voice. Amazed and
looking into that face above him, he thinks, "He doesn't want to kill me!" Then, as
his gaze falls on the dead ones, the blond man looks at them too, with something like
regret in his eyes. "They would have made trouble," he says, and they both stare at
the bulky bodies of those once-robust sailors, who would never "make trouble" again.
Only later does he discover that the blond "angel" had drugged his drink the night
before when he had been on watch. He had not "made trouble," so it had not been
necessary to kill him.

When Jan was brought up on deck by his captor, he found the ship
swarming with strangers. All their own men had either been taken captive or killed. Some of them still struggled in the grip of the Pirates. Griff
was one of these, and Jan only had time to look him in the eye before they
dragged his friend away below to the hold.

The Captain lay on deck. There were several wounds in his great chest
and the blood from them was seeping up into his beard. Jan bent over him
and could see that his eyes still moved, yet he wondered if that good man
could survive such a mortal wound. He did not have to wonder long. The
Pirates lifted the Captain's body onto a plank and pivoted it over the rail.
Jan heard the splash below, and his heart sank with it. He had been a good
man, a good Captain, and he realized how they had totally relied upon him.
What would happen to them all now?

As he and the blond man walked the deck, they were barely given a
curious glance. It seemed the Pirates did not worry overmuch about such a
little fellow as he, Jan thought, but he took comfort in that. He kept out of
the way and observed as much as he could. That is how he overheard that
the gentleman whom he called "Sir Knight" was being held captive. He
understood enough of the motley language the Pirates spoke to know that

they thought he might be ransomed, or that they might be rewarded by the Spanish for his capture.

Once they had the crew secured, the Pirates set about looting the ship, and at first, they found little to their liking. There was cloth on board to exchange for spices, but they were hoping for more than they found, although they were pleased with the spare canvas, for they needed that, their ship having been heavily damaged in the storm. Finally, by tearing out a locked panel in the wall of the Captain's cabin, they found the strongbox of money, and their raging ceased.

The new Captain, a Frenchman, has taken over the tall ship. He is thin, sharp-faced, with salt and pepper hair. His beard is so sparse; it looks as though he cannot grow much of one. He leans on the rail looking away from what is going on aboard ship, and rolls pills from a loose powder, swallowing them. He seems to have an illness - and the sourness of that and his nature is written on his face.

He keeps trying to find out what the destination of the ship was to have been; why they do not have more merchandise on board. When Jan was asked, he was puzzled, for he was ignorant of the purpose of the voyage. So, searching his memory, he repeated what Sir Knight had said about their being on an errand of God. "Phaw! Religious men," spat the Frenchman, as though that explained the whole of it.

Jan, intent on survival, became ever more vigilant. He overheard bits and pieces that he could understand and learned that the Pirates had hidden their ship (a sailing sloop, not a tall ship like theirs) on the other side of the island. It had been badly damaged by the wind. On discovering the presence of the Dutch, they had spied on them in secret. Finally, they had sent the two men - the blond and the black man - to pretend they were castaways, so that they would be taken on board the ship. Once on board, at the time arranged, they were to kill those not on deck and distract the Captain and deck hands, while the other Pirates came on board. It had worked well - only two Pirates had fallen in the fight. One still lay below deck, groaning with pain, while the body of the other one had been dumped over the side. Jan had witnessed this sea burial. It was done without ceremony or sympathy. All of them had gone about their business as the body splashed into the sea. Perhaps they had not known him well, thought Jan.

After the discovery of the strongbox, the Pirates were in a celebratory mood. Some were rowdy - flaunting their victory. The blond sailor kept Jan with him, guiding him roughly, but protectively, through the crowd on deck. Although the others cast curious glances at him, they did not dare to trouble Jan, so he knew that the blond sailor was either feared or respected. He was relieved - yet he was on guard, lest this "guardian angel" should change his mind and move to harm him in some way. Jan saw that as he talked among the men, he spoke in different languages, and read their Captain's log aloud for the French Pirate, who could not read that language. To Jan, he seemed a cut above the other men - an educated man. He decided that this was the reason he had the Pirate Captain's ear, and his respect.

Later that day, the two of them, Jan and the blond man, were on a small boat, rowing to the island on an errand for the new "Captain." Jan studied him as they rowed. Instead of tying his white-blond hair back into a pigtail, as most of the others did, he wore it loose. It hung at the base of his neck in dingy tufts - shaped untidily by the wind at sea, and from the habit of rubbing grease into it (as did all the sailors), to train it away from his eyes. His eyes were light green, and Jan could see small brown specks in them when the man leaned toward him in the boat - yearning toward Jan, it seemed, as he would toward a friend. As though he wanted forgiveness, he told Jan he did not like to do the murder, but since the Pirates would have been out-numbered, his Captain had ordered him to. Jan said nothing, and looked away from those pleading eyes.

Then he gave it up, and asked Jan where he was from, and if he had family at home. When Jan told him about his mother and grandmother, he nodded as though he understood, and then he asked, "And your father? What about him?" Jan stammered, "He died . . . I don't remember." The man was amazed - "But you don't know who he was? You never asked about him? You little simpleton! Didn't you ever wonder about him?" But Jan was reluctant to talk about his father to this man. He sensed his tender memories should be protected from the worldly view.

James was his real name, the fellow said, though the Pirates called him a nickname (the meaning of which Jan never knew). He told Jan that his home was a beautiful place on the banks of a slow-moving little river, where the grass was soft and green and smothered with purple flowers in the spring. Jan stared at the man who could do murder in the morning and speak of the beauty of tulips in the afternoon. James, whose face had turned soft, looked at Jan, and then said, "You look like my brother. What age are you?" Jan answered, "Fourteen years."

The oars went slack for a moment as James silently calculated the years he had been gone from home. Then he said, "Yes, that would be about the right age" he said, then changed his mind and frowned, "No, he would be older now."

He started to row again. His eyes turned sad as he thought of that pleasant home by the slow little river - of a sweet time of long-ago, never to be recaptured. It was quiet, except for the creak of the oarlocks and the oars stroking the water. Jan, too, was busy with new thoughts. It was true, what James had said - he was a simple boy with simple thoughts. Perhaps he had been stupid, but he was learning. He had learned a good deal by observing the natures of the people he had met since he left home. Some had been bad and some, good - or so he had thought. Now, he realized this man in the boat with him was both bad and good, and he struggled to understand how one could be both. He knew he needed protection, for the Pirates did what they pleased - their Captain being a lawless man himself. . . . But how could he be a friend to someone who had murdered his shipmates? So, his moral soul struggled within him to accommodate this new complication in his life.

The tall ship still lay within the leeward side of the island, where it would not be readily seen by sea-going ships following the coastline. It had somehow taken on a derelict look, although there were men aboard. The following day, because the Pirate Captain was fretful and anxious to get both ships afloat, he ordered everyone, except a watch, to work on his ship. The captive crew - subdued now - was unshackled and rowed out to the island. This was when Jan discovered Griff was still alive, and he rejoiced to see him, but Griff looked at him with dead eyes, not like his old friend at all. Jan was overcome with shame by that look - for wasn't he being treated like a child's pet, while the crew with whom he belonged had been beaten and trussed up in the dark?

For a few days they all worked on the Pirate ship and slept on the island at night. Their ship remained at anchor on the other side of the island, with two Pirates aboard, as the watch.

Their crew had been kept closely guarded by the Pirates, but those men grew lax in their duties, just as they were lax in their morals. Some of them, Jan had found, were unwilling captives who had participated in that rough game but hoping an opportune time would come when they could obtain their freedom, or, like James, they were so deep into that life that they felt compelled to go on. Others enjoyed piracy. Jan thought he knew who those were.

Jan was free to come and go, but only within the view of James, who was here, there and everywhere as overseer of all work. Finally, he was able to join the crew of the tall ship as they sat around the fire one night. They looked at him with grim humor, and professed they were glad to see him. As they sat there under the stars, they concocted a plan. They wanted to get to their ship, subdue the men aboard and weigh anchor. It seemed a good time, since there was only the watch aboard, and they were quick to act upon it, when the pirates were judged to be asleep.

There was only one set as guard over them and he was negligent and sleepy. But it was a very strange thing. Just as they had slit the guard's throat and were racing for the water to go to their ship, a tall tree, apparently loosened by the storm, fell with a great crash and woke all the Pirate crew.

Jan, who had hesitated a few moments behind the others, had seen the tree go down and heard the crash. . Then he was running, but his heart was beating fast and he was near to crying, for he could see the hopelessness of the situation for the others were already catching up to his shipmates. Suddenly, fingers ran through his scalp, and as he was lifted up and jerked to a standstill, he felt his hair was being pulled from his head. "Behave," James hissed in his ear, "or they will slit your throat." He pulled Jan into the cover of a copse of trees beyond, and shook him hard.

The noise of the clash between Pirates and sailors came to their ears. James paused to catch his breath, for Jan had not been easy to catch. He had been afraid for the boy, and it showed in his pale face. "Do you think they need a little boy like you?" he gasped, "We need to make a pact - you and I, boy. You will not run away until we are at port - then you are free to go. If you try to escape," he explained, "the Captain will take out his anger on me." He paused as he wondered if Jan would care about that, so then he tried another threat. "If you do not agree, you will be imprisoned with the others." He looked deep into the boy's face, illumined by flickering moonlight shifting through the branches above them. "Do you know what happens to some of the prisoners?" This last did the trick - Jan, remembering the wise words of the Master, nodded and said "I swear." From then on, he and James were allies.

* * *

They set sail finally, with the Pirates in control of both ships. Most of the Dutch crew, including Jan, were left aboard the tall ship with the Frenchman and some of his men. But Jan didn't see Griff anywhere, and he worried about him. The Dutch crew's food ration had been severely curtailed, so that the Pirates would have enough to carry them through to the next safe port for them. Some of those ports nearest this island were under the control of the English and Dutch and they are not so friendly to "buccaneers" these days. The Frenchman told the Dutch they had cut their food supply so that the Dutch would not have the strength to run anymore. If they "behaved well," he said, then they would be well fed. They did not believe him, and smoldered in silence for a while.

Because they had no weapons, and were greatly outnumbered on each ship, they did not mutiny, yet they began to whisper against the Frenchman, and, since he did not seem to notice their complaining, their murmurs became bolder. Still, the Frenchman did not do anything against them, but stared out to sea and rolled his pills. To all appearances, he was a sick, weak man. After some time, when the complaints had become audible to all, they were made to realize, too late, that they had made a grave mistake. He was not at all a weak man, but a hooded serpent and they had trod on his tail one time too many. . . So, when they did not expect it, he turned suddenly and struck back.

They knew, when he turned, that a blow was about to be dealt, for his face was strange - His eyes were lit with hot fire, and the oddness of his voice, when he spoke, struck fear into their hearts. "I am tired to my teeth," (he enunciated the Dutch words very clearly for their benefit) "of your grumbling and sour faces!" They waited, tense and uneasy as he cast his eyes about for a victim to make an example of. Then he pounced upon that unfortunate sailor who stuttered. He strode across the deck and seized the terrified man by the cloth of his shirt, and roaring that he was sick of his stuttering, he ordered his men to cut the fellow's tongue out. Then there was much grappling and confusion on deck, as the Frenchman held the other Dutchmen at bay with his sword and the other Pirates showed their knives, so that they would not dare to interfere. After the bloody deed was done, the Frenchman himself nailed that gruesome thing to the mast, up high enough so that they all could see it as they passed by. "Now, there will be no more trouble," he said, more quietly, and his face was serene and glowing, as though the poison had gone out of him.

The Dutch were horrified, and some were greatly guilt-stricken, for they had complained aloud and the stutterer had never said aught but to reply to orders in the best way he could. One of the crew (who had complained so loudly) rushed to the rail, so that he might vomit into the sea. At that moment, the ship swayed, so that blood from the stutterer's mouth followed him across the deck, running between the vomiting man's legs and coating the soles of his boots. The sick man looked down in horror as it trickled over and he was even sicker.

The stutterer was purposefully ignored by the Pirate crew who moved away one by one - and the others were afraid to move. Finally, one of the stronger and more experienced sailors took mercy on the victim and hoisting him up in his arms, carried him below and did what he could for him.

There was no sound from the stutterer and his body hung limp as a sack as they went, leaving a trail of blood across the deck behind them. The Pirate Captain, placid now, watched them go, but said nothing. Jan looked at James, but that man's face was unreadable, like a stone; his eyes staring out to sea.

The Pirate Captain had kept Sir Knight prisoner, in the event that he might ransom him when he reached the islands where they were bound. When they were well out to sea, and the other hands were busy, Jan furtively sought out the place where they had put him, and whispered encouragement to him. That gentleman was weak, for they only fed him enough to barely keep him alive, so that they might save their food, but he was glad to see his young friend. From then on, whenever the opportunity arose, Jan would steal away to speak a moment with Sir Knight, to keep the man abreast of what was happening aboard the ship, and to take him bits of food that he could save from his own ration, which, in turn, James had supplied to him.

* * *

Jan is sitting on the bowsprit, the sea spray hitting him in the teeth. There are tears in his eyes - not just from the wind and spray. They are in the Caribbean Sea. The air is warm, and, at first, it sickens him. He is young though, and he soon becomes adapted to it. In spite of the circumstances, he is curious about where they are going, and what the Pirates themselves will do when they get there, and what they will do with the Dutch crew. Some of the Pirate crew are merely sheep, quickly doing what they are told, with helpless eyes. He has learned that some of them were prisoners, too, picked up somewhere along the Frenchman's bloody voyage.

He can tell that the Pirate Captain - always a nervy man - is now anxious indeed, because this is a Dutch ship, and the Dutch are all over these seas and control some of the islands. If they catch him within their domain, they will have no

mercy. He has changed the name of the tall ship, and very daringly sails her into
the islands, on a direct course to the Spanish-held isles.

The port in the West Indies was not like any city of Europe, for it was full of color and noise, and had no large buildings. To Jan, it seemed littered - with trash, loose timbers and people of all colors and languages, in strange and colorful dress. It was as though all the flotsam of the sea had washed up there. The Frenchman was careful before he docked, looking nervously through his spyglass, to see what ships were in the bay. He was reassured by what he saw, but even then he sent a small boat into port to see who was there before he ventured in. Some of his peers could not be trusted to leave him his prize of the tall ship and its plunder.

Not a word had been spoken to the Dutch as to their intended fate. Carelessly, their captors, led by the Frenchman, all streamed across the gangplank onto a long pier and the Dutch slowly followed with trepidation, expecting to be stopped at any moment. But, to their great surprise, they were simply ignored - it seemed they were to have their liberty! But, their first exultation was tempered by the question; where were they to run in this Spanish ruled island? Wherever they went, the Frenchman could lay his hands on them if he wanted to, but it seemed he did not care where they went, now that he had both ships safe in harbor.

The Frenchman sauntered off to deal with the Spanish authorities. The glib story he had conceived was a mockery, but one with which he was sure they would connive. Sir Knight was still aboard the tall ship, watched by a changing guard of a few of the Pirate's men. The others, Pirates and sailors alike, streamed into a place called "The Silver Shell," there to congregate with like-minded men.

James walked into the town with his arm on Jan's shoulder. He had been very quiet since the affair of the stutterer's tongue. Now, he led Jan to a boarding place and talked to the inn keeper in Spanish, dropping a few coins into his hand. Then, he turned to Jan and said, "Well, lad, this is where we part. You will be taken care of here." Then he fumbled a little as he pressed some coins into Jan's hand. "This is your pay," he said. ". . . Seaman's pay." Then he said, "Look, you, never go onto a Pirate's vessel again. It is better, perhaps, to die than to be a slave of such a man. There are ships that will come here - merchants' ships, such as the one you were on. They will be foreigners to you, but you can go back to your country on one of them." Then he turned his back and walked away. Jan never saw him again, even though the boy was in the islands for some years. It was as though he had disappeared into the air.

Jan had thought Griff might be dead, but finally he saw him, dirty and shabby, released from the Pirate's smaller ship. He was sick, and would not talk about what he had endured. Jan's heart was sore for his friend and tried to comfort him. Now, their situation was reversed and he was the leader of the two. He returned to the inn, and in spite of the language difference, made the innkeeper understand he wanted his money back, that he would not be staying there. The innkeeper protested, pretending he could not give him the money but Jan had been through hardship and was now a hardened youth. He leaned toward the innkeeper in a bold and threatening fashion, and the man reluctantly gave him the money, except for one coin, which he stubbornly insisted on keeping. Jan turned away as the man flailed him in angry Spanish and spat at his back as he left his door.

Griff and Jan surveyed the waterfront, and found it a busy and dangerous place. They were nearly run over by a careening barrel that had escaped the dock loaders. They found an empty hovel to sleep in, to rest until they were recovered from their ordeal. There were many such make-shift shelters on the beach, put together by sailors to take their ease until they put to sea again. There was food for the asking, for they were thought to be

Pirates. Nothing was denied to those cruel, yet generous men, they discovered. Fruit and bread could be had for nothing. Jan, quick to discover the advantages of this disguise, acted the part, bold and swaggering, gesturing and signing to make up for his lack of Spanish. Griff stood aside in wonder that Jan could be so bold, but Jan had changed, too.

The two youths wandered about, seeking information, listening to conversations for words they could understand - so that they could determine how best to find their way away from there and back to a safe port. All of the mariners there were a mixed lot; mostly Spanish and Portuguese. Jan knew it was important to learn their language as soon as he could, so he set about listening and learning.

It was not many more days before Griff and the rest of their old Dutch crew had found work for passage aboard a ship bound for a neutral port, where they hoped to find a Dutch or English ship to carry them home again - for, after this adventure, all of them yearned to see a familiar and beloved face before they set to sea again. They naturally assumed that Jan would come along, too, but after some thought he declined. It seemed to him that it would be a rough trip, for the cold-eyed Captain of that ship did not seem to be a sympathetic kind of man, and the sailors were harsh Spanish Catholics; antagonistic to the Dutch. Griff did not care, but Jan was not willing to go back to the sea, yet. He had found (to his surprise) that he liked the islands.

Jan in the islands is a very different person than the boy he was when he went to sea. He is becoming a man now and his nature has become languid, like the islands. He is strong and stocky, his upper body built up with work on the sails, and he works loading on the docks and at odd jobs for enough to live on. He enjoys the sweet fruit to be had in the islands, and remembers the boarding house of

Amsterdam where such things sometimes appeared on their table. He grows so much that he can no longer fit into his shoes, so he is barefoot. It doesn't matter, because it is warm here and he is carefree. I see him on a small, raft-like craft which has a make-shift sail of faded red material. His hair looks faded too - bleached from the tropical sun. He is brown and sturdy. On this little raft he has made, he traffics from one small island to another, fishing and scavenging for food; finding odd things to trade or sell. On these islands, if one is not a Spaniard, one cannot make much money. The only way is through trade or piracy. He is evasive - on guard so that he will not be captured and put upon a ship to be a sailor.

Sitting on his raft, he drinks from a jug, and contemplates how he enjoys the life here. It is easy to get enough to eat, and, so far, he has been able to handle the dangers. He has bought and learned how to handle a knife for his own protection. A toothless old sailor had taught him how, and cackled to see how well his student had learned. He was not a nice man, though, that sailor, and once Jan had learned the skill, he avoided him thereafter. He is very adept with the knife, and the islanders know it. He can throw it from some distance so that it will stick in a man's guts, if the need arises. He practices openly, the blade flickering in the sun as it flies through the air to land in the sack of sand that is his target. Never does he miss, nor do bystanders miss the message he is sending. They know he is sharp-eyed, with a keen wit and fast responses. So, he is safe enough . . . or so he thinks.

The way to overcome a man with a knife is to catch him asleep. Jan was awakened by a rough grip and hauled to his feet before he could lay his hands on his knife in the dark. His attacker was a stranger, a sailor by the look of him, and Jan started to fight him, but another sailor joined the first, and he was beset. Above the noise they were making, he heard the familiar thin whine of the Frenchman. "Cease, boy, we only want you to do us a small favor, then we will return you to your bed." Giving it up for naught, he surrendered himself, though he was sure they were taking him to sea for another unholy trial.

They tied his wrists together, carried him down to the docks and aboard a small sloop. Then one of the sailors, having helped them cast off, left them. The Frenchman handled the sloop while the sailor held a knife to Jan's throat. "Now, lad, you will do as we say and everything will go well with you, see? Do you agree to be still?" asked the Frenchman. When Jan nodded, the sailor removed the knife and helped the Frenchman with the sails.

When they cast off, a small skiff, secured to the sloop by a rope, bobbed along behind in its wake. Why they wanted him Jan did not know, but obviously he was not being taken out to sea in such a rig. The Frenchman was piloting the sloop around and through a chain of islands; all inhabited, from the look of them, until they came to one which had an eerie, wind-blown appearance. No sign of life disturbed its landscape. There was no natural port and it was dangerous navigating. At this point, the French-man untied Jan and said, "Here is where you do your work, boy," and ordered him up the slender mast with lanterns to hang there. "Sharp eyes, now, and look below for the reef. There is a gap between in the bay there, just large enough for this vessel to get through. Watch for it and guide us through." Then his voice lowered to a hiss, "If you let us break on the reef, I will kill you. If you guide us though, we will soon be finished with our little chore and you may return to your bed."

This sort of navigation was new to Jan, and the mast was but a spindle compared to the tall ship, so that it was difficult to scale, especially since he had become heavier since he had last done that kind of work, but with the help of the lanterns he soon saw the opening they were looking for. He guided them without any guile on his part.

It was slow work, for the space was circuitous and narrow, very tricky to navigate. Then, as they were rounding a curve into the bay, the sea was suddenly clouded with a "sea garden" which glowed and moved beneath the surface, so that he could not tell where the reef began and ended. He was taken by surprise, so that for a moment, he was confused. Then he called out a warning, but it was too late - the hull had scraped across the reef below.

The men below cursed and scurried about while Jan slipped down from the mast. He stood quietly as the two men strained and grappled with a pole they had carried for just such an event, to free themselves from the reef. It was easy - they were able to come loose of it with no damage that they could see, but the Frenchman was nettled. His tension grew while they were forced to wait until full daybreak. He paced and stared at Jan, his eyes reflecting a strange green light by the glow of the lanterns. Finally his fury overcame him, and strode over to Jan and slapped him, cursing him all the while in French. Jan had no doubt it was a curse, and knew it was for the mistake he had made.

This was the first time Jan had ever been slapped, even by his grand-mother when he was a child. She had been a gentle soul. He had been surrounded by gentleness. Now, as the slap stung, for the first time, a rage filled him which made him feel as though he were growing from the inside out - about to split his skin and tower above the Pirate, like a giant. He felt he could strike him down - that spindly, whining man - but his mind gained control and advised caution. There were two of them, and they were far away from any settlement. So, he damped the fire within him and bided his time, though the feel of the Frenchman's palm on his skin lingered for a long time afterward and his mind buzzed with angry thoughts. The Pirate was like a wasp - dealing unexpected, sharp stinging blows, verbally or physically, at a moment's notice. Always before, he had feared him, but now he began to hate him with an adult hatred which admitted no fear.

Once more, as the day broke, he was ordered back up the mast. This time, he could see better, for the glowing, floating garden had dissipated from the clear blue water, so that they made their way within the waters of the island and anchored. The sailor began hauling in the little skiff. Jan waited to see what would happen next.

As the Frenchman and the sailor loaded the gear they had brought into the skiff, Jan paid sharp attention to what they had brought. The French-man himself loaded a heavy sack and there was a small spade. Jan had seen that kind of spade used by the islanders to dig turtle eggs, for there are many turtles in the islands and their eggs were delectable, but he did not think the Pirate was going to be digging eggs.

There was an excited glow on the Frenchman's face that Jan took note of, for in the end, it was only they two who went ashore, the sailor remain-ing with the sloop. Jan rowed the skiff around the perimeter of the island as he was ordered, until they were out of sight of the sloop. There was a high place and a dead tree which seemed to attract the Frenchman's gaze, and he directed Jan to bring the skiff up on the beach below it. In spite of his predicament, Jan's curiosity grew.

When they had beached the boat, the Frenchman reminded him that it was a deserted island and it was useless for him to run, for he would starve there before he was found. "We will take you back to your home, boy, just as I promised you," he said with a grin, acting as though Jan were a friend, rather than someone he had just humiliated. Jan could see that the small island offered no sustenance for the casta-way - there were neither planted fruits nor a habitation of any kind, just thick brush. So, he waited and watched. The sack the Pirate had brought along was wrapped at the neck with twine. Jan could see, from the way the Frenchman held it against his chest, that there was a heavy weight inside the sack.

The Pirate did not like being stared at. He handed Jan the spade and barked at him, "Walk ahead, boy, we do not have forever," then he turned around to look through his spy glass to scan the sea, from whence they had come. "So. . . . He does not totally trust the other man. . . . Why, then," thought Jan, "does he trust me?" and he remembered how the Frenchman had always treated him as though he were of no account.

They had left the beach and entered the tree line and brush, when the Pirate warned him not to break any of the branches. They were to leave no trace of their passing, it seemed. Walking behind, he directed Jan to a place with bird droppings on the ground, for there were several large sea eagles' nests in the trees above. Here, they stopped and the Frenchman set his load down upon the earth and counted paces out from the trunks of several trees. Then, he directed Jan to dig a hole just beyond a fork of tree roots. While Jan worked, he kept one eye on the Frenchman, who had untied the sack and rolled out its contents - a small, tarred-over keg. He smoothed it with his hand in a fond manner before he set it on the ground. When he'd decided the hole was deep enough, he bade Jan to get out of it and step away. Then he nudged the keg with his boot, so that it rolled into the hole.

As Jan filled in the hole again, he felt the Frenchman's eyes boring into him, for now he knew full well what the keg contained and why the secrecy. Within that tarred-over cache were riches - coins taken from the tall ship whose Captain was slain, and from many other such victims. As he worked, Jan smoldered inside, for there was a fire of rebellion within him against the Frenchman. He had carefully memorized all he had seen - recording the number of paces and the look of the trees — just for the power of knowing this evil man's secret.

When the job was done, they both brushed over the diggings, and scattered dead leaves over it, so that the ground looked undisturbed. By then, it was broad daylight. They stood for a moment and their eyes caught at each other - Jan struggling to keep his expression blank; his knowledge from showing in his eyes. The Frenchman's eyes were hard; his mouth tight - though; "Walk ahead, boy," was all he said.

In that way they returned to the skiff, Jan hurrying to keep several paces ahead, the hair on the back of his neck standing up, because of the man following behind him with the shovel. On the beach again, they waded into the water with the skiff, made their way back around the island and back out to the sloop where the sailor waited for them. Here, (as he was well aware) Jan made his last useful contribution to the venture when he directed them once more through the narrow passage. Afterward, his doom stared him in the face. Warily, he came down from the mast and waited for it to happen.

He stood facing them, not daring to look out to sea.

It was peculiarly quiet, except for the squeak and squawk of the rigging and the thudding of his heart. The burly sailor stared back at Jan. The Frenchman shifted his gaze to the sea. Still, they did nothing. And Jan realized they were waiting for something.

Time dragged on, and he could scarcely focus his eyes without their jerking, for the nervousness within him. He had even begun to hope the lie was true - that they truly would return him to his shanty. . .

Then the Frenchman moved away from the tiller. Reaching into the skiff they towed aft, the Frenchman raised an oar and handed it to the other man. Now there was no doubt about their intentions - for as the sailor came toward Jan with it, his intention gleamed from his eyes and pleasure was writ on his face. But he bungled it, for Jan eluded him. The boy maneuvered around the side of the sloop and cast a frantic glance over the sea - looking for land on the horizon. He did not jump overboard, for he was stalling for time - waiting until they were within swimming distance of land. For a time, the cat and mouse game continued: the sailor creeping forward wielding the oar, the boy slipping away, clinging to the side. Still, not a word was said between them. The only sounds were those of the sails and the scuffling of their feet. The Frenchman, too, was silent, seeming (as was usual for him) to distance himself from this irritation.

The sloop was gaining speed - for it was a fair day - and a green island loomed toward them, its beach reflecting the sun, blinding Jan for the second it took to measure its distance. . . . Still too far away. But the Frenchman had finally had enough of watching the sailor made a fool of, and seizing a rope, he came forward on the other side of Jan, to put an end to the affair. Trying to keep them both within his vision, Jan caught another glimpse of that beckoning spot of green that was yet so far away. He had no choice, though, and as they lunged toward him, he jumped overboard.

They are upon him as the water closes around him . . A loud noise, "thwack" . . . echoes in his head . . . an oar waving above him . . . At first, he starts to sink under the stunning blow, then wills himself to remain conscious and alert. Then shooting pains start . . . He is momentarily blind. . . . Still, his fingers scrabble against the hull, seeking a hold. . . The blows continue, striking his hand so that he lets go of the hull . . . then a hand comes down on his upturned face, pushing him below the water. . . Holding his breath, he struggles. . . a rope . . . someone is trying to entangle him. He evades it, but then there is a stinging pain in his calf. . . . He pushes away from the hull and sees a flash of metal reflecting in the sun . . . stabbing at him. He gasps for air, then sinks in the water, going limp, drifting downward, ever lower . . . so that they will think he is dead and leave him alone.

(They wait and watch to see if he rises, but his body floats below like limp seaweed. They are satisfied that they are rid of him. It has not occurred to the

Frenchman that the boy can swim, since most sailors of his acquaintance did not know how.)

Through the shifting waters, he can see the dark hull above moving away. The side of his head throbs; his lungs are aflame from holding his breath so long, Still, he fakes it for as long as he can bear it, which seems an eternity. . . Finally, the surface of the turquoise water is broken, just barely, by a shockingly white face, the nose and mouth of it gasping for air- then it disappears below the surface again. The next time the whole head surfaces, and turns, looking for the enemy, but they are well away.

His breath is easing. Ignoring the pain in his head, he looks for his salvation - the island. The sight of it consoles him. As he takes the first strokes toward it, he sees a trail of blood behind him in the water. It is flowing from a cut in the calf of his leg. His heart leaps with fear. He is reminded of the stories he has heard of the man-eating fish. Horror thrusts him forward with a sudden burst of speed toward the island.

He tires too quickly. . . He was already tired from digging the hole and the struggle with the men. A glance behind him shows no more blood in the water. The wound must not be so bad, for the water seems to have stopped the flow.

He reminds himself that he is strong, his body well-muscled . . . With more confidence, he swims strongly again, his strokes slowing to a steady rhythm. Always, he keeps the island in view, yet it never seems to come nearer. . too far. . . oh, it is too far away! He is not used to swimming such a long distance. He must stop and rest, his chest burning, his head throbbing. He gives himself up for a time, floating inert, buoyed by the sea . . .

The sun's warmth rouses him, he rolls over in the water, turns toward the island, and swims toward it again. . . Several times in this way he rests and swims . . . For a time, he fears the current is taking him away from the island, but soon he can see it really is nearer, and he is heartened by the sight.

It is hard for him to move at all now. . . His arms and legs seem made of wood . . . too tired . . . He does not think he will make it after all. . . . Yet, just there, just ahead, the island lies . . . Its silver beach is beckoning him to come and lay his weary body down there. . . Safe. With all his heart and mind he yearns toward that beach, and wills himself onward, but his body will go no farther. . He floats again, trying to ease his cramping arm, trying, by force of his will to send new life into his limbs so that they will move him forward in the water. . . just a little farther. . . just over there. . . His trembling fingers reach out toward that island vision, as though he could almost touch it . . .

Gently, the wash offshore rocks him. . . lulling him toward the peaceful end he has accepted . . . Then - he feels something - a stirring of the water near his legs, signaling the passage of some large thing. A thought seeps through the clouds in his mind - man-eating fish! He rouses himself, staring into the amber cloudiness beneath him. There, a dark shape circles his nether parts and comes nearer. . . Now it is brushing against him! His heart leaps with terror, urging his poor weak limbs to flail the water, a feeble attempt to push himself forward and out of the thing's reach. Even this spurt of energy is soon gone. He cries out - a moan of despair - for he did not want to die in this way. . . The dark monster is emerging now, just at his waist. . . He can see it plainly, yet his exhausted brain cannot, at first, identify it. . . It is a strange-looking object, large, flat and wide . . . not a fish. . . It is hard and insistent. It nudges him again, as if there were no room in the sea for them both. Rolling in its wake, he can see its appendages . . . and so it is revealed to his great relief - Only a great sea turtle! Perhaps going to lay its eggs in the sand of the island, he thinks.

Yet, the turtle does not go on ahead but remains by his side, partially submerged; insistently scraping its great body against him. Exhausted, his arm reaches out to cling, gratefully, to that broad back. . . Ah, rest . . . a place to rest. Then the turtle moves upward and forward - carrying his depleted body with her. His face rests

fondly against that broad back, as he breathes freely the precious sweet air, no longer
having to struggle to remain above water.

The turtle's movement is like that of a rowing boat, with rhythmic thrusts they
move through the rocking current of the island's waters. Soon he is nauseated, for he
has swallowed a lot of sea water, and vomit spills from his mouth over the back of
the beast . . . Still, the great turtle does not take alarm and dive for the deep, but
surges forward with strong rowing strokes. On and on she swims with her strange
burden. The surf is rising, adding its momentum to that of the turtle to wash them
toward the island. He begins to hope that he may make his arms and legs move
again when they come into the shallows, yet he is weak indeed. . . The arm with
which he clings to the turtle is trembling with the effort. . . Yet, he is grateful, so
thankful that his heart fills fair to bursting and his eyes fill with tears. God, he
thinks, has seen him in his time of need and sent this wonderful creature to save him.

The next he knows, he is lying in a fishing boat . . . rough wood against his
skin. A face bends over him. It is an alarming face, a bad eye with a drooping eyelid
and bristling whiskers - but the voice is soothing, although he cannot understand
the words. His touch is gentle. There are others. . . They bend over him where he
lies upon wood and nets, and then he is carried like a child out of the boat where
it lies on the sand and laid in the shade of a tree. . . They are talking to him, but
he cannot respond, and doesn't understand. . . Then, suddenly, it is quiet, for they
have gone away. From where he lies, he can turn his head and see the beach. His
vision is blurred but he tries to watch for the turtle, expecting her to come upon the
sand below to lay her eggs.

Later, when the fishermen returned, they could not tell him anything
about the turtle, for they had not seen her when they had seen him lying
in the shallows and pulled him into their small boat. They shrugged. It
was a mystery. They had brought others with them to see the man they had
found washed up by the sea, with no ship in view. They spoke a garbled

language, but, to his surprise, they understood his Dutch, for the lord of this island was Dutch, they said. Once again, he was hoisted up and carried away inland, to the home of the one they called, "the Dutchman."

On the leeward side of the island, there was a house - a fine house for this country - and there lived the Dutchman. His sugar plantation covered the acres which could be planted, and the islanders either worked on his plantation or they fished. Jan was taken in graciously and put to bed. He told the man, whose name was Jakob, that he had been beaten by Pirates but did not tell him why. The Dutchman may have been curious, but he did not ask any questions. He was a quiet man.

The days stretched into weeks and then months - for where was he to go? Jakob was a good man, generous to his guest. Jan was reluctant to ask for a boat to take him to another island and he did not know where he was, so he set to work for the Dutchman, fishing and working the crops to repay his keep.

The boy's presence gave Jakob something to interest him. He talked to him about the business of the plantation and that of trading. Jakob traded with the Dutch islands and had offices there. Finding that Jan was little educated, he began to teach him to read and write in two languages. Since Jan was such an apt pupil and avid listener, Jakob's reserve melted away and he became as enthusiastic as his student.

With the giving of his knowledge, the older man became more alive. The pleasure he felt in these talks eventually became love for the boy. There would be war in Europe soon, he said, if there was not already (it took some time for news of Europe to reach the islands). He showed him maps to illustrate what he was talking about. Jakob had round maps, for he said the earth was round, like two bowls put together. So Jan saw how the islands looked within the sea, their proximity to each other and to all the other countries of the world. He was struck by this illumination. His ignorance was pierced as though by a lightning bolt and he was left forever changed. He was amazed to find that the earth was mainly sea, with lands dropped into it - little dumplings thinly scattered in soup. At first glance, it gave him the same feeling of trepidation that he had experienced in Amsterdam, when he first stared at the sea - for the world was huge indeed, and from this time, the sea took on even more importance to him.

Jan's visit with Jakob became a sojourn of several years and during that time he learned a great deal about the region and the trade and politics of the world. It seemed to lonely Jakob that he had found a son.

Eventually, Jakob had began to talk about himself, and the story he told to Jan was a strange one. He had buried his wife and children in the Dutch islands. Then he had moved to this island, and remained here alone. His heart, he said, was buried in the islands. His wife had been the daughter of a rich slave-owning family of Brazil and had been spoiled by them, so that she was arrogant and impulsive. Her behavior with her family and friends was charming and affectionate, but her manner with her house slaves was peculiar. She had grown up with some of her slaves, and since her family's plantation was remote, with few visits from her own kind, they were the people most familiar to her.

The Dutchman, looking back on it, said it must have been difficult for her to assume her role as their mistress. Her treatment of them was erratic. Sometimes she would be far above them - the iron mistress, aloof and superior. But at those times when she was needed a good deal of time in the kitchen and stores, then she would revert to the behavior of her childhood, when these same slaves had been her companions. On those occasions, she would become one of them, gaining their favor and their friendship - an unseemly behavior for a plantation mistress. Of course, sometimes they would not remember their place as her servants and would dare to treat her as merely a woman. Then, when she found herself in that position, she would turn upon them. It was as though sometimes she said to them sympathetically, "Yes, I am not like the others, I know you, you are such as I, a thinking, feeling human being." Then, when their hearts were warm toward her, she would freeze such feeling with some spiteful act or would draw herself up and lash out at them. It was as though she taunted them with, "I am no different than you, yet, I can tease and provoke you just as I will, for you are mine to do with as I will."

As was the custom where she came from, she always wore a dagger in a sheath on her belt (more of an ornament than a weapon), but it did not save her. A black man (they said he had loved her - a hopeless, cruel love) turned upon her and stabbed her with a kitchen knife, while she berated him over the game he had supplied for their dinner. She had been kind to him as one childhood friend to another, but then she would spurn him as he grew bold. The African never understood it, just as he never understood why he had killed her. (Much later, when they had captured him, he said he had been driven "by devils" - which is what he actually believed, for had he not felt tormented?)

For a moment only, all the house slaves stood aghast - staring at the body from which blood (some surprised by this proof that she had been merely human, after all) ran and spilled its way across the sloping brick paving. They did not spare much time to puzzle over what she had been to them, but quickly armed themselves and had soon slain all those in the household (all those who would surely require their deaths in return for hers). Then they ran into the jungle, determined to survive.

When Jakob had returned, he had no family left. So, he had buried his wife and children and gone away. Closing the door upon a too-terrible memory, he had come to this island where he had started anew, (". . . for what is a man without work?" he asked Jan) but he had no desire to start another family. Once he had told Jan this story, it was never again spoken of between them, for it unmanned him to speak of it, and that was embarrassing for both of them.

When Jan thought of it, the violence in the islands disturbed him. The warm and lazy lands floating in the sea were all quite beautiful - wild and pleasing - yet it could become a suddenly fearsome place. It was a very different country than that small spot in the Netherlands which had encircled himself and his grandmother in inner peace and warmth, even while that time had been one of cold weather and hunger. This part of the world seemed balmy, serene and full of abundance, yet, in reality, it was fraught with danger. His own experience with the Pirates and the stories told him by the Dutchman awoke Jan from the idyllic vision he had begun to have of the place. He was never so comfortable there from that time.

Jakob now spoke of all he had henceforth held within himself. His ambitions and ideas for trade were revealed to Jan as his affection for him grew. They sailed to the Dutch Islands at regular intervals, for Jakob to trade and conduct his business. Already, he was thinking of giving Jan a place in that office. Then, at the space of two years and six months, a great storm struck the islands, bearing down most on those to the east of them - which was fortunate for the plantation of the Dutchman, and, as it turned out, for Jan

* * *

. . . .*The sky looks peculiar; the wind shifting . . Talk of a storm escalates along with the wind. . . Jacob's men go down and beach the boats well into the tree line, turning them over and tying the hulls down to the base of the trees. The sailing ship is harder to manage, but all of them working together succeed .It is over by the next day. When the sea has finally calmed they get out the boats and make a tour of the islands. Everywhere is disaster. Their own island has been spared the brunt of the hurricane, but the islands east of them have sustained heavy damage. Dwellings and buildings are flattened. Those who survive are scavenging for food. Many have died - sailors, Pirates, Spanish, English and Dutch, alike. Among those mentioned as dead is the French Pirate Captain, who was trying to save his ship. Bodies and pieces of bodies are everywhere - brown and bloated, floating in the water. . . The big fish have eaten their fill after this storm.*

The Frenchman was dead! The news satisfied Jan's desire for retribution; for justice. And it was good that such justice had been meted out by God, rather than by himself. The news made him think again about the keg that they had buried, for he had never really forgotten it. Was it still there?

When Jakob and Jan sailed to that deserted island, Jan found the spot, even though there was a lot of damage done to the trees and the aerie had been blown away. At first, he thought the keg was gone, for it seemed to be deeper in the ground than it had been - but then he struck it!

When it was broken open, they found it was full of gold coins; a few silver ones scattered among them. Jakob refused any part of the money, for by this time, Jan was the son of his heart. Jan needed the money to further himself in the islands, he said. The question of whether it was robbing another (for they were both men of principle) was settled in this way. Jakob pointed out that some of the coins were Dutch, saying they may have come from the merchant ship that Jan had sailed on, which had been stolen by the Pirates. If Jan wished, he said, he could return that money to the Dutch East India Company. But most of the coins were of other realms, (who were not allies of the Dutch) and who knew how they had come into the Pirate's hands, he said. He advised him to keep the treasure and use it for good, for if he lived his life for good, out of that evil doing would come goodness. Just as, Jan thought, good had come to him out of the Pirate's attempt to murder him. He had been saved, and in such a way that he knew he was blessed - that God was aware of his minute presence upon the earth. He had been brought to Jakob, whose worth in his life could not be measured, for he had taught him so much and loved him as a son.

Soon after this, Jakob decided to return to the Dutch Islands, and apprenticed Jan in his store there, to learn the business of trade. Soon, with the advice of the Dutchman, Jan bought his own goods, using the Pirate's gold. He learned quickly. Besides having learned to read, write and how to do sums and measurements, he soon spoke three languages fluently. While he learned the business, he drew upon and added to, his knowledge of human behavior (for had he not been an observer all his life?). He became quite rich in a short time, partly by capitalizing on the vagaries of man and the politics of nations. In short, Jan was an insightful dealer, but still an honest man.

After a few years in the Dutch islands, Jakob died and Jan, his adopted son, buried him and grieved. After this loss, he began to grow restless among his fellow-countrymen. He had noticed that the Dutch did not seem to blend with their island surroundings, nor with the other races of people in the islands. The jarring contrast made Jan start to yearn for "home," as he had begun to think of it. He told himself it would be best to locate himself in the Netherlands, to better enable him to trade in the African-Indian areas of commerce. So, when he was able to leave the business he had inherited in other hands, he boarded a ship bound for the Netherlands.

Jan was still a young man when he returned to the port from where he had started his great adventure, but he was changed beyond imagining. When he had left Amsterdam, he was a child whose experience of life was that of a lowly weed sprung up in the narrow crack of a country path. Yet, he had not allowed timidity to overwhelm him; rather he had made himself go forward into the unknown.

Now, upon his return, his stride was confident; his accommodations comfortable. He was talked about as extraordinary, even among the very rich of that city, for he was a "child-prodigy," they said, in the trade business. Of course, he was no longer a child, but he still had the face of youth and he was known to have started as a lowly seaman upon a vessel from that same town when he was but a lad.

So, all around the city, the talk spun and schemes were made upon how he or his business could be used to their advantage. They soon found, however, that Jan's open and youthful face was misleading. He had learned a lifetime of knowledge in the few years he had been absent from the Netherlands, and little remained of the boy he had been - that simple trusting youth from the country, whose acute observation was centered only on the sunset, his grandmother's face, or the steam rising from a bowl of soup. That innocent boy was still there, but already overlaid with many experiences, like the flesh of an onion.

Two of the lessons he had learned he carried with him throughout his lifetime. He had learned that man was a crucible in which sin and goodness were melded, so that although a man must strive for goodness, he could not expect perfection from others, but must be tolerant of their failings. And, of course, early in his travels he had learned that a too-gentle soul, especially one small in stature, must learn to protect and advance himself by shrewdness. Then as he became strong, he must hedge his power around him like a fortress. Yet, through it all, he must hold tight to honor - for if he had no honor, he had lost his good soul.

Jan, still looking very much a youth, is striding down a street in Amsterdam. His gait is still that of a sea-faring man, his steps long and wide. His gaze sweeps upward, appraising the rows of fine homes - brick with top-hats on, for the upper story with a single window is merely an ornament - not another floor at all. This amuses him, for what use is such a trifle? It was a vanity only, as though the builder and owner professed to have another story on the house, yet all could see it was a mockery. He is looking at these fine houses of brick and stone, thinking of what he shall build for himself, when his attention is taken by a pretty girl in a lace cap. She is sweeping the stone steps of a house when he passes by, and he is aware that she is looking full into his face, which is unusual with girls of good families, but when he looks into her face, he can see she is only being natural. She is not brassy-bold, nor is she pretending to shyness. He doesn't stop, but turning around so that he can continue to admire her, he walks backwards a few steps. She is fresh-looking, slim and beautiful; standing by the step in the dewy morning like a newly-opened flower. Her blue eyes which follow him down the street are intelligent and bright, and sparkle with good humor, a reflection of his own. Her lips part, the corners tilting upward. Her mouth is the color of the pink nacre inside a sea shell. Silent laughter rises within his bosom, for it seems they share a happy secret apart from all the others in the street.

Several times after that he goes by and sees her there. Finally, he wastes no more time, but goes to the door to call on her. They who live there ask if he has come to see the daughter of the house, for they think it is for her that he is asking (and it would not have been unwelcome, for he is talked about - known to be ambitious and well-set already for his age). But no, it turns out he has come to see the servant girl, and they glower and are put out with him. He does not care for such as that, for he has found the girl who gladdens his heart.

His chosen girl's mother, a seamstress, was the widow of a man who had been prosperous, but gave credit with an open hand, so that after his death, the widow and daughter had to seek work to support themselves. They were good quality people and had a comfortable home which the widow had feared they might lose before Jan came on the scene. When Jan and her daughter married, he moved in with them (his wife being as practical as he was) to save money. His business flourished, and his warehouses grew.

After some years, he was able to buy the house next door as well, and his office was downstairs. The symbol he used for his office, warehouses, and eventually, his sailing ship and trading offices in the islands was the sea turtle - tortuga - which, he said, was his good luck.

He was a busy man. He invested, bought and sold, imported and exported - flour to the Indies, bringing back home rum, sugar, spices. Others - older men - watched to see what he did so they could follow his lead, but he was a private man, discreet in his actions.

I see him in his office, playing with something that sits upon his desk - This is a large stemmed basin shaped like the earth divided in half, wrought of gold metal, ornately worked with leaves and waves and supported by a great sea turtle sculpted at its base. The basin is filled with water, and miniature ships float upon it - replicas of his own and those of his company. This gives him pleasure in idle moments. He gently blows upon the sails of the little ships, and watches as they scud across to the other side of the basin - a far-away look in his eyes as he dreams of other days, of adventures he had far away.

He and his household are regarded as upright, respectable people. He says with pride that his wife is beside him in all things. She of the twinkling eyes welcomes those with whom he does business in a room on the third floor of their house. From the windows there, they can see the wharf where he has his warehouses. He has a limp - brought on by the knife wound - which has gotten worse with age, the scar tissue thickening. But this is a small thing in a life blessed with goodness and a reminder of all he has to be thankful for. His home is spacious and comfortable, pleasing to the eye - but nothing else, for he will not have the vain trappings of the rich. They have a gracious, well-furnished dining hall where they often have guests to share their bounty. His wife knows when they have soup on the table, that it must have lots of meat, dumplings and vegetables floating in it for him to be satisfied. She still marvels that the smell of hot yeasty buns will bring him, this well-fed man, to the table in a famished condition; nearly shaking with hunger. But in the morning, he likes to break his fast in the kitchen with his children; sharing their porridge. Their table is messy, for the little ones tilt their porringers into their mouths and in their eagerness the porridge misses the target and dribbles down little chins and is smeared upon their aprons, but he doesn't mind. He laughs and wipes them clean, for they are his greatest treasures, these little apple-cheeked faces he cups in his hands.

* * *

Dear Richard -

To answer your questions, recording what I "see" is easy enough, but I have great trouble trying to compose them into a traditional book. They just won't conform. I can see many details that I find vastly interesting, but other things, such as names of people and places will not come sometimes, or I will get several names for a person. In that case, I found myself ad-libbing by giving them names and then feeling guilty that perhaps I shouldn't make things up – that "I must keep it honest." Then, of course, I asked myself why I thought that – as though this information isn't coming from me at all, but from some outside source. And then I would be afraid, because, if it is not coming from me, from whom or where is it coming? Do I sound confused? Yes, I am. Ultimately, I have decided it is coming from me, but I think it may be gleaned by me from elsewhere. Richard, I know this is weird. It makes me nervous, yet I feel honored and excited at the same time. The stories as they unfold constantly shock or surprise me, making me cry over my keyboard once in a while, my heart seized with emotion. Even if they are never published, they have been a great adventure for me.

Anyway, the best way for you to understand is to read some more stories and let me know what you think I should do with them. I have several more now but must edit them. I write notes as I see the scenes and then combine them in what I hope is the right order, trying to do justice to the description of what I see. That's not always easy. They are coming thick and fast now. If I lag behind with one, another story will jump in before I am finished with the previous one, so that I am no longer sure of the "correct" chronological order. Also, I have discovered that words are not sufficient for internal, spiritual, things.

I have considered that maybe I should keep them to myself. Yet, that seems wrong somehow. If one receives a gift like this, shouldn't it be passed on? Does such a thing happen just for the one person who receives it? You know I am not a member of an organized religion, but I have said many prayers over this. What am I supposed to do with it? Does it have any value to anyone else? And if so, just what is its value? In meditation, I got the word "Scheherazade." Although it seemed familiar, I confess I had to look it up. Perhaps, like the fictional author of Arabian Nights, I must save my life by telling tales.

Perhaps these people (if they actually existed) simply need or deserve to have their stories told.

Here is a story I can relate to personally, which I suppose could imply evidence of a previous incarnation of my own. The character is a sculptor, as I am now. In fact, I have not long ago completed an alabaster carving, a tableau of an angel and man. I love wood carvings but I don't work in that medium much. I can't say I felt any acute sensitivity to the assault, but perhaps some sympathy to the hypocrisy of religious establishments. I have always wanted to visit Switzerland, which may have been the site of the cloister. I was completely ignorant of Alsace-Lorraine, or "Alsatia." I have not found a "Sainte Marie," in Strasbourg or any reference to an historic city garden in which a red, red rose may have been grown.

The Little Nun

An early time, in another country - I believe it is called Alsatia, in some place called Strasbourg-St. Marie (or something that sounds like that). I see a man wearing a shirt with no collar, tucked into short, knee length pants. These pants are leather, with a fine network of cracks across the surface. These are the pants he uses to work in. There is something like suspenders that hold up the pants, but they have a horizontal strap across the two vertical shoulder straps, in front as well as back. He calls this contraption "Hawsers." He wears very thick soled boots with some sort of laces around stud-buttons, no eyelets.

The next time I see him he is dressed for church. His thin, sandy hair is slicked down and he wears a shirt with a high stiff, immaculate collar; a lacy neckcloth at his throat. He wears a dark coat which has tails in back, but is short in front, and I see a waistcoat with a bit of watch chain hanging, thick stockings and sort of slip-on shoes with no laces. He is still wearing short pants, but of a nice quality material, and an odd, tall hat tops off his costume.

This gentleman and his wife have their own pew in church, which is basically a high-sided box with a door. Inside there is a low "genuflecting" bench in front of the seat. The small child with them wears a stiff brocade gown, which is made bouffant by starched petticoats, and a snug, brimless cap, tied under the chin. She is uncomfortable and makes faces because every time she moves her arms the seams of the heavy material of her gown scratch her tender skin. The mother is trying to teach the little one to kneel on the low bench, between them. The child feels miserable and crushed with the stiff garments poking into her as she is forced to her knees and she cries. Her father is understanding and doesn't like her having to wear such uncomfortable clothes.

When they sit down again, the mother takes out a rosary and kisses the cross. She also wears a sort of bonnet with no brim, very like her child's, but with a little row of fine embroidery at the front edge, and little cords tie it under her chin. It is made of such fine, thin fabric that I can see the impression and color of her ears pressed against the material. Her blouse, which is made of the same material, is nearly submerged, except for sleeves and neckline, in a vest and skirt made of a fine heavy fabric, embroidered all over with small pink flowers. She has, not one, but two elegant dresses for church, and for this she thinks she is fortunate.

When the service is over, the mother scoops up her child and they make their way down the aisle to the rear of the church, pausing here and there for amiable conversation with the other parishioners. (Although they speak another language, I think that the woman is addressed as "good wife" and her name.)

A servant girl appears from the rear of the church and takes charge of the child from her mother. She has brought along a strange-looking infant carriage; hoodless, low and scoop-shaped, with only two small wheels. The child is placed in it and wheeled away, like a little empress. In spite of the finery she wears, the little face seems small and peaked. She is older than her size seems to indicate, and not robust.

When they exit the church, there is a priest, or bishop waiting outside beyond the door. He wears a black gown, with a round, brimless cap. This cap is also black, with touches of red, and a little white, embroidery. It is pieced, like a pie, making 5 or 6 sides, flat on top, with a tassel on a cord that hangs from the center of the top of the cap. When he bows a little in talking to them, this tassel dangles over the side of his face, and instead of adding dignity to his personage, it makes him look rather silly. I can see that the church is in a city, because there are fairly tall, impressive buildings nearby. (Note: from examining photos, this may have been the Church of St. Thomas- it wasn't the Cathedrale de Notre Dame)

*The family gets into a carriage, the servant girl and child on one side, their
backs to the driver, with the couple facing forward. The mother leans over and says
something to the child, (one word sounds like "Danka or Dunka"). Perhaps the
language is German, but they also speak French.*

*Perhaps the family name or the Christian name of the little girl is French or
German for "Rose"? Somehow Rose is a strong symbol in this story.*

*The man is a craftsman and merchant. I see him making something. He is
twisting a thick cord of rush matting in a circle, like a braided rug, and hammering
a kind of staple in it as he goes, into the wooden bottom underneath. When it gets
to the right size, he puts a low curved back onto this seat, and covers it with leather.
This softer matting together with the leather molds to fit the bottom of the user. In
this case, this is a high stool with spread legs, and a foot rest. It will be used by men
who sit a lot, working in a counting house.*

Her father's trademark was a red, red rose. This rose appeared on the
sign outside his shop door and was inscribed on the bottom of his furniture.
The shop had a fireplace in the back where he worked, and sometimes people visited with him there. The floors were rough, thick wood, and there
was a window in the front by the door. Anyone entering the front door, and
up the one step, had to pass by a hound (rather like a kind of greyhound,
but stouter, light gray in color, with sharply cut ears, folded over at their
tips). The dog would get up hopefully at the entry of each visitor to the
shop. He was let in by the fire only when winter had really set in and it
was cold. Otherwise, he stayed outside in his habitual place to the left of
the door. The street out front of the shop was cobbled right up to the shop -
there was no sidewalk.

The light from the one shop window fell on a counter standing there.
He made money in another way, besides furniture-making. Behind the
counter and to the left, there was a small casket, opened by a key on the

ring he had. Inside there were articles of value, such as jewelry. He was discreet, and bought or loaned money on such articles for the aristocratic class. They knew he was discreet; therefore many used him whenever they needed money. He had accumulated a comfortable fortune this way, but he was a wise man, so he was careful not to flaunt it and lived a circumspect life.

They had a small place in the country, besides the town house. The servant girl in the town house was the daughter of a couple who were care-takers of their country cottage. Their house in town consisted of the shop belowstairs and the living area above. His wife was satisfied, for she liked that place where they lived. There was a balcony running the length of the upstairs in the back of the house, which overlooked a large, formal public garden. It was a very pleasant garden to look at and to stroll in, and there were roses, including a "red, red rose," growing there. Not everything was pleasant. The people of the town emptied their chamber pails into a tiled drainage ditch, which in turn emptied into the canal. Water was sluiced into this, to carry it onward, as the pails were rinsed, but it was not healthy. Flies gathered on it. This was not by their house, but nearby. Those who had to pass by the ditch held their breath and hurried on their way.

The wife liked the color blue and often wore a royal blue gown, which enhanced her beauty, since she was blonde and blue-eyed. Her hair rarely saw the light of day, usually being under a cap of some sort. It was darker around the ears, where it was pulled away and gathered up into a knot in the back. Although it was fine, thin and straight, it made an attractive curtain around her face when it was combed out at the end of the day. She had to knot it tightly, because it was so straight that it would escape all but the tightest knot; so the fine strands tended to break, and it was uneven and shorter than was usual for women of her day. The caps helped to keep her hair neat, but it was also the custom to wear them in that part of the country. She was pure Deutsch or German and usually spoke that language.

When she was quite small, the little girl loved her mother best and liked to be with her in the kitchen. Sometimes she helped with little chores, but often she would come to stand by her mother as she worked, leaning hard against her, her cheek pressed into her mother's skirts, just dreaming.

Once in a while, after gaining her mother's attention, she would ask (in that little wispy voice that touched her mother's heart) if she might have her palm read again. Then her mother would stop, and a little impatient, she would hurriedly wipe her hands. Then she would stoop to take the little hands, palms up, in hers. Then she would go over the story once more.

"Petite, it is so: The left hand tells what one can be. It is God's pattern for this life. The right hand tells what one has already done or what has already been decided for one's life." Then she would continue, eventually becoming engrossed herself - because she was impressed with what she saw in her daughter's hand. There were indications in the lines there that the girl would achieve something far above the average, and when she had seen these lines in the infant's hand, she had been proud, as a mother naturally would be. Because she held this exciting secret in her heart, she had succumbed to the temptation to tell the child what she had seen. Now she was regretful that she had done so, for the child wanted the story over and over, and she hadn't the heart to deny her.

The problem was her husband would not approve if he knew, and the neighbors would be shocked if they knew she did such as that, since it was considered by some to be witchcraft. She had explained to the girl that it was just an old custom among those from whom she came, and that there was no harm in it, but just the same, she always cautioned the little girl not to mention their secret to anyone, since they might not understand.

That was not her only worry, though, for she had seen something in the child's hand that she didn't speak of to anyone. She interpreted it as a possibility of great suffering, or tragedy, occurring sometime during her daughter's adult life. She had studied both hands, searching for a way to defeat that fate; to guard her child from sorrow. She could not decide if there was anything that could be done, but she thought perhaps if the child were to have a strong husband, someone within the class of money and power, and had children, then she might be protected from this tragedy. So, this dream for her daughter became her heart's desire.

Over the fireplace at the back of the shop, I see a row of little carved wooden figures. The man is sitting on a low bench, straddling it, and working with a draw-knife on a piece of wood, producing curls of shavings on the floor, which he scoops up from time to time and puts into the fire. Two children sit on high stools beside him as he works.

Sometimes if he was working in the evening, his two children came down to visit him while he worked. This night found them there, in their usual places by the fireside. He asked them questions and they answered politely, sitting upright and fairly still. The boy, blonde and blue-eyed like his mother, felt restless and had to restrain himself. He was larger than the girl beside him, although she was older than he. She was petite, and was called so by the family and neighbors: "la Petite" - a name which she would retain all her life.

Her hazel eyes gleamed, golden in the firelight as she watched her father work. This was her favorite time of the day, and she was content. She liked it especially if he were carving one of the little figures. Her eyes strayed often to the row of them on the mantel. One was of the local shingler, the man who did roofing, and the bowed figure carried his burden of shingles and tools. The shingler was very pleased he had been "done," and often came by to see it. He would come in and stand in front of the fireplace, gazing upward, smiling toothlessly; shaking his head in awe. To anyone who happened to be in the shop at the time, he would gesture proudly to the image of himself, and marvel aloud at the skill of the craftsman. He had proved to be good advertisement. The carvings were all plain polished wood, not painted, and the little girl loved the curves and intricacies of them.

She sat, still and content, as her father talked to them. Mainly, he would ask questions and they would answer. They were well brought up children and would hardly speak if not spoken to first. The girl was a charming little figure, in a bell-shaped skirt, blouse, vest and little cap from which extended her long blonde braids. She sat perched on the high stool; her feet extending to about half-way down, and her little hands clutched the sides of the seat, as she waited.

Finally, the father put away what he was doing, and took up a figure he was working on. A soft sigh of satisfaction escaped from the little maid and she stirred a little on her perch. This was what she had been waiting for. It was a crucifix, and the figure of the Saviour was amazingly finely detailed, even to the crown of sharp little thorns and a drop of blood on his brow. The boy's restlessness was getting out of control by then, and he squirmed and shuffled his feet, bumping the stool legs. This gained his father's attention and he offered to let him hold the knife and to show him, with a block of softer wood, how to carve.

You would have thought he had stabbed the little one (and indeed, she felt an actual stab of pain, she who had always yearned to be allowed to do just that, but had not dared to ask). Her father was shocked at the noise when she wailed aloud (she who was usually so quiet), and was truly amazed when she confessed, between snuffles and nose wiping, that she hungered to work with the knife and wood, and wanted so much to make the figures, like those that he made. She looked up at her brother, so big and strong and - to her - stupid. With a wave of her little hand toward her brother, she protested, "He is not really interested; all he wants is to be a soldier."

The father, though startled at first, was moved by her passion, which he recognized as perhaps greater than his own, for the craft. However, he knew carving was not an acceptable thing for a little lady to do. Her mother, for instance, would most certainly not want the girl to do anything unladylike, or to cut or callous her little white hands. He surveyed the so-small creature in front of him, and was at a loss, as to what to do. But he cupped her hands in his, and told her he would think about this problem.

* * *

I see her mother, her gown covered by an expansive apron, stirring something that is cooking in a large pot on what appears to be a tile stove. She then lifts a copper can with a wire bale, about 2 quart size, and pours wax from it onto the tops of something preserved in crockery jars. The jars look to be about the size of a pint and a half. They are made to have wire bales, and some did, but one is broken off. She covers each up with wax, and continues to pour wax, even to dribbling it over the rims of the jar; completely sealing them. Then, I see the father come into the kitchen and rummage around, to the mother's protests. He is salvaging some of this beeswax which the mother uses. He forms it into a lump and this, together with a little, duller knife which he uses for cobbling their shoes, he gives to the little girl to practice with.

La Petite did not mind that her mother was insistent that she learn all the housewifely things - such as sewing, cooking, cleaning. As long as she was permitted to work with her father in the evenings before the workshop fire, she was content. She even enjoyed the work her mother taught her, or at least, that of fine embroidery, lace-making, and cooking. Her mother had

no cause for complaint against the child, although she was not at all reconciled to the carving and tried to hide it as long as possible from the neighbors. However, pride struggled with embarrassment when, eventually, the
new carvings on the workshop mantel were noticed. Visitors turned them
about in their hands, admiring, yet noticing the differences in style and
craftsmanship, so that eventually, they discovered that "la Petite" worked
with her father after hours. After dark, people coming home would stop
by the window and peek through the slit that showed at the edge of the
drape, to get a glimpse of father and daughter, their images emphasized by
the firelight, working quietly and contentedly together. They were always
charmed by the scene and would nod their heads and walk on by, smiling.

She had her own carving stand now, which turned on a wheel, and she
sat erect on a tall stool made just for her. Her father preferred the bench.
He would glance up at her progress now and then and would come to give
advice, but only when he thought it was necessary. It was interesting to
him to see "what comes out of the child" (as he described it to his wife),
without much interference. The skill was not easy for her to achieve, but
she knew, with fierceness, what she wanted and was able to keep before
her inward eye the image of the finished piece. She was sorely frustrated at
times, but hoped her father would not see, because she thought he might
not allow her to continue if he did. Actually, her father had come to cherish
those quiet evenings in the shop, and his daughter's companionship. The
mother often had to call downstairs, to chide them for their lateness at bed-
time. So, the daughter learned many useful things from both parents, but
she knew nothing of the act that brought infants into the world.

As the years went by, the girl was carving more religious figures. She
was intense by nature, and so those subjects were attractive to her. Also,
her mother found her daughter's pastime more acceptable when she could
perceive that it was a Christian thing to do. The parish priest, also, felt it

was acceptable and lent his (somewhat detached) encouragement. However, when it became clear that due to her absorption in her craft, she was an oddity in the marriage market, the parents discussed what was to be done. The mother's secret fear made her wring her hands, but it seemed beyond her power to change anything.

The only other avenue seemed clear, and was not unacceptable to the girl - the cloister. It was not that she cared much, one way or the other. She liked the housewifely arts, but attracted no suitable beaus. This was not entirely the fault of her unfeminine work, but also because of their some-what ambiguous social position. Her father was actually of the merchant class, yet had attained wealth beyond the average of that class, and was patronized by the elite for the money he was able to give them, in secret and when they needed it, in return for their valuables. However, for this very reason, they would not condone an alliance of their offspring with that of the Merchant's daughter, no matter how much they respected his wealth and furniture-making skill. He knew their weaknesses, their secrets.

In fact, a lot of the carving on the furniture coming from his shop dur-ing this time – that which was so admired, was done by the daughter. As she stood, her sleeves rolled up in the warmth of summer, grappling chisel and mallet, her father, observing the rippling muscles in the upper arms of his daughter as she made wood chips fly left and right, was seized with misgiving. Perhaps he had made a monster of his child. Perhaps his wife was right - she was too odd and unfeminine - a peasant. But this was only momentary, for he knew she was still petite and charming, even dainty, when she wasn't at her work. His wife was the one who worried. She was totally German, and the German people were not adverse to good, peas-ant stock. She was, however, very conscious of French attitudes, since they had French clients, papillions though they were. A good marriage for their daughter was important to her. It was indeed a problem.

The merchant had a talk with his daughter, and finding she didn't have marriage in mind, (actually, she had not thought much of the future, being content with the present) he arranged to have her live in the cloister of the bay, at least temporarily, to see how it went.

* * *

I try to see her in nun's garb, but nothing familiar to me seems right. I do not see a headdress. Then, it comes to me: She is wearing a dark, translucent veil. It is long, thrown over her head and hangs down to the waist of her white linen gown. I don't think they wear the veil in the privacy of their quarters, but only in public - outside the cloister - or when they are among some of the visitors to the order.

I see her against a background of angels, like a forest of carved wooden wings. She is still a small person, but as she stands there, against this formidable background of her own creation, she seems not so insignificant (as she is often thought) after all. I think this is a bas-relief in wood, executed for this order.

It was, perhaps, a wise choice, since in the cloister she was able to practice her craft openly, and it was admired by the other nuns as a gift from God. When she eventually accepted the veil, her father gave her considerable dowry to the order. In truth, the order was not considered a very dedicated one, and their rules were lax by comparison to many such nunneries. Their women were mainly daughters of the elite and of rich men of business. Her mother died soon afterward, of a pestilence. She had gone believing her daughter was in a safe place. Then, La Petite's brother moved into Germany to take up his inheritance from their mother's people. Her father, alone then, and thinking his daughter was well taken care of, remarried, sold his business and moved to their country place. There he eventually became addled, having to be led around by the hand, muttering to himself in the garden. So, you see, there was no one to save her from what came next.

* * *

There is a man who is in charge, who is cold and mean. He has a long head, tight lips, graying hair. He makes her cry. I feel this man is really wicked, disgusting. He comes to the door of the cloister, and shuffles his feet on the mat inside the door to clean his shoes. When he enters, there is a chill that comes inside with him. All these women feel the cold when he comes, no matter what the weather. Then there is a great feeling of dread throughout the house.

At first, when the new priest came, they were, if not exactly happy (for, they said, he was an old sour-puss), they were at least amiable and determined to do what was right and proper toward him; praying the extra hours, fasting when he decided it was necessary for the good of their souls.

The longer he was with them, however, the more disturbed the atmosphere became. The placid nuns became aware of guilty feelings that had not surfaced before. They began to realize their shortcomings; their sins. Therefore, it was always a relief when he straddled his pony to make the journey back to the city and the diocese there. The time he stayed with them was longer each visit, and more grueling - more given to fasting and soul searching. He would take them into the darkest room - the one they normally used for a cold-larder - and there in the dusty gloom, he would berate them over the frailties of womanhood; of "Eve's great sin". . and would beseech them to wring their souls of every sinful thought, every conceivable sin of omission. Tearfully, their confessions became longer, as imagination supplied more "sins." Eventually, they were unable to shake off the feelings of guilt, even when he was not there, and they shuffled lifelessly down the halls, starting up at noises and looking behind them. Where before they performed routine chores gladly enough, actually enjoying themselves in constructive work, now it was duty - even atonement - and therefore, drudgery. Now they were oblivious to the beauty of the cloister and its estate in which they had formerly rejoiced, because they worried constantly for the safety of their souls.

As for the little nun, he seemed greatly troubled by her work – A female was unworthy of such a high calling, the execution of sacred sculpture. He spoke of this, his voice low and rumbling with worry, to the head of this female household. He would have taken the girl's tools away, but the "mother" persuaded him to let her dispose of them, "to a workman in the village," she said, where they would be "put to good use." Then she hid them away in a chest in her room, telling him they had been disposed of. This small sin was done for the greater good, she believed.

* * *

I see he has a short whip of some sort. There are several thongs in it that are only a little over a foot long, each with a knot on the end - for self-flagellation. It is cold in the room - a chapel, with high ceilings. It is silent and empty of anyone except these two. The sunlight streaming in from the windows illumines her as she lies there, nude, with her eyes closed. She is stretched out on her back on the altar dais, a sacrificial lamb - the loosened pale gold hair so very long - the sun picks out the individual strands of that glistening stream where it trickles down her very white, frozen body.

He also is nude; his back studded with patches of wiry black hairs, as he stands below the altar and sprinkles her body with an instrument which I think must be a censor. On the end of the handle he holds is a pierced knob, from which the drops scatter forth, to strike her skin with cold, stinging drops. After this, he brings the whip, lays it across her torso (do I detect a shudder from the small body?) and then he steps up and straddles her. She remains inert, as though dead.

He bends forward and bites first one nipple, then the other. In spite of the discipline she has learned, she flinches - it is very painful. There are other, older, teeth marks on her body. His voice is loud; threatening. He speaks of sacrifice, selflessness, the sin of being a woman, the sin of Eve being the downfall of mankind. He penetrates her, forcefully, his voice droning on without pause, warning all the time not to "mind" what he is doing down there, not to think of it. She must think merely of the pain, of the sacrifice. He was helping her to achieve perfect grace, perhaps even Sainthood. They must all be grateful to him for guiding them to a higher plane of spirituality, though no woman can ever be as near to God as man. "They are the baser sex," he groans, his voice escalating. Trembling, he screams, "They tempt man! They must atone for their sin!"

At the end, there are marks across her body, and beads of blood ooze from teeth marks on her breasts. She has had time to learn, and has succeeded somewhat, in not letting the violence penetrate into her inner being, where "she" really resides. He cannot get at her mind and spirit. Thus, she feels, with a strange elation, that she has not been touched. Still, tears flow down the sides of her face as she lies there - a sacrifice - not to God, oh no! - But to the beast. She knows better than to open her eyes until he is gone. He will be disgusted with her, as usual. Although her body stings and there is pain in places she tries not to think about, she is relieved because she knows it is over, once more - until the next time.

Afterward, she always went to her private chamber (for which privilege her father had paid dearly). There she would mechanically strip herself down and cleanse her body. First, she would fill and stand over the tin basin. Then she would turn herself toward the little window set in the stone wall, and look outward toward clouds and treetops, dreamily, but unseeing, and wash and wash. Though her body would sting as though already in the fires of Hell, she wouldn't think about it, and had found, as time went on, that she could even ignore it. Eventually, it would be time to bathe her lower parts and legs, then, much against her desire, she would have to look away from the window, and pay attention to the process. This area was always slimy, and she shuddered as tears ran down her face, but even then she would not think, but only washed and washed. After that, a powerful sleepiness would overtake her and she would lie on her cot and let it come. They would not call for her that day. The next day she would awaken and go about her routine, not remembering.

* * *

She has something growing in her belly. It has become large, distended and feverishly hot. . . . It is so beautiful here, where she lives. She walks, slowly, awkwardly, down a gentle slope of green, sweet grass and wildflowers, to where it merges with the still, cool water of a bay. She is drawn to the water, as to an oasis in a desert, for she is hot, parched. Once there, she wades in, fully clothed. Her soul despairs, her body needs relief. She slips down on her haunches into the soothing water, cooling her hot, tight belly. There are weeds and rushes growing at the water's edge, and her shoes slide in the mossy, muddy bottom, but she does not care for that. She is past caring for much of anything. Her hair is hanging in little strands beneath the pinned-back veil, and she is crying softly, her clothes floating out in the water. I see, immersed in the brownish water, the plain unbleached linen of her skirt. It is so real - the floating linen and leaves undulating in the amber liquid. . Then, I see blood as well - spiraling up from below and seeping into the coarsely woven fabric, adding its red stain to that of the brown water. (It comes to be that "They," or someone has accused her of being pregnant, but that can't be! she says, stunned by this ridiculous insult. How could she have a child, who is not even married? She is very ignorant of such things.)

She was shocked by the sight of the blood in the water, and in horror, she tried to struggle up, but being so heavy, she slipped backward, striking her back against the rocky ground behind her at the water's edge. That, combined with the pain in her lower body, made her lose consciousness.

She lay there for some time, a dark lump at the water's edge, before a peasant couple came by and saw her there. They hurried forward and bent over, examining; identifying her. The woman was excited, and chattered and lamented in French. They knew the little nun, and were fond of her. (At her home, in a box which held her "treasures," this woman had a little drawing of her child that the nun had done, and was most kind, she thought, to have given her.) They knew what had happened to her. She was pregnant by the vicious priest who supervised the cloister. They knew what went on in the cloister, even though visitors were not allowed while he, that monster, was there.

They looked back toward the stone structure as they spoke, spitting out angry words toward it in an angry stream. The building stood alone in a background of a meadow, set apart from the village. They debated what to do, the woman wanting one thing, the man, another. A glance at the sky that was becoming rapidly overcast, hastened their decision. The woman won control and, that settled, she directed the man as he hoisted the limp body, "Simon, don't let her legs hang down, so." They did not raise up her gown to check her condition, there - where they had dragged her out of the water - after all, she was a nun! The idea of doing such a thing would have shocked them. They could not leave her there to be seen in that condition, for the same reason. The weather had turned, the wind was up and a swirl of raindrops spattered them as the woman raised her skirts around her calves and urged the man to hurry with his burden. They scurried across the grassland toward the nearest shelter, which was a shepherd's hut.

The roof line was very low, and they had to duck their heads to enter. It was dark inside, and the woman shooed a lamb out of the way as the man carried the nun to a cot built into the side of one wall. There he laid "the little one" down. There was a lamp hanging from an iron swivel hook in the wall. This they adjusted, and lit with the means of a tinder-box the man had in his coat. The woman bent over the nun's misshapen body, straightening and probing. The man, feeling suddenly awkward, hurried away outside, leaving the woman to take over.

She rolled up her sleeves and took a look below "la Petite's" wet skirts. A sharp intake of breath and a muttered exclamation came from the peasant woman. Her eyes stretched at the ominous sight barely revealed by the lamp. There was no time to strip the wet garments from the woman on the bed. She had seen this sort of thing before and something had to be done immediately. She forgot the lady was a nun. She only saw a female in great trouble and she was a peasant who had always done what was necessary.

It was not easy. She had to force the birth; pulling and straining until her arms hurt and trembled, but it did not matter. Finally, it was over, and she stood and clumsily dried the back of one hand on her apron, so that she could wipe the sweat from her brow. Her arms were trembling from the strain and bloodied to the elbows. There were twins, but both dead, "and God Bless," said the woman under her breath. They had been long overdue, she thought - from the look of them - and were blue. She was relieved and thankful - it made things so much simpler.

Soon, the tiny room seemed over-full by the villagers crowded into it, or peering through the door. The nun, semi-conscious and feverish, slept between clean coverings that someone had brought. Her clothes had been taken away for drying. There was a fire in the crude hollow made for it, under the hole in the roof that took away the smoke. The sight of her lying there, so small, her hair, long and lovely, spread out around her, tore at their hearts. They were shocked at the soft youth of her, her beaten-down inno-cence. She was just a girl who could have been their own daughter.

The peasants debated furiously, occasionally looking toward the object of their discourse with fondness. What to do was the question. They were united in their wrath, which raged against the priest. They knew if the nun returned to the cloister, he, of course, would know what had happened and would scour the village to find the child, or to threaten them, since he would know that they knew. He knew how to make them miserable. Meanwhile, the same things would go on in the cloister. It was not right, they stormed. In hissing undertones, they discussed this latest sin, this crime against God, which was allowed to go on "up there." Soon, both the rising of their voices and the heat of their anger made the stuffy little hut unbearable, so that they moved out into the starry night to continue their discussion.

They exclaimed that they did not understand the church. As for them-selves, they knew they were only simple people, but, by God, they did understand wickedness. So they raged. They liked the nuns, they hated the wicked priest. The church, they knew, would do nothing. They, peasants only, were poor people, with no power. Yet, it was a strange thing, for as they raged, they realized they did have power - they felt it rise - and at its apex, they decided they would do away with the damned priest.

* * *

I see the priest, straddled on a small shaggy horse, his legs dangling, for there are no stirrups. He rides leisurely down a dirt path that leads up into leafy woods. There the men fall on him, beating in his head. They catch his mount too, and, after some discussion, they kill and bury it also - both in the deep woods. For if the mount is found, they reason, the church will send someone to find the priest in this location, whereas, if it is not found, they will not know where he was when he disappeared, for the priest travels far. They feel compassion for the beast and hate the necessity of killing it. They feel no remorse at all for the priest, who was, they exclaim, "a son of the devil himself."

No one in the cloister knew the truth about the death of the priest, and no one questioned or discussed it. There was simply a tremendous relief. During the time of her pregnancy, the other women had conspired together to hide her condition. Suggesting she was ill, they had sequestered her in her room. And indeed, she was quite ill. After the release from this curse (as they expressed it and thought of it), they gladly waited upon her during her recovery, assuaging the guilt they felt for being unable to protect her. The little nun blossomed, but slowly. It was a gradual process, but eventually, she became strong once more. The nuns gave her paints and board, and later, when she had regained her physical strength, they returned her carving tools to her; so that she could do the work that she loved.

Her devotion to the villagers was intense. She felt a great sense of loyalty and love toward them for taking care of her in "her illness." Although the nuns were her companions, she really felt more love for the world beyond the cloister - the freedom of the flowering fields and the people of the village.

Finally, a replacement priest came. For awhile he was closely watched, although he didn't know it. He was a mild-mannered, older man with a fringe of fine white hair, pink cheeks and nose, and a habitual expression of abstraction in his light blue eyes. Very organized, efficient and largely oblivious to the inhabitants of the cloister - concentrating solely on the business of the order - he was exactly what was needed most at the time that he arrived. The recent history of the house would have horrified him had he known or even been able to imagine such events. This priest was most often at his worktable, surrounded with paper, pen and ink, and he did not prolong his stays there.

There was a man - a mere mortal, the shepherd of a flock - who loved the nun, although he knew it could not be allowed, of course, to become a carnal love. Still, he continued his adoration into their old age, and he often brought her offerings of carving wood, when he was able to find it. She, whose wounded memory was vague, lived a rich, full and rewarding life, and her works, both charitable and artistic, were well-known in the area. She left behind many friends and devotees when she joined the angels whom she loved. As subjects for her carvings, she always seemed to prefer angels - they are, after all, beautiful, powerful - and sexless.

* * *

Dear Richard,

This Scotsman's story is the most frustrating and intriguing for me. It had so many little details and weird sounds - words that I can't figure out, and snatches of pictures that I have agonized over (like what the heck is "du or dhu?") - not to mention my joining in the suffering of the character, and he suffered as a way of life, it seems. This story is the one that broke me of trying to research to be sure that *this could have been*, and if so, to see if all the facts were accurate. I realized by the end of it that I couldn't possibly put all these pieces together. There are way too many loose ends. There were a few very exciting parts for me, in that I was able to actually verify that some details are historical fact, but many others, I could not. The "Cock of the Rock," or "Raven," actually does fit with one McDonald of Glengarry's crest, and I had the names "Donald and Ronald," so that encouraged me. Also, they had a connection with the Western Isles. However, I have not been able to find out anything regarding a battle in which a light-haired McDonald clan ancestor was crushed by a crowded mass of soldiers and horses, nor whether the dark one actually did die lying "in a field of blue gentians." I don't know if gentians grow in Britain. I don't even know if wolves existed in Scotland at this time, what kind of weapons would have been used, whether the details about the land birds and snares are accurate, etc. and etc.

I am guessing that this took place about the 16th century, but I could be off a hundred years!

This whole story seemed very strong, poetic and lyrical to me, which is fitting since the main character was such a man. His "presence" really affected me.

Anyway, I wish I could find out more historical data, but have given it up. I realize it would make a better story if I could fill in the gaps with imagination or historical facts, but somehow I just can't do that. It will have to stand or fall on its own. Perhaps I should just discard it? Wow! Even as I say that, I can practically hear this old Scot bellow, "Nae, nae!" He was quite a man, fit for an epic. Strong energy, I guess some would say. I doubt I can do him justice, but he wants to be heard, it seems.

Maybe these visions are not my own previous incarnations after all. Richard - now I have moments of fear that I may be a medium. Please tell me you don't think this could be a real possibility! The idea that ghosts might be using my mind terrifies me.

The 'Plaint of the Scotsman

I see a Scotsman. I know he is a Scot because of the way he talks, although I can't understand a lot of it. He says something . . . his voice sarcastic: "Tis noo grr-ret thing to be a Stewart of Pillbury (or perhaps it is Tillbury?). Also there is something about Langdon, or Langston, and "Grenick?" His tongue has many twists and turns as does his mind - for he is a cunning man. He has had to be, in order to survive. I try to understand the strange words and names, but because I simply can't, I will just write them down the way they seem to me, and describe what I see.

* * *

There had been a mist claiming the wee hours, but the breeze has blown most of it away now. It is strangely silent and a sense of the present moment reigns; a kind of suspended animation. A group of clansmen are waiting on the rise for the fight to begin. Their leader, this man called "Malcolm the dhu," is sitting on a rock. He seems a part of the rock - like a stone in the stream of life. It seems nothing can move him when he is set to do what is needed, or to attain that which is his soul's desire. He is a strong, resistant force; very calm and seeming without fear- no nerves - only his feathery hair gently moving in the wind. I have the impression all fear has been ground out of him through the years, with all he has been through. A rough life he has had — so that now he cares little for death.

From habit his hand brushes aside the kilt he wears exposing a hairy thigh and knee which bear the scar of an old wound. Absently he rubs this reminder of a previous battle while he waits and thinks. He is a handsome man, burly and large-boned. There is no fat upon him. His beard is kept short, for otherwise it would be a most wild and blooming thatch of whiskers. His hair is no one color, but a mixture of blond and red. It is so fine and light; its feathery wisps float about his face in the ever-present breeze, as though he were suspended in water. His arms and legs are also covered with lively, curling hair; bleached by the sun and weather. The high-topped boots he wears are made by the boot-maker of the clan especially to fit him. These are of good leather and in the unique construction of this particular boot-maker, in that the tongue in the boot is so long that it extends beyond the height of the boot and hangs out and over the top of it, ending in a fringed cuff in the front. The thongs with which they are tied are first threaded through the cuff at the top of the boot, then criss-crossed around the leg downward to tie at the ankle. He seems to be dressed in his best, for he wears a spotless white shirt with long sleeves and a round collar, a lace- trimmed bit of the same material gathered at the throat, a bonnet, a tartan garment wrapped, girdled and thrown over his shoulder (I am not sure where this begins and ends). I am surprised at this white shirt, for surely this will be dirty work, and will ruin his clothes, but he seems so impressive . . . and then I realize that this is the reason. He wishes to impress the foe, and emphasize his position as their chieftain. He turns his head, and the sunlight flickering on his eyes set off sparks of brilliant blue. Surveying his men, he sees they are still ready and willing for what lies ahead.

They are an impressive sight as they stand there on the tussucky ground, their weapons and metal badges glinting in the sun as it comes and goes behind the clouds. They are clean and dressed in their best for this occasion, like gentlemen - yet, they are strong, hardened men with fierce eyes and wild, weatherworn faces.

The terrain is scrubby, rolling grassland. There is not another living thing within sight, and they might be the only beings on the face of the earth, from the look of it. They "loom large, not like mere mortals, yet so they be," these Scots, as they stand there silhouetted against the sky on this ridge of their beloved hills. There is absolute quiet as they wait - the only movement is the light wind gently moving, stirring, lifting the fabric of a neck cloth; tendrils of hair. I am overcome with the drama and potency of the moment. He himself - this Malcolm - is quite aware of it. He feels a strong sense of self and power against such a background, yet there is something more - something timeless. It seems as though they will be there today, tomorrow, forever. . . It is a strange quality of these hills of Scotland. As they stand there, I have the thought, "It is ever like a stage, where the actors enter, perform and exit - until another drama unfolds." Perhaps it is this mystic quality that makes them take themselves so very seriously.

They had arranged to meet their foe on this ridge, and had walked across the fields to arrive early. It was their right to be first, since they were the ones who had been challenged. Malcolm got to his feet, and walking over to a scrubby tree which abounded there, he reached up and broke off a low hanging branch. Then he snapped off a twig with lobed leaves, inserted it into his badge on the tartan worn across his chest, and passed it on to the others standing there, who also broke off pieces and put them in their bonnets or on their tartans. Then, he bent over the ground and the others gathered around him to watch. Fist, he cleared a spot of soil free of grass, then he drew a circle and within the circle he drew S-shaped serpent, with dots for eyes and a forked tongue. This was a superstitious custom of their clan when they prepared for battle; so old that its origins were no longer remembered.

The time drew nigh. At his sign, they formed a line along the ridge, all eyes looking forward to another ridge on the horizon in front of them. Malcolm was very composed and his calmness seemed to settle his men. He held a large two-edged sword with a broad blade. On his left arm, strapped on just below the elbow, was a small, padded shield, made of thick, hardened leather. Most of the other men were also equipped with these. A few men among them carried cross-bows.

As they stood there expectantly, the empty horizon was suddenly filled with a line of men, a mirror image of their own. A small, petty, battle this - there were only about a score of men on each side. Malcolm, though ready to do what he must, had not wanted this fight between kinsmen. Over the gulf between them, the sides surveyed each other with cold eyes for a few minutes in total silence. They might have been statues, except for the stir of hair and kilts in the breeze. Then, Malcolm gave the greedy one another chance to save face and go home. He spread his arms wide, baring his chest in an open, trustful stance - the sword in his right hand pointed downward into the soil. His words, harried by the wind, nevertheless reached their destination; "Mayhap best not to fight this day. . . The blood is hot, but it is clan's blood. . no outsiders here, we are all one family. Think over this thing."

Then the other, the puffed-up one of from the Stewart clan, braced himself on spread legs, angled his sword across his chest in battle-ready stance, and growled his reply, (*I cannot understand all of what he says, but it sounds like: "We will nae allow the likes of ye to rr-uele Glen (Ardoch or arnoch?) Mair"!* As soon as the last defying word left his lips, the archers on both sides knelt and fired their darts at one another. The others on each side just stood there a few minutes while being fired upon. (This was an act of defiance and courage. They would never bow themselves to seek cover. The wind made marksmanship poor, anyway.) Then, after this preliminary, they got down to the meat of the battle. Throwing down their tartans, and slim in their tunics, the clansmen of both sides let out a roar which echoed over those hills that had heard this sound so often that the earth braced itself for yet another drink of blood. Brandishing their swords, the blood in their veins providing a drumbeat for the pounding of their feet, both sides raced downward - into the little vale below and between them. There was a great noise as they came together. Clanging swords, the groans of the wounded and dying, and shouts of the living, wrangling Scots - rose up from that bowl of earth . . . and soon that bowl had blood in the bottom.

Malcolm, holding his great sword in both hands, deflected most of the blows from his opponent with the shield on his left arm which he held foremost. During the heat of it though, one of his fellows backed up and pressed against him so that he had no space to maneuver and he only barely averted such a blow. The sword hissed like a serpent across his shield, and like a serpent, it took a bite of his ear and grazed his cheek. Disgusted by his mistake, he muttered something under his breath, but he fought on without pausing.

They are all bloody swordsmen. I see Malcolm standing over the wounded "Stewart" who is lying on the ground. He feels no slight compunction to have mercy. One of them must die - It will not be himself, for he has behaved with honor throughout the affair. He stabs the enemy in the abdomen and twists the sword, swiftly disemboweling him, so that he will quickly die. All around his clansmen are about the work of killing. They do not hesitate to hew heads from torsos with chopping blows of their swords, first to the one side of the neck, then to the other. . ."Why?" I wonder, shuddering at this horrible scene with no mercy shown - and the answer comes, "Because it is the custom; it is their way."

* * *

When the battle was done, Malcolm was still once more, as his few remaining enemies called a halt, acknowledging that they were beaten. What a sorry sight! he thinks. Once roaring, with eyes flashing they had come against his men as though they would easily eat them alive. Now, only a scraggly handful of them were left. Their eyes shocked and staring they picked their way over their dead, which littered the glen. Then they huddled together, looking like lost and crumpled birds after a storm. As they stood in the midst of the slaughter and looked around at their dead and dying with stunned, disbelieving eyes, Malcolm was disgusted with them. He thought, "So well had their new leader misled them, that they did not even imagine they could lose!"

Then, he too, now that it is over, surveys the scene and for the first time since I have seen him, he is overcome with emotion - hot with anger toward the Stewart - toward that man who had married within their clan and had brought about this slaughter through his greed. "What a waste of clan's blood!" he cries aloud. Now, the viper in their midst was dead, but he could not totally rejoice in that fact, for he knew the canker which that rebelling branch of the clan felt toward his would not be eased now. No, it would be worse, in fact, for they would grieve for all these dead sons and fathers.

His defeated kinsmen had begun to gather their wits and their dignity. One of them intruded upon Malcolm's reverie, saying they must have men enough to bury their dead. (The implication was, if not for that, they would have fought on until the death of their last man.). Malcolm acknowledged this as truth with a nod and silence - for he would allow them their self respect. But he was very weary, and was about to turn away, when suddenly the youngest of these rebellious cousins, whose humiliation had stoked his anger and made him bold again, thrust himself forward from the elders of that little group and cried out.

Malcolm turned back at the sound and focused his attention on his face. The lad still had the down of youth on his cheek and tears stood in his eyes. His defiant, emotional words spoken in a child's breaking voice trembled on the air like a fearful, electric butterfly . . . fluttering outward to stir and pain the hearts of those who gathered there more than a lion's roar would have done. He vowed they would return to fight again one day, Malcolm and his men all stood silently, awkwardly, watching the lad weave on his childish spindly legs, seeing fear and defiance come and go in that mother-loved face. Malcolm's face was stony, but his sore heart was whipped afresh. When it was his turn to reply, he was careful to measure his words beforehand so as not to scorn this cousin as a callow youth but to give him the respect due a man.

"Well, come again then, whenever ye will," was all he said, his voice soft and calm. Though the words were a challenge, his tone and manner soothed the boy, who turned away. Before the youth had gone many steps, though, his grief broke over him, and his relations gathered him in and they all went away home, with him bowed over and crying. . . Just a lad after all, thought Malcolm - dreading to tell his mother what had happened this day.

Malcolm knew it had just been brave talk from the lad, for it would be a long time before they recovered from the wounds inflicted by their older, more experienced clansmen.

They are tired, but not exhausted, for these clansmen are used to battle. All during their lives and that of their ancestors it had been necessary that they be ever ready to fight. They busy themselves - chopping down scrubby branches to strap their dead and wounded to - and drag or carry them back across the moor toward home. They have a small two-wheeled cart, drawn by a work pony, and this they load their weapons into, the swords stacked up like lumber. There is no good way to carry these swords of theirs. They are too large to strap on. They don't, to my wonder, take very good care of them, but use them more as mundane tools. It seems their value is not so much for their sharp edges as for their weight when wielded by strong Scot's arms. When lined up for battle, it is their custom to hold these swords across their torsos, diagonally, so that the blades catch the sun's rays and reflect it - hopefully striking awe into the other side's hearts. Besides, if their enemies are somewhat blinded by the light, they cannot make out the numbers which stand there. They did not do that in this small battle, because it was an in-clan fight, and the numbers of each side were even and the men within each were well known.

Malcolm, as their chief, rides on the back of the little cart as they return home, his legs dangling over the back, his feet tapping the ground with every bump. He is quiet, listening to the comments of his men. Their words are over-laid with relief that this unpleasantness is over and they have won. At first, they cover the ground with strong strides, but as their band draws nearer to home and their women-folk, their talk subsides and they are quiet. Their hearts are heavy as they think of what they will tell those who are waiting in vain for their men to return. But had it not been their duty? And had they not died valiantly? So, then these hardened men fortify themselves against the onslaught which will soon be brought against them by the waiting women and children. For those hardened fighters' hearts are stripped bare of their armour in the presence of their loved ones.

I can see a long construction of stone and mortar. It is a walled enclosure - a fortress. At one corner there is a square tower three stories high. This is called "the keep." At the right side of this tower, the wall jogs inward and a door is there, which cannot be readily seen face-on. This door opens into a quite narrow passage between the wall and that side of the keep. This dark passage was thus designed to discourage an armed intruder, who could be waylaid easily from the inside as he sidled along the passage, his arms and shield down. From this short passage, one enters into the courtyard, and from there one can enter the door to the keep, which is the main house. Along the other sides of the wall, to the left and behind the keep, additions have been added where others of this extended family live.

Besides the dwelling quarters within the fortress, there are cottages scattered on either side of the road before and beyond it, where others of the chief's family live. When danger arises, the families that live in these houses flee to shelter within Malcolm's fortress.

Now, as the clansmen return from battle down the road to their village, light-colored dogs and small boys come gamboling out onto the path to meet them. . . . Excited and fearful at the same time, the women follow - but with slower steps, and full of dread. Shading their eyes with their hands, each one is reluctant to look up, to see whether or not her menfolk return.

* * *

While caring for the wounded, the clan comforted themselves with the hope that this battle would give them peace, at least for a time. It seemed they would lose but two men and their talk reflected the relief they felt. The Stewart who had led the other group was of another clan who had married into that branch of theirs, and crude ambition had led him to challenge their leadership. They spoke to each other of how his greed would have bled the life out of them, and of how their chief, Malcolm, had hated to take the lives of his own blood-kin and those who had followed behind this usurper, but it had been necessary. They should not have followed the outsider to do battle against their own kin. Now they were in harmony once more. All of them could return to their peaceful, homely routines - could hunt and fish without worry that someone would come out of the trees behind them, with a broad axe to lay open their heads.

Malcolm did not join in the talk. He was quiet; his thoughts were more cynical - his vision focused on the future of his clan. He did not fear the threat of renewed violence any time soon, in spite of the threat by his young kinsman. It was expected that something of that kind would be said. It was sad, yet noble that such a youth was the last defiant one. The lad was on his way to becoming either a valiant foe or a friend. In Malcolm's opinion, no worthy man would have taken such a whipping without threatening retaliation. But, although it had been an empty threat, there was still danger in that quarter, and his thoughts dwelt on that. His heart was heavy for the young wife of the leader, Maigret, who had bairns at her skirt, but he knew her close kinsmen would take care for her, and, eventually, she would find another man to protect her and look after her interests. A better man this time? But who would it be? There were few to choose from within the clan. And it was this that worried him.

His thoughts turned to his sons and how he had trained them to be fierce fighters, to know when it was necessary to fight, and how not to provoke one, if it was not necessary. Through the years, their clan had been severely reduced in numbers, so that they must cleave together and increase their size if they were to hold to their lands, else they would not survive. (This desire; the continuation of his line and that of his clan, was as much a part of Malcolm as the blood in his veins.) Who would have led them if he had been killed today? None of his sons were ready to take on this duty. Ronald, his youngest, was hot-headed and must be taught to follow the lead of the eldest. Then the idea came into his head. He simmered it a while then decided he would call a clan meeting, but first the burial of their dead or dying.

* * *

It is a strange picture I see, and in fragments. I don't really know if this is Malcolm's clan I see, or if it is their ancestors, for it seems this custom was one which their ancestors practiced. I can see their women preparing the dead. The bodies are fully clothed and laid out on a flat rock upon stones, like a table, or a bier. The women fold the dead hands over each breast, and looking up toward the sky, chant to spur the spirit heavenward, for they have a firm belief in the immortality of the spirit. Then they build a ring of fire around this bier which will leap up and consume the flesh. Afterward, they will remove and clean the bones. "Ashes to Ashes, dust to dust. . ." the grieving women sing, swaying with the monotonous rhythm. The bones will be made into a pile and all of them will be buried with the others of the clan, all as one, united in one grave. It seems a strange combination of barbaric beliefs mixed with Christian, but these people - his mother's seafaring race - are proud that their heritage sets them apart from some of the other tribes of Scotland. Malcolm is proud of his other ancestors, too - those of his father. On both sides he is descended from royal blood - some were the barbaric warriors - the seafarers, and the others were genteel "of the manner born."

* * *

This is a new vision, yet it is still the same Scottish story, for these are ancestors of Malcolm the dhu. I think to understand more about Malcolm, I must first see a little of his history, for he is most strongly aware that he is a link in the chain of his line, and that his descendants must live on to perpetuate the greatness of his ancestors.

The Blackbird or Cock 'O The Rock, Malcolm's Grandfather:

I see a young man of slim and elegant build, with long narrow hands. He is richly dressed. His tartan is mostly blue, green, black; with a little yellow and a fine red line run through. This pattern is made into a snug vest worn over a round-necked shirt with sleeves that are puffed at the shoulders. His head is capped with sleek black hair and his beard of the same shining black is quite short and neatly trimmed. His bonnet is adorned with a silver badge and a black cock's feather - a symbol of fierceness in battle. Eyes of a deep, vivid blue dominate his face which is framed by a ruff ornamented with a brooch-like "jewel"; a gold chain glimmering beneath it. He does not wear a kilt, but pantaloons and hose, for he is often on horseback. He is a noble Scot, a fine, illustrious gentleman, worthy of the king's notice - perhaps regarded as a prince in his land. He is called "Cock O' the Rock," (the "Rock" being his castle) and more often, simply: "the Blackbird," or "the Raven" - the raven being a symbol which is associated with his house. He is somehow tied to the English . . . loyal to the rightful king. He rides a fine white horse with a silver-grey mane and tail and some dappling of grey on the rump and shoulders. The silver fittings and ornaments on his bridle and saddle have been given him by the King. He has whippets - well trained for fetching - and falcons for hunting.

The "Blackbird" is wealthy and has married well. The terrain of the land on which he lives, lying more to the south, is not as rugged as where Malcolm will later live. Here, life is easy. He and his family live in a massive but gracious home - a castle with a square tower set in the middle of its front section. Here there are plenty of servants and time for frivolity - here the Blackbird plays his lute; making up songs.

There is a little blond woman, heavy with child - walking about in the gardens in front of this castle. She is mistress of the "Raven's Nest" or "The Rock," and at present, she is supervising the drying of freshly-dyed woolen yarn. Many women - gentle ladies and servant women of the household - are busy draping enormous, damp skeins on the shrubbery and on linen spread on the grass, to dry. The gray stone dwelling creates a background of comfort and ease - the scene before it, filled with color and beauty; the flowers in the garden, the gowns of lovely ladies as they move softly over the grass, their vibrant ribbons of yarn they are spreading out upon the shrubs and sheets. It is a nice day, and this female activity seems to be enjoyed by all, for the garden buzzes with their lively chatter and humming of ballads.

The chore finished, the servants retire indoors and the ladies gather beneath the trees to refresh themselves. There, on rugs and cushions laid out for them, they tarry softly, idly talking - some at their embroidery, others gently napping. Unobserved, the wind turns about and clouds blow in, bringing a sudden swirling of wind and spattering rain . . . . Then, fluttering female voices rise in protest and laughter as the women scurry about, snatching up the yarn. Racing against the rain, they run hither and yon, gathering the huge skeins into bundles and great baskets. The teasing wind enters into the playful mood, plucking at the colorful skeins and the gowns of the ladies as they skitter about, wafting their laughter aloft so that it sounds like the distant tinkling of bells.

A delightful scene, but their mistress should not rush about so. All of them so distracted they do not think to stop her. She stumbles on the stones and falls on her side upon a sharply projecting rock. She cries out, and the women rush toward her, the yarn forgotten. She looks up at the breathless women clustered over her, their clothing misted by the rain, beads of water clinging to their curls and veils, their alarmed faces a reflection of her own - for the stone has struck her belly where the babe lies. All solemn now, they carry her inside and put her to bed. There she lies for some time, her bruised side sore and painful. Then the child makes his entrance and it is a difficult birth.

This event was an omen, the midwife says, that the child would have to make his own way in the world - that it will be hard for him, his path will be "rocky". . . and so it was.

Since the Blackbird was connected to the English, he fought with the English early on. (His descendants groaned later that he had chosen his side wrongly)

There is a battle . . . . blinding red and flashing metal . . . lines of men in red tunics, wearing conical helmets of shining metal and marching very close together, holding their glittering spears upright. The Blackbird, looking very stern, is with them, riding his handsome white horse. He wears chain mail and armor, as do the others who can afford it. . . The Campbells were supposed to be friends and allies, but spoilt the lot. There are three days marching, and crossing water, the noise of a horde of armed men and horses' hooves splashing through water - rumbling cannon wheels. . . When they reach dry land again they beat upon the earth like a drummer on his instrument, so that those peaceful peasants - alarmed at this ominous sound resonating from the earth - cower in fear before they actually see the source of it . . . MacLeish or MacLean of Stewart Clan - is restless. There is something about the Isles, and a Duke of Argyll.

(I think that at this time of the history of Malcolm's people, they were Catholic, but were not devout. The "blackbird" did not like the church because, he said, they coveted all the lands and possessions of the people, and couldn't be trusted. As it

turned out, this was well said, for "The Raven's Rock" was a place of beauty and abundance not escaping the lustful eye of a man named Malloy, a representative of the church who dared to call himself a Christian - a man who was really a preda-tor; a wolf in sheep's clothing.)

In a dip in the earth, a place between two hillocks, the blackbird is standing - facing a loose rocky slope at about his eye level. He seems calm, but looks around warily before he digs into this cairn. Removing some of the rocks, he hides a leather bag of valuables within it. As he replaces the stones, he looks about him again and, seeing no one, he rides away.

Unknown to him, he has been spied upon. At the crest of the hill above, lurks an older man, a highlander, well-bearded and wilder looking - a contrast to the young, neat, lustrous-looking Blackbird. He had been on the slope beyond, minding a flock of goats. He did not do anything then, but later he comes back to this place, and stands pondering a moment, looking at the cairn, absorbed in his thoughts. He is poor, but he knows the danger and dishonor of his deed, for he knows the blackbird well and is supposed to be an ally - but temptation is stronger than he. Removing the stones, he finds and removes the bag of treasure. This was ill-gotten gain, a curse on his house. I think he is a Campbell. His tartan is bolder and brighter; red, yellow, with a broken black line.

The Blackbird, a lowlander, had come north to enlist an army to his side. Inside the bag were precious stones: a large grey pearl, gold coins, a ring with a large smooth ruby, and a heavy silver chain with pendants hanging from it (a necklace which holds some special significance). (After some thought, I think this vision may have been symbolic; that the grey pearl was a castle, the coins; riches, the ruby ring; a symbol of leadership or the king's support, and the silver chain of pendants may have been a chain of islands or families of a clan from the islands.)

So, because of a traitor, the Blackbird failed to recruit the clans in his support, and was dishonorably trapped. Because of lies against him, he lost the king's support and was imprisoned. While, there in that place of shame, even while others worked for his release, he was taken with a disease. He was still a young man when he died in the "old woods" - a deep forest. Others were helping him homeward, but it was too late - there under the trees in a bed of blue gentians, the blackbird breathed his last.

At the same time that his lands were being divided between his heirs and the wolves, songs were being written and sung to the honor of the once proud "Cock of the Rock," the "Blackbird" who died on "gentian hill". . "Ah, the sweet-sad beauty of it," they would say as the picture was brought vividly to mind - their blue-eyed, raven-haired prince, the life breath gone from his body, lying there in the deep woods upon a bed of blossoms as blue as that of his own dear eyes . . . Just as a blackbird fallen from one of those great trees - his song no longer heard in the forest.

Donald "The White": The Uncle

The Cock O' the Rock, or Blackbird, has a relation, perhaps a brother or half-brother who rises to leadership when the Blackbird dies. It was left to him - this one called "Donald the white" to save the family fortunes, to build for the future of the clan. He too, is slim and elegant, but he is a contrast to the Blackbird, being blond. His straight hair is pulled back from his face and tied. He also wears a bonnet with a black feather, but his tartan colors are different - mainly green, black . . perhaps a little blue. (With the death of the Blackbird and the loss of part of their domain, the tartan was argued over and the pattern was changed and lost to another.) This man, great uncle of Malcolm, is considered a man of beauty, and has a beautiful wife. She charms her admirers when she laughs, as she often does. Her lips are naturally red and soft. Her eyes slant downward at the outer corners; thick black lashes cast seductive shadows over the dark blue orbs they rim. The hair of her head is a rich, dark brown. Her children are darlings, kept prettily dressed, and she adores them. This perfect couple is romanticized, and songs are written about them which are sung to the lute. Those whose hearts love the unjustly downtrodden are waiting for him to assuage the demanding ghost of his "brother." He is expected to take up the banner and lead his people to vengeance. Even those who have naught to do with it urge him on, allying themselves for their own ends. Too young to be a legend, all this adoration and sudden responsibility goes to his head, and clouds his judgment. He is foolhardy, and later, it would be said "he played with vipers."

I see him standing on a ridge overlooking a glen in which maybe 200 or so men have gathered. They look up to him, listening to the words he is shouting. He is a vibrant, persuasive man; cajoling them into taking up this battle. He is eager to fight and armed with a sword - not a large, two handed one, but a smaller one that is sheathed at his side as he rides on his horse - another, smaller blade is strapped to his other side. Back and forth he strides, gesturing. . Then his final cry - which sounds like "Yaw -HO!" and again, "Yaw-HO!". . . And capitulating to his charm, the men take up the cheer.

In the midst of the battle, something is gravely wrong. Donald is astride a horse, while around him there are soldiers on foot, locked in hand to hand combat. Beyond the mill of the warring people, those on the fringe of it push inward until they are all squeezed together like a wine-press, so that some cannot even raise their swords above their heads, and are helpless. The combatants press unbearably against Donald and his whinnying horse. His bonnet is torn and he loses it. As he turns his head I see his face . . . It is dirty; shock is written on it. It is like he is in a vise - his mount cannot move, nor can he dismount. All his men are also locked in this horrible crush. Moans and protests fill the air. His suffering supporters have ringed him in all around, but somehow, he is torn from the saddle. His right leg, cruelly twisted, remains in the stirrup, that part of him pushed below his hysterical horse, is trampled. Eventually, he somehow manages to get free and drags himself under and away from the compacted horde. Beyond a veil of dust raised by the trampling and trampled warriors, I see him sitting on a boulder with his leg outstretched before him. He is no coward, but when he unties the thongs of his boot, he signs and shudders, and for good reason. When the boot top is peeled back, I can see the shin bone projecting from the skin, its jagged white edge gleaming through a bloody mess.

Too young, he acted rashly, precipitately - he "struck too soon," said those who analyzed it later. They said he was quelled by an "Iron Fist" - one whose gauntlet appeared on a banner in the thick of this battle.

* * *

Malcolm's father: Cullen

There is a man striding along, in distress of some kind. He doesn't look well He is unkempt, oblivious of all external things. A flock of blackbirds swoop down toward him and he, short of patience, flails his arms at them; to scare them off. . . They glide away. It seems they are an omen to him, and add to his distress. I wonder what is wrong with him, and who he is. He mutters to himself: "Noo friends to bide the time with, Noo friends at-tall. Tisnee is the one to thank for that . . . a pu-ir man, with naw left." "Culloch mair" . . . comes to me (I don't know what this means). His health is failing. He doesn't see well. I understand that this is Malcolm's father. I do not get his name but will call him Cullen. In appearance he is somewhat like his son, with the same vigorous, curly hair, but he is blonder, and has a thinner, paler face which seems drawn and bitter. But though he looks a paler version of his son, he looks much more like a warrior than his father, the Cock O' the Rock. Suspended on a chain around his throat, where it lies high on the chest bone, is a Celtic cross. He is wearing a chain mail tunic, with a sword strapped to his side.

Cullen grew up in his mother's old home in the higher lands, which he later inherited. It was an irony that this place used to be an abbey, for his mother embraced the Protestant religion, and her children followed likewise. It is not so much that they were fervent followers of the movement, as it was that they did not like to be dictated to by the Catholics, in the manner of their past. They had been bullied out of their little kingdom, and Cullen, like his father, the "Blackbird," did not take kindly to that.

All of his family were, by now, stubbornly independent and rebelled at the first sign of domination.

Although they had been rich, by the time Cullen was a man grown, the clan was poor. Yet Cullen was strong and vigorous. He drew the loyal clan in around him; then built up an estate of his own. His first marriage was to Anabel. The marriage was a good one, both for the unity of the clans, and because it brought money into the fold. Perhaps it was not such a good match of personalities.

Whenever Malcolm thought of his mother, Anabel, it was always his favorite memory which came to mind. She would be in the garden, with children at her skirts or in her lap. She loved sunshine, gardens and children. She would sit there on her bench - her heart and eyes full of the fairness of it, while, unbeknownst to her, it took herself to complete that scene of perfect beauty. She would hold her face up to the sunshine and would draw off her veil to bask in its warmth. Free from its covering, her light auburn hair fell in waves down her back and shoulders. (Malcolm's heart turned over at the remembered vision of it, just as it had done when he was a small boy resting his cheek against her knee as his eyes idolized her.) Ah, the goodness of his mother! The glory of her hair! How the sun's rays made a halo around it, setting off sparks of gold and flickers of flame! Her chattering brood of children, leaning inward to her - their source of warmth and love - would suddenly fall quiet and stare in awe, their grubby little hands timidly reaching out to touch those gleaming strands of unearthly fire. It was as though the sun had reached out to reveal their mother for the angel that she really was, and they - soiled and anxious little earth-creatures - stood off a bit in worshipful adoration. But then she - oblivious to that holy aura - would look down and say something homely in that so-familiar voice they loved, and they would rush in to clamber over her again, reassured that she was only their mother after all, and not some celestial being. Malcolm, however, would continue to stare - impressing this scene upon his memory for always, remembering her just this way - transfigured loving mother and angel beauty - for, to him, she was above all others. Nor did she ever fail her children. Although she'd had many, she had been a good and loving mother to each and every one.

* * *

I see her - this Anabel - within an ornamental arbor, which has heavy vines growing on it. She is young and voluptuous - female; full of vitality. Her husband, Cullen, playfully hiding there, reaches out and draws her in, smacking her on the lips. She giggles and protests half-heartedly. His laugh is deep and lusty. He covers her neck and mouth with little smacking kisses - tasting the sweetness of her.

Before and at the beginning of their marriage, Anabel had been in awe of her fierce, passionate, so-intense man; impressed by his noble blood line and very quick mind. She didn't, however, understand Cullen's desire for power and the politics of the land did not interest her. She was just a simple woman with simple tastes; quite satisfied with what they had: her children, home and comforts. He, on the other hand, could not be satisfied with what was there before his eyes.

He could have learned a lesson from his wife who held peace in her hand like an offering. Hers was a gift he never accepted - a blessing he was never able to enjoy. As his ambition grew and he wanted more than she, he began to weary of her company sometimes; thinking her dull-witted. Instead of turning aside into a peaceful pasture he continued stubbornly down his rocky road, becoming both a driving and driven man - pushing all before him toward his goal. Ever before him was the enlargement of his estates, perhaps even the restoration of that territory which had been his father's (Yes, so he dared to dream - so unreasonable though that was!).

As the years went by, his sweet wife began to suspect that intelligence was not always the same thing as wisdom, and being thus enlightened, she began to see the flaws in her husband. So, they progressed rather separately, along their life's path. She, a gentle spirit prone to meditation, observed life and human errors and gained inward strength, while her husband - racing as he was toward his unattainable goal (which, when measured against hers, was the inferior one) - degenerated in spirit.

* * *

Oh, woe, there is a small, slim woman with dark hair. . . She is lurking in the darkened gloom of the castle, whispering to Cullen, seducing him - a small viper in their midst.

There was a kinswoman, named Tisnee, who came to live in their household. Cullen became involved with her, even before the death of Anabel. When Anabel had joined the true angels, Tisnee became his second wife. So, the sin of adultery was compounded by a mistaken marriage to one who brought out his worst faults. It was, perhaps, no coincidence that at that precise time his downfall began.

After the death of his adored mother, the continued upbringing of Malcolm, his brothers, and sisters was done by the other women in the household, Tisnee taking no interest in them. Malcolm grew to hate her - her with the bold black eyes. To him she was a harlot who had taken the bloom from his mother's cheeks and sent her to an early grave. He took care to avoid her, though sometimes they would come face to face in the great hall, when he would tremble with anger as she stared sidelong and sharply at him from those hated eyes, silent, but daring him to fly up at her.

To Malcolm, it seemed that, without his mother's love, the sun had gone beyond the clouds and the flowers had withered away. He felt cold and abandoned and turned to his father, making attempts to waylay him for that talk and light affection he had hitherto shown to his children. Soon, he saw it was no use, and gave it up. His mother had been his heart; his father, his hero. Now he had lost them both, for Cullen was as distant from his children as if he had been in another country. There was a far-away look in his eyes and his mind was stuffed full of his dream. Still, he was his father and Malcolm the youth wished to be a man, so he stood apart and watched his sire, closely observing Cullen's dealings and learning where to pattern himself after him. He also learned where not to do so, for he was his mother's son in many things. He appreciated the simple things life had to offer and was an honest, open soul, so he rejected the subtle, covert ways of his father.

He also devoted himself to accumulating knowledge from the other men of the clan and from books. It was the latter which finally brought him that which he had desired - the attention of his father. Cullen, pleased and surprised to find him in his book room, urged him onward. He brought out the family tree and impressed upon his son the importance of the continuity of the line, going over the lives of each of their illustrious ancestors. The boy observed the look of his father; excited by his flashing eyes and intense voice, his heart wrung by his beleaguered, weary face, and all the while he basked in the warmth of his father's great and awesome shelter - for he had his arm about Malcolm's shoulders. It was obvious that family continuity was important to Cullen and since Malcolm was touched to the heart that his father had taken notice of him, this moment took on rare significance in the boy's mind. He stared, enrapt, at the names penned upon the parchment his father held. The ink scrawls blurred and wobbled beneath his eyes as he strained to envision each image beneath the name - to see those living folk who had lived graciously and heroically and wished to perpetuate their kind. And when, through his father's narrative and his imagination, he saw them clearly, it seemed as though they, too, looked to him: Malcolm, their Successor - It was up to him to make sure no link was broken and to regain their lustre and renown.

Always Cullen had been alert for ways of reclaiming his father's lost lands - waiting, and planning. He had accumulated a great deal during his first marriage years, and the clan was largely satisfied and at peace. But after he yoked himself to Tisnee, the dream of reclaiming his father's lost estates burst from its bounds, becoming a monster which overpowered him. He became a reckless schemer and endangered it all. Tisnee was clever and devious - plotting and scheming always. Together, they burned a path to destruction.

Although he had always been ambitious, Cullen had still been an honorable man. Now, because he listened to Tisnee too often he became - not just a plotter - but cunning and sly. The clan lost respect for him, since they admired a straight-forward man; one honest in his dealings. Soon, they were saying he was ruled by his wife and they became wary; not knowing his mind.

Cullen, with his ripening devious nature, preferred to play politics to achieve his ends, but would rise to battle in a moment, if it would further his ambition. Since the clan was not solidly behind him, he was frustrated time and again. When he wanted to race out and flay his enemies, he was often forced to stew by his fireside, instead.

One hard year followed on the heels of another, so that through the years, there was less and less richness in the lands and homes of the clan - until by the time Malcolm became chief, they were lucky to have food in their mouths. Tisnee had pulled down the man who could have accomplished much without her. Everyone agreed Cullen could not have remained in the single state, as he was the kind who much needed a woman, but he should have looked elsewhere, they said. If he had, the history of their clan would have been very different.

Even he realized, in his later years when he was ill and lonely, that Tisnee had deceived him. By then, she had become a sour, mean and disappointed old woman - a shrew - whom all (even Cullen) avoided. Then, he reached out to his family, but by then it was too late - his sons had turned their backs on him. Only a daughter would help him off with his boots and would bring a hot drink to warm his old bones - but alas! When he looked into her eyes when she'd brought him the cup, he saw naught but pity there.

In what should have been his prime he became old and weak - a tiger with his teeth drawn. In one last effort to reclaim his lost lands (so sick he had to be helped onto his horse) he went out to battle for the last time It was a churning mill in which he broke his neck. They carried him home to bed and, even though he lay dying, they turned away from him in scorn and disgust - for they suffered bitterly over their losses.

By this time, the family had begun to believe they carried a curse - a bane – to be harvested from generation to generation. They were now poor indeed. There was one thing, at least, in which they rejoiced - Tisnee had proved to be barren. They were glad, for otherwise she would have found some way for her offspring to inherit what little was left when Cullen died.

In the end, Cullen had lost more than he had gained. His children had lost faith in him, his relatives had abandoned him and, in the final summing-up, the only thing he himself had added to the family's inheritance was the Protestant religion - and his heart had not been fully engaged with that. His conversion had been, for the most part, retaliation against his father's Catholic enemies. Clearly and without mercy, these truths came to him now in his last days as he lay on his bed, unable to move. Before they had not been able to catch up with him, for he was a man of action, and impulsively on the move. Now, the only part of him which was still alive - his brain - worked ceaselessly; conjuring all the scenes of his life heretofore. At first, he stared at these visions with bewilderment, wondering, filled with self-righteous questions beginning with "why". . . and that door in his mind cracked open, and the answers came battering through - the truth that would make him ashamed at Heaven's door. (He had never halted his onward surge though life for long enough before, to hear that small voice, nor would he have listened, then, for he would not lay aside his will, his determination to achieve his passionate desires.)

So, during those days as he lay paralyzed and defenseless against it, the truth washed over him. He saw himself as he had been - not as he had felt he was. After he had viewed these mental revelations with horror, he was moved to repentance. That he was not even able to speak his apologies to those he had wronged added to his torture. Now he could see things clearly. Now he finally knew all the errors of his way! Now! When he was utterly helpless to rectify any of them! Though he lay in anguish, his mind was merciless - it played his pitiful story for him, over and over again. He could only stare - so unwillingly mute - at those of his family who came to stand by his bedside. His unblinking eyes - straining to convey that fervent regret welling up from his comfortless soul - reflected such a deep abyss of sorrow that they all turned away from it, troubled. Finally, (when he had, perhaps, achieved a proper level of remorse) he looked up to see Anabel standing by his bed, and when she smiled and bid him come, his soul leapt up with gladness and humbly he went with her as she led him onto the lighted path.

His passing was a great relief to himself and everyone else. Just as the midwife had foretold, his way had indeed been a rocky road.

Malcolm's Story:

"Clon don daeraugh". . . " (it sounds like) There the keep lies. Don't be <u>too</u> good, for goodness can be a weakness," this man says. "Keep up thine arm, for readiness to battle is strength, and the way to prosperity." . . "Ever Vigilant," is his motto.

It is a poor country and the people are hard-pressed to find food. He loves it, though - this man of the earth. The sight of it, in all seasons, thrills his being. It is beautiful, in a sad and lonely way - most heart-rending in the mist, which softens the cragginess and gives the barrens a sweet, dew-kissed look. The scrubby trees are then a soft, gray-green, the far-stretching heath a myriad of shades and textures. . . The meadow bells humbly hang their heads with the weight of the moisture, and then . . . "Look!" . . . he whispers. The hart is there - and then gone, in a moment - so that one thinks one has imagined it.

Malcolm the dhu, or "the black," was forced to leave the place of his birth. He like Moses, led his brothers and sisters to the new land, and there they defiantly pushed roots into that rocky soil. (They left behind his youngest brother, who had married outside the allied clans and was considered a traitor. When Malcolm thought of him, he had to clear the bitterness from his mouth and spit upon the ground.) They had no choice but to leave, since their father had lost everything that had remained from the estates of their grandfather, the ill-fated Raven, but they shook the dirt from their feet and called back curses as though they were glad enough to go. They carried little with them except the memory that they had once been a noble family; rich and well-bred.

"Land, land!" was always the quest in Scotland. Even Malcolm was not free from that yearning over their lost estates, but, unlike his father, he was able to shake off that vision and devote himself to building up what they now possessed - this land which was the inheritance from his mother, Anabel, and the leadership of that clan.

Most of the family lived in "the keep," a fortress of stone built around a square tower. The rest of the clan lived either in those dwellings they had added within the fortress's stone walls or in those cottages which lay beyond it. At dusk, they would all gather together for a meal in the great hall and tarry to discuss day to day concerns. At this drawing-in time the hall would be full of the young ones, playing or lounging in front of the great fire. When they had sated their appetites, their elders would sit in the glow of the fire and wax soft as they basked in family companionship. At these times, if a child leaned against one's knee and yearned for a story, the story-tellers among them would resurrect those legends out of their illustrious past. Then their dead ancestors - full of pain and glory - would come alive among them; their shadows moving within the flickering light of the hall. Sounds from the hearth - a falling log or the snapping fire as it ate its way through a too-green limb would startle the children from their reverie and, their eyes stretched large, they would all creep closer to their elders. The story of the Blackbird was their great favorite but Malcolm (though he yearned over the tale in his day dreams) had difficulty telling it to the youngsters. He knew he betrayed himself in the telling of it, for his voice would tremble with emotion, and he was reluctant to pass on the bit- terness which that great injustice had sown in the minds of his father and his kin. Other tales were easier to tell. There was one in which a dragon played a part. Even the elders were no longer sure what that one meant, but it was a glorious tale, strange and eerie - and these Scots were not skeptics. It was in this way of story-telling that their history was recorded - in the minds of their children and grandchildren.

Because they set great store by the dignity of man, much of their con- versation became debates about what they considered the correct or right- eous - even the noble - thing to do. Sitting by the fireside in winter talking or making and repairing their tools, was a congenial pastime, but for the most part, they were men of action and grew weary and stale without a greater outlet for their energy. Though it promised hard work, all looked forward to the warm season.

* * *

In the spring, when the soil awakens, they all turn out to the gardens to toil; men, women and children. I see Malcolm clear a small circle on the ground and when it is just exposed dirt (fine, soft stuff) he draws a circle in it, spaces a marker to the edge and spits into the center. He then looks up at the sun. The drop of spittle in the middle of the circle is coated with fine soil, but still forms a bead. When the sun comes around the marker, the bead of spittle suddenly flattens out and is absorbed into the soil. This is the sign that it is time to plant.

They clear brush, burn off the dead growth, and turn the soil up to the sun. Every year it is the same; they rise to their work with hope in their hearts once more, that this year will be the one when Sweet Circe will come and drop abundance into their laps. Scattered wisps of smoke rise above the rock walls which enclose the garden lots. The odors of smoke and freshly turned soil mingle in the air, and Malcolm breathes deeply, delighting in it. He is assessing his small "kingdom" with some pleasure, rather than regret, for he is a man of simple needs - a man who loves his people and this land of Scotland. His people are poor and, at present, all begrimed - for they are digging in the soil with the pigs and the soil is still mined with stones. Every now and then someone will find one and toss it, (if it is small) or drag it, (if it is of some size) to add to that wall which was been formed through years of this labor. Although this scene is repeated each year, they never seem to run out of stones. Still, the barriers help to fend off the blowing, chill wind from the garden. These walls extend outward from the keep, forming wings from the living quarters all the way to a steep hillside at back. This hillside is prone to rock slides, and fallen boulders have formed a "scree" - a welcome defensive barrier which meets with Malcolm's approval. Any enemy fool-hardy enough to climb down from that direction would loudly signal his approach, if he were lucky enough not to break his neck, first.

Within the walled-in garden and orchard, they have a kind of fruit tree, which they cherish. It bears a small apple - tart and spicy. The children are not allowed to climb in those trees. Anything that produces food in this place is highly respected and well tended; its seeds saved and replanted - for it was a hard land.

There are cottages outside the main house and the walled-in area. If trouble comes, those who live there will remove themselves to the main house for safety. The keep itself is three stories high. . . . Coming through the door in the front wall, down the close passage to the courtyard, and entering into this ground level door of the keep, I see that the floor is merely dirt, and there are some slit-like windows high up on the walls where one cannot see out of them. Then I see - extending diagonally across the wall from the ground - narrow ledge-like steps, hardly more than toe-holds, by which men (archers I suppose) might gain access to these windows. On the second level, which consists of a great hall only, there are more narrow windows and on the third level there are larger windows - for light. Some of these look out over the enclosure at back, for this is where the family resides. I am dismayed that the windows have no glazing, since surely they freeze in harsh winters, but then I see that the women work at tapestries by the light of the windows in good weather, and use these and wooden guards, or shutters, to cover those drafty holes in winter.

Outside their windows lay high grassy ridges and plateaus. There were very few large trees in the elevations. They were clumped together in the rims of the glens below. Standing on one of these high plateaus (his favorite view), Malcolm could see an extraordinary expanse of landscape below, where a shining body of water - a serpent of fluid silver - made an undulating path across it. Above, green hills and golden ridges cast shadows in patterns of blue and grey, shifting as the sun moved over the earth. On sunny, mild days, magnificent clumps of clouds would be piled high in a vivid blue sky, but on windy days the clouds would be swept across the sky, as though by a giant broom. Falcons wheeled overhead, searching for rabbits, hedgehogs and ground-nesting birds.

Though it was true the land was poor for farming, it still provided for them in its way. His clans hunted small game with a sling shot. Sometimes, one would issue a challenge to another to try their marksmanship. The most difficult target was one of the kites which circled high overhead. It was said that the man who could fell one of those with a sling shot was a man, indeed.

* * *

There is a kind of long-legged bird with rough, burry claws that nest within the hedgerows. On the ground beside the hedgerows, the clansmen set out a long, narrow strip of soft netting, the weave of it loose and easily snagged. When this bird simply walks across it, his claws are almost hopelessly entangled. Boys are set to mind these nets after they are spread, for it is a slow job. It also requires much netting for the women to weave on their loom. "Ah! But the flesh of (this fowl) is so sweet!" say the men - who have little to do with this job but spread the netting.

They have several swine among their livestock. These were kept sheltered near their dwellings for protection from the cold and wild beasts. They were thin and rangy, for it was hard to find food for them in the long winters. A few scraggly fowl (prized, not just for their reproduction, but for the rare extra eggs they offered up stingily in spring) ran and scratched around the premises and were well housed in winter against the raw wind. Fortunately, the clan lived not far from the sea and could always get quantities of fish - dried or fresh - by barter, usually. Fish was cheap and good food. They fished the streams around them also - one man on each side of the stream holding a net of their own making. In some (celebrated) seasons past, the nets had been fair to breaking with the load of their catch. They supplemented this with beef and (less often) game.

On the rare occasion when they had a milk cow, (the calves usually drained their mothers dry, the cows not being of a breed for a long "wet," or milking time), then they counted themselves most fortunate indeed and used the milk in puddings and with fruit. The milk was not rich in butterfat, so butter was rare, but they were able to make a kind of cheese, white and crumbly, which they sprinkled into other dishes. Their cattle were small, shaggy beasts, with curving horns and beautiful dark eyes. To protect them in winter, they had looked for those narrow hollows - a natural bowl between two crowded hills and down in these crannies they had built a projecting shelter onto the one slope; the opposite slope also providing its protection against the buffeting wind. During this season, the tender calves or milk cows were brought in and sheltered within the byres of the keep, where they were hand-fed by the women and children. There was little grass for their cattle to share, so they deliberately kept their numbers low. The goats, on the other hand, were not particular as to forage, and they fared better. Besides the meat they provided, the women of this clan, known to be very clever with weaving, made cloth from the shorn hair of these hardy beasts.

It was much more difficult to grow grain or find herbage. There was a tall-growing wild herb which the women looked for in spring, when they would pick its tender green leaves to cook with meat.

That timber which was lawful to cut was meager, yet there was a resin which could be found, crystallized in little lumps within the cones of a conifer which grew there. They would gather it and when they had warmed it near the fire until it would spread easily, they would fill in those holes and tunnels made by beetles in the timbers of their buildings. It not only filled the holes, but repelled the insects. This was a fall or winter job for the clansmen, when there was little else to do.

* * *

Even though it is a hard land, I sense his great abiding love for it - the look, sounds and feel of it in all weather and seasons. He loves the storm - it makes his blood rise. He rejoices in it. He watches the clouds build and darken on the horizon and then come rolling forward across the moors - a gray curtain of power sweeping toward him - taking his breath away. He is always looking toward the West, and the sea.

He is a poet. It is natural, since he loves the earth and exults in its beauty. Some lines come into my mind, which I feel are a rough translation of a paean to spring that he wrote:

When April spreads her skirt of flow'rs,
no longer do we spend our hours
tucked away in chimney's corner.
The winter chores are now laid by,
no longer will the bull-bat fly
to hide himself in ceil beam's gloom.
Come out, come out! Rejoice! Rejoice!
The God Almighty's Spirit voice
is heard from yon wee birds and bees.
His breath, life-warm, upon the soil
brings us once more, to joyful toil
that we may flourish on the earth.

In the privacy of his small room, seated at a table by the light of the window, he records these lines neatly in a carefully hand-bound book. In the quiet of this room I can hear his quill scratching, as he composes "paeans" or poems of praise to the land and his God. Unlike his father, he is a "true believer," reading his copy of the Gospel daily. He becomes moody when he is confined to the keep, so he busies himself in this way, but sometimes it is because he simply cannot help himself. He will be so overjoyed by the bloom of earth and his love of the creatures living upon it that he must rush indoors and write his feelings down.

At first, I marvel that he can be a sensitive poet and also a merciless killer on the battlefield. But then it comes to me that it is not to be wondered at, for death is as natural as life to his people. They must face their mortality at an early age, for many die at birth or while quite young - sometimes in horrible ways. (Their country has been war-torn for as long as any can remember.) They know death can come at any time and have come to terms with it; have prepared themselves for it. Out of this well of sadness within each of them, shared by all of them, has come a fierce and hard desire to absorb all that life has to offer their senses. They must taste, feel and drink it in - must turn it about within their souls; savor it, add to it and expel it, coated with their own songs of sorrow, of joy, of love. To them, it is not so much how long they live, but how they live that counts. They strive toward spirit, valor and courage, for as long as they breathe.

As for mercy, Malcolm believes if he spared his opponent in battle - if he did not fight to the best of his ability - it would dishonor them both and deprive his foe of a praiseworthy death. He says, "One must go into the afterlife with as few burdens on the soul as possible."

The Lady of the Keep

Green-gowned is Moira, Malcolm's wife, her light brown hair has a glint of red in it, and she is lightly freckled from the little sun they have in summer, when she must work in the garden. She wears much underclothing, for it is cold in the keep, and, no matter how many stockings she wears with her thick-soled boots, her feet are always cold from the stone floor. She has borne many children - so many it seems her life has always been a chain of love-making and child bearing.

Like his father before him, Malcolm evoked awe from his wife, partly because of the high-standing of his forbears, partly because of his education and intellect. His writing was a thing private from her, but he sometimes sang to her the songs he had written. When these ballads were about her or their love, she knew a happiness her breast could hardly contain; for the swelling of her heart. Because she did not have his gift of words, she could not tell him how she felt, but it did not matter that she was tongue-tied and silent. He could see it in her misty eyes; her overflowing face.

Although he thrilled her inner self, her body, too, was ever weak and responsive to his desire, even after she had borne so many children. How his blue eyes flamed with his passion - even his beard and hair seemed to spark with it. Her heart leapt up in her throat when he looked at her that way, at those times, for his love was a consuming, spiritual thing, not merely physical - and she willing gave, indeed, invited him to take from her whatever he needed.

There was also a purely physical aspect, a natural lust for one another - a feast not unlike that of the celebration of harvest, and a full table after a hungry winter and spring (something they knew quite well). In no other outlet of their lives did they find such complete relaxation, as they experienced after this spontaneous and exhilarating expression of each to the other. Out of this union there were seven sons and four daughters. There had been more, but they did not survive. Now in her middle age, Moira, though she was neat in her clothing, did not think much of how she looked - nor did she need to. Her man had been known to be overcome with the look and feel of her, even when he had come upon her working in the cow byre. Heaving her up, smell and all, in his strong arms, he had taken her in to bed her. On such occasions, her excitement usually equaled his, although she felt he was not always well-timed. Now that they were older, their lust arose not as often nor blew so hot as formerly, but it was still a satisfying delight, and comfortable, because it was unchanging in a life made up of sometimes disturbing changes.

Three of their sons, all married, lived with their families in the keep and cottages beyond. Their little village was crowded with expanding families. One daughter was still unmarried, but this did not worry Moira yet, for she was good in the work of the house, and seemed not to champ with the need of a man. Three daughters lived with their husbands within the clan, but outside the village - on their lands which spread out over the surrounding hillsides. The second eldest son had removed himself to an old place some distance away which had belonged to one of their ancestors; a ruin which he was rebuilding; replanting an orchard and making the fields tillable. ("Hard work, but admirable," Malcolm had told her, but they and their two small children had little to look forward to, was Moira's thinking.) They had taken two couples with them to help them build and they would all "blend their hopes and lives together there in the wildness," her husband assured her.

Malcolm loved the land so, that he couldn't see the hardness. Sometimes she thought he even loved that too - the hardness. It was hard for all those who were left in the keep and cottages, with so many mouths to feed. She thought it would be better if some of them could leave and take up their residence elsewhere. There had been talk of leaving Scotland, as some others in the clan have done in the past, but this land and their kinfolk pulled hard at their hearts. Still, the anxious business of providing food was so wearisome that the thought of leaving lingered in their minds. Moira was torn. Her heart wanted her children around her but her mind told her they would be better off elsewhere, with a new start. But, whatever they did, she herself would stay with Malcolm - for she knew he would never leave Scotland as long as he drew breath.

* * *

Malcolm has called a meeting of the Clan, after the battle on the ridge which was my first vision of these people. I do not think they all bear the same surname, but they are all kinsmen. They have come from all parts of their domain, from all over these hills to meet together in the great hall - not the defeated ones, of course, who are nursing their shame and feeling their loss - yet their presence is felt as strongly as if they were there in the seats of honor, for they are the focus of the Clan's discussion.

Malcolm's two brothers-in-law are there, and his brother. This brother is named Ronald, as is the son of Malcolm. He has dark hair, and is just as hairy as Malcolm, but broader of girth. Black, shaggy eyebrows springing from a projecting brow give him a scowling expression. He is slower to act than Malcolm, and more cynical. He has a chronic, nagging pain in his belly, which explains a good deal, but he does his duty and does not shirk.

During the feast, Malcolm is buoyant - basking in pleasant sensations. There is dancing, drinking and the great hall is filled with noise - voices raised in jest, laughter, the rattling of plate and cup. He is happy, glowing. His people acknowledge him with respect as he, dressed in his best, he moves among them. Moira is there, her eye on him while she sees to her duties, and he can feel her love. He is grateful, satisfied with his blessings. For their family, their home - which is perhaps not fine, but substantial. Although this deep room can be a gloomy pit in winter, it is not so today. His survey approves the huge tapestries - their shades of red and green leaping out to mingle with the sun beams which have found their way into their midst. Drawn to the window, he looks out on that beloved land-scape, bathed in warmth today - topped by scudding clouds. Ah, yes, he is pleased with his life at the present moment. (The wound in his face is nothing to him.) All is well, so far.

As is his way, he abruptly turns to his clansmen who have gathered around him, and when he gains their attention; he makes his speech. I do not understand what he says, but I see their faces - they are shocked, ill at ease. What does he say, in his

quiet, self-assured voice - what is this thing he has given much thought to? "Tis no
wrong to take what good luck sends," he says to his bewildered kinsmen. He spreads
his arms wide as though to reassure and gather all of them, his beloved people, into
his heart, where they will always be secure.

The clansmen, all dressed in plaid tartan and bonnets, were suddenly sober as they stood before Malcolm, listening. For the most part, they were simple unschooled countrymen, and could not always see for themselves the problems which lurked beyond the present day. First, he went over their feelings with them, for well he understood their minds. They were reminded how they had been loath to come up against their kin, misguided as those had been by the outsider. They even understood the thing that had started it all - a deed done long ago, when those kinsmen had lost a stretch of land which lay toward the sea. This was one of the areas where the frost did not settle so, and had yielded good grass for their cattle. Because it was necessary, they had been obliged to share this land with the rest of the clan. They were not willing, and this grievance became a canker in their minds, and was encouraged by the outsider who, the rest of the clan said, thought too much of himself - "a fine fellow" they used to call him, mocking his ways.

The men stirred, restless with the guilt they felt for having shed clan blood, yet protesting that they had had no recourse. One of the older men spoke up, saying their kinsmen had been lucky, for he reminded them that in former years, they would not have stopped with the rebel leader, but would have slain the son, also (who was, in this case, only a child). Amid groans of protest, the old fellow said, "Ah, well, that is what would have been done in the old days." Malcolm, in revulsion, said adamantly, "That may be so, but I will never raise my sword to strike a bairn, may I be cursed if I do."

Now that their attention had been gathered and guided to this point, Malcolm told them his thoughts on the matter. Those rebel kinspeople lived in a stronghold on land which lay higher up than their lands, on the lowland moors. He pointed out the advantages of merging the two house-holds, one higher, the other lower, linking their lands for common graz-ing property of the clan at large - the look-out of the upper house being a defense for the lower. He was ever forthright with them, and was honest when he shared his thoughts. It was unfortunate that his own sons and oth-ers of the clan were already married and could not come for the widow, to do the honorable thing and wed her. But since this could not be and know-ing the bitterness of the remaining members of that family . . .

At first, he alarmed them when he suggested taking possession of the other place by force, and putting his son in charge. It went through their heads that he might, after all, have an overweening ambition like his father. It was not so. He honestly thought this would be wise all around. "We could look after our kin-folk," he said, "and could give the women our protection. There are piddling few men left there now, not enough to take care of the women. True, they are bitter now, but if they were forced to live amongst us, and we treated them gently, they would soon get over it." He protested impatiently against the guilty faces he saw before him, "There is no shame in being served by this deed. In this way there would be contin-ued peace, whereas," he warned, "if we do not do this thing, those cousins might bide their time, still nursing their rage, until the young increase in years, marry outside the clan and so gather their strength anew. Then, once again, they will roar down the valley to do us harm. They might do this," he said, "because now they have two bitter causes to remember - the loss of the grassland and the blood of their men. What say you? Are you with me in this? Do you want continued peace, or will you imperil your children in the future?"

The debate went on for hours. They would have had the right to take over the home and lands if the conquered ones had been of another clan, but it was not done this way for feuds within the same clan. "Truly, it is a dangerous situation," Malcolm stressed upon them. For one thing, where would Maigret, the widow of the fallen leader, get a new husband? She was the heiress. These clansmen knew Maigret well - knew that she must be wild in her grief, and, even now would be loudly denouncing them to her family and calling for revenge. Her kinspeople would survey their household and know their weakness - their shortage of men. If those cousins were left to their own devices, they would look elsewhere to fill that shortage, and where would that be? Not within the clan, since all their suitable young men were married. Unfortunate, but true. They had no one to offer for Maigret. No, Maigret's family would look to other clans to provide a husband for her - one with menfolk who would raise arms to fight for them, and, with Maigret's call for vengeance spurring them on, would do this as early as possible.

"Who will it be?" asked Malcolm of his men, and nodded when he saw them look at each other with the knowledge in their eyes. "They will look to the Melvyns," Malcolm said, and they nodded, and stirred restlessly, for they all knew this was a surety. "And what then?" he said as he challenged their minds to follow that natural chain of events. The Melvyns were strong and aggressive and cold of heart when ambition was stirred. So far, the Melvyns had no real interest in their clan, their interest lay elsewhere. But if they married into the clan through Maigret, then, they would turn their interest to them, or rather, to their estates, and they would be a mighty force to deal with. Yes, they would soon rule them all, thought those men of Malcolm's clan, and as they stood staring into that future, their eyes sparked and their hearts leapt up in anger against them - those Melvyns - those cold and merciless sons of Belial!

Even if, by some stroke of luck, Malcolm pointed out, Maigret's future husband was not the Melvyn's heir, that remnant of their clan would still fall into some other, alien, hands and would be forever lost to them - making the clan's territory smaller still, instead of enlarging it, which was always their goal. Whereas, he continued, if Maigret and her household were under their "guardianship," they would not need to look for protection elsewhere. Then it would be at least a year - perhaps two - of bereavement, before Maigret selected a husband. Anything could happen in a year or two - they could reckon with that then. The point was to exercise a position of absolute control over this rebel family.

In deciding how it was to be done, the discussion moved on to taking the household by force, and this notion did not appeal to most of the men. "The king would not like it," someone said. "The king," snorted Malcolm, "what does the king have to do with us here?" (*Muttering against the king, it seemed he said, "the bastard"*). "He wouldn't know of it," he said. "The king doesn't involve himself in clan affairs. If this is peacefully and quickly done - if we are sweet and gentle with Maigret and our vagrant clansmen - it will not come to the king's ears, except as another clan affair."

When they had all agreed a peaceful takeover was preferable, they gave some thought to the remaining males within Maigret's household who might be sympathetic to clan unity. Finally, they decided Duncan could be approached and talked with, if it were done soon. Since he was lame, he had not come to the battle. His lameness was a good excuse, but they knew he had been against warring within the clan. He, as the eldest of the remaining men of the household, was now the acting chieftain and, although he was sure to be angry now, he was a sensible man. It was wise to offer an olive branch, a peace offering. They decided against Malcolm's idea of sending his elder son and his household to live there at this time. If someone of the clan was set in place of Maigret's husband, it would be considered usurping, is what they thought. Malcolm advised softly: "A little enmity now is better than war later." But he conceded to the collective judgment, that they must wait until the fires of their cousins' anger against the clan subsided a little - but not too long, he advised, and they agreed - else their cousins make some agreement outside the clan and bring everything down on their heads.

* * *

So, the clansmen delayed . . . and fate turned against them, for by the time they met secretly with Duncan, the pot was already brewing in another camp. The husband of Maigret's aunt - of a clan whose territory was east of theirs - heard of the feud between their members and exercised his mind to use it in his favor. For years, this man had nursed a secret lust for control of the territory of Malcolm's clan. Now he was happy that luck had given him an excuse to meddle into their affairs. From this beginning, a plot was hatched which grew enormously, gathering to itself numbers of men who gave their loyalty to each side, eventually even attracting the interest of powerful men who, though they were outsiders, yet also meddled in the expanding intrigue. Thus, a small family fight eventually turned into a great mass of confusion which could not be managed by Malcolm or by the intervention of those allies he had called upon. Finally, claiming he was now coming to the aid of his niece and to that of the "true religion" - the "uncle" struck. Beware of vipers who twist the truth so that they may satisfy their own desires!

* * *

It is night. It is pitch black with no stars out at present. Outside the wall in front of the keep, Moira is stoking a fire which has been lit there for the two nights past. It is a beacon to guide either a messenger, or the menfolk home. At the sound of hoof-beats, she turns away from the fire. Its flickering light gilds her profile as

she stands wringing her apron in her hands, her mouth agape as she stares at the
messenger approaching - for how could it be good news, as out-numbered and over-
powered as their menfolk had been?

The messenger turned his horse and rode away again, rapidly disappearing once more into the blackness. Throwing her apron over her head;
wailing as though she had been gored through with a mortal wound, Moira
stumbled blindly toward the keep. Others had come out at the sound of
hoof beats and her moaning. Moira's daughter led them, her voice thrown
out in alarm, "Mother, what tis?" With her arm around the weeping
woman, the women lead her back into the keep. They enter that place that
seems so empty now, though filled with all the women and children of the
clan and smells of ale, babies and wood ashes. The eyes of the women and
wakeful children are enlarged by fear, staring behind them into the darkness outside, for this fortress which had offered them safety before cannot
shield them now; not without their men to guard it.

All the women gathered together behind the enormous tapestry which
divided part of that cavernous room from where the children were sleeping
on the other side. Their arms wrapped around themselves, they nervously
discussed the news: The men were gone; fled to Ireland - all of them who
are not dead; for they knew some of their men must still lie on the field. For
the sake of the peacefully sleeping children, they did not allow themselves
to cry out but some began to babble. Moira, in a voice soft and grieving
like a ewe-dove, said, "They can nivver coom bahk, nivver. Oh, what is to
become of us?" She thought of what Malcolm had said, with his own lips,
"They will not harm you, love. Do you think I would leave you if I thought
harm would come to you and the children?" A thought came to her with
a thrill of horror and she gasped, "Surely they wouldna slay the children?"
At this, all the women surged together more tightly. Their eyes huge in the
light of the candles that they held in clinched, white fingers, they stared

into the unlit shadows of the room, as though they saw the enemy already there, lying in wait to slay their lovely bairns.

Then they gathered their wits - sharply - for were they not Scotswomen? They should be grateful - at least some of their menfolk had escaped, though they had gone away - driven from their own land and homes. What to do? The women had been told to leave immediately to join them there. But, alas, over in the corner watching them lay Elinor, one of the daughters of Moira and Malcolm - her time had started most inconveniently. The pains of her labor were hard, but slow, too slow. Moira went over to sit with her, to hold her hand and to tell her the news. Murmuring and weeping together, the others waited. How long would their enemies wait to come and take their homeland and what would they do with them if they found them there? Moira herself made the decision. If Elinor did not give birth very soon, they would carry her on a litter. They had to get themselves to the seacoast and from there to Ireland with the help of fishermen who would help them. It was arranged and so it would be. It was not far to that country, and only then would they be safe. So they waited, all of them praying that Elinor's child would come quickly. Meanwhile, they gathered around the long dark table in the great hall where, their brimming eyes and stricken faces dimly illuminated by the flickering grease lamp, they pushed what cold food they could find into their mouths - not tasting, but stoking their bodies for the trip to the sea and beyond.

* * *

(Wolves s . . . Are there wolves in this country? I keep seeing wolves - gray and vicious, slinking and sniffing the ground for food. . . They are starving.)

It was just before dawn when the crowd of women and children assembled outside for their departure. Elinor had just arisen from child birthing, the news having hastened her pains. They had bound her flaccid belly and wrapped the babe. Now they felt hard-pressed, terrified that their enemies would soon be here to claim their lands as their own. They had gathered only what they considered their most precious belongings to carry with them, but when they discussed which items in their accounting were the most valuable to the clan, it was found that one such treasure was still inside - Malcolm's writings. Some bent to lay their bundles upon the ground but it was Elinor, the one who was only just up from birthing, who yet insisted she would be the one to go and fetch the book. Malcolm used to read to her when she was small, and made up rhymes for her pleasure. So then, it she who hurried back to get his things, leaving her sweet new bairn (even now still red and smelling of the birthing bed) wrapped and lying on top of one of the bundles. The attention of the others was on her as they reluctantly watched her go back into the keep. Wishing she would not tire herself in that way, they murmured among themselves as they anxiously waited.

They heard the new bairn cry out - but it was such a wee cry! They turned toward the sound - some with smiles on their faces that the little one had found his lungs - and were only in time to see a gray shadow slink away into the darkness, the infant wrappings trailing whitely behind. When they realized what had happened, all screamed as one and that shrill and endless scream brought Elinor hurrying, stumbling, out of the gate - book and papers clutched in one hand and holding her belly with the other. Her mouth opened but she did not ask. Her babe was gone from where she had laid him and her mother, brandishing a torch and a club was just rushing into the dark woods. Some of the other women followed, some stayed their ground and clasped their own weeping children to their breasts. "Wolves" and, "the bairn" were the words which Elinor heard and understood. Her eyes starting from her head in fear, her face as white as the moon, she flung what she carried to the ground and rushed forward on her mother's heels.

The women were not the trackers that their men were, and it was still dark. Oh, the useless frenzy - the heartbreak - the horror of that mental image of the wee one being eaten by the horrible beast! Each mother moaned, as tormented and spurred afresh with that inward vision, they crashed around in the brush, looking in vain for signs by the light of their torches. Elinor's wail rose higher as she thrashed about, straining her eyes to see beyond the normal ken - to pierce the darkness beyond her torch. Moira slapped at her, and admonished them all to hush their noise so that they could listen closely for any sound. Instantly, they fell silent - straining to hear a tiny whimper or movement in the brush. But, though they crept about for a time in the light cast by the torches, their hearts sank within them as the uselessness of it was borne in upon them. The moon (fickle light!) rode in and out of the clouds and the wolf was fleet-footed. Yet that dreadful image persisted - horrible . . . horrible! And so they continued, picking their way over moor and scrub, straining their eyes into the darkness for some flicker of movement, all mothers' hearts reaching outward, yearning, and praying.

They could not leave - not yet. Moira knew if they did not wait for daylight, the daughter would never know for sure. All her days she would be haunted by the thought that she might have overlooked her child, that he might have been yet alive and lying in the scrub somewhere. Yet the fishermen would not wait at harbor for them. So, she decided to send the others on, to tell the fishermen what had happened and to implore them not to leave until she and Elinor could arrive. So the others - fourteen women and their children - departed. As they walked to the sea, they spoke in shocked undertones about what had happened, because it was truly amazing that the wolf would have come up like that, bold as brass. Some thought perhaps it was an omen - but then it was a starvation year. Perhaps, the bitter women said to each other, those who had forced them from their land would starve, too - and they walked on in silence, each taking some consolation from that thought.

Moira and her daughter (as disheveled as a mad woman) arrived that morning at the little harbor. She had been forced to pull the crying Elinor along most of the way, to keep her from going back again to her useless search. They had made it in time, and there was much relief, mingled with sympathy, from the waiting women already in the boat. The restless fishermen had already started to leave several times, only to be stopped by the cries and wailing of the women. Several of these women were very beautiful, and it was fortunate that it was so, for tears from their pretty eyes as they made their appeals to the men had worked the charm. They had stayed against their will though, because, they said, "This thing has been broadcast everywhere and those who take the losers' side could now be in trouble." Now, with Moira and Elinor aboard, they did not spare the oars and sail.

I can smell salt air, mingled with a strong resinous fragrance, like that of pine or fir trees. Then, I see a very beautiful little glen surrounded by these tall, fragrant trees. There is a pool of water, encircled by ferns and green mosses. Malcolm's face is reflected in the pool, for he is squatting there looking into it. There is a scar extending up his left cheek as far as the left eyelid, where it puckers a little, but this is an old wound. He is still physically strong, but his face - and even his hair - is ashy, like the fire has gone out of him. He arises and flexes his body, which has lost flesh and looks sinewy. He wears a ring and a metal bracelet on one brown upper arm. He clenches his fists and raises them toward the sky. The tendons in his arms and neck stand out like cords. Though he does not make a sound, the eerie effect is that of a silent scream.

Dusk had fallen and Malcolm's men were tending a bonfire upon the rock shelf overlooking the sea. They threw on more branches and sparks flew heavenward, where stars were showing at last, heralding a break in the rain. They were worried and impatient with waiting, and kept looking out to sea. In their days here, they had constructed crude shelters by driving small, straight tree trunks into the ground and covering these with branches with evergreens and mosses. This had kept off the wind and much of the rain, which had continued with few pauses, adding to the despondent mood which sat heavily upon them. They had been murmuring and were beginning to admit their despair, when the stars, and then the moon appeared from behind the clouds. Just then one of the men said he thought he saw something floating on the horizon and they rushed eagerly to the edge of the bluff, staring out to where he indicated, but they did not dare to hope yet.

A little later, as they craned their heads forward, straining their eyes to see into the dark, the little ship sprang into view. A few more minutes and they joyfully verified that it was the one they looked for. The women had come! Then, in no time at all the ship's sails were lowered and the captain, manipulating the anchorage, threw up a line for them to secure. Soon, the women were climbing upward. Seeing the dear face of his wife, Malcolm knelt on the ledge, eagerly reaching out to help her upward. "Moira!" he murmured - moaning, rejoicing, all at once. Holding her head against his throat where his pulse quickened with joy and relief, he whispered his love into her hair. She being weary and overcome, felt faint, and gladly surrendered herself into his arms.

He drew her to a seat near the fire, (for he saw that she was shivering) and he stooped there and held her hands as she wept and, knowing her as he did, he knew there was something wrong with her. He quickly scanned the group, but seeing that all those he had expected were there, he looked back at his wife. She struggled for breath and managed to say that something had happened that had made them late in coming. She had been strong for the time required but now his loving strength made her faint, and she stammered like a weakling as she lifted streaming eyes to him and told how they had lost Elinor's babe to the wolf. Then the mother of the bairn herself came forward and thrust his writings into his arms. She was no longer sure of this offering - this gift she had demanded to be the one to return to him.

Father and daughter both stared down at the bundle, dumbly. For this, she had given her son. His heart turned over with a mighty pain as he thought that her son would be alive, but for that. And what was it? Only a stack of paper on which were written simple, perhaps vain, words by a failure of a man. As he looked at it, he was deeply ashamed, indeed, it seemed obscene. His urge was to cast it from him - to thrust it into the fire. But into this violent turmoil within his mind, there came suddenly, a soft and warning voice which stayed his hand. He could not spurn this gift from his daughter - this gift for which she had paid so much. In a moment of illumination, he realized if he did so - if he devalued the reason for which she had turned back into the keep and left her son in harm's way, her guilt would be unbearable. So then he did what was expected, no matter the churning within him - despite the urge to reject, to destroy those poems of love, of hopeful, brighter days. It may have been the most difficult thing he had ever done - but he did it. He pulled himself upright before his daughter eyes; then, with solemnity and grace, he blessed and comforted her, saying "Thy loving gift for me has cost thee dear. . . But daughter, I thank thee for thy love, and give thee mine. We will heal each other's wounds with our love and, with God's grace, there will be more children to call thee mother and adore thee, for thou art a good woman."

(And in the back of his mind, he was surprised that such words still came to him, even now in such bitter, painful days. But he was a just man, a Godly man, a man who put Love first.)

But there was no time for grief now. He urged his daughter to put that loss behind her and be strong. His gaze took in all his clan gathered around him. They would all need to be strong, now. Elinor said nothing; but as always, her father had eased her heart and cleared her mind. Now, as she returned to her husband's side, she looked up into his sad and loving face, and was grateful that he, at least, was left to her.

The women had already found that although some were wounded, all their men were still alive, and this both amazed them and gladdened their hearts. Malcolm knew the value of a strategic retreat in dark of night, when the odds were impossible. It was "no shame," he told them, for family was more important than possessions. They fell silent; sculptures gilded by the firelight - all united by one sobering thought. It was true; all was lost to them of the material kind. No possessions had they, only each other and their mingled spirit and strength.

Then Malcolm, though he was sick in spirit and weak-hearted, gathered the remnants of his own courage, blew upon the coals of his inner fire, and once again rallied his flock. There under the stars they took the oath of loyalty to each other and to their clan, and, in their desperation their hearts warmed strongly to each other. When they had made their vow, they raised their arms and roared as one man, that they would never lie down and die, but would fight for their honor, their family and for their generations to come. They would survive. They would overcome!

This, though, was a new kind of battle. When they looked about them, the alien country plucked at their spirit. Scotland was mother earth to them, and they had known no other. They were as lost as they would have been on the great sea. They were fighters, but here - whom or what to fight?

It was not a question now of confronting an enemy with a human face, but fighting for survival in a strange land - for food and sustenance in the years to come.

Malcolm's spirit has been injured - like a battered and fallen bird it cannot right itself to fly again. He beats his breast with a closed fist when he is overcome with that sorrow which will never leave him. His heart is still in Scotland with his ancestors. I feel for him. The sight of him breaks my heart. "Why?" he continually asks of God. Examining his soul minutely for sins, he honestly feels he has always done what was required of him and has never forsaken his duty. He has lived life as a true man - as a Scotsman should have done. Were not his comings and goings an open book to Heaven? He had naught to hide - so then, why had he failed his people so miserably? Why had he not been able to stop that gradual, but unceasing decline in the fate and fortune of his family and clan? "Why?" He cried to Heaven, which only kept its silence. Abandoned on this alien shore, his mind worked busily with this puzzle - his lonely face always turned in the direction of Scotland.

The clan have managed to obtain a little land and built on it with their hard labor. He has built his little house upon a spit of land which leads into the bay (for they could make their living from the sea, he said, if the land failed them). It is green here, with good grass.

He looks different now. He has let his beard grow longer, but it is not only that. His steps are heavier and the beautiful fire has gone out of him - yet there is a rock-hard tenacity left that shows in the deep lines of his face. He will not let his poor people down now, but will do all he can to direct and advise them when they seek him out. His simple croft might as well have been a castle, his rough-hewn chair on which he sat for clan meetings; a throne, for in the eyes of those people, if he but knew it, he is still crowned in untarnished gold. With this last great loss, they had gained new insight into his greatness, and are filled with unshakeable respect and deepened affection for the man who had led them here. But alas, he would not allow

himself to see the reverence they bore him, for he blamed himself for all their adversi-
ties. Oblivious to this comfort which he has at hand, he wraps himself in misery and
loneliness, so sure is he that he has been torn away - not just from Scotland and all
he had known and loved - but, in his most desperate moments, even from the arms of
his once-loving God. Somewhere, somehow, he has gone wrong. When he looks back
over the years past, the way he had used his time on earth seems so futile. Truly he
is in exile!

With the passing years, Moira draws ever inward, confining herself to the
inside of their cottage, where she sits in the chimney corner knitting stockings for her
grandchildren who have gone away. Her hair has not turned grey but it is dull.
She doesn't speak much. Her gaiety has left her, for she has given up. She has left
Malcolm to his grieving, for he can no longer see or feel her presence.

Then one day, quite suddenly, she is gone . . . and he awakens with her pass-
ing. Then, when it is too late, she has regained his attention. Then, he realizes his
greatest mistake. They could have comforted each other, had he not been so absorbed
in his own pain. How could he have neglected his wife so? And she the great love of
his life! And with this added weight of remorse, the burden he carries becomes too
great to be borne.

Finally, (so they said) his great heart burst - like a red flower it suddenly bloomed within his chest, and the stream which issued from it - that
blood of proud and noble lineage - carried with it all the regrets. The flow
came up and escaped through his mouth where he lay under the trees and
poured itself into the soft soil of Ireland. He was finally purged of the pin-
ing for his homeland, for Moira, and the burden of shame he had heaped
upon himself for his inability to provide land for his children and security
for his clan. He did not understand, until his eyes glazed over and his soul
stepped into the afterlife, that in this unwilling separation from the land
he had so loved, he had actually taken the first step to gaining his most

cherished desire - that of longevity and better fortune for his clan. Because he had loved Scotland so well, he would never have willingly moved. Yet it had become necessary for them to do so, if his line were to survive. Already, at the time of their exile, there had been a plan in motion - a plot which would have caused their total destruction if they had stayed on. Unknown to him, his God had reciprocated his love.

Now, his sons, daughters and grandsons looked toward a better future. Not only were they young and adaptable, but they had a fierce desire for *Life*, and with the wisdom, fortitude and passion of their dead chieftain, they set out to gather it in; to discover and enjoy all the blessings it contained. They, then, were the seeds saved from the harvest of that hard and rocky soil of Scotland, eventually to be planted in the new and fertile soil of America - seeds which contained the blood traits of their grandfathers, together with the uprightness of "Malcolm the Just," as they were always to call him thereafter. "In the end," his children told their children, "he had naught to hold in his big and generous hand - naught of that kind which he could offer his people, and that grieved him sore. But that which sprang from his heart and mind has greatly blessed us all."

Malcolm, during his sojourn in Ireland, saw his ending days as "Travail, travail, as a woman in childbirth" At times his grief and toiling of spirit would overflow - spilling onto paper as psalms written with sober reflection, alternating with writings launched upon furiously - in a fit of helpless passion. It is unfortunate that these writings - these "heart songs" - were lost to man, but they were heard by God and are thus still alive and remembered - for they are recorded on that slate of human endeavors which is never lost.

* * *

Dear Richard,

Dear friend – Through this story, I have concluded that *music is the sound of Love.*

This whole experience has been extraordinary for me and has increased my yearning for spiritual growth. I used to pray: I talked to God. Now I meditate: I get quiet and hope he talks to me. With meditation – listening for that still, small voice of enlightenment - I have concluded that it doesn't matter about reincarnation. I suspect that the past, when it is gone, is as if it never was. Time is an illusion, right? As such, then, reincarnation doesn't really exist, except as a learning construct of our own doing. Therefore, I would never try to convince someone of the validity of past life experiences. I hope you are not suggesting we publicize them as such.

Actually, I am wondering if these stories might have been gleaned from others' experiences, to which I have some empathy. You know – someone else's memory bank that I just tapped into, Universal Consciousness and all that. What do you think? Don't some people call it "the Akashic Records?" Where everyone's life experiences are stored? Maybe I was transported to other times, to observe other people in the stories they were creating. Sounds simple.

I had no name for the main character, the musician, in this story. Something popped into my head and I used it. It may be similar to his name, a joke or a nickname - *if he actually existed.* And here we go again. Let's address this now. Although I've been concerned that my stories should be accurate and not misleading, ultimately I have decided that I shouldn't worry so much about "the truth" of the story. When I think about it, perhaps no life story is totally true. It is only a perception, remembered by a person who sees something through their judgment. Do even bare historical facts exist? Perhaps as dates and names, but events? Well, everyone sees a different story, a different world, based on their past experience and therefore, biases. There are glimmers of golden truth scattered here and there in our life experience, if the mind is seeking it; if we are ready for change, to advance.

All this aside, I do think it is important how the characters in my stories *see* it, in order to understand them.

"Only a story that unites the brotherhood can be useful. Only that story has truthful perception." (This came to me during meditation. If I'm crazy, so be it. I'm in too deep to care now.)

The Unknown

I see a man coming along a street that is encrusted with snow and ice. He wears a fur hat and overcoat, and wrappings over his shoes and legs. He enters a rough-timbered building - an inn with the name, "The Three Feathers." Instantly, he feels better, for it is warm inside from the fire and the hot breath of all the convivial ale-bibbers gathered within.

He orders a rum drink, and the barmaid heats it with a metal rod on the end of which is a crescent shaped disk. This has been placed on the fire's hot coals. When it is red hot, it is plunged into a small keg of rum. From this a mug is filled. This is a specialty for cold nights such as this. . . I believe this is in or near, Hamburg, Germany.

As the night progressed, he got drunk and cavorted around - dancing, belching aloud. He flirted, as usual, with the waiting maid . . . making ridiculous faces. . . Goggle-eyed, lips puckered up and extended like a fish's, he pretended to be ready for her kisses. His friends, rollicking companions all, roared with laughter. He was very funny as he stood swaying, arms swinging loosely at his sides, pursed lips extended to an extraordinary length, eyes bugged and rolling lewdly. A good-natured girl, she played along and spurned him, telling him to move "his silly self" and finally shoving him, whereupon he fell to the floor, doubled up as if in a spasm of pain, his arms crooked over his head to defend himself from her "merciless blows," as one mischievous eye peeked out at her through long, wagging fingers. He begged for mercy, moaning that she had killed him. He was a hilarious gawk - all elbows and knees. When his friends could laugh no more (for their sides were sore), they begged him to play for them. He staggered over to the harpsichord (it seemed he could hardly walk, for the rum in him), and sat himself down.

The music this night was, as was often the case, what he had been composing, and would "try out" on his friends. Everyone was attentive and the "drunken" musician was suddenly sober. They said he was a genius, and his music was taken seriously. All eyes turned to look, all ears to listen as he worked his magic on the instrument. Sometimes when he was playing in the evenings, he would forget they were there, as some part of the work in progress would snag his attention like a pestilent thorn and he would have to work over the passage until it ran smooth, or sometimes, in the midst of a piece, he would suddenly weep and pound the keys in frustration. His friends would then turn aside, awkwardly pretending to be drinking and talking among themselves and not paying any attention to him. Eventually, he would wake up from his reverie, when he would either begin again, or would make his way to the door and home.

This night he did neither, for his work had gone well and he was in good humor. After much well-wishing and back-slapping from his friends, he retrieved his coat and hat and went out the door to the inn mistress's call, Good-bye, "Herr Rougstrum."

(This is the way the name sounds to me. I think it is a joke they play - that this is not his real name . . but I cannot get what his real name is.)

* * *

Sometimes he didn't go to the inn in the evenings, but would stay at home and work odd hours, for several days straight. When he did go there at the end of such a stint of self-denial, he would go with a head full of steam. After the usual orgy of being the center of attention, he would sometimes fall asleep on the floor by the fire, or with his head on the table. The innkeeper would throw a cover over him, and let him stay the few remaining hours before daylight, when she would give him breakfast and send him home again. During these breakfast hours, she had gotten to know him well, and even though she was proud of him, she was also deeply sorry for him.

All of his friends shared a mixture of compassion and pride toward this man. He was a misfit and a tortured being, therefore, they felt sorry for him, however, they knew he was very talented and as such they felt he was above them – for they were "common" people.

His father had not respected his son and had shunned the lower classes, so now the son embraced them in his revolt against his dead father. Not all of his friends who gathered at the Inn were lower class. Most were small business people of the town (bourgeoisie). Some were singers in the opera who would join in with his music when invited.

This habitual outing at the end of his day was all in fun - it was silliness, but it was good - a relief after the work of the day. He would come into the inn with tight knots in his belly and tense all over and when he left, it would be as though he had been purged, his body cleansed with the rum and fellowship. This was the way he felt this night - completely relaxed, a new man. Sighing, chuckling, he made his way up the street to his home, the blood singing in his veins, his warm, happy breath steaming on the cold air.

When he arrives at his destination, he enters under a gothic arch that projects over the front door. The house is dark, but inside candles are lit in the entry hall and there is a fire. He takes off his wrappings there, hanging them on a clothes tree and leaving his shoes on the floor. I can see he wears a chain around his neck and from it hangs a pendant in the form of a golden ball, which I think has something to do with his musician's status. In the room to the right of the hall, he lights his pipe with a candle and goes to work on some papers. I think he writes music for a "symphorium?" A small concert of symphonic works? As he writes, he beats time with one foot to the music in his head. When he finally goes to bed it is on the cot in this same sitting room, not in the bedroom upstairs. I believe he is also a cobbler - making shoes by day. Otherwise, he would starve. (He says, "There is no money in making jokes, playing the fool")

There is a woman who lives with him. He must be intimate with this woman, yet I don't feel any love or affection emanating from her. Whoever she is, she cleans his house. I see her mopping, throwing water from a bucket out the door. She has no time for his trifling ways. She has no sense of humor and doesn't understand the complexities of the man. Yet, he remains enthralled with her, even though he knows her limitations. It is as though he pretends she is a puzzle yet to be solved - that there is something more to be discovered about her that she withholds from him. So he cannot let her go. She on the other hand, is sometimes flattered to be desired by him, for he is gaining a reputation as a musician. This makes her proud, even haughty, among her small circle of acquaintances - besides, she also lusts for him, so she stays. (The body must be fed, she often says to herself, and this seems to be her motivation in life, to be fed, clothed, and physically satiated.)

The name that comes to me is Marie Clothilde. Golden-haired, she seems to crackle with goldness, like the high points of flame in the fire on the hearth. Each strand of her hair is a fine, sparkling golden wire, too thin to measure - sometimes escaping the confinement of a piled-high hairstyle or from under a round, ruffled cap. Her eyes are as blue as bee-flowers. He is fascinated by her, but often admits cynically that her inner self is not what her outer self says she is. She has a habit of looking at him sidewise, somewhat disdainfully. Outwardly, she seems to be a dream being, with a seductive woman's flesh. He thinks she is wonderful to the touch, with smooth, firm flesh over all her bones except ankles and wrists, which are small, but sturdy. He spends time just studying her - and I get a vision, as she looks in the nude: round, high breasts, long narrow waist, tapered darker blonde vee of pelvis, white thighs, legs well-shaped, but fairly short. Trying to see what she normally wears is not as clear: a blouse with a fine lace collar joined at her small waist by a full, bell-shaped skirt. Her skin seems creamy gold too, her cheeks of a peach tint, except when she is angry, then she is flushed with purplish red - as snappish as a little bitch dog. When she is like this, she punishes him with her tongue, the cap on her head shaking askew from the violence of her anger.

The musician has dark blond hair, varying in length as he does not always get his hair cut when it is needed. Marie cuts it, while he makes amorous advances. She cut him once, deliberately, while he squeezed her and wouldn't cease. This only inflamed and delighted him. (The haircut was delayed for quite a while.)

His cobbling business, which he conducts in the front room to the left of the hall, was left to languish if he was rapt in his music. He would even lose track of the days. Marie would bring food and leave it at the door, for she was not allowed to enter, or even to knock. If he became conscious that he was hungry, he would open the door, look around for sustenance, grab it and shut himself up again. Sometimes the food would still be there for the mice at the day's end, when she would either throw it out, grumbling at the waste, or eat it herself, in spite of its staleness - for she was French, and stingy, he said (actually her father was French, her mother was Swiss). He had met her in France while he had been a student there and brought her to Hamburg with him- supposedly as his housekeeper, but everyone knew she was his mistress.

His family had been well-off (not aristocracy but petite Bourgeoisie) and respected in their community. To the disgust of this son, his father had been well-regarded as an upright man, since he had given a good performance as a congenial fellow among his peers. The sons had been well educated, and the musician had finished his education in France and had traveled to Vienna and other countries in Europe.

In the privacy of his home, his father had really been a horrible man - caustic, critical, and non-loving. A very angry man, he often struck his family with stinging blows, both verbal and physical. (*Here, I can see him, thin hair standing out in wisps, he is shaking, his green grape eyes bugging out with his rage. And this is the frightful image that is dyed onto his son's memory when he thinks of his father.*) As a result, when he was grown, his son would do almost anything to be liked or loved by others. He was driven to produce music that would bring him the respect he craved. Yet, he was not above groveling on the inn floor, in jest, to entertain and gain affection from his friends. In short, to gain love, he seduced others with his music and wit.

His mother had been dominated by his father. After years of marriage, her image and impact on the family had been ground away by that millstone which was her husband, until finally, she seemed to be merely a blur - a pale reflection of a human being. He struggled sometimes to remember her as an entity in her own right, but he thought he must have lost contact with her when he had been very young, for that is when he last remembered her speaking to him in an intimate, homely way - mother to child. About that time, she had simply removed herself - if not physically, at least mentally. She had simply retired away from them all, like a turtle into its shell. On those necessary occasions when the family gathered, her shell was there, but *she* was not there. There was no life within her face, and her dead eyes avoided contact with her husband and children. She had a maid-companion-guard dog who looked after her, and to whom she gave instructions regarding the household. Therefore, when it was necessary, the children heard, via Altruse that such and such was to be done. He was aware of a sense of abandonment, like that of being left outside in a storm. Buffeted by his father, he ached for the sweet presence of his mother and yearned to be held in her arms, even when he was too old for such a thing.

Once when he was small, he had witnessed a baby bird forced from the warm shelter of its nest under the low hanging eaves of their home. The mother bird had, for some reason unknown, ejected the naked, helpless creature, so that it fell into the shrubbery below. He was shocked, but thinking this was surely an accident, he had carefully rescued the pitiful little weak-necked bird. Then, climbing the wall, he gently and lovingly returned it to the nest. The fussing mother bird returned to her nest under the eaves. The boy retreated, and watched. Once again the mother bird mercilessly pushed her offspring over the edge, this time to land on the cobbled walk. The boy rushed over to examine the bird, and finding it dead, a tiny eye crushed, its head bloodied, he became so enraged that he tried to seize and kill the wicked, fluttering mother bird, but, of course, not succeeding. Sobbing hoarsely, he once again scaled the wall, where, this time, he tore out and destroyed the nest - furiously stamping on the twigs and string with his little boots until the bits and pieces were scattered over the courtyard. The heaving of his small chest gradually calmed, his complexion cooled as he watched the bits borne away in the breeze. Tenderly, he buried the unwanted nestling in the garden, and then he sat down and cried, for it had truly broken his heart. . . yet he knew not why it had done so.

(I see in my mind, an angel, his guardian, sitting beside the child to whom he is invisible, trying to comfort with his spirit, the heart of this child whose life is so hard, because it is devoid of love. His lament, and that of the child, are heard in

Heaven and compensation will be made, if the soul of the child will rise high enough to embrace it.)

* * *

He travels away from Hamburg for periods of time, to perform. When performing, he wears a wig and clothes woven through with golden threads. I can tell he sweats a lot, and can feel his tension, although he looks calm enough. He would die before he failed on stage. He can't make even the tiniest mistake, EVER. He loves his music so it is not too difficult to be the slave to it that he must be, in order to achieve mastery over the instrument and himself. Sometimes he thinks it is killing him, but I sense that is his own fault, because he is obsessed with earning respect and recognition from it. It is not his gift, his talent, but this obsession that is ruining him.

He drank heavily when he was despondent. The only time he felt really good was when playing music, when he had just written a good piece, or when the audience really fawned on him (his desire for applause was insatiable).

During his best performances it seemed a wondrous spell would come over him. The first time this occurred, it was a little unsettling, but later he welcomed it. When this happened, it seemed he was disembodied, as though he floated before his instrument, no longer conscious of the seat beneath him or the pressure of his fingers on the keys . . and then the music would seem to pour from him. . . Effortlessly it flowed - like a pure and sparkling waterfall, not just from beneath his hands but it seemed from his very soul. He could tell when it was beginning- this phenomenon. It was always triggered by a passage of the music that he especially loved. First, it would seem that his heart within him would leap upward, suddenly, like a startled dove rising heavenward - and then he would feel a great warmth as this thing within grew and expanded . . . ever upward and higher this thing - his spirit - soared, until an almost unbearable zenith was reached when he would become very nearly breathless. And then, at just this point, a tremendous surge of powerful energy would fall upon him - from his head downward through all his limbs, followed immediately by an awesome sense of union, and then *ecstasy,* when his whole being would seem to explode, with sparks literally flying from his body. The final culmination of this was a saturation of immense, all encompassing love that he would feel, both for the music and for his audience. This phenomenon was so vibrant, so *real* to him that on the first occasions when it first made itself manifest, he looked down at his hands and body, half-expecting to see those sparks of fire, but it was difficult to tell with the gold thread costume and the blur of tears in his eyes.

The elevated feeling which always followed this phenomenon would continue into the festivities after the performance, and after the first few times this had happened to him, he looked for some similar response from those who had sat there, listening. Gratefully, even tearfully, he accepted the heartfelt appreciation of those who had been moved by his music. But gradually it was borne in upon him that, even though he had felt something wondrous had happened, most of the audience seemed indifferent. Oh, they said the conventional things, the polite things - twittering, smiling, and fluttering their fans - but it was only from their mouths. He could look into their eyes and see that they had no *feeling*; at least they had certainly not shared in the magnitude of what he had felt. He was appalled - and confused. Was he deluding himself? Did he have real talent? If so, how could these noble, educated, upper-class people not appreciate it? This doubt haunted his mind much of his years. He finally decided that these rich patrons were fickle and were harder to please than the common people. The nobility professed to love him, but sometimes he thought the best of

all times were with his friends at the Inn and the conviviality there - for
they did not expect as much from him.

* * *

*I don't think he ever played a piano. I don't think they were used yet. He played
the harpsichord and the clavichord (which he didn't like) and some instrument starting with a "Ver" or "Ven" sound. As a knobby-kneed student in short pants, he was
first acquainted with this instrument in someone else's house - a very rich place - and
there he fell in love with music.*

His mistress, Marie, became ill, with consumption or some such thing -
the physician wasn't sure. She looked terrible, her once pretty hair dull and
thin, her face that of an emaciated old woman and she lay abed most of the
time. A friend and neighbor came in to see to her sometimes. She advised
her to stand up, to defend her rights to her man, before the dark-haired
woman got him. Marie would have laughed if she had been able to take a
deep enough breath to do so. All she could do was stare unbelieving at her
friend and reply bitterly, "Look at me! What do I care for such things? All
I desire is to die, and the sooner the better!" But she yearned over the safety
and care of her daughter. She spoke to the musician about it before she took
the last rites. He would, he promised, always take care of their daughter
and never send her away. It showed how little she knew him - that she ever
worried over such a thing. His heart raged at the thought. He would have
cut off his hands before he abandoned his daughter.

A priest came in when the sky had turned dark. They lit candles, which
reflected on the face of the poor woman in the bed. She seemed to fade away
already; her face and hair as white as the pillow. She was helped to raise her
head enough to kiss the crucifix, and soon after, she was dead.

The daughter was looked after very well. She was the first human being to totally love the musician, yet he was not really aware of that, indeed, he could hardly recognize this kind of love. Although her physical needs were well supplied, she had lonely days, spent with only her nanny and a spaniel he had surprised her with on her birthday. Her nights, however, were not always spent snug abed like other little girls. Sometimes they were fairy tales, of which other little girls only dreamed, for her father had taken a fancy to having her there at his performances. The musician's audiences were amused at first, by the little girl who was dressed so regally and seated in the balcony box.

After the music, there were always those unreal-looking people who would come to see her, and she would try her utmost to stay awake until then. (She was bitterly disappointed if she fell asleep before.) When the music ended, there would be a great noise and then a rustling and drone of voices and her excitement mounted as she fought to stay upright. Then, to her great joy, they would float into the box, like wonderful huge butterflies, all-over gold, silver and glittering jewels. She thought of them all as princes and princesses (they were too big to be fairies) - the gentlemen hovering, the beautiful ladies bending over her, bringing her sweets, chucking her under her chin. They were cooing, sweet-smelling, bewigged figures who did not seem to exist in the daytime - at least she never saw them when she went out with the housekeeper to do the marketing. She was always looking for them, but never saw them elsewhere. Sometimes during her daytime walks, some pretty ladies would wave to her and call her by name. They would be dressed in very pretty clothes and she liked them, but she did not think they were those magical nighttime creatures.

* * *

He had sought to marry once; a dark-haired woman of good breeding. But there was a barrier - he had a daughter by his first woman, who had been a mistress, not a wife. The dark- haired woman had refused him, because of the daughter, and his "profligate" ways. This had amazed him. He saw himself as an innocent, and no harm to anyone. He was by then a musician of some renown, and as such, was greatly respected - and yet she refused him!

I see her, the one he had once courted, in middle age; the dark hair is now threaded with gray, her once sweet, youthful face has taken on a stern, unyielding profile, such as normally seen stamped on a coin. Her once lithe figure is now thickened, her bust - boldly thrusting and rigidly corseted - gives the impression of a ship's prow. Headstrong, she forces her way through any storms that dare to challenge her. The husband she chose instead of the musician is tall and as stern as she. They are two of a kind, both smug in their righteous way of life, so sure of their rightness in all things; unyielding. It is a good thing she and the musician were not married, or she would have eaten him alive. (Yet he foolishly grieved for years over the loss of her!)

I am transported to a great gilded hall where the musician has just performed. I see the patrons of music coming into a kind of lobby, where they negligently toss gold coins into a receptacle. They are very grandly dressed and bewigged - the women in very high hairstyles. They appear jaded - bored. I think they are turning on him. He may play well, but he does not play by their rules.

He cares little for the manners he must have in order to be accepted by society. He is arrogant enough to think he should be accepted for his talent alone. His daughter had been regarded as an affront to the woman who was courted by him and so, gradually, the child is perceived as an affront to them all. They frown on her presence in the balcony. He is oblivious to such things. Since that lady, one of their peers, spurned him, he has begun to lose favor with the society of music patrons. They are insulted because they had been prepared to accept him into their society, but still he flaunts his bastard child and keeps on with his bawdy ways.

* * *

The Unknown - The late years

He was no longer as popular as he once was, yet there were not so many musicians as good as he in these times, so he continued to get by. The decline in his popularity puzzled him. He became morose when he realized that many of the patrons of music, though rich and educated, did not really "hear" the music, did not really *feel* it. His visits to the lower classes' drinking and musical houses became more frequent - his clowning more sad than funny.

I can see him out one day, he is not wearing a wig, and his hair is thinning because he is older now. Perhaps he is a little tipsy, for he slips on the ice and falls on his arm. . . Ah! His hand! He lies there, in pain; slides his arm out from beneath him. . . With a great sinking of his heart, he knows his hand is broken. The pain in his heart is the greater by far, because he fears that his future as a musician is now destroyed.

A friend comes to his aid, gets him to his house and calls a physician. The Physician examines the badly swollen hand, probing for fractures. The musician is very upset, urgently demanding that the doctor rise to his utmost capability for the mending of his hand. But, the physician is shaking his head, his voice strained as he says: "I do not know, Herr _____, so many little bones, you see, so many, little, bones." He advises him to keep it stretched out flat - immobile. He gives him a potion, and then wants to bleed him of impurities. When the doctor and the friend leave, the musician's loud howl of helpless despair follows them out the door and down the stairs. The friend hastens his steps, and the physician shudders at the sound, for he is truly sorry for him.

He continues to cry and lament for years afterward. The hand has healed, improperly - the fingers stiffly spread, he works to loosen it and tries in vain to play the harpsichord. I see him despairing, tortured - a tragic figure draped forward over his instrument, wailing and weeping . . . for what does he have now?

After he broke his hand, he no longer went to the inns to see his friends, and withdrew from all society. He felt they couldn't care for him now, for he has nothing to offer them. He could not play music, and therefore he couldn't be gay with them. So, he stayed home and grew old. He cobbled shoes once more, because he had to earn a living. He wept and groaned over his work. What was worse; he deliberately mutilated himself in his misery. When using the awl or hook he would gouge himself in the offending hand, with self-hatred. He truly hated himself, for he felt he was worthless. Some of his friends brought in extra shoes, and kind words, but he looked rather wild, his hair stuck out in wisps, like he had been in a blustering wind. In response to these well-wishers, he only ducked his head and mumbled unintelligibly - a once cocky jester suddenly become awkward and shy; a "bawdling." Finally, he was left alone, since that seemed to be what he wanted. Then he sank further within his self pity.

He has a grandson by his daughter. The grandson has always loved his grandfather, strangely enough, even in those bad years, when the grandfather raged against his injury and lost career and this grandson was an infant, he had wanted to go to his grandfather. The old man walks slowly along a path and the blond-haired grandson runs up from behind and slips his small hand into the "good" hand of his grandfather (He is always careful not to hurt "the poor broken one," so stiffly held by the old man's right side.)

His daughter was the one who stuck by him. She took him home to live with her in the country. She was then grown and married, with children of her own. She was not in poverty, but they had meager means. They may have scorned him in the town, but she was still proud of him. She and the old man spoke French together - it was their private language.

He was a trial, even to her, for he was so changed from what he had been. She became tired of grieving over him, and, prodded by the display of his continual self-pity, she finally spoke in a forward way to him (for usually she was more respectful - he was her father, "the Maestro," and she was a farmer's wife). One day, she was standing in the kitchen area, kneading bread for the baking, her arms floury to the elbows. He was his usual mournful, decaying self, sitting by the table, staring into the fire, and moaning about having nothing to live for. This hurt and angered the daughter. Her patience run out, she was provoked to say, "What is your life, eh? You say you have nothing?"

He was startled at her tone, and looked up questioningly. She said, "Do you see?" She pointed two floury fingers at her eyes, "Do you hear?" (a flick of her hand to her ear) "Do you speak?" (A flourish of her hand from her mouth into the air) This hurt, and he cried out - "But I cannot *play*!" Before he spoke, she had anticipated his next phrase. She nodded, and joined him in the lament she had known was coming, "But you cannot play." She looked up at him, as she vigorously kneaded and slapped the dough against the table top. "I cannot play . . . No one in this village can play. Yet we *live*! There are other things." She paused, then waved her hand over the contents of her warm kitchen, as though including the whole of the cottage, the warm fire and smell of good food cooking, the kittens, and the children playing nearby. "Do you see contentment here?"

(And it was strange, but his eyes were opened, as though he saw, for the first time, what his daughter had. She whom he had thought was poor, was instead, richly blessed)

She continued to chastise him, "It is why you like to be here, no? You like to be near contentment, even though you cannot have it - (she pressed her fist to her chest) here. I cannot make music, yet I am happy. I have my children, a good man, a home, work for my hands. It is not special work, I will never be distinguished, but it is *good* work. I have *Love*!" Here she abandoned the dough, wiped her hands on her apron and leaned on the table to look into his eyes. "You have no one - you drive them away - all but me. You have no love. You throw it away and live for yourself. . . All in here - (she tapped her head) everything is you, how you feel, what you can or can not do." She sighed, "I do not agree with them - that you are being punished for your profligate ways. But, there may be something. . ." She paused, her brow wrinkled in thought, "You may need this lesson to learn, Pere. Perhaps you must rise to this - accept it and find another way to be useful, another kind of work. You cannot indulge yourself in this way." The thud of the dough onto the table was the period to her speech. "That is all I have to say - finis!"

He was stunned, rather than indignant. She had rarely spoken for so long and had never before been so hard with him. He thought about what she had said for a long time. He did not believe she understood musicians, but she seemed to understand people. So he thought, and finally he repented (even performing the penance for the sin of pride demanded by the priest). After this discipline, he became more aware of the others. He tried to help with the chores, to relieve his son-in-law of as much as he could; doing errands for the daughter (though these trivial tasks seemed like small, biting mites to his pride). He was humbling himself, but he still felt bitter. Venturing out into the countryside to perform this penance, he met people whom he had previously avoided. It became easier as he went along. To all their neighbors, "Rougstrum" was only a crippled old man - shy, but decent. He had lost all the frivolous exuberance of that young fool in Hamburg.

Herr Rougstrum did not know, of course, the anguish the daughter felt for him - the times she had cried into her husband's shoulder, as he held her sweetly. Her husband was a good man, simple but surprisingly deep in his understanding of human feelings. He knew his father-in-law was an educated, worldly man, and he was only a farmer with rough manners, yet he understood somehow, that the great man had been stripped of his greatness and his passion and had been left with nothing with which to replace it. After thinking on this for some time, he took his father-in-law out to the woods where it met the field, where he showed him a sapling of a certain type and flexibility. "Bending is better than breaking," he said, and he saw the scorn in the old eagle's face. Nevertheless, he went on, cutting the sapling. During the evenings following, he kept company with the old gentleman by the fireside. Without saying a word of explanation, he carefully worked the sapling into a bow, and cut and shaped slats of ash wood from which he crafted a sort of fiddle - a country instrument with which he was familiar. He used horn for the bridge and bone in the section at the end which held the ends of the strings, which were animal guts. All the while, the musician feigned disinterest.

Finally, one evening, the son-in-law drew the bow across the finished instrument, making crude, but mesmerizing squawks into peasant music, charming all within the family circle. (His wife saw the flush which rose up his neck as he gathered his courage to play before such an audience, and she loved him for it.) He eyed the old man, the maestro, over the bow and gathered boldness as he played. He was encouraged as he saw the gleam in his eye, the covetous look that he cast upon the fiddle.

The old man had tried other instruments, but had soon given it up; for nothing, in his crippled hands, would yield beauty of sound like that he was used to. This, for its crude simplicity, was not beyond him. The simple peasant songs on the simple peasant instrument, were crude, but with a certain charm which interested him - he saw its possibilities. His repulsion - that of the fine musician against the raw and undisciplined was overcome by something appealingly primal in this music.

Just when his interest was most piqued, his son-in-law, to the protests of his children, laid the instrument aside for the evening. He yawned and was headed for his bed, but turning back to his father-in-law, he off-hand-edly offered him the use of the fiddle any day he "was pleased to be amused by it." The young man was thinking, as his father had often told him, that "a little of something is better than a lot of nothing."

Secretly that night, the old man rose from his pallet to try his bad hand on the bow. He could not rest until he could see if it was possible. Painfully, he cajoled the stiff fingers into the curve necessary to clasp the bow, and gradually he saw how it could be done - by compensating - by moving the fiddle more, and the bow, less. He crept silently back to bed, satisfied.

It was not long before he was comforting himself with strains of pure music in the woods behind the cottage, where he had found privacy. He did not want anyone to hear his first crude attempts. He was not that humble, yet. Eventually, the country songs were interspersed by songs of his own composing which were eerie, sweet, but very sad - their drawn out tones lingering on the twilight air. He was fascinated by the natural components of the instrument, the horn of the ox, the bone of the dog, the guts of the sheep, and the tail of the horse. He imagined that the music vibrating from the remnants of these unfortunate animals was an expression of their souls, telling the joys and sorrows of their lives, and mixed with his, a man now as primitive and forsaken as Adam, they were all united in a symphony of tragic, earth-born spirits. These songs, simple and pagan though they seemed, stripped the nerves bare, pierced the heart of the unseen listeners, and transported them from the extremes of the joyful exultation of being alive, to the deepest, grieving groan imaginable - that of bright spirits trapped in earthly bodies.

As she stood in the doorway listening to the music coming from the woods, his daughter broke her heart with crying because of the sad sound of it, until her husband explained to her that it was good for her father to make these sounds that came from his soul, that it was what he had been needing. He, the son-in-law, was awe-struck that the old man could make such sounds come from such a limited vessel, and for the first time realized the true greatness of the man.

It was not so long, of course, before the music attracted listeners. First the goat herder became an audience for the musician in the woods, and during the days following, was joined by others. Too timid to call attention to themselves, they gathered quietly, sitting on a log in the pasture beyond the woods. At first, Rougstrum, when he noticed them there, was filled with heated passion that they would dare to intrude, but the passion of anger had also, by this time, been tempered by his awareness of the feelings of others. Brooding, but silent, he turned his back on them and continued to play. Some months went by, and the little group on the log gathered courage and began to grow, and other make-shift seats were added to accommodate the newcomers.

The daughter and her family were reluctant at first, to intrude, but when they saw he had not yet displayed his temper, they joined that rustic audience. She was happy and proud, her neighbors regarding her with a new respect. These country folk took this time after chores to listen to music played as they had never heard it before. They recognized their favorite tunes, but the tones seemed fuller, richer. The lilting melodies drew them

close to the heart of the musician. They strained to enclose within themselves those stranger sounds which were the musician's own composition,
and were moved. He began to seem special to them (indeed, they felt they
loved him!) - he with whom they had hardly exchanged a few words.

He, in turn, was not, as it seemed, oblivious to them. He was aware
of a curious struggle within himself as he adjusted to their growing presence. Anger, shyness, embarrassment, finally gave way to a small tingling
of pleasure, which became awe, and then, gratitude.   Then finally one
evening, when the sunset was especially precious, he turned for the first
time to face his audience. They caught their breath, for they sensed something of importance coming. He looked at all their faces, expectant and
yearning toward him and his heart was deeply touched. Then he lifted the
simple tools of crippled hand and homemade fiddle, and from those came
such an outpouring of love, such overwhelming passionate music, that the
group of peasants in the pasture were heavily struck by the force of it. So
stunned were they by such music that for a few moments, as the last strains
died away in the waning sunlight, these survivors of the storm could not
move, but sat rooted, some tearful, some agape, until finally, they roused
themselves as one man, and surged toward him. . . But then, they stumbled, and halted and were awkward, trying to express what could not be
expressed in any language, and feeling hampered by their countryman's
jargon. To stop them, he held up bow and fiddle and stepping into the
clearing where they waited, he said, "Now, my friends, dance! We celebrate
Life!" Then he artfully skipped the bow across the fiddle in a jubilant country jig, and smiled as he saw them shrug off the weariness of the work-day
and joyfully dance to his tune. As these new friends whirled and laughed
with the skipping music he made, he watched with a warm and full heart
and thought, "What power! What riches! What a Gift!"

* * *

Dear Friend,

Thank you again for your encouragement and support. I realize you are concerned about the salability of this kind of book, and I am concerned for your sake, but I don't know what to do about that. It is what it is. Maybe it shouldn't be published? Richard, my background is so conservative. I can't possibly tell my relatives about these experiences. I know you said I would not be considered "flaky" in New York or California, but I live in the Deep South Bible belt and I think if we publish this, I will have to use a pen name and remain a hermit. Yes, I know, the publisher will expect the author to go on a promotion tour. Don't you think we could forego that?

I am glad you say we can label these as fiction. I think that may be accurate since we don't really know what they are. However, I now believe these are brief stories of individual lives; each is a summing up of deeds and accomplishments, of learning and love. It seems clear from these summaries that a lot of things we may think are important at the time, at the end are not and are therefore vague in our memories. Some things we might have thought trivial at the time, become the real gold nuggets to be stored away. Why? I can only think that somehow they involved love, forgiveness and learning - what we are here for.

I am worried about you, though. It is not as though I am a psychic or anything. Yes, I do have little flashes now and then. Some seem precognitive and were related to national events. Some I have never understood, since they are obviously symbolic and have to be translated. Others I have understood and they are personal; I guess you could say they are guidance.

I don't have anything others don't have. We are all equally blessed by a fair God.

As you know, Richard, I am not highly educated. I am only a high school graduate, although I have a lively curiosity that demands to be fed. I am a painter and sculptor who sort of "wings it." I learn from nature and do what comes naturally. It took me a while to get to that point. I thought I had to go through the impossible art scene, doing anything for publicity, proclaiming how great you are and cultivating contacts - and one does if one wants to be famous. However, if fame is not important, one is free to do and be whatever one is, right? Yes, I know - very fine words from someone who is lucky not to be the breadwinner of our family.

I used to worry a lot about what I should be *doing* – what was my life's work? It seemed I wasn't doing anything important, nor was I "successful" and I was always very aware that *life is short, time is fleeting*! It finally came to me that I should just be a lily of the field. At first, that didn't seem to be enough. I was disappointed with that answer. But I thought about it for a long time, contemplating what a wildflower is. It doesn't worry about tomorrow and accepts whatever arises, flourishing in the sun and rain, rooted in the soil of earth. It doesn't worry about what it is, how to find itself, what is going to happen to it. It blooms in its own time, gives off its perfume, maybe sows a few seeds. It doesn't worry about who might come along and inhale its perfume and enjoy its beauty. It doesn't feel wasted and depressed if there is no one to appreciate it. It is what it is, complete in God, being the essence of what He gave it.

This next story began very vividly. I could hear leaves under foot, could feel the cold, could see his legs coming down the wooded slope, could feel his steaming resentment - later the icy chill coming off the child's bare bottom, etc. Everything was *very conscious*, you understand. Some of the political details, darn it, were not so clear.

This is the first story that I can say involves "important" people - at least, important in the eyes of the world: Kings and Queens, no less. Yet, this man was disgusted by the corruption and deceit he found in that arena and retired from it to lead a simple life with the people he loved. It may have cost him materially but he gained great peace and joy from his decision.

Although I have moved past the importance of reincarnation, you asked me to tell you any connections between myself and the stories. There is a peculiar thing I have done for many years. Whenever we are driving down a road, I sometimes, kind of automatically, check the roadside for what might be a baby thrown out. You know, the garbage bag moving, old box, etc. We hear about that kind of thing sometimes. It is not that I do it seriously, but idly - like just in case. Like I wouldn't want to miss it and not save an abandoned child. I don't like to admit this secret foible, but it does relate.

As far as research on this one, although I established that this must be the English king Edward I and Eleanor of Castile and their household, I finally gave up on establishing details. It is verifiable that because the main character's mother was Spanish she could have come to England with Queen Eleanor. That she married an Englishman and therefore remained in England, I can't prove. I don't think the main figure was really a jester, only that he saw himself as one, and resented it. He was gifted in humor and wit, but had sarcastic thoughts about those he entertained. If he had a title, I don't know what it was. Perhaps that wasn't important to him in the end. I haven't found any evidence that he actually existed, nor do I understand who this "maiden of nobility" was that he impregnated when they were both in their early teens.

Since I told you I have little success with dates and names, I can't understand why I got the date of the beginning of the story. It just sprang into my mind and I wrote it down. Perhaps it was an aberration, maybe it is accurate. If I am gleaning from his memory, he might have cherished that day as a very momentous one in his life, and therefore it remained there glowing bright.

Wayside Child

I see a forest path . . . . I can hear something scuffling in the wet leaves that litter it - footsteps. Someone is panting. Boot-clad feet come into view . . then, long, thin legs. It is a lanky man, all limbs and loose-jointed - clothed in dark colors. The cloak he wears swings out behind him as he hurries down the hill toward the sunlit meadows beyond. Patches of snow still lie in the long blue shade of the trees so he is glad to come down into the valley where it is warmer. It is early morning and the date is December 7, 1305. He has come from the direction of Kent over the Cotswold Hills. I have the impression that this man is "a jester," although he is not dressed as one at this time. (Whether he is really a jester by occupation, or he simply sees himself as one, I do not know.) He is not in the light mood one would expect of a jester this morning and seems to be absorbed with gloomy thoughts; grappling with a decision of some kind.

I can tell that he is very conscious of the cloak he wears, as though it burdens him. Yet, it is not really the cloak itself, for, although it is lined with a short-napped fur, it is light. It merely reminds him of those rankling duties he does for the people he serves. That, not the cloak, is what really lies heavily upon him. That is the weight he would like to throw off. This resentment he is feeling has been a pot boiling for some time. The little he is rewarded for those duties galls him. Even the loan of a horse for the final lap of this journey had been out of the question, and his legs are tired and strained. It is unusually cold this morning. The early chill seeps through his cloak and the thin clothes and hose he wears beneath -

adding to his dissatisfaction, for he knows he would be more warmly dressed if he were not kept in such humbling circumstances. Besides all this, he has grown impatient with the pretense that he must always hide behind. Yet his loyalty to the king wars against these thoughts, and he chides himself. He should be grateful for the cloak. Although it is not luxurious or thick, it is better than nothing. It was given him by the prince - soon to be king - a reward for service he has done him. Unfortunately for his peace of mind, he remembers what this service was when he tries to be grateful. His dark eyes turn hard-looking. His mouth twists into an expression hard to interpret.

This journey was another service rendered for the King, something involving sex, or a mistress, the third party was "a Kentish woman?" Then a very strange thought - his thought- comes to me, that it was "a man - disguised as a woman." No, not a real man, but a strong woman - "a man in woman's dress," he calls her. The king must quiet her - will not die and leave her empty-handed. She has a daughter to care for and her needs must be met. This jester does not like her, hates dealing with her. This was a late-formed attachment of the king, and strange in a way. The jester wondered how he could have benefited from it. But he was not privy to the king's personal affairs and it was not for him to ask. She could be alluring, he supposed. "Green Sleeves" . . . She loves singing ballads and has a deep, lovely-sounding voice. "The voice of the serpent," sourly thinks the jester, "who will soothe you, lull you, then leap upon you and swallow you whole." He hated being the go-between for the king and this woman, but was not the king his master? And did he not look forward to all that the king had promised him? For this is what keeps him locked in this burdening servitude — the promise of better things to come.

In this way, his thoughts chase themselves through his mind as he trudges into the valley, and this is why the cloak - though light - is a burden that lies heavily upon him. It is a symbol of his bondage to the king and his house, and the unpleasant things he must do to please them all.

The path divided. "Left or right?" he wondered, but something urged him to take the right side. He was delaying his return by wandering the countryside so it mattered not which road. As he plodded along, he allowed himself the daydream of finding some sort of honest work in a remote village and never returning to the king's service. (Yet, in the back of his mind, he knew he would be summoned, and if summoned, he must return.) "The man who is obedient to authority bears a yoke," he thought, and sighed.

As he wandered aimlessly, so his thoughts also wandered - scattered and without direction.

The road turned gravelly and the soles of his boots were thin, so that he felt the rocks through them - another small mite added to his long list of grievances this morning. He stopped by the wayside to rest. With a sigh, he sat on the ground and emptied the grit out of his boots. Both his mind and body were weary when he stretched his long body out on the grass. It was still wet with melting snow, but at this point, he didn't care. All he wanted was some mindless sleep. He dozed, twitching occasionally - short intervals of sleep interrupted with steadily increasing noise as the hour grew later: human voices, cart wheels, birds singing, a cock crowing - the clatter of beasts and people making ready for another day's labor.

Finally, he was roused by the sun that had risen above the treetops and was now shining onto his face, making his cold skin tingle with warmth again. He was very groggy, and felt worse than he had before. He sat up and tried to revive himself, stretching his eyes and blinking to remove the greasy film that seemed to have settled over them. There were more people moving about now, taking their wares to the village market. A man with a barrow full of rotting cabbages rattled by and said something to him. It sounded, to the sleepy jester, like "pretty child," and his foggy mind wondered what the fellow could mean. He continued to sit there, for the warmth of the sun on his back felt good and his damp clothes no longer felt as clammy. He gave himself up to that pleasant sensation for the moment – just basking. Soon, however, he could no longer ignore that disturbance in his belly that urged him not to dally. He was hungry.

As he stirred himself to rise, there was a slight noise behind him and craning his neck around, he saw an infant girl squatting there in the wet grass just behind him. She must have been there for some time, watching him like that. She had a stick in her hand and she was jabbing it up and down in the thawing ground as she squatted there, looking down at it and then back up at him. He was surprised and looked around for her folk, but saw no one. Her hair was curly but unbound and she looked neglected, for she was not dressed for the weather. Her feet were bare and her gown looked thin. He thought she must be very cold and his heart was touched by such a pitiful sight. The compassion he felt showed itself in his eyes and transmitted itself to the child - for in that instant, her face twisted and her little mouth stretched into a wide line turned down at the corners. Although she still made no other sound but that of the stick jabbing into the dirt, tears began to roll down her cheeks.

Greatly moved, he asked her gently where her mother was - her "folk"- no response. The child just snuffled and rubbed her hand against her running nose, smearing her face. The jester jumped up. Being a fastidious man, he came to her in order to wipe her face on her petticoat - but lifting up her dress, he saw she had none. His mouth fell open, for he was deeply shocked to see that she was naked beneath! None of the usual many layers of clothing that normally covered an infant were there. "Poor child!" he murmured, "with naught but the thin dress to cover her from the chill" and he could see that she was chapped and raw in places. Then he realized he had been gaping open-mouthed and thought, "Poor soul, now she will be affrighted, too." While he was wiping her face on the underside of her dress, she clamped her arms about him - not in the yearning way a normal child would. This was a dead-eyed creature with a hard and desperate grip. He hesitated only a moment, then accepted her into his arms and rose to his feet. Seen up close, the skin of her face was bluish and waxy and this filled him with fresh alarm.

At first he pulled her dress snug around her to warm her as best as that garment could serve and wrapped his arms around her as he walked around looking for her folk. He was still thinking that the girl had wandered from her bed in some nearby cottage. The countryside was by now all astir with people and he asked all who passed by if they knew the child or her family. But, no one knew her - which struck him as odd indeed. The child did not simply sprout there. He joined the stream of folk making their way to the village, and hailed anyone he saw coming from that direction, thinking she may have been from that place - but still, no one could tell him who she was. He was anxious and at a loss for what to do with her. He looked for rescue from those passing faces. Some were sympathetic and kind when he told his tale, but they simply nodded and went on their way. Finally, it fell on his mind that they thought all was well, for wasn't she in good hands? That was when he realized the full extent of what he had done. He was now possessed of this child. If he did not find her family he would have to take on the care of her, and at present, he was not fending that well for himself alone.

An old wife, looking warm in her abundant skirts and wrappings, came and stood before him, gushing over the child. As he related how he had found the infant, she nodded with comforting understanding. She talked and talked and made a cooing like a dove, but when he offered her the child, she quickly cooled and took herself off. Irritated, he thought "Old biddy . . . all she wanted was to satisfy her curiosity." With difficulty, he pulled his cloak from beneath the child who had attached herself to him like a briar, and tucked her inside it, wrapping its fur around the both of them. "Now," he thought, "I look like I have grown two heads!" and being quick to wit and humor, he smiled, but the smile disappeared with the next thought: "She probably has lice, and they will take up residence in the fur." That idea disgusted him, but he resigned himself to it, for he also had a tender heart. The cold emanating from the child's wooden body lying upon his breast made him shudder, but before long she began to thaw and soften against him. By the time he stumbled into the village, she had sunk below the cloak, fast asleep, flat and limp upon his breast like a fallen sparrow. He, too, was quite warm now with the sun and the exercise and he was very tired besides.

As he surveyed the village folk for a possible rescuer from his situation, he was attracted to a young woman who was standing in front of her step, sweeping out her doorway. This done, she busied herself displaying her goods for sale before her door, coming in and out, her arms laden with baskets of vegetables. Her hair was red-gold, making her look warm. Perhaps her heart would be, as well. He tarried beside her, wishing to talk to her and thinking he would buy a few russet apples to quiet his stomach. Then, when she had said the first words, (for she had spied a curly head now peeping up from the breast of his cloak) he felt it was proper to speak to her. He gave the tale of finding the child all the drama and pathos he could bring to it (and he was a gifted story-teller). He was pleased by the shock and sympathy he saw plain on the woman's face and further encouraged when she beckoned them into the warmth of her home.

By then, the child was wide awake. From her nest in the cloak she stared around the room in which they found themselves. There was a fire on the hearth, and the jester made his way to a lump of cloth and stuffing which was clearly meant to sit upon, and perhaps to sleep on. There he sat heavily down and opening his cloak, he released the little bird. The child had not taken her eyes from the fire since her first sight of it, and its light was reflected in her eyes and made sparks in the curls of her hair. She did not move from his lap, but she let go of her tenacious grip upon him and sat very still - staring, trance-like into the flames.

The woman was stirring about, making a posset of something hot for the child to drink, but hearing the jester exclaim, she turned around. The child had suddenly fallen flat. As though her limbs no longer had any use to them, she lay completely limp - sprawled across him and the couch, nearly sliding to the floor. The jester reached for her, and pulled her upright - yet her limbs remained slack and her eyes rolled in her head. The woman hurried over and peered closely at the child in the gloom of the cottage, which was lit only by the fire. She lifted the child's dress and examined her naked body. The ribs stood out, the belly sank in. "Pah!" she said. "This child is not only cold, she is starving!" Then she returned to the larder to get the makings for a meat broth with herbs, instead of the posset.

Soon there was a savory smell coming from the pot in the fire.

The child recovered from her sudden weakness but then she was over-warm from the heat and the steam filling the little room. She lolled against the jester, feeling sick. The woman was slicing bread and cutting vegetables into the soup. . . . Chop, chop, chop - that and the crackling fire was the only sound in the room. The jester was lost in his thoughts, until a trickle of water seeping through his clothing and hose brought him awake. Startled, he cried out; "Heigh now!" and jerked the child up, setting her onto her feet. Her toes and feet curled inward awkwardly when they struck the cold, hard stones of the floor. She whimpered; a shiver went over her face, and her mouth drew into an "O." "Ah!" he said, sorry indeed for setting her down so hard (even though she had wet on him) for he suspected her poor feet were pained from the time she had spent in the cold.

(He had no way of knowing that the child - starving as she had been - had eaten snow, lots of snow. It had not filled her and had only made her cold inside and out. But now that she was warm, her bladder would not hold out any longer.)

Seeing what the problem was, the woman rushed over with a pail and snatching up the child, she stood her in it until the spate was over. Then she wrapped her in a rag and shoving her back into the jester's arms, she emptied the pail, refilled it with water and sluiced it over the spill on the stones. It was all over quickly and efficiently. Then, she returned to her work, leaving the uneasy jester gaping at the liquid disappearing between the cracks of the unmortared floor.

He saw the woman eyeing him as she prepared enough food for them both. She wouldn't feed only the child, and not him. Yet, he had a sense that she begrudged the extra portion of bread and victuals. She handed him his plate and seated herself on a low stool before the child, where she began to feed her gently from a cup. When she was finished, she said she would first bathe the child and then let her eat again, for she could not hold too much at first. When the woman rose, he placed a coin on the stool. She saw it (he had taken care that she should), though she acted otherwise. While she refilled his beaker and took away his plate, she was in better humor and the coin had disappeared.

He was impressed with this young woman, for she seemed naturally affectionate. "A good mother," he thought. So, while she made ready the bath, he took heart and asked her if she would take the child, to mother it, for, he told her, he had no wife and no real home. She was taken aback and he could see her thoughts chase themselves across her face. At first, a gleam appeared in her eye and he was pleased, for he could see she was considering the possibility with favor - but then, all of a sudden, her expression changed and it seemed as though a door slammed shut in her mind. Through clamped lips (which foretold what her answer would be), she refused. Her husband, she said, would never stand for it. He would not understand where the child had come from and would not believe this tale. No! It was a "work of worry," she said, and would not do. He opened his mouth to protest but shut it again, for she was adamant. He would have to take the child on with him, was what she said.

She did not quite trust him after that, and made him stand by as she bathed the child in a warm bath, for she was afraid he might disappear when her back was turned, and leave her with the child after all. Neither was her manner toward the child the same then, for she had steeled her heart against loving the girl. As he drank his cider and watched the bath, his lingering hope that the girl might win the woman's heart and change her mind died away. He was dismayed that the child did not yearn toward the woman, as he would have expected any babe to do. Instead, from beyond the woman's broad back as she knelt and ministered to her, he could see her peeping face. From beneath wet curls her serious eyes stayed fixed on him as though to pin him to the spot. Still, she made no sound, but a pale little arm and hand stretched out toward him, plainly pleading. Her little fingers were busy - opening and closing, opening and closing - as though she wished to grasp and knead his heart in her little hand.

After the bath, the woman made a napkin for the child, showing him how to tie it, and giving him another to use, she said, when the other was wet, so that one could be washed. He stood frozen as she went on about it, for he was gripped with fear. It was impossible - that he should take a child along with him on his tramp, to change its sodden napkin, to wash it. What was he to do? Indeed, if the woman had turned her back then, he would have gone, so she was right about that. But she kept an eye on him while she busied herself. From some place, she had found a little petticoat and woolen stockings for the child, and devised, with a few stitches, some woolen cloth into soft slippers for her feet. She instructed him severely not to put the child down - for the slippers and hose were not to get wet in the melting snow. He was to carry her - (this burden he had taken on - fool that he really was!) all the way in his arms.

Before he took himself off (for he could see no help for it), he instructed the woman that if the child's sire and ma'm should come to look for her, she must send them to him at this place. (And he would have written it down, but of course, she could not read and there was naught in the house with which to scribe it). "Then remember the name, and sure, you will remember the place," he said. When he told her where they could find him, at first her eyes widened and her face cynical, for she would not believe he lived in the king's quarters. With sarcasm he said, "I am only a lowly servant of the king and live above the stables." (The apartments there were finer, he knew, than anything she must be imagining, but no matter.) "Edward Parminter," he said, "just ask for Parminter."

Then, he could tell from her smoothed-out face that she was relieved and he could imagine what she was thinking - Ah! The child would be all right - they were going to the King's castle! Anyone would be safe there! He snorted at the ignorance of people. The irony of it! How little they knew! But, simply because he had plucked this child from the wayside, now it seemed his path led irrevocably back toward that life from which he wished to flee. Fate had drawn his lot for him. There was no escape. He must return to the castle and take up residence once again as a fool.

She helped him tie up the child to his back in an old shawl - like a harness - the cloak over all, still covering them both except for their heads, but now his arms were free, which was a relief. Then he was on his way again, this time knowing the route he must take.

As he traveled onward, she would lay her face next his shoulder most of the time, beneath the collar of the cloak. But sometimes he could feel her raise her head and the stretching of the cloak as she popped her head out the opening to see what she could see. When she heard any unusual noise his figure changed from a hunchback to a two-headed monster, he thought, with a quiet laugh. He was always one to see the humor in things. As he walked along, he began to think how, when he arrived, he would tell about this journey to anyone who wished to be amused.

A peasant farmer and his family gave him a ride in their wagon, and when they reached a town of some size, he threw them a coin and left. There he found an inn where he and the girl could get warm and fed. There was mud everywhere. No snow now, but all was amelt. Since they were nigh onto a town, this place was busy with people and horses groping in the mire. Some careless fool bespattered his cloak with it, and he was fussing about that when he entered the door. The innkeeper was an old woman - her salt and pepper hair was sparse and escaping its knot. For some reason (which he wondered about) one side of her face was drawn downward - the mouth, cheek, and the skin around the eye - all sloped down to one corner as though it would slide off there. He freed himself from the infant, set her on a stool and cleaned his cloak while the innkeeper fetched food and drink. When he looked up from that task, he saw her standing over the child, and it looked to him as though the old woman was handling her roughly. Not trusting her, he sent her away and cared for the child himself. Carrying her to the tall-backed settle next to the roaring fire, he began chafing her hands and warming her small stockinged feet gently between his palms. Soon, her eyes lost their focus and she slid sideways, falling heavily asleep again. It seemed she would never have enough sleep. He covered her with his cloak and stood there a few moments, looking down at the poor little infant - wondering from whence she had come and what had happened to her family. The firelight lent her small pale face a warm glow and picked out glints of gold in the strands of her hair, allowing him to see the possibility of future beauty - if health would return.

Meanwhile, the woman had come back and stood at his elbow with her hands wrapped in her apron, looking down at the child. When she spoke into the silence, her voice was raspy and irritated him since it intruded upon his peaceful study of the infant's face. She was saying that the girl didn't have enough clothes for the weather. He said he knew that and then he told how the infant had been abandoned by the road. What expression passed on the woman's face upon the telling of the tale, he could not say for sure, since it was warped awry. She moved past him and bending over the child, she examined her clothes - fingering the thin material, lifting the child's skirt and looking under it to assess the petticoat, woolen stockings and the slippers that had been given the child by the young woman of the village. She left then, but soon came back with another petticoat and boots; both too big. The child didn't awaken as she put on the petticoat - even when she lifted her by the legs to tuck up the top of the garment, to make it short enough. Then she showed him the boots, saying, "Although they are too large, they will do to keep her feet warm, and the damp out." "But," he said, "her feet may be too tender." "What meanest thou?" she said. So he stripped off the rough woolen stockings and showed her the child's purpled feet, saying "the cold had blued them" and he worried she would lose her toes, if she did not die of it. The old woman bent over and stared closely, then she hurried off, shuffling her way to a dark corner where stood an odd-shaped cupboard. Soon she returned again, this time with a balm, "Something she has made herself, likely," he thought, but it smelled all right - like herbs and rosemary - so he did not object as she gently soothed the little feet with it and wrapped them up with cloth much softer and kinder to the child's skin than the woolen stockings had been. Then she replaced the soft stockings and slippers. Even then, the child did not awaken, though she stirred and sighed.

He was touched that the old woman - for all her ugliness of face and voice - seemed a good body after all, so he asked her if she wouldn't like to keep the child with her, to fetch and carry and, eventually, to help with the work around the inn (for the old lady looked in need of it). But she grimaced and refused, saying she had a wasting affliction that was now fast making away with her. She would not have much longer on the earth, she said, and when she went the inn would go too. She had "no family to care for it," she said (pointing to the girl) when she died. Then she turned to stare at him piercingly with her one good eye (a pale blue orb, but not unkind) and said, "Besides, it seemeth God hath chosen thee for the task." He was taken aback and - as he absorbed this sobering thought - his eyes went to the child and lo, she was awake and staring at him too! He was a superstitious man, believing in signs and omens. He would not put away anything the good God had laid upon him. So, he considered; perhaps the child truly was meant to be his burden to bear.

The two supped together, the child sharing his soup. He watched her as she supped the liquid from the bowl. The way she had - of fishing out the bits that clung to the sides with her little fingers, and eating them most daintily - charmed him nicely. When she was satisfied, she quietly set the bowl aside and looked up into his face. Then, for the first time, she smiled. And oh! That smile! – "Ah well," he thought, "I am trapped now indeed!"

It was not an eventful journey, after the appearance of the child, and he made rapid progress toward that castle where the royal family was staying at the present time. His bitter thoughts had faded and were replaced with wonder that a child should be left by a roadside, and why. He took to heart the admonition of the innkeeper, that the child might have been given into his care by The Almighty, so, throughout the remainder of their journey, he set his mind to the task of fitting her into his life. All pretense he had made earlier - of leaving the king's service - was now abandoned.

Perhaps, he thought, a lady's maid would oblige him with a bed some-where for the child - in the kitchens, maybe, where she would be warm and fed, and perhaps put to work in the royal household. Surely that would be a good thing? What could be a better place for a foundling? Yet, as he thought about it, he was reluctant to place the child in the hands of some of the servants of that nether world - the labyrinth of chambers below-stairs, where ugly things sometimes happened to the unsuspecting. This thought led to other, unpleasant ones, like the chain of events which led to this journey. Yes, ugly things happened to all people, no matter what their station. Perhaps it would be best, however, if he could find a place that he could share with the child, so that he could see for himself that she was well cared for.

* * *

Who is this man? I wish I could see him more clearly . . . . Then an image comes: Dark hair and eyes, long head, proud nose. He has his Spanish mother's face.

His thoughts turned to his mother; the stories she had always told him - the experiences of a child of nobility, so rich then so poor when her folk had died. The king of Castile was no better than the English. The best he would offer her was to be lady in waiting upon his daughter when she went to England to become queen. ("Too young!" his mother had told him when she reminisced about what her mistress was like in those days. "Just a little girl who knew no one there but herself, and a sad time she had becoming a lady-queen.") Well, he thought, now she is dead and there is another queen, but his mother had stayed on for a while in the queen's service. Early on, she had married an Englishman - his father. The old queen's people had not been loved by the English. His mother had been lucky to have had this marriage arranged for her so that she could remain in England, but bad luck had come again, he mused, since his father had died shortly after his own birth.

He could not imagine what life would have been like in Spain, nor anywhere else but London, for that is where he had always lived. Even when his mother moved to the Cotswolds, he had remained behind. The farm in the Cotswolds - his inheritance from his father - came into in his mind's eye. It was his mother's home now, but she was still away in London, so he had stopped on the way from Kent to the castle, to check on affairs there. He took pride in the stock he bred on their farm. His practice of matching all the best specimens of cattle and sheep had proved that their offspring were usually superior to the flocks of others who let theirs breed indiscriminately. It made sense to him, yet not to all. Some thought his practice of selection would "thwart the will of God" - and this puzzled him, for weren't people classed and kept separate, to breed only within their class? He would have a "royal family" of sheep, he thought, and grinned at the irony, for, it was his secret opinion that the royal family was a poor lot.

The farm was a pretty place, he supposed, but so small - so rustic. It didn't interest him much now. In his mind were visions of a grand estate, with a fine manor - an estate more worthy, he thought, of the service he had given the king and his household - of the title the king had bestowed upon him. He smiled as he dreamed of it - of how it could be and how he would develop the farms that would belong to it. How he would shed the jester's mask for good and all, and just be himself - a lord of his own lands, a pleasant host, but no buffoon.

He scowled again. What had started him on the path to the position he was in now, was his mother. During her years of service to the queen, his mother had been extremely reserved and stayed to herself. When she walked the passageways in the castle some whom she would meet there - especially the servants - would shrink away or scurry out of her sight.

She could not help it – didn't even know why it was. When he had first noticed this, he had been quite small (for he could remember being lost in the folds of her skirts as he walked beside her) and - seeing their expressions and haste to depart - he was puzzled. He had looked up at her - a question on his lips - but when he had seen her face, he understood. Her public face was not the private face she showed to him alone in their apartments, where it softened with tenderness. Out there, in the corridors of these "foreigners," her dark look was so serious and piercing that they were a little afraid of her. They would have said she was an evil woman - would even have accused her, perhaps, of being a witch, except that everyone could see she was a very religious woman - always praying, counting her beads.

She had probably been more uncomfortable in her new land than her little queen had been. She had not known the language at first, so; "Better not to say anything, than to chance saying something wrong," she would think. Even when she had learned their speech, she had never trusted the ways of those at court. She had been brought up and trained at the court of Castile, so she knew the twisted ways of those who surrounded the powerful. His heart had ached for her, for he knew it was due to her outward manner that she had no friends and was always alone. Yet, he also knew that she could not change herself. How she had attracted his father was beyond his imagining, yet they had had a loving match.

While he was still a small lad, (plainly seeing how things were with his mother and learning by her bad example) he set about making himself a pleasure to be with. By the time he had become a youth, making others laugh had became a natural part of that. He did not fully understand it himself, but his elastic face served him well in this. Ordinarily, his expression was terribly sober. His long face was pale and smooth with no ripple of emotion upon it, although his dark liquid eyes had the look of sorrow within. But then, he would smile, and the change was so extraordinary, that it captivated any witness to it. His grin would stretch so wide and so far upward that it cast awry all the features above it - his thin cheeks would rise and pop up like muffins, tilting up the outer corners of his dark eyes, sparkling with a very mischievous glint. . . . while, above them, his dark brows would shoot upward, forming enquiring arches high on his forehead; even his ears seemed to extend themselves outward in a comical way. This total transformation from the long, serious Spanish face to such an infectious, funny-faced grin was so startling that it made people laugh outright, and - even if they had never met him before - they liked him immediately.

He also told amusing imaginary tales - sometimes naughty, often outrageous - of things that (supposedly) had happened in the castle. He became a darling of the palace, and his "silly" antics were told and retold among the servants and waiting maids and laughed about until inevitably, this had come to the notice of the king, who had him brought in to amuse him. This soon became the king's habit when he needed his spirits raised and was "too sour," as one of the young princes had had the gall to tell him. The king was no fool - he could plainly see that behind his farcical manner, Edward Parminter had a "sneaking" wit and brilliance that he only wished his noble advisors possessed. He became fascinated with the young lad, and was always curious to see what he would do next.

* * *

There is a large straw-filled "hobblety horse"; a wooden-framed skeleton, plumped with straw, covered with hide and painted. This had been a nursery toy, but the young Parminter was so clever with it that they had brought it to court in London, where he was expected to do a certain skit over again with each visit from the King. The horse had not improved with the years, but the shedding straw made it funnier than ever. He had tried to make it a little different each time, but it didn't really matter. The King laughed until he cried, always, and begged all to

see how funny it was, explaining it to them until it was robbed of its comedy. . . .
"Never explain a joke," thinks Parminter.

In this skit he would parody a certain sometimes-foe of the King as he rode into
battle. He was clever at mimicry, and with the years, had become a far better actor
than he had been in his callow youth (far better than any of them realized), so
that the skit had improved with time. His legs were longer, too, for he had grown
tall and thin, but that made it funnier, too. His legs akimbo like a grasshopper, he
would straddle the paint-peeling, straw-shedding horse, calling out that he saw the
king, and would ride out to do battle with him. Then, he would slide about on the
horse's hide as though the man were a bumpkin, and, rolling his eyes, he would state
(in a perfect imitation of the man's voice) those foolish words he had memorized long
ago that still made them all laugh.

Eventually, all the royal family had made young Parminter's acquaintance. The crown prince would speak to him, and Parminter's favorite princess had laughed whenever she saw him, for he would "play up" whenever
he caught her eye, in the ways he knew she enjoyed. The royal family's
portion of the castle was another world from that assigned to the servants,
which consisted of their quarters, kitchens, laundries and sculleries. Parminter enjoyed all of it . . . Up and down, here and there he moved through
the castle, making faces and jokes about it all. Everyone came to accept the
unique freedom he enjoyed. So, it came about that he had no set place, no
defined class within the castle - he mingled everywhere, with all levels. All
of the inhabitants of the castle had humour in common - they all wanted
to laugh. All of them - stable boys, scullery maids, ladies in waiting, peers
of the realm - looked toward him with bright, expectant eyes whenever
and wherever he appeared - waiting for the funny faces or sharp wit. In
his youth, this had been a joy, but in later years, he had found it to be a
disappointing thing - that they would see him only as a jester. Perhaps, had

he foreseen this in his childhood, he would have peddled his wares more lightly, but by then it was too late, for by that time he was - officially and entirely, the king's own fool.

But, with the bitterness there was also a secret pride - for there had been some private matters he had attended to for the king, of which he was not ashamed - to the contrary. He was thought of as only a fool, but the king knew better and sent him with important messages into other parts of Europe, for he could not trust all those men who served him. But, increasingly of late, the errands that the king (and now, the prince) was assigning to him were not honorable - like the one that he had attended to in Kent.

* * *

"The Jester" and the child have come into a town. At first, I assume this is London, but that seems wrong, somehow. It is a land of cliffs and wind, near water. There is no wind at present, and the sky seems shrouded in wool. It is just before dark, though the sunset cannot be seen beyond a dirty, yellowish haze. The town, formerly a small village until the king had built this new castle nearby, is cupped in a depression of the landscape. As Parminter and the child make their way into it, the noise increases. It is the usual mixed sounds of wheels, hooves, hucksters hawking their wares, the tinker beating upon pots and pans, and when they walk by the fortune teller's stall, there is the rattle of the curved bones he used for this and the dismayed gasp and cry of his patron when his fate was spelled out to him. . . . There are also the usual odors - of vegetables left over from the harvest and now smelling more pungent than they should, of dried herbs and medicinal roots; and above all this, hovers the smoke. The downdraft that plagues this place carries the smoke from the many street fires and chimneys downward, where it shrouds the cottages and shops, so that the air is dark and smoky and makes the child cough. It is a dirty-looking place to Parminter's eyes. He prefers a green landscape - that which is fresh and open. He hails a barrow man and prevails upon him to carry the child and

those purchases which he then makes in the market, for they must have food ready to eat. The child chews on a bit of bread as they rattle down the stones of the street. He has stripped off his cloak and made a nest of it around the child in the barrow, for it is not as cold now, and the exercise is making him overly warm.

The castle is on a green hill, facing the sea and wind and they are yet building on it – it is of timber and stone. The area surrounding it seems jumbled, dirty and poor. The people expect no better than they have always had, yet they are swift to proclaim their king as a strong protector and rally to him. Those Englishmen whose natures stamp them as fighters love this king and choose to live near his call. There are dreary, tiny habitations set upon the cliffs - animals and people dwelling together. One would think the wind would blow all the misery away, thinks Parminter, yet it stays. There are some nice manors out on the fringes of the town - pretty places. He yearns toward one such place and would like it for his own. He always goes there upon his return - where he stands before its gate and looks longingly down the little winding lane toward the house in the distance. It is vacant of heirs at present, but he knows the king will not think of such as he when he gifts this estate. He sighs and contemplates his future as they make their way onward and upward to the castle. Behind him, the barrow is starting to make an ominous clacking noise, regularly punctuated by wheezing from the peasant - a fitting harmony for his mood.

As they came within view of the castle, Parminter's thoughts turned to assessing his king. He was a warrior and dominated the whole of Britain. Roaming outward from its core he would fall heavily upon the countryside, and subdue all those who would rebel. Then he would throw up great piles of stones - his fortresses - upon each conquered territory as though to anchor the country firmly under his foot, leaving soldiers to safeguard each conquered bit. The weight and size of this castle where they were staying now, was a fitting monument to this king. He had failed, however, to completely manage the wild Scots. Yet, although his king was less than perfect in his eyes, Parminter would hate to see him die - as he thinks he surely will, soon. Then the crown prince will be the new king - the prince who had been a sometime- friend in their youth. Edward was his name, also. Parminter had never called him that to his face, of course. The old king was better by far - wiser, saner. The crown prince was dangerous, and Parminter dreaded the day when he would sit upon the throne.

It was dusk and darkening fast when he stood once more before that huge edifice. As he gazed at it, his heart became as one of the stones, and a chill came over him. No matter, he told himself, he would go about his business and delay, delay, avoiding the crown prince as long as possible. He paid the barrow man, shouldered his purchases and looked down into the child's face. What a mite of a thing she was - staring up at the great looming hulk of the castle! He wondered how it appeared in her eyes.

Within the castle walls were the usual noises of the inhabitants settling in for the night: clanging metal, thuds, and - as they made their way to the back where the stables were located - there was that unmistakable, pungent odor and sounds of horses stamping and snorting. The child was charmed by the beasts; reaching out with one small hand to the big dappled grey. "That one belongs to a prince, my dear," Parminter said and the great beast rolled his eyes toward the child - the whites of them gleaming in the twilight. With a swish of his tail and stamp of his hind hooves, he conveyed his royal impatience to be fed his oats.

Parminter avoided those who looked in his direction and did not engage anyone in conversation - but made his way in quietly and quickly. He had no desire for the royal family to know he was back as yet. Later, he would find the child a place and seek permission for her to stay. This could be obtained on a much lower level, he told himself. There was no need to tell the king.

A sleeping boy was sitting slumped against the stable wall - Parminter nudged him awake and in a soft and lowered voice, told him he would have a fire. He and the child climbed the stone steps to the upper level of the wing that held the stables. Then he summoned his servant woman to come and make a meal.

There, in the one large room where Parminter stayed when he was here, the two of them shared that simple but satisfying supper, accompanied by the crackling fire. Afterward, the child lay content on the straw tick the woman had made up for her to sleep on. Her hunger had been satisfied and she felt wonderfully warm beneath her sheepskin - even her bones were warm, now. She lay flat on her back, not moving, welcoming the blessed heat into her body. Only her face was turned, so that she could see Parminter where he lay on his couch. Assured by his presence, she was soon asleep. Parminter, however, lay awake. Though he was still, his eyes were restless. Unfocused, they flicked back and forth - wandering the ceil beams illuminated by the flickering fire below. His mind was busy, too - running back and forth — for he was still seeking an escape from the trap he was in.

The king was his master, yet must he not also obey the crown prince, although he despises the man? How far should loyalty go? The king may be dead before the year is out . . . . What then? He could see the handwriting on the wall. When the old king was dead, those who lay in wait to manipulate the new king would make their power felt. The crown prince had poor judgment. He had never been able to see beneath the masks people wore - there was nothing but doom ahead for such a king. Parminter sighed in despair. As king, the prince would make a slave of him - having him do things for him that went against the grain. He would lean on him - as he would on anyone who would prop him up - and then he himself would go down with that fine new king, caught up in the net of intrigue and treachery that was already being woven - a black fate.

* * *

It is early morning - He stands before a window cut into gray stone. Framed in its arch are the soft, mist-muted shades of England. He can feel the mist within the room, too - cool, damp, yet refreshing. The snow has melted entirely away as though it had never been. There are the usual sounds of awakening - clanging of metal pots and tools, neighing and snorting of beasts . . . Out onto the road winding through the hovels below staggers a sleepy peasant - his hat clamped down upon his head, his tunic rumpled as though he had slept in the stables the night. Parminter's eye is drawn down that road which winds onward through green pastures and disappears into the blue, blurred larches in the bog on the horizon. A cock crows, and another takes up the call . . . birds of all kinds adding their treble notes to the summons of the fowl. Parminter breathes deeply of the cold air, which, like the countryside, is pure and clean and soft . . . His heart lurches toward it. How he longs to be out there and away!

But, he sets this thought aside and turning, he goes to one corner of the room where there is a cubicle built into the stone wall. Here a quantity of straw is stored for use as mattress filler, floor covering or fire starter. Plunging his hand beneath the straw - his hand closes around something which he has hidden there. It is a round pot of silvery metal - the shape of it is rather flattened and the lid has an elongated knob, which fits neatly between his fingers as he cups the lid in his hand and then raises it. His movements, even in this privacy of his own chamber, are a bit fur-tive - his manner that of a man with a secret. Within the pot, there is a seal and sealing wax. Moving to a table near the morning light, he sits and writes, then rolls up what he has written, heats and applies the wax and carefully presses the seal into the warm glob. Leaving the chamber for a moment, he finds someone whom he trusts and sends this message to the court. They will recognize the seal, and it will be received by the king. (The king will know who the sender is, but the servants and others will not).

No one in the court knows about these secret messages he carries for the king, except for one woman who has the king's confidence. . .

I don't know who she is - but I can see her. She wears a loose, flowing robe, a wimple, and a rosary - almost a nun. A soft, middle-aged face, rather sweet, she nods her head as she listens, pale blue eyes beneath lowered lids . . . I can see a strand of her hair pulled out from under the cloth. Although it is never seen in public, it is light red-blonde. The king cares for her good opinion, though what he must do to receive it often grieves him. She can be severe. Who is she? . . . She is like a sister to him.

This castle is this "nun's" domain - she is there sometimes, anyway. This is in Wales, but the royal family is there only temporarily and then they will be off again. It is a resting place for the king for now.

Later that day, an overdressed page with a self-important manner and tight mouth hurries along to that wing of the castle to summon the jester - It is time for the fool to make his return to court. The corridor is very dark. Even though it is daylight outdoors, it is still night here, in spite of a row of torches along its length. Though they are held a good arm's length out from the wall, these torches do little to alleviate the dark beyond a few yards away - instead, they cast their flickering light upon the dusty edges of stone and cobwebs fluttering outward on the draft. There are straw mats underfoot, which are not changed nor cleaned until the dirt has obscured the straw. Then they will be removed, the place swept, and new mats laid down. There is a strange odor to the place which I cannot identify - the nearest to it that I am familiar with is that of rancid fat, straw, mingled with something else. Parminter does not like any castle in the winter, thinking it is better in warm weather when it is opened and fresh air can pour through it and cleanse it.

When he and the page come into the room, one of the princes is there. He is always ready to laugh at Parminter, and when the jester comes in, he greets him with a wide, open-mouthed grin - ready for the repartee` to begin. He is not disappointed. Immediately, Parminter's presence is felt, as he begins his seduction of the audience. Everyone at court hushes their noise and leans toward him. They are his to do with what he will, at least for this short space of time. His demeanor and *expression change totally from the man he had been "off stage." His face is alive and mobile, his gestures vivacious and graceful. Soon, they are absorbed in the tale of his travel (carefully edited to exclude what might be unwise to reveal, studded with vignettes of peasant life. "The fool has been on a rustic holiday," think those amused listeners at court. The thing that most interests the king Parminter saves for his ears only. He doesn't have long to wait. The others, even the prince, are sent away, and he is alone with the king, who, though he did not show it to the others, looks especially ill this day. The battles with the Scottish scum, had confounded him and made him weaker, so that his illness is now worse than ever. He sits propped up on cushions - his battle scars standing out against the ashen color of his skin, one leg thrust out before him. One thing that has not changed, he still has the gray, piercing eye of an eagle, thinks Parminter, who doesn't flinch beneath that gaze. He does not pity the old man, nor does he love him - but he respects him. Bending his grasshopper legs beneath him, he sits on the floor beneath the royal couch, so that the king's head will still be above his. Then it is time to speak of the matter in Kent.*

Some days went by, and no one had come to claim the child, so Parminter kept her out of sight in his lodging, warning her not to peep outside the door. They were to return to London soon and then he would make some suitable arrangements. He was relieved that the girl was thriving, with no ill effects that he could see. (A miracle - perhaps due to the intervention of the jester, the storekeeper, the innkeeper, and the angels of Heaven.)

LONDON

The child is running down a great hall, afraid, crying, looking for "her gentleman" (the jester). When she had awakened this morning, she could not remember what he had said to her earlier when she had been so sleepy. She only knew he had gone away and she was alone again, in another strange place . . .

Looking about her for something familiar, she beheld the huge tapestry which swelled and ebbed alarmingly in the draft. All around, the great stone walls soared upward to where they disappeared in misty gloom - the ceiling being lost in the darkness. Appalled, she stared agape far up into that dismal "sky," her little head thrown back so far that she lost her balance and staggered backward. Just then she thought she saw some creature flying way up there, and she screamed. . .

Now she is running down the corridors - looking into each room she passes, to see if he might be there. Servants drawn by her screams are coming down the corridor toward her. Angry voices echoing up and down the hall are saying things she cannot hear. Then as she peeps into another great room, she sees a gentleman seated at a table, wearing a soft felt hat. He looks up from his reading and is startled to see a strange child standing there. Rising from his chair he comes forward, a question on his lips. His dark eyes beneath raised brows do not look unkind, yet she is afraid. Softly moaning, she retreats into the hall, her back coming up against the wall. The stones behind her are cold and hard, and all around her, and coming nearer, are strangers, staring with harsh eyes. Crowding in, they hover over her. Sliding down the wall to the floor, she sits - knees up and crying - eyelids squeezed tightly shut to hide from all those strange, frightening faces. . . .

When she heard that familiar voice, her heart leapt with gladness. She opened her eyes and ceased her grieving - for it was he whom she was seeking! He was bending over her, his voice soothing, yet he seemed a bit upset. The young gentleman in the conical soft hat was with him, full of curiosity, his eyes bright. It is a tale he will hear from Parminter's own lips, and soon, he vowed. The child in his arms, Parminter turned back toward his room but then changed his mind and went to the kitchens instead. It was warm there and he had friends who would see that the child was fed and kept in sight until he could come for her again.

After hearing the tale of the child and having their curiosity satisfied, the kitchen servants were immediately united in sympathy for the child - partly because of their fondness for Parminter. He left the child in their safekeeping while he returned to explain to the prince. The servants allowed the child a straw tick to sit upon - out of their way, because it was a busy place - the king's kitchen. So there she sat upon her little tussock, under the table near the fire. Beneath that great table it was like a small, cozy room, and she felt more secure in that smallness, hearing the homely, easy talk of the kitchen help and warmed by the great fireplace where food was cooking and delicious smells were rising with the steam. She could not see the faces of the people above her and this was comforting too, for she had seen too many strange faces today.

She listened to their voices and watched the homely feet of the cook and maids as they moved around the room and the table. Two of the feet were young and slim - as dainty as the voice above them. Another set was thick and knobby - slopping over the outer sides of well-worn, distorted slippers. A pair of elderly feet, flat, tired, swollen and bunchy with layers of stockings moved more slowly than the dainty, younger feet. The voice that went with those was slow, too. The child, not understanding the accent, listened to the tone of the plodding, long-suffering voice as it seemed to soothe the more agitated, higher-pitched voices overhead. A small set of boots, split and dusted with soot scurried into view, then abruptly stopped, scuffled, and raced off once more, dragging a clanging scoop shovel behind them. The little boots were hastened onward by a shrill, nagging voice from above. After a while, the child's quiet contemplation of feet and voices was interrupted by a face that appeared - upside down - and asked if she "would have a bit." She stared agape - bemused by the sight of the upside-down image with corkscrew curls bouncing down on either side of it. . . . When she did not answer immediately, the intriguing face disappeared, but the maid soon reappeared, this time kneeling and right side up, and placed beneath the table a cup of broth and a piece of bread. With this "bit," the child arranged herself for comfort, squinching her feet up onto the straw, for the stones were cold, even so near to the fire. As she sat sipping and nibbling, she gazed into the flames and was content enough; remembering that the gentleman whom she thought of as "hers," had vowed he would come back and he had been true to her so far.

The prince (for it was was indeed a royal member whom the child had surprised at his reading) was enthralled with Parminter's tale of the lost child, and was amused that the Jester had become a father. It was a good joke, and provided opportunities to jibe at Parminter in the days to come - enquiring how it went, and what he had learnt in this endeavor. Parminter, after the initial shock of the child coming to the attention of one of the members of the Royal family, had risen to the challenge; as usual making the most of this situation to make his superiors laugh at his wit. When he woefully related the tale of the infant wetting his clothes, he was droll - a fastidious fop bewailing his fate - yet, at the same time, he was touched with remorse as he prated on, for the poor little one had not been able to help herself . . . He did not mind being laughed at, but he did not like making fun of the child.

As the days went by, it seemed it was not a bad thing, after all, that everyone knew about the child. The jester was relieved, for he had been uneasy and had feared for her safety. The prince saw to it that "a fair young maid of comely face" (so as to appeal to the child, he said,) took her from the jester each day and cared for her as she went about her other duties. The duties of this family maid were light - providing for the royal wardrobe; seeing that it was in order and clean, repaired or refurbished with laces or other such trimmings. As a result, the child was soon attired in proper infant dress - plain but warm and sufficient for an upper servant's daughter. And this is how they all came to think of her: "the jester's daughter."

No one knew from whence she had come, nor did they know her origins. In my vision her family was bound for Scotland, and was set upon by thieves. Her mother, a parson's daughter, and her father, an English soldier, had been slain. Her nurse was old and fragile, having been her mother's nurse, and not young then. The shock had made her lose her mind, so that she wandered about the countryside with "the bairn," hiding at the sound of any voice or footfall, until she had finally died of exposure. Unfortunately, she had not sense enough to dress the child warmly against the cold before she breathed her last. In fact, she had plucked the clothes from the girl as she went along; leaving them in the snow behind them . . . as she let her shawl and bonnet fall, also. Yet they had covered an amazing distance from the point where they'd been set upon. Because of this, no one ever made the connection of that incident with the girl-child who had later come to court in London. . . . Eileen. "Ei-leen" the old nurse had screeched into the wind as she wandered, "Ei-leen." (Was that her own name or that of her mistress or of the bairn . . . or was it even a name at all?) However it was, when they had prodded the infant to remember a name, she harked back to that terrible scene and the keening nurse, and with trembling lips and tears in her eyes, she'd cried out the word - mimicking her nurse's voice. It had sounded to them, like: "Eileen," so that was her name thereafter: Eileen Parminter . . . though Parminter liked to call her "Briarie," since she had clung to him from the first with the clasp of a thorny briar rose. She much preferred that name, too. It had no frightening memory attached to it.

All of the torches in the corridors of the castle were kept lit by a boy whom Parminter had befriended. He was always on the move about the castle and - being a lad of intelligence - saw and overheard a good deal, information that he shared with Parminter. Sometimes, when Parminter was away from his apartment and the torches were all lit, the boy would come to keep Briarie company. To entertain her, he would show her tricks he could do with a bit of yarn or, he would take out the squirrel's tail he kept in his pocket and placing it on his knee, he would stroke it - showing her how he could make it move like it did when it was on the living animal. This had frightened her at first, but when she had looked into the boy's face she could tell there was no harm in him. So, then she relaxed - and chuckled at the undulating bit of fur - her first laugh since her trials had begun.

Sometimes when the boy came he brought a bit of food to entice the mice into the light where the child could see them. He would scatter the food and then they would sit in silence and wait. Before long, the little mice would peep out, their noses strained forward and whiskers quivering as the smell of food drew them out - but, suspicious, they would hesitate - their tiny black eyes straining into the darkness for an enemy lurking there. This was the crucial, exciting part. Both children would sit stock-still, unblinking, hardly breathing. Soon, hunger would win out over caution and the mice would dart across the stones at the edge of the wall until they reached the lamplight where the boy had laid the bits. They would watch, spellbound, as the greedy little animals seized the crusts in little forepaws and stuffed themselves until their cheeks were crammed and bulging – but still ready to scamper off at the first movement or sound. Briarie would always remember that scene illuminated by the lamplight - the quivering little beasts with dust bits clinging to their fur. . . . their tiny forepaws so dainty and quick as they stuffed and chewed as fast as they could - their tiny black bead eyes glittering nervously and crumb-dotted whiskers trembling with fright.

* * *

Time passes and finally Parminter is found waiting, one of many who visit their king for the last time. They are crammed within a makeshift chamber, a series of tents put together on the roadside - for the king who was always blazing down the roads to build his kingdom had finally been stopped enroute by the hand of God. The dying monarch's breathing can be heard from across the space - a loud, alarming rattling which rises above the murmured prayers intoned in low voices by those religious. The king is framed in by drapery and burning candles which lead off and away from his feet as though they light the way to Heaven. To one side there is a fellow squinting and sketching - studying the monarch even as he dies, in order to do an effigy for his burial place. Parminter himself can scarcely breathe, for the crowd and his sympathy for the wheezing King. It is too late to insist upon a paper to secure his title to the estate he has been promised. It is not likely that he could have done so, anyway. No one ever could force the King's attention to something he considered unimportant to himself.

The King called many to him, in order to extract from them their promise to remain faithful to his house - (an act which clearly revealed his unease at leaving the crown prince in control of his empire). Parminter stands in line among these and when he reaches the king, he kneels beside him. His face on a level with the King's, he looks up to regard his master's pale and dying profile and his calm is shattered, for he is being stared at by one very alive and piercing eye. The large head of the king has not turned in the slightest, but this one orb has slid to the near eyelid corner facing him, and it bores into his, transfixing the startled Parminter, who stares - mouth agape. "I know you," the dark, piercing eye seemed to say; "not as a king do I know you - but as one passing soul to another." But then, the moment was gone, the eye turned cloudy, the gaze turned inward and the sinking monarch, with trembling lips gasps his desire that Parminter should remain to do his duty to his son also, just as he had stood constant and faithful to himself. Then he is silent. Parminter waits, but that is all. No mention of the estate, no thought of reward for such a faithful and discreet servant - just the expectation that he remain in thrall to his son as well. With bitterness in his heart, Parminter mumbles only that he will try, but he does not pledge. Then, rising from his knees, he scans the pale face of his monarch, waiting for the all-seeing eye . . . the protest. But the king does not seem to be aware of any omission.

He escapes from the chamber, is glad to be free of it - the emotion, the suffocation, the dying king whose weight of loyalty had become hard to bear. The air outside is cool on his face, his body feels light, his steps unimpeded, but there is a tinny taste in his mouth as he reflects that, out of all the others who had stood by the deathbed, his loyalty had always been taken for granted. He walked away from the camp, mounted his horse and started toward that place where his mother waited for news.

As he rode, his mind groped with the idea he had formed in the chamber: It had seemed to him that the old King, sapped of all his mortal strength during his few days of dying, was stripped of any worth he had ever possessed. He was only a pitiful shell - no longer an awesome king but just another man in his nightclothes begging for entrance into Heaven. What had this king been to his country? he asked himself. He had possessed a cunning mind, but not keen. He had not instructed, nor led his people to greater learning, nor would he be remembered for his benevolence, or religious piety. But wasn't a king valued for all he had left behind? So, what had this king left? Extended borders in some areas, fortresses hemming in the empire . . . laws hemming in the people. But didn't any common squire hedge in his land and protect his own interests - hoping to secure his descendants for those generations to come? It was true that, in doing these self-serving things, the king had with one hand, protected the people of England, but he had also been very willing to sacrifice many Englishmen with the other hand, with not a thought given to the human cost of battle. He mused over that - was the greatness of the king - perhaps of all kings - only his force of will, his physical strength? Was that the only worth of a King? (He was to puzzle over this new illumination for years.)

Then his thoughts turned to the future: What of the new king?

Although the old king had often been away from home, he had sired sons and daughters with both his first and second wives. The crown prince had been left to the care of women, and did not attract the notice of the King until it was too late. Parminter remembered vividly the King's return from a long absence, when both he and the prince were of an age to be considered coming into manhood. The King strode forward into the chamber where they were all gathered and his eyes searched for the youth who was his own blood. Alas, he could not immediately decide which one was his, for the room was filled with people - several youths among them. The prince, young Parminter, a cousin of the prince, were all very near the same age.

The king's eye glided over Parminter (a sturdy and tall lad but wrong coloration - too dark of eye and hair and his apparel bespoke his lowly position). Then his eyes lit upon the cousin, and they gleamed - of course! This fine young man was his son! - and he started forward to embrace him. A murmur of embarrassment rose from the family group. Then the king's sister blocked his path and, courteously, most kindly, she directed him to his own son, standing most unobvious apart, a spindly fellow - his complexion weak and pasty, most unlike his fighting, energetic sire. The king stopped abruptly, and studied this specimen. From the confusion on his face, it was apparent to all that he could hardly believe it.

For some time after that, he had sought to introduce his son to the company of men and youths who were rough and sporting fellows, and Parminter had been obliged by the king, to take the prince out into the archery ring. Here, they had gone through their paces under those tutors who schooled the king's men in their battle skills. Parminter had not minded. He had always enjoyed archery and had looked forward to hunts with members of court. The prince had done well enough, but Parminter had known he would fail when it came to drawing blood from some living animal with soft eyes. Which was odd, Parminter thought, because he knew the prince could be cruel too. More than once, when they were children, Parminter had seen him slap his sister when they had quarreled over some object of his desire - yet he had often seen them holding hands. Edward had always seemed possessive of his favorite, blonde sister - perhaps the only female he had ever yearned after.

Yes, he was altogether a puzzling creature.

* * *

Grief strikes the palace. Out with the old, in with the new. Lace and pannikins instead of sword and shield. What a waste for England! Those who are acquainted with the family grieve twice - for the old king and for the fate of England under the new one.

The new queen is proud, reserved. She had brought some favorites with her to this country - Now, those "friends" draw in around her, hedging her in to protect her. They add their plots and plans to the pot which already boils. The widowed queen cannot influence her, for she is young and trusts only her own people. Parminter had thought and hoped that perhaps in his lady-wife's bed, at least, the young king might find himself to be a man, but if this was the case, it did not extend beyond their private chamber.

In former days, when the old king had returned home after an absence, it was a cause for celebration. The new one - well, all were cast down when he was in residence. Still, for awhile he was given loyalty because he was the son of the old king. He counted on that loyalty - even expected it. That is why he was surprised when it fell away from him like the sand in an hourglass.

Parminter kept himself informed through his sources of information so that he could be forearmed against anything that should arise which might prove to be a danger to him. He was careful to act rather dim-witted when necessary, for those who manipulated the king glared at Parminter some-times, as though they feared he might be a threat to their position. So, he made himself say silly things that would make them think his head con-tained no thoughts of consequence - that he had no brain for intrigue, nor wit for anything beyond jokes. Yet, the cleverness of his jokes sometimes belied his acting, so that not everyone trusted his mask of naive innocence.

As the years went by, Parminter was kept dangling - partly by his own conscience regarding his loyalty to the King, partly because of promises unfulfilled - for he still had hope that Edward II would confirm his dis-puted title to the estate he had been promised by the deceased King. He was not given respect, as he was formerly, for those gaining power under such a weak King regarded "the jester" as nothing, and, if they thought about it at all, wished him gone from among them. The people he had regarded as friends were taking sides - some with the vultures, others dis-appearing from London - easing back to their estates and abandoning the royal family.

One day he realized that he was now in the same position his mother had held - that which he thought he had avoided. What irony! Friendless and lonely, he confided in his daughter. He explained to the young girl the complexities of life within the ruling class. He talked to her much as he would to an adult, since she hung on his every word. He had become sour, and it grieved her to see him change. She listened, plucking his sleeve and turning a yearning face toward that fellow she loved. From what she had observed of the intrigue in court life she had learned how perverse human nature could be. She could not be the complete cynic he was though, for hadn't he plucked her from the wayside - a trampled flower left to die? Had that not been a miracle? Was he not an angel to her need? He was the other side to the human coin - the good, deserving side - the one he did not talk about, but was. She always listened to him with a full heart, and as she grew in stature and experience, she answered him wisely. She smoothed his nerves and woman-like, unscrambled his thinking so that he was able to discern the thread of truth - the path he should follow.

Parminter - taking care to remain on the outer edge of the arena in which nauseating evil on both sides was being committed - observed from this distance as events moved steadily toward disaster - The King was afraid; was threatened. They had studied him, and knew him well - he was frail of heart and they were predators. The Queen, though charming, seemed over-proud upon their ascent to the throne. It could be she was just afraid, and hid behind this haughty reserve. Still, she began to listen to bad advice and her head was turned. The King was inept and knew it, so he became belligerent to hide his fears. One day, he drank from a cup and it made him ill - then he was doubly afraid. Fearing (and rightly so) that he was surrounded by enemies, he nervously questioned every situation that arose. His face - his eyes round and straining from his head - told the world he was afraid. The Jester's jokes were no help, for he resisted letting down his guard for long enough to laugh - to be at ease. Parminter's cautious words of advice seemed not be heard. The king's fears infected Parminter, who must try to shake them off after he had left his presence. After awhile, the strain of being expected to fill his father's boots, and being what he was, became too much for the King. He gave in completely to weakness and oblivion. This is when they - the vultures- fell upon him. By this time, he was easy prey, for as long as they professed to be his friends, he would grant them anything they wanted.

* * *

Parminter was sitting to a meal - it was too hot and he felt very uncomfortable, but saw no help for it, for he could not be disrespectful. His back was to the fire, and it felt nearly blistered.) The area in which they dined was closely hemmed around with folding screens - treasures, probably, yet he resented them for the infernal prison they made for him. He was pretending to enjoy his food, but he secretly studied his host who sat at one end of the table - a man who was enjoying his food, as he did most things. He was not eating quietly, but made a good deal of noise with his chewing and smacking, and belched naturally, easily, since he saw naught wrong with any of that. His short black beard was bedewed with little beads of grease from the meal. Occasionally, he would smooth it with an already greasy hand, as though the weight of those spatters bothered him. His beard was a good deal darker than the hair of his head, and quite glossy - probably from this habit. When his hands become so greasy the morsels started to slip from his fingers, he removed them to beneath the table where, sliding them under his tunic, he was nice enough to wipe them on the underside of it, so that he would not soil the outer side of the velvet garment. The tunic, however, had a dark shininess on the upper side since the grease of many meals was working its way through to the surface.

This habit of his host had captured the amused attention of the jester, who was contemplating a satirical parallel to the situation. Then, his eye fell onto her grace at the other end of the table, and he thought she must be sadly affected by her husband's manners at table. She was the opposite, in appearance, to her husband. A dainty flower of the field - weak of stem, for she looked as though she could snap in two in her hearty man's embrace. Her pale thin face had discontent writ upon it, though she covered it well. Her hair was pale, also - braided and bound back from her face; caught in a jeweled net. She was a small lady, her frame thin though distended in the middle at the present. He found her feet and hands fascinating, for they were abnormally long and narrow. He watched her eat daintily, the long, thin fingers picking at her food like knitting needles. Her feet remained well above the stone floor, enclosed in soft, warm slippers and resting upon a warm woolen, much embroidered pillow set upon hot bricks. (She was the reason for the overheated room.) She was a dutiful lady, looking well to her husband, household, children and the needs of the church (which one was most important to her, he could not guess, for since she had married she gave little away of her feelings). She looked so frail; it was hard for him to believe that she had borne such large and lusty children. She did not look at all like the lively girl he was charmed by some years ago. Now she seemed drained of blood and vigor - so sour. Back then, he had never noticed the extraordinary length and narrow width of her feet and hands. Sometimes he wondered if he had been blind - or perhaps those appendages had not yet grown to such a length?

When his host, the Baronet, looked up from his dinner to gaze upon his prized wife, Parminter observed the pride and affection glowing on the man's face. "What a wondrous thing this is!" thought the Jester, as his eyes were drawn toward the recipient of this emotion, to see that the lady had caught her husband's warm gaze upon her and seemed a little startled. But, after a little flutter of uncertainty, she steeled herself; acknowledging her husband's show of devotion with a faint, slightly twisted, smile.

He was plebeian, she; aristocrat, thought the jester. But the man was very good to her; devoted and generous. It was not his fault that he had not her refinement which years of breeding had brought about. He was a simple farmer, who loved his fields; his crops.

The wife signed to the servants to bring the cloths and hot water to wash from their meal. . . but the jester thought - "Too late!" and wondered why the lady had not had them brought on earlier, and spare her spouse's clothes. The host rose from his chair and walked around the table to raise his lady to her feet and kiss her hand; then he escorted his guest to another chamber - the lady silently disappearing along the way.

The Baronet clapped his arm around the jester with a hearty squeeze as they made their way to his "library." "A joke," thought the jester, for the man was hardly literate. However, he had to admit that the fellow had waded his way through enough of the works of the friars (and 'twas hard work for him, he thought) to improve his education.

There is a boy, a son of this couple, a dark and husky boy. The jester loves him like his own. (Ah! but then it dawns on me. . . .Perhaps he is his own?)

I am thinking this lady is of nobility, perhaps even a princess, though called "lady" now. In their youth, when she had been blooming and had a sweet smile, she used to follow Edward Parminter around in the corridors. I think the boy is the result of their ignorant (and awakening) youth - Parminter being barely into puberty. I suppose no one knew who the father really was. I think they did not suspect Parminter. She was hastily married to this older man.

(But, why, if he knows, or suspects, that the jester is the father of the boy, does this man seem to cherish him as a friend? Because, if not for the jester's folly, he would never have had such an opportunity! "A handful of gold" - is the way he sees the boy.)

The Baronet does cherish his lady - whether for her position, or for her good qualities, the jester does not know. These visits are very uncomfortable for Parminter. He finds his erstwhile child-lover repellent, her husband's strange affection for him, embarrassing.

As for the husband, he thinks he does not have to worry about the chastity of his wife. He thinks she is properly subdued - and he knows that the jester's young ardor had died almost as soon as it had begun. He can safely invite Parminter to his house and seeing them together, gloat over his good fortune. The son - his son, legally - will never call Parminter "father." It is a good joke on the jester. Yes, he is happy with his lot. He, who had been looking disaster in the teeth, had been presented with a windfall of wife, estate, title, and - in a short space - a ready-made son. No matter that Parminter's son was the heir - All their children (his own offspring together with the bastard) would be well taken care of. No one would ever hear the truth of the matter from his lips. Oh, no! He was a shrewd man, and well satisfied with the bargain.

If the two men could have seen into the heart and mind of the lady, they would have been astounded. She sat there - remote and cool - her face and manner giving not the tiniest sign of the pain in her heart that these visits of her childhood lover caused her. She knew Parminter thought the spark had died within her - as it had with him - years ago, but he was quite wrong. As she nibbled and sipped - seeming to be oblivious to anything beyond her duties to her table - within her breast there seemed to be a large, hard, ball of hurting. She had compressed and rounded the thing until it was manageable, and when he was not there it could even be forgotten. But each time he returned it was there again, threatening to burst through her ribs. She was careful not to meet his eye when she looked so vaguely in his direction, but when it was possible - when out of the corner of her eye, she could see that his attention was drawn elsewhere - then, she filled her hungry vision with his face - so handsome, yet more than handsome - so very dear! So, while her face told them nothing at all, her heart clamored for him.

* * *

A man is wailing, overborne . . crushed with grief - why?? Soil . . . something to do with owning land, and losing it. . . He thinks he has been stripped of all he had in order to satisfy another's lust for his estate. Deep, deep sorrow, futility . . . I see the Baronet - his face an agonized grimace - saliva runs from his stretched mouth - his face already wet with tears . . . Surely this is more than the loss of land? Yes, I can see his wife with a sword to her throat, because she and his children have been taken from him by force . . . . All gone, all gone. He curses the king who took his land to bestow it to another, then took his family away from him to another house. He has been accused of something but it is all pretense, a charade played out so that

the king could reclaim his so-called "sister," for now it could be said she and her
children must live under "the king's protection."

Later, his body hangs from a tree at the edge of a field, the branch from which
he is suspended springs up and down, from his sudden weight and jerking limbs.
He had acted very quietly, but now the leaping scarecrow body frightens the birds
away. Screeching they fly over the fields beyond, fields which had been his, and the
last sight of this earth that he had beheld before he died. Stretched out before him
and imprinted on his dying vision lay the soil - acres of good, rich soil, tilled and
awaiting spring planting.

* * *

After a few years under the new rule, Parminter was revolted by the
king's actions and had grown sick of the intrigues at court. It was not possible to feel sympathy for such a king. His behavior toward the lady he called
his own "sister" had been especially unsettling. As crown prince, Edward
had never known the truth behind this girl's grossly unbalanced marriage.
He was aggrieved - not for her sake, but because he had lost her. He had
sulked about it in secret for years, and finally, now that he was king, he had
settled the matter with lies and farce. Now, she was back in his grasp, and
he was soothed. It seemed to satisfy his perverse side that she was forced to
look only to him for protection; that every little thing she had came only
through his "mercy."

Still, Parminter could not seem to get free, shackled by loyalty, habit
and his yearning for the estate he had been promised by Edward the first.
He still hoped that Edward II would openly acknowledge his father's
bequest. Because he did not yet have this validation he needed, he had
not dared to build a dwelling upon it, for fear of drawing attention to
himself - He would have had to deal with the stares and questions of those
who would like to take it away from him. There were two parts to the

estate - a fine manor and lands nearby, and a farm in the hinterland, with no residence. The manor with its land was an enticing bit, yearned for by someone in power, with the king's ear. He was an educated, worldly man, much admired by the king and queen, who could not - or would not - deny him. So, since Parminter could not bring himself to force the king's hand, he dallied at court, using his cunning and wit to ingratiate himself with the king, hoping he would eventually see the matter in his favor.

The waiting and frustration seemed endless. Eventually, he was plagued with ailments and his face was drawn and white - not much of the spirit of the jester was left and it was difficult to play the frivolous fool. Finally, when Briarie was about eight years old, he thought it necessary to take her to the farm in the Cotswolds to be raised by his mother.

Wayside Child (cont.)
Briarie:

Growing up in the Cotswolds, Briarie blooms . . . a little maid - pretty oval face, very full lips, round mouth - a kissable rosebud. Her blue eyes look enquiringly at the world and those with whom she is surrounded, but she still rests her faith on Parminter. He is her bastion who has never abandoned her. In that rural place, she has schooling enough for her station. She can sew and embroider fine work, and knows the housewifely arts. She admired the icons in the churches and would like to imitate them. Her efforts of painting are hidden away, so that they will not be seen, for it is not considered "proper" for a lady to do this, and she is meticulously proper. She satisfies this desire to make art by embroidering tapestry pictures - using many colors of silks, if she can get them.

She is still cautious as she performs her good works and careful in her associations. She has seen what has happened to the jester when he went afoul of powerful folk. She removes herself from those in power, and will have none of the climb toward it, preferring the safe, uncensored life of rural Cotswold - far from the eye of the monarchy. She has been a good and dutiful daughter - showing in all that she does, the powerful feeling she has for her father and her "grandmother," who has taught her so much, and protected her, even once placing her body between herself and an attacker. She never forgot that. Briarie is filled with love for the woman who fought for her safety. If it had ever come to such a pass again, she would have fought with the spirit of a lion - would have even given her life for Parminter or his mother.

Finally, Parminter had not been able to stand it any longer, and allowed his mother to initiate the climax. Madam Parminter was saddened over the new king's state of affairs, for she had been fond of him when he was little - having known him with her heart (that organ which sees the possibilities in another, rather than his flaws). Still she would not have returned to court to beg from him were it not for the need of her own son. She had asked for naught from the old king when he was alive - now, she would like to see her son receive that which was rightfully his, that which the old king had promised to be given him. Even though before the death of the old King, it had been placed in the management of another it should have been her son's. Although he nearly despaired of it and said he will never have the titles to this boon which had been promised, she felt she must try. The prince had once been fond of her, too, when he had been a child at his mother's knee.

They were attacked on the road, returning to his mother's house. Madam Parminter and Briarie had been in the wagon, he riding alongside. The weather was cold and misty, so the top and sides of the wagon were covered, but Brairie and Madam Parminter heard the noise of approaching riders, the jangling of stirrups and upraised voices. They had to struggle for balance when the wagon stopped so suddenly - then the tarpaulin was ripped back by a man with a drawn sword. "Oh! The shock of it! To see the villain standing there like wicked death itself!" was how Madam Parminter later described it, but she had recovered quickly and levered her body to cover the child. At the same time, she raised her arms to shield them from the swordsman. When he waved his weapon, her hands snatched at the blade to prevent it from striking them (an automatic response which had been unnecessary, since their attackers merely wished to frighten, not to murder them). Then, the tarpaulin was thrown back over them, and Parminter was swept away with their attackers. By the time they were able to alight and run around to the other side of the wagon, she and Briarie could see only their backs as they rode away. Madam cried out something - she knew not what, but it was a plea from a mother's heart - a plea to spare her son. As she watched them disappear into the distance, her cut fingers dripped profusely, staining the gown she had been given by the late queen.

Their driver, aged and infirm that he was, was not harmed, so that he was able to take them home again. Huddled in the corner, widow Parminter wept all the way - to Briarie's distress. She tried to comfort her in her little girl way - with soft, feathery words and gently stroking the back of the lady's hand. But, her attention was more distracted, her eyes were riveted on the blood which seeped unceasing from the alarming wounds on her grandmother's fingers - it was ruining all that lovely lace and her best cuffs that she had worn to see the king. She had watched as grandmother sewed the cuffs into her sleeves, admiring the beautiful lace which had been carefully laid away for just such a fine occasion as this visit to the king. Briarie, impressed by these treasures which had come from the old queen, had admiringly traced - with one fingertip - the outline of roses in the delicate mesh. Now, blood was ruining that cherished gift from the late queen, and grandmother does not seem to know or care. Instead, she is sighing, weeping; whispering to herself that she must intercede with those she knows for his safety and for his release. "What evil games men play!" she says, when at last she notices the child's face, awash with silent tears, turned up to hers.

They took him so that they could "talk" to him - to warn him not to cry for what he could not have. Afterward, he was returned to the king, so that he could have the message from his own lips, and therefore, believe it was true. He was only a fool, they said, so they did not spend much time on him. The threat toward his "daughter" and his mother had been enough. They had seen behind the mask he usually wore, and could tell from the mouth fallen open, the worried eyes. . . No, he would not give them any trouble.

When Parminter stood before him, trembling and made awkward by his anger, the young king had already been primed by those unprincipled men, so he had his speech rehearsed and felt sure of himself. His voice was soothing, gentle and his pronouncement was (he thought) reasonable.

He asked Parminter to be reasonable, too. He questioned why a mere servant of the king had been promised such an estate in the first place - an estate worthy of a nobleman? It was unreasonable! He implied that Parminter's claim had somehow been a mistake - his sire, the old king, could not have known what he was doing. (He had no knowledge of the duties Parminter had performed for the King - of the trust he had placed in him.) What could Parminter say now, when the old king wasn't there to uphold his claim? Who would protect his mother and Briarie if he spoke? So, he stood mute in the full knowledge of the futility of protest.

Encouraged by his silence, King Edward was quick to console, eager to make some restitution. He had always enjoyed this man who could tell such funny stories and was so charming to be with. He wanted to retain his friendship, as he wished to retain all his friends. He did so like charming people around him. Therefore he smiled cajolingly and pressed upon him, with white, soft fingers studded with rings, the scraps left of his father's promise - the title to the other part of the estate; the farm in the hinterlands and some lands adjoining it in addition. "Take it, take this in exchange," he urged, "and be soothed. It is a fine farm and more land than you would have had." Edward felt generous, but Parminter knew it was a poor substitute for that valuable piece which had been stolen. Yet, even as he thought of spurning it he seized the titles - for he had declared to himself that he would not leave with nothing at all. Then, with gall rising in his throat, he bowed and left the royal presence - shaking the dust of the place from his feet and swearing to be through with castles and kings forever.

As he rode back to the Cotswolds, Parminter's thoughts raged - against the men who had waylaid him and had deluded the king - using him as a puppet for their own desires - and against Edward himself, who was so easily led - preferring to live in a dream, rather than reality. He harked back to their boyhood days, and told himself Edward the second was spoilt.

His father, the old eagle, had gone out to rob the nests of others and had left his own aerie to be befouled. The heir had been raised in the company of doting, fluttering women, except for one who was also cruel. She and her husband had emasculated young Edward. "Thin-faced, mean bitch!" he thought as her face rose before his mind's eye. As a boy, Parminter had always avoided her. All that time, her husband had been behind the scenes - biding his time, watching, assessing the puny prince aright. Now, their time had come, and they were reaping their harvest. His thoughts erupted into voice; startling his horse, he howled a curse, "May God damn their souls to hell for that is what they deserve!"

All the way home, his thoughts enslaved him in bitterness. He had heard those at court say that Edward "wasted his seed where it could do the kingdom no good." He was thoroughly disgusted with the Royal house. They were all depraved, in one way or another. . . . Nothing straight about any of their dealings. A rotten house - its stench seemed to follow him from milepost to milepost. He cleared his throat and spat heavily on the ground, as though he could rid himself of the foul taste of it.

It was some years before he could forget.

(Eventually, even those who had been glad enough that the king was weak and pretended to be his friends in order to use him for their own purposes, had finally reached a state of revolt - or revulsion - against him. . . and, ironically, it was these same people who had become his most virulent enemies - calling for an end of it. In the end, not only did they cancel his reign, but they made sure he could never reclaim the throne!)

The Farm:

A flowery field, red poppies . . . other, less bold, posies among them. . . Parminter is walking knee-deep in them. He is hot and sweating from stored anger and tension but this is easing as he surveys his humble "estate." He has always loved poppies. On the hillside before him is a stone tower, a pleasant place . . . so sweet . . . surrounded by fragrant wildflowers. Beyond it are blue hills, below is a pleasant valley which would be filled with golden grain in season (and so he allows himself to dream). A slight breeze ruffles his dark hair and cools his face. It seems to bestow a blessing on his decision. It would be well to be away from those who ruled the new king - away from all the plotting and subversion. He would come here and bring his adopted daughter. His mother perhaps, would join them. He must set to work to build onto the lone tower which stands there on the hill. "Yes" the breeze whispers to his hopeful, rising spirit, "Yes!" it can be done.

* * *

Like a tinkling bell a young woman's laughter rings from the hill house and echoes over the pleasant valley - it is the girl-child, Briarie - now a young woman. I can see that she is happy. . . . Her smile stretches her face for joy, her eyes are alight with love - the love she has for a young man. . . He is dark, like Parminter, and tall and slim. She wraps her arms around his and walks snug against him. He is merely a villager - for his family are merchants - but he is noble in her mind. He and Briarie are visiting her father's farm as they do often, for it is not far from their village home.

There is a table set under the trees, overlooking the valley. It was brought there a long ago, and is never put away now, but remains in that spot - season to season. The first summer that they sat there and whiled away the time had been so satisfying that he will not allow it to be moved, for they might destroy that gentle atmosphere it evoked. If the table rots, he will build another on the spot.

They spend many contented hours here. All is green, for summer has returned once more, so they have eaten their meal and, as usual, they tarry to enjoy each other's company. Briarie's children race in and out through the trees, then down into the meadow to play. In the quiet after their passing, she can hear that familiar gentle rustling of the wind in the leaves above them. It is like a sound she remembers from long ago - the swishing of the ladies' skirts as they hurried down the hall to see to the needs of their queen - a scene which was vividly impressed on little-girl memory - although somewhat dimmer now. They were dressed in beautiful gowns of vibrant-colored, exotic materials, their faces pale, indistinct orbs under tall caps hung with veils - that lovely gossamer that floated behind them on the breeze from their passing. It was all so far and away that now it seemed merely a child's dream.

She looks across the table at her father. She knows he does not yearn for that time. His face is serene, with just a few thread-like wrinkles to mark his age. No longer is he given to excessive scowls or foolish grins - just quiet good humor; a twinkling eye. He is a calm man, a rustic fellow now - never talking about his former life. It is as though he never had one other than this. She remembers but refrains from talking about it except for those little reminiscences they share that please or stir their hearts. He still likes to tease her that she sank her thorns into him and made him her prisoner.

He is the peacemaker here. The people in the parish come to him to arbitrate their grievances. His manner is mild but he is wise, and educated beyond them, since he used to listen to the lessons of the king's children.

He feels her look upon him and when he turns, his dark eyes light up from within at her smile. No, she has no doubt that he is satisfied with his lot, and her heart fills to overflowing with love and pride in him.

Parminter surveys his world - his family - and his heart hurts with the enormous gratitude he feels. The view is lovely - the valley and the surrounding hills in colors of green, blue, gold, and when the wildflowers bloom, there will be vibrant red. His house is plain, and they have forgotten his name, but he lives a full life. True, the work is hard - his hands are callused - but he has found it is good to exercise the body, and good for the mind to live in such a setting. They have plenty - bread and cheese, milk, ale, fruit from the orchard. . . Simple foods, simple joys . . . his daughter and grandchildren. . . His wife, a dark plump woman, laughs at him and ruffles his hair playfully while she leans over the table to refill his cup.

He sips and savors. Ah, yes! He is content. The grand folk have all forgotten him, and what a blessing that is! Such a delight, this feast beneath the rustling trees; a scene always repeated - to his great joy - with each warm season. He would not give this up for all the world's riches. Freedom - that was the main thing. . . and with that freedom came a sense of ease and love. And their love was free, too, passed around among all who feasted at the table - his wife, his daughter, her husband, and their children. Their love flowed all unbound, not tied up within, not parceled out grudgingly, nor fearfully, nor saved to be given out as favors under certain circumstances. No, their love was restful, free and flowing. It, too, moved on the breeze, mingling with each one there, reviving, refreshing them while they were bathed in it. "Ah," he thinks, as he leans back, stretches his long limbs and opens up his soul to that sensation "and what a lovely bath it is!"

* * *

Dear Richard,

I have several more stories at this time. I was editing them and then this one came. I am guessing that it came last and in the "wrong" chronological order because it contained a lesson I need to deal with in my life at the present time. If this is my past life, Eastern teaching would say this is "unfinished karma" for me. I have always had conflict with organized religion. I was born into a family deeply rooted in an evangelical Protestant church. I was disturbed by that church's "superiority" – their judgment and condemnation of others who did not share the same theology. However, I could also see that harshness was smoothed out at times with mercy and forgiveness when the words of Jesus were allowed in.

I knew you wanted to publicize this book as past life memories of my own, and you know that I didn't like that idea. I thought the reason for my reluctance was my integrity; that I must be sure that everything is accurate. But, I know that can't be done because of the ambiguity of whole sections or events that I see and don't understand, not to mention lost or cloudy details. Also, I don't want to *teach* reincarnation because I sense that all our life experiences may be illusory. But when I got down to the roots of this reluctance, I realized the real reason was my fear of attack. I think I was more afraid of being attacked than the danger of not maintaining my personal integrity. I couldn't help feeling I would be persecuted over this book. And then this story came.

Now, I have decided that if I do the best I can with what I have, I will still have my integrity. The Protestant southerners I grew up with may be shocked by my "heresy" and my relatives may never speak to me again, but I have to overcome this fear at this time. What is more, I have to forgive any perceived attacks and let it go.

This story deals with the persecution by "Christians" of certain free-thinking people for their beliefs of that period. So, as we are exploring reincarnation, this could be a strong indication of a "past life" of my own. Anyway, I knew I needed release from this problem and asked for help.

Then, today while meditating, I received the answer. I saw a staircase and I am on it, but instead of going onward, I turn around and look back at the step behind me. When I do, I am overcome with shame and scorn for the stupidity that step held. I am fussing at it, lecturing it for its inferiority.

"Bing!" I could plainly see that without that previous step I would not be there on my present step. Of course, this also told me that the step on which I now stand also holds mistakes for which I will have to accept correction before I can go upward. Condemning the previous step and those who must be using it is, in effect, condemning myself. Even though I may not remember being in that particular problem area, I had to have been. If fact, I realize I am stuck on the step I am presently on by looking back and not focusing on where I am headed. I perceived this as a ladder away from the ego world and upward into enlightenment or "Heaven." We are all on it, on different steps but all going to the same place, in our own time. I also realize I am not really higher up than anyone else. I had better not scorn the guy behind me now, because when I turn around, he may be ahead of me and I may need his assistance. Who knows how long my journey may be and whether I might have to descend and begin again on another level?

But I can't worry about that. I have to focus on today, the present step.

I can't tell you how peaceful this realization has made me. I hope I can now leave behind the torment I had hidden away, but which this story revealed.

Anyway, here is a story that is not so pleasant and may indeed reveal something about myself and my own need to forgive.

Stargazer

For some days I keep getting flashes of a gray stone house on a knoll, surrounded by brown vegetation. There are no trees immediately around it. It is a two story dwelling or perhaps three if the lower one is right on the ground. It is unornamented; just a gray block of stone with no porches or appurtenances that I can see from the front. Yet it attracts me with its simplicity, its straight flat face. There is bright sun, fiery sun in my eyes that makes me think of "Sunny Spain."

Another day: The first thing I see is a vine twining over stone. It has small pink flowers on it at this time but somehow I know small fruits will follow which can be eaten, although they are very tart. A woman approaches and she bends, struggling under this hanging vine that forms an arch over her head. She is not truly fat, but has a comfortable belly beneath her long, dark-colored gown. Her skirt has a flowered pattern that somehow I feel focused on. I wouldn't think a peasant could have such a fabric, hand-figured in this manner. Then it comes to me that she did the embroidery on the fabric of her skirt herself, work at which she excelled. She makes all her clothes, is a skilled seamstress. A voice chatters in French here, yet I had thought she was in Spain. She is of the petite bourgeoisie? She is comfortably well-off. Her husband is dead, had been a merchant? On her head is a stiff white hat or bonnet. This "bonnet" has a flat hoop of a brim projecting outward and framing her face, and a skirt at the back of it covers the nape of her neck. It may have been a linen cloth and a white box hat of some kind on top of it. I can't figure this out, because I haven't seen anything quite like it before. She wears an apron, a kind of overall, in her house, but not today when she visits this place.

She is not supposed to be here.

She is fussing to herself, mumbling against the vine and bits of stone underfoot that cause her to stumble. She is not well-shod for walking in the rubble of this place, the stones making their sharp outlines felt through the thin shoes and several layers of hose she wears. The pain of walking on them echoes the pain in her heart. She thinks, what kind of relentless hate was this that would cause people to tear apart a stone building, working mindlessly and tirelessly, fueled by their rage for days until the building was rendered uninhabitable? She looks upward, for it had been a tall house, seen for a far distance across the fields. Now only parts of it remained and that was vine-covered. But even if it had not been ruined, she felt she could have done it with her own hands. In her mind, the house and the property somehow had been the reason she had lost him, her beloved father.

Yet, it had been his legacy, and it was not fair that he had not been able to enjoy it all of his life. He had worn velvet as a child (she had a portrait of him thus, with his dog). While he'd lived here, life was good and wealth was theirs. It was not for herself that she minded so much, but for her father, whom she had loved so. She would have given it all with both hands, if she could have kept him.

She raises her fist and curses the house, flecks of saliva on her lips from the force of her anger. She paces angrily, then gives in to despair, leans against the house, weeping bitterly, and letting go of the anguish. But it does no good. Making her way across the rubble, she moves left to the wall of the old building. The lintel is ornately carved. She runs her fingers over the carving in the stone that frames the doorway. Her memories flood and flutter a heart so sore that she gasps from the pain of it.

She lifts the hem of her dress. Under it, pinned into a fold of her petticoat she has a key. She unpins it and uses it to unlock the door of this house. It would have been impossible for her – in woman's dress - to scale the ruins and remain unseen otherwise. She does not want to be discovered here, so the key was necessary. Most of the upper part, the roof and part of the upper story, part of the left hand side of the stone walls, are gone. She enters a large room, closes the door and locks it behind her. It is littered and dusty, derelict and sad. She knows it well, since she lived here as a girl. Then she goes right to the end where the fireplace is, looks at something lying there with writing on it. As I watch her, her face changes rapidly with her mood: At first, her mouth is bitter and tight, then her face softens as her eyes look inward at some pleasant bit of memory, only to crumple up with grief again when her inward vision returns to tortured scenes.

About midway through the room there is a narrow staircase built against the wall. There had been other rooms beyond the staircase, on that side, but this is ill-defined now. Slowly, carefully she climbs the stairs to the second story. Pushing at the door, which hangs crooked and sadly gaping, she goes straight down the hall where there had been a window. She had always loved looking out this window, but now what was left of the wall has fallen outward, leaving a crumbling hole instead. The scene outside is the same, however - a patchwork of cultivated fields and wooded tracts and over all a blue, innocent sky. She stands there a moment, wondering how it could look so innocent when it was traversed by such devils masquerading as servants of God. Such sin done in the name of the Divine! Then she turns away. I hear her panting; her breath is hot and short as she heaves herself along. I feel I am hovering very close indeed, almost inside her. I don't want to be so close. She is a very sad and angry woman. My heart bows over with her sadness. She needs to forgive.

There are the remains of two rooms on the right side of the hall on this floor. She opens the door to the one next to the window, farthest away from the stair and is greeted by a gust of cool air. The wall is broken up on the window side; and she judges it unsafe to enter here. Within the next room there is a carved bed. It was too large to remove and would have had to have been dismantled (there were problems with that, or the vultures would have taken that too). It's hangings, once handsome, now look ragged and poor. That and a chamber pot on a low stool beside it are the only furnishings in the room. The floor coverings are gone and all the tapestries have been removed from the walls. The stone floor in her memory had always been a bit uneven in places. The floor coverings had helped to provide a safer footing. She does not go in, but stands gazing for some time. This had been her father's room and is, therefore, holy to her. There is a window at this end of the hall, also. There had been other rooms on the other side of this floor but little remains now, all dangerously crumbling away. The men who had come here to kill all the heretics would have liked to have kept the house, she knew, but those people within the community who had been frightened by her father had taken the matter into their own hands. They would tear down as much of it as they could, this "wicked nest" of a man they had perceived as evil.

I can see it now, as she sees it: A graying man stripped naked, his wrists and ankles tied down, spread-eagled. They came at him with a fiery brand — to "scourge" him, to draw and quarter him. He was killed as a heretic. Violence, clothes torn from her aunt, who was dragged out of the house, taken before some authority where she was humiliated; spat upon. She, the girl, was there somewhere in the darkened background. She had shrieked her protests but no one had heard her, not even her aunt. Much noise, chaos. The boy, her half-brother, was thrown onto the fire.

This was a religious thing, and a lot of her bitterness and sorrow comes from the fact that she still practices the religion of those who did this to him. I think she cannot be blamed, for she would have been treated the same as her father if she had not professed to it, so she meekly gave in and outwardly has assumed their form of piety. Piety! What a jest! A parody of sacredness in wicked demon's guise. She thinks they are incredibly stupid, these religious people. Revulsion consumes her, loathing rising, strangling her whenever she is confronted with this hypocrisy — both theirs and her own. She cannot shake the fury she has with them, for she lives with it day by day. If she could thrust it from her, this hateful duplicity, this religion she wears like a most scorned and hateful cloak, she would be well. But she cannot do so. She lives within its "protection," imprisoned by that which caused her father's torture and death. So, she is bitter and this gall has leaked into her body, laying waste her bones and sinew.

"The house of the heretic is laid waste and only the crows will nest in it," they had said. What utter fools they were! And are – for some of these fools still live at this time of her visit and she must see them whenever she attends the church or shops in the market. The house, of course, was not part of the plan. They, the ones behind it all, had wanted the property for themselves, including the house. They had not counted on the local people destroying it. They had come here to wipe out the heretics and to steal the property of those they could accuse. But some of the common folk had been spooked by the alchemist practices and astrology of her father. He worked by the light of oil lamps in the cellar, late into the evening. They had seen him working in the depths of his house, the lamplight gleaming oddly late into the night, working secretly on his experiments, studying works of strange people from other lands. They said he was a creature of the night. He studied the stars but to them he was doing God knows what. As they wondered what he was doing, their fearful imagination supplied lurid dreams of what they supposed he did. They declared such odd things had to be of the devil himself. "They" wondered what he was doing down there at night. It had scared them, those lights from the cellar, in evenings when most were abed. What innocent work could take place at such an hour? He never spoke about what he did. He thought if he did it would weaken his mysterious work; would take away some of its magic. She believed they had imagined him turning iron into gold and couldn't bear the thought that he could have it and they could not. So their fear grew, fed by insane rumors. Still, it probably would have come to nothing had it not been for the crusade against the heretics. He had been caught between two forces, the ignorant class of people who feared him and those relentless crusaders who looked for any slight in order to destroy.

Miraculously, she'd been saved by a friend of her father; a merchant with credentials who was not from this place where her father had lived. He had smuggled her home with him, as though she were a relative traveling with him. She was lucky that he had been there that day; that he had recognized her and that she had not been recognized in the chaos. After some time in his household, they were married. She was grateful to him. He was older, and even though he was aggressive in business, he was a kind man. He was not a dreamer like her father. He was practical. Although he had respected her father for his intelligence and liked to debate with him about philosophy and alchemy, he knew the way of the world - the way it had always been and, he said, the way it would always be. No nonsense for him. Ironically, although he was without blemish in the eyes of the church, he was actually much more of a cynic than her father had been. Yet, they did not talk about that, he and she. He was outwardly pious and required that also of her. Yes, it was the way of the world – the safe way. And now that her father was gone it was also her way.

(I will call her Marigold, since she has yellow hair. I have done some research and it would appear from the clues that I have, that this was either in or near Languedoc, which was on the border of Spain and once ruled by Spain, but later was largely independent until it was taken over by France. It would fit with the "Cathar" or Albigensian crusade in which many thousands of people were tortured and killed by Christian crusaders. Pope Innocent III offered the lands and possessions of those he labeled "heretics" to any who would take on the crusade to wipe out the Albigensians. Marigold's father was of Aragon heritage and did not consider himself "French." The noblemen of this region were tolerant and he had an understanding with them. He respected their authority more, I suppose, than that of the church hierarchy. But mainly he had been oblivious to church politics, his nose in his study, his work, his business in trade. In the end, his ties with Spain had not helped him. I think he was in authority, a mayor, perhaps, or a councilor.)

She had not had a mother. She thought of that woman as her father's first wife who had soon thought better of her marriage. It had been a terrible mistake, this woman had said. After the birth of her daughter she had pleaded with the church and her husband. She requested that she be allowed to go into a nunnery. To the church officials' surprise, her husband gave her permission. She could not have been allowed in, otherwise. If she was unhappy, he would be a fool to force her to stay, he said. What would that accomplish, except more misery?

The little girl didn't mind much, for her aunt was there, her mother's sister. Unfortunately for her father, he hadn't thought much at the time about his decision, about being celibate thereafter. He was cursed with the lower cravings of man; was not a saint. The clergy, hypocrites that they were, would count her mother as unmarried, yet they would not absolve her husband of the marriage. Any association he began thereafter would be a sinful affair, unsanctioned by the church, devoid of marriage, until the death of the first wife. No, he was not a saint. The aunt had a child. This happening did not at all disturb Marigold, who loved her aunt, who was gentle and kind, affectionate to all. But this "sin" further increased her father's infamy among his neighbors and those distant ecclesiastical "superiors" who heard rumors. Actually, it gave them ammunition, for he had academic friends who would have protected him if it had not been for this flaunting of the values of the church. Those in the church in higher places could get away with such things, but no, not him. What hypocrisy!

And hypocrisy is what he had hated and rebelled against.

He took Marigold aside in those times, to attempt to explain to her the weaknesses of the church, and his discoveries regarding the Divine nature, for he believed he should share this, this inheritance, with his offspring. Surely, he reasoned, the gold of spirit was a greater portion to leave his children than estate and privilege.

He hardly noticed his wife's absence. It had never been a love match and he had his work, his science – astrology, alchemy, philosophy. These things took all his thought. As for God, he believed in a divine presence that kept all these things in order. God, whose time and patience was limitless, was the Celestial Juggler with many mysteries left up His sleeve, offering man only tantalizing glimpses, inviting him to solve it if he could. It was these mysteries that he sought to peek into, begging to be let in on the hidden . . What? What was it? He didn't know really. He only knew there *was* more - much more, and he needed to follow the clues. Each day, reading and pondering the writings and beliefs of others, his thoughts would alternately skim or plod along as he sought the truth within. Suddenly, at a point when his thought had lapsed into perfect stillness, he would meet at an intersection with the mind of God and for a moment a burst of light from Heaven would illumine his mind.

He liked to say that man could plot the ways of the divine, could make a world of symbols for the real beneath; could make names for the nameless. But the world was merely a mask on God's face, a curtain drawn over Heaven. And it was well to remember that time and space could be stopped by that awe-full stillness of God.

Oh, yes. He believed in GOD.

Some days he wandered absently, with sparkling eyes that made her think he had made a wondrous discovery, that he had plumbed the depth of another miracle. Outside on cloudless nights he studied the paths of the stars. (The meteor he had seen when he was young had thrilled him and left him marked for the life he later adopted.) On such nights he lay on a blanket on the ground, staring overhead and talking to himself. Those who saw him there, when they went to find some stray livestock or fetch a midwife on such a night, said he was mad or possessed.

She, his loving daughter, awakened by the moonlight illuminating her room, would patter across the cold stone floor to her bedroom window. Sometimes, if she were lucky, she would see him there and would creep out to lie beside him. On these magic nights he would tell her how the stars influenced the affairs of men. But even the stars and planets were only the symbols of greatness, of that which lay behind it, within it. They were the manifested. The truly great was the Mind that made Manifest. This she never understood and gave up trying. But, Oh! The peace and glory of it, lying there under the stars listening to her father's patient, low voice, following his finger, the flourish of his fine hand as he pointed out the constellations, the phases of the moon (always her favorite heavenly orb), the planets, telling her in his gentle voice what the auras and streaks around them meant.

He studied astrology and alchemy: the changing nature of things. He was a brilliant man for his time. He had bound pages of works, some from Arab libraries others in Greek. One was on stars and symbols. In his three-dimensional world he looked for symbols and signs that were clues to the higher realms in which he believed.

He wanted to experiment - to unravel mysteries. Sometimes he could see coming events in the reflection of their pond, among the floating clouds and sky reflected there. Too bad he hadn't foreseen his own danger, but it had come upon them so quickly. Suddenly he was called "a beast among men." Some even spied upon him in private moments, to have a look at his feet. They looked for cloven hooves. Their fear infected even her at the same time that she knew better, knew her father was a kind, good man.

He would examine the parts of a flower with her – the wonders of nature – the design of it repeated all around. He said that all of God's creation was in that flower – if he could unlock that mystery, he would *know everything*. She never understood what he meant. But he was not what they said. He worshipped GOD, always begging to understand more of His ways and man's destiny. He tried to explain to her the oneness of all things, the inner dust that is many faceted, manifesting itself in a great variety of matter, yet itself was one. If this oneness could be changed from one manifestation to another, the material itself would change. From dust we came, to dust we must return, he had said. The inner spirit, or inner dust, was gold. The inner life was that which was living particles, and set in motion by God himself, it was, in fact, God. True treasure, genuine gold, was found within. Immortality was within. The outer layer, the darkness, was without. That which is seen by man's eye was lead, or darkness. The goal was always to release that within, to free the light to shine into the outer darkness of matter. (In this way, perhaps, he had agreed with those "heretics" who taught the duality of man.) This was a very ancient teaching, he said.

He was guided in this study by more than one master of the art, and by those who had studied ancient manuscripts. Those men from Arabia and other exotic places had come to talk with him and stayed for some time when they came. All this frightened his neighbors. Those dark-skinned, strangely- garbed men eating at their table had set off that chill breeze of fear. Oblivious to gossip, he had avidly discussed with them the thoughts of Aristotle and the great Arab scientists and philosophers. They told her father about things, the astrologer's stone and such. They had laughed together; shared their interests, their "toys" – scientific gadgets that both amused and fascinated. He had a set of lenses interconnected in a series, so that one flipped down over another, until the desired precision and clarity came into view. Marigold was expected to be on hand only to bring the guest refreshment or to see to his comfort, but covertly she had listened and learned.

She thought she could detect the gold within her father, while he was aglow with his faith, telling her these secret teachings. His eyes gleamed and even his hair sparkled and rose up from his head like an aura of red-gold. He had a misty look on those occasions that further convinced her that he was a special man- not a magician, as he was accused of, but some-how unearthly. She thrilled with the knowledge of it, that her father was touched with something beyond other men. No, the others with whom she came into contact every day were not at all like him. They were dark and stupid; incredibly gross by comparison.

He talked about Peter Abelard. He believed in the love of God, that God forgave all and that true freedom came from that. He did not believe the church had the right to condemn. He hated what they had done to Abelard, and although it went against his belief in forgiveness, he carried a secret grudge against Bernard of Clairvaux, who had begun the hunt for "heretics." Yet, although he had studied the works of many, and respected some of the beliefs of the Albigensians, or Cathars, he had remained loyal to the church. That's why it he had found it incredible that they had turned on him in the end – a man of science, quiet, self-effacing and home loving.

The man who had saved her from the horrors, that friend of her father's, had been good to her. He had taken her into his home and after his wife died, he had proposed marriage to her. She had accepted with gratitude. His wife, small, dark-haired and too weak for the world, had trusted her with her children. Marigold had taken over the household, the children, and the care of the wife. It had been easy to step into the shoes of mistress of the house when the poor lady had finally drifted off in her fever. She, the first wife, had been properly tutored in how to leave the world and enter into heaven by those churchmen who had come to her side. Poor lady, she'd been only partly cognizant of them, mumbling in her fever, asking for water and peering into the dark for Marigold, her support in her need.

His children who had seen her care for their mother and received their daily care and attention from her, had easily accepted Marigold as their second mother. It was continuation in the flow of life, of her life, also. She was already equipped with the memory of this man at her father's table with his other visitors. He had laughed with them, debated with good will and struck bargains in trade at their table. Her father had owned properties and storehouses involved in the purchase and sale of goods. He had once taken her to the sea coast, to this very man's home. She had loved the smell of the sea. So her marriage was also a continuation, because it was a tie to her father. It had been contracted with ease because of her memories.

She had borne no children. Perhaps it was because her husband was no longer young. She was a good stepmother to his children; kind, attentive, alert to their needs. In return they loved her and continued to cherish her after their father's death and into her old age.

She was never able to talk to her husband about what her father had disclosed to her. She could only touch on a few vague references about stars, science; nature. Anything more and he would be respectful but instantly distant. Thus she soon learned that he saw her through different eyes than those with which he had regarded her father. Her father had been an eloquent, amazing man. She, although she was his daughter, was merely a woman, the caretaker of his house and children. But also, this man, although he loved to debate philosophy, was blind in some ways, unable or unwilling to understand the deeper way. (*If she could have seen into his mind, though, she would have seen those horrible images that came back to him each time he thought of her father - of darkness, flames and blood. He was not a warrior, nor did he think any cause, other than defense of his family and property was worth murder. This he had to keep to himself - a lonely man yearning for peace in a world of warriors.*)

She took an interest in his trade, for he was a prosperous merchant at the seacoast. He traded not only in articles of necessity but those precious things which only the wealthy could afford. Fabrics were her main interest - lovely silken transparencies with gold threads woven through, satin imported to be embroidered locally. He needed her advice in those. She arranged with needlewomen and advised the styles to be used which most appealed to those women who could afford them. These fabrics were so

costly and so amazing that to cut them unnecessarily was strictly forbid-
den. The fabrics themselves became the main adornment. The styles of the
time bowed to the dictates of the materials and showcased the fabrics in
swaths, draping, folding, pleating cunningly in ways that most revealed the
richness of color, weave and embroidery. With time, such fabrics became
her expertise.

One day he had taken sick, and weakened away – and she saw him for
the first time as a frail old man. It seemed so wrong that she couldn't get
over it. He had always been so solid, so strong; needing no one. He died.
And, suddenly, she had an odd sensation of suspension, as though her feet
were no longer planted on firm soil. She became uneasy. Only then did
she realize her dependence on him. On his solidity, she had grown with
courage and had been allowed to give of herself to all around her. She had
always been conscious of gratitude toward him. She had not realized she
had loved him. Now she knew.

By this time his sons were grown and were managing their business of
trade and the grandchildren were growing up. Soon, she knew that things
were well in hand, so (abruptly it seemed to her children) she turned her
back on the wealth of her deceased husband's estate. Let the young deal
with the problems of guarding possessions from the vultures, she though.
She was weary and yearned for peace. And so she retired to a cottage in the
foothills. It was a simple place located near a well-worn path taken by both
peasants and gentry. There she sat and observed. Human nature amused
her when it was not vicious. She lived alone, unencumbered, free to think
her thoughts, to pray. Her stepchildren and grandchildren saw to her needs.
Food, necessities and money were given her freely as it was needed. Not for
her the amassing of earthly treasures, only those treasures within. For all
during the years as a merchant's wife and widow, she had held deep in her
heart that core of teaching she had remembered from her father.

* * *

Poor soul! In her age, Marigold has large, swollen hands. There are deep wrinkles around her knuckles which are painful and feel stiff. Her skin stings outside, inside she has aches and pain when she touches anything. Her feet are in similar condition. She wears shapeless shoes, with eyelets to lace up the middle, over the arch of the foot. Lots of hose, I think. Again, her garment is ornately embroidered, done at a time when she had been able to do such work with her hands. She wears a cap on her head, but it is not the same one that I saw before. It has curled corners in front. She is standing on a slope, looking down into a valley where there is a castle-like building, stone with two gothic turret-steeples. I see it in a vivid flash. It is very solid and impressive, but not overly embellished. I think it is a cathedral. It seems to be in a green valley. She does not live here. As she looks at it, she is thinking about the crusaders and wondering when they will return.

She had a good deal of time to think. A rich merchant's wife had not so much to do, and after she became a widow there was more time to remember her father and his teaching. What he had told her, how he believed, seemed much more important to her after they had killed him. It was what she had left of him, and it was precious. She needed to understand, yet knew there was a great deal that she could not, nor would she ever truly understand. After years of meditation on the things she had overheard or which he had shared with her, she had narrowed it all down into a certain kernel of his philosophy. This she kept quietly in her heart, discussing it with no one, and took it into the hereafter with her – for she had known no one in the world who wanted it or could put it to use.

The teaching of the Stargazer (student of philosophy, astrology, alchemy, and religions of the world) as understood by his daughter:

The essence of our existence on earth was thus. God in his creation gave life freely to his son. His son was all that he extended. All forms of life came from this one extension, but remained one with God, from his mind. Then came "the fall" - the alien thought that arose from a segment of this life form that there could be separation from God, an existence apart from him.

The fear and self hatred that came from this thought, this thought that was thought in isolation, apart from the mind of God, had created a faux world, an illusion that did not exist in God's reality. Because it did not exist in God's mind of creative thought, nor was it his will, the world *perceived by man* was not real. God's son, Adam, slept, and dreamed of this world, cursed by fear, death and isolation from God. God's spirit gave his sons what they thought they wanted, but kept his will intact. They would not truly be separated, but would exist in that dormant state until their will became one with God's again. In this existence they would learn their way to Heaven, to be reunited with God again. Therefore, the earth, with time and space, was a lost world, and would continue so until we laid down our arms against one another and against God. Forgive, Jesus had said, yet we don't really know the depths of Christ's forgiveness. We only understand what we see with our eyes and hear with our ears, and in such a world as ours, wasn't that based on a falsehood, created in violence against God? There was a greater dimension, beyond time, a still place where God himself dwelled, and as her father spoke of this, his voice would trail away, his eyes went inward to search for it, that Heaven on earth that he was always seeking, yet sometimes despaired of ever finding.

Duality, he said, was not exactly as taught by the new religion. It had been formed by separation from God. This was perceived as satan, or that which was anti-God. It was that part of man that harbored hatred, fear, and guilt - that which hated man and would kill him for his guilty sin. Christ was to be the Messiah, the savior. Christ was the one who had succeeded in finding his way back to God and who had returned to save his brothers, by making the path, figuratively and spiritually, so that we could all join with his spirit and awaken from the illusion.

The Christ was born into the man, Jesus. (In this her father held fast to the Church.) Jesus the Christ came to redeem us from our "sin" (that which was called by other names in other countries). All was forgiven. We could now be healed. We could now accept joy instead of fear and hatred. All we had to do in return was to allow the forgiveness of Christ, to relinquish judgment against our brother. This was necessary so that the collective consciousness of man could be exonerated. We were one. We must forgive as one. We were all in the mire together, and must forgive to be forgiven. We cannot judge, because if we do, that judgment is kept alive in our consciousness against ourselves. In order to free ourselves, we must free each other. Love must be the victor. And God is Love.

How can that be? She had once asked him. If a man steals from his neighbor, should we let it go and just forgive him? He will be punished because that, he told her, is the law of the world. But God's law is the greater. The neighbor may reclaim his own, the law may punish the thief, but Consciousness must forgive him, the offended neighbor must realize he himself needs forgiveness and in order to be forgiven, he must forgive the thief, who is his brother, who cannot be divided from him. That is the consciousness of Christ. We must take on the consciousness of Christ, he said, again and again.

The church, he told her in a harsh voice, had kept the treasure of Christ, his forgiveness of sins, in their own hands and away from the people. Instead of diminishing guilt they had raised it to a high degree and held it over people's heads, filling them with fear, and then telling them they could only be forgiven through them, the church leaders. Thus they had stripped Christ of his precious salvation and kept it hostage, to be doled out as they saw fit. They placed themselves between God and his sons, telling the sons that their church alone held the key that opened the door to heaven. Bah! He said, incensed at the gall and stupidity of such men that they would expect guilt and groveling to them as "the disciples of Christ," would expect the toll of guilt for expiation of their sins. Christ was blameless and experienced no guilt. And that! He exclaimed, was what brought about his death. They, the collective "satan" could never bear that! It would be the end of it. No, he must be killed, murdered, so that guilt could exist, so that satan, the rebellious entity of collective man, could continue to live on in the earth. She did not understand this, but she sensed he was right about the church using guilt for their own ends, and that they themselves were tools of satan when they did this. Some things he said frightened her, though, for attacking the church was surely heresy, and the church killed those accused of that.

She had since thought much about the lack of guilt of Jesus. It explained the fury of the crowd whose rage could only abate by annihilating him. She had wondered why people would kill an innocent man. But, that of course, was why - he was innocent and knew it. He had no guilt. The guilty must see guilt everywhere and in everyone. The guiltless were guilty. The collective consciousness of mankind, aligned against the forgiveness of God, could not exist without guilt.

When her father was killed, this was brought to her consciousness in an extraordinary way. It was almost as though he had sacrificed himself for her understanding. The guilty hated those who had none. Her father showed no remorse for his "sins" that he had committed against the church. He had not committed any against God or Christ, he claimed. Thus he committed his soul to God and his body to dust.

She thought his time had been too short, for surely he had much to share with others. But, did they want it? Apparently not. There were those of his friends who had studied and debated with him, who cherished his insights. This was worth his life, was it not? This knowledge was carried forward, if not in written word, perhaps at least in conscious thought? Wasn't all that was good in this world saved for all mankind? She wondered if his thoughts would perhaps be found in the dreams or visions of those yet unborn. She prayed that it would be so. Only those like her father could save the world. Most men were stubbornly turned away to their own devices of pain.

And, she often wondered, while he was tortured and murdered, through his pain and horror – had he forgiven his "brothers" who were doing this to him?

She still goes out to make purchases, to do errands and duties. Whenever she makes her way back home and enters her house, immediately her little maid comes to help her take off her wraps, her shoes. She puts on an apron, slippers and goes to the settle by the fire, which is blazing and warm-looking. She lies on the settle, with cushions. Her maid brings her soup. She sits up, but she can't hold the spoon, so the maid gently feeds her, she slurping it up (this is not considered bad manners). She is grateful and tells her maid she is a good girl. The patient maid has blonde hair just barely showing beneath her cap that ties under her chin. She wears a rusty black gown, with natural ecru-white apron. Her skirt is a wrap around arrangement, very full. A lot of things she wears tie around her waist, which makes her uncomfortable. (I got the name, Marie, again)

* * *

Here she is again. There are stalls and sellers everywhere. I think it is a fair. I see a man, a knight or soldier, on horseback charging through the crowd in her

direction. There is a boy in his way, whitish blonde hair, "witless;" he drools. He
must have been the lowest of the low, for he wears a brown, long, rough fabric shirt
and no shoes. This horseman is going to run him down as though he is nothing. He
is an arrogant, unfeeling clod - ironic since he is a "Christian" knight or serves a
knight. But that is why he is arrogant. He is superior to the masses. Her mind
protests, this is wrong, an unchristian thing, "He is nothing in your eyes, but he is
still a child." It all runs together fast here. She puts herself in the way to protect the
child, the man and horse's bulk shoving her aside. The man does not care that she is
in the way, for he is high and mighty. But even as she falls she sees that the horse's
eyes roll, he not wanting to hurt her, to trample her. She falls against a market cart.
This cart has four upright narrow posts at each corner. She falls against one, and
it snaps. The broken upright gores her in her spine, a grave injury. Bystanders are
distressed. Some of them know her; know she is a harmless old soul. They come to her
aid and take her home. She was paralyzed then, but mercifully, infection set in so
that she did not have to live in that condition much longer. Her maid, ever faithful,
nursed her until her time came.

In her mind, this was another thing for which religion was to blame.

She had had much time to think while she was arthritic and unable to
do much. Then when she was injured, she suffered yet more and did little but think and dream. She thought of what her father had taught, and
finally it occurred to her that even he had not learned all of what he taught.
He had not found it easy to forgive the church for its failings, its false
teachings, and its judgment. She had inherited this from him, along with
all that wonderful wisdom. She had found it impossible to forgive them for
what they had done to him. Now she knew that they - she and her father -
were guilty too. People went as far as their learning allowed them to go.
They knew not what they did.

She could do nothing but think while she lay paralyzed and dying. Only her mind worked. Her condition was urgent. She needed to review and condense all she had learned from her father, yet there was something more. She observed her faithful maid as she attended to her needs. Before this, she had not delved deeply into the person who was Marie, but now she could do little else. The quiet girl came and she went, into her line of blurring vision, out again, back and forth; doing what was necessary to keep her clean, fed, alive and still seeking, still hanging on to life's thread until she could understand and let go. Then, in one expanding moment, as her maid's face hovered over hers once again, something said *"look!"* and she understood. Marie. Marie was the key to this moment of understanding. And so then she focused, fully, on Marie.

Marie was woven into the fabric of the church. She was a peasant who did as she was told, believed simply and sometimes wrongly. It galled her mistress when her maid seemed a stupid pawn in the church's grasp. In the past, she had sometimes snapped at her for her sheep-like stupidity. But she had restrained herself in these last months. For she had learned all people were groping for truth, in their own time, in their own way. She had often wondered why Marie stayed on with her, seeing to her gross bodily needs, when there must have been a better place for her. Why did she stay, patiently feeding her soup and turning her; changing her bedding? Why did she stay?

It was true that Marigold had been kind to Marie, had taken her on and been generous to her. But she doubted that Marie thought about duty much. She was not analytical. She had enjoyed mulling over the gems of philosophy that Marigold had shared with her on occasion but it was like giving language to something she already knew. Spirit recognized truth, and Marie's spirit was as great as any that walked the earth in bodies. Princes and Popes could learn from Marie. She went along with the shabby construction that was her world: The church, the customs, the inequities - all these were the backdrop of her life and it made no sense for her, a simple creature, to try to make it otherwise. She could only be what she was and try to flower in its harsh soil. Marie had a treasure - that gold that Marigold's father had taught was "the way." She was in touch with the true divine spark within.

Marigold, feverish and fading fast now, had to laugh at her discovery. Marie, for all her worldly ignorance, served Christ well. She looked after her mistress with a simple acceptance of their circumstances. Outwardly, she was indeed limited to what she had been taught, but within she was unlimited. Her heart was free, her soul unbound with the love she had for her mistress and nature – for all of life. When faced with the choice of judgment or love, she always shrugged and chose love. She found it easier so. Marigold always marveled that Marie never seemed to worry about the future nor did she grieve long over the past. She lived timelessly and acceptingly. One day flowed into another like a steady stream and she accepted it as it came, glad for the good she saw in it. She was a flower of the field, doing what came naturally to her; bending with the wind, holding her face up to the sun, glad of the rain. She knew that life was fleeting, that flowers fade and die, but she had that grand hope that they returned to their source, their God.

And so, at the end of her life, Marigold, daughter of the brilliant scientist and philosopher - she who was educated in the great arts, speaking several languages and a seeker of truth - learned her last lesson from her illiterate maid.

* * *

Dear Richard,

I first had the thought that this story took place in "Tunis," not Tunisia as we would call it today. I didn't know exactly where this was, so I looked it up. As usual, some parts of the story seem lacking in substance, while some details are vivid.

As for details that might be related to me personally, I do love colored gemstones with a passion. I despise what my eye finds "ugly" and I love creamy or golden stone architecture.

Actually, many years ago I had an experience that really startled me at the time and I find it actually relates to this story. I was standing in our paneled dining room that we had recently painted an old gold and cream. I thought it was beautiful and peaceful and I was just standing there, loving that. Suddenly I had a visual flash, a vision, I suppose. I saw men in a spa-like pool. A few of them, wearing white tunics, were standing on the paving around it. The surrounding stone was all cream and gold. Even though it quickly came and went, I had the distinct impression of great peace, of quiet joy and brotherhood. It didn't know what to think of it and I didn't tell anyone about it then. I think it was the first time I had seen one of these flashes that I have begun to see since. As startling as that was, you can imagine how I felt when I was well into this story and realized *I was there*! I had returned to that scene I had glimpsed all those years ago!

Ah! Another discovery: *Beauty is the face of Love!* But the question here is, where is beauty, really? Is it what we see or that which creates it?

The Crown

The Disciple

I see a young man - "a Greek." He has black hair, a short, groomed beard, and wears a striped tunic. His fingers glitter with rings, so I assume he is wealthy. He stands on the outer fringe of a crowd that has gathered to hear a follower of Jesus Christ speak to them and answer their questions. He is a man complete unto himself and does not need to push and shove his way to the front to show his importance, nor to indulge himself with unnecessary emotion.

This Greek is an intelligent, educated man and is able to grasp the meaning of resurrection - death of the material life and rebirth into a spiritual one. He relates this to the lessons of nature; such as that of spring and winter - the caterpillar and the butterfly. He is a dreamer and a thinker and ponders all he has heard from the Christian; then he forms from these teachings a pattern for the correct way to live - the way according to Christ, as he sees it.

* * *

The people called "the Corinthians" had gathered around him like moths to his flame. Not only did he have the heat, the fervor, of the new convert, but he was educated beyond most of them. Yet, because he scorned "intellect" in favor of wisdom, his words were simple and easily understood by all. He now stood among them clothed in the simplest garments, unadorned by the affectations of the rich. They saw the rightness of his way, and nodded to each other as he spoke. "It is not the outer man, but the inner man to whom we should give our attention," said he who now called himself a disciple of Christ and of Paul.

The only affiliation between the Corinthians and the other churches of this time was the goal of communion in perfect love. As the Disciple said, "It not only changes the inner soul of a man but permeates the atmosphere around him so that all are benefited by it. Love - who can stand against it? It is sweet, it is subtle, but Oh, the power of it!"

His father was confused. Of course, he would be, since he had never taken religion very seriously. Now his son babbled on about things he did not understand. He was alarmed when his son started selling off all his possessions. He followed him around the house trying to reason with him, and quoting Euripides - which was of little use. This stranger - his son - called himself a "disciple," and practiced love in all his dealing with others. It was difficult to argue with that. He had always believed that one should follow one's convictions - should always search for truth. Since his son seemed to be doing that, what could he say? So, in the end, all he could do was stand by and observe (with a mixture of dismay and respect) as his son exchanged his wealth for provisions to establish a community of these believers of Christ. He had said he would build a place where he and his assembly could remove themselves from their old habits and concentrate solely on living this new philosophy. He did not understand why his son didn't think they could do it here in Greece. Though he was still uneasy when his son finally departed, all he could do was embrace him and wish him well. (Both father and son believed in peace.)

The Corinthians would have followed him anywhere by then. It was a long journey - first across the sea then by cart - to the place they called "Tunis." When they finally arrived at that bit of wilderness that had been offered them, it was evening, and too late to start building their sanctuary.

As his disappointed little flock stood there looking out over the empty sweeping landscape, the Disciple understood their mood. All during the inactive days of their travel they had been anticipating this moment and talking about it together . . . their enthusiasm had been building with each mile of the journey. In their projected imagination they had begun their work right away. Now, as the sun dipped low in the sky, they felt deflated.

He detached himself from them and moved away. Squint-eyed and curious, they watched him as his dark form moved against the brilliant orange sunset. Bending over a pile of rock and, touching and smoothing the stones with his hands, he selected just one. Then he looked to the sky; the sun and, scanning the landscape, he stepped off some paces - counting as he went - first one way then another. After a final look at the sky, he set the stone in the spot where (he announced) the building would stand.

Perhaps it was odd that their hearts were comforted, for it was only one stone planted in the soil, yet it seemed a decision of importance had been made and they had indeed begun. Then in the gathering dusk they silently thanked their God. When they looked again, the brilliant red hues of the western sky were gone - leaving a purple sky. In this way, "Evenstone" got its name. The stone was left exactly where he had laid it, and the building was erected around it.

(That same natural, uncut stone, selected by the sensitive hands and artistic eye of the Disciple could always be seen thereafter, as the center of the intricate pattern of worked, smooth stones which made up the floor of the anteroom. It was a unique color with a mottled appearance. The Corinthians were never to see it's like again and marveled that he should have laid his hands on just such a stone for the first building block. It was a symbol - and the Disciple was fond of symbols, as he also was of symmetry, order and (most of all) beauty - for (he asked himself) was not beauty an expression of Love?

* * *

Eventually, Evenstone became an Eden on earth, for it was a place of serenity, and thrillingly beautiful. Set upon an elevated, grassy plain in the middle of the wilderness, it was a glory to behold in its framework of dark cypresses - deceptively simple, elegant in line, with beautifully wrought arches and corridors. Because the stone used in the building was native rock in shades of mellow gold and cream, it blended with the landscape in which those colors predominated. It was, perhaps, appropriate that the structure was most beautiful when seen from a little distance, bathed in the setting sun. It was beautiful at all times, but it was magic then. A mist would come up from the cooling earth; creating a shimmering veil through which the golden, sun-tinted stone seemed to glow. Coming upon it at any time of day, the traveler would hesitate and stare. At first glance it would not appear to be a magnificent structure - certainly no castle or regal residence. Its lines bespoke a simple place. . . There was no excess of ornament anywhere, yet the visitor - no matter how barbarian he might be - would sense that it was somehow most unusual.

A master planner and designer, the Disciple had made everything to please the eye. During the building, he had stood looking out from each door and gate, to make sure the view from each would be a visual feast. If this man of love hated anything, it was ugliness - it grated on his sensibility; actually bringing pain to his eyes and causing him to squint and recoil.

The location of this "Eden" was a place of seven springs. By the time the sanctuary was finished, two of the springs had been enclosed within the central courtyard; the others flowed outside the building's walls. Some of the outer springs fed a pond, which the brothers had enlarged and stocked with fish. It came to be known that the outer springs and pond were common ground - the use of them free to all who came this way - because the

Corinthians quickly made peace with all the nomadic races who lived in this country, and would give anyone shelter.

One of the springs in the courtyard supplied a fountain. Laid on top of the pipe through which the spring flowed, was an ornate, horizontal cross worked in metal. Each of its four arms formed a waterspout. This fountain with four branches provided water for all those who lived there. The little pool which lay beneath the fountain overflowed into a sluice that filled two larger stone-lined pools. The first pool - just within the room where food was prepared - was for drinking and cooking, and the overflow from this first pool ran into the second, which filled the baths in the atrium, and the overflow from that was channeled back into the garden. The arches within the building and the courtyard were reflected in these pools, and this also was pleasing to the eye. Because of this irrigation, the gardens within Evenstone's walls overflowed with vegetables, many herbs, (including Hyssop, which they called, "the blessed herb") and fruit trees, some of which were cleverly espaliered against the courtyard walls to protect them from the wind.

It gave the Disciple satisfaction to be able to point out that the fountain of the cross was symbolic of the resurrection that nourished them, both spirit and body. One of the brothers had suggested the planting of rue around this fountain pool, but he had said, no, that rue was for sorrow and regret and that they could not regret Christ's sacrifice. No, he said, they would rejoice in the fact that Christ still lived. So, instead, they planted mint; for "rebirth," there.

The mint grew richly in the damp, dark soil around the pool's brim. When one came to fill the cup with precious water and bent humbly to receive it, the cool breath of the mint - mixed with the mist of the fountain spray - would bathe the tired and thirsty one so that he would be doubly refreshed. He would pause a moment - to inhale the cooling scent . . . to feel the mist upon his dry skin. Soon the busy thoughts with which he had come to the fountain would no longer be remembered and he would be thankful for all such "small" blessings. Thus the fountain might have been the greatest element within Evenstone. And the Disciple was well aware of the effect of this and of all the other elements of Evenstone that would help his people attune themselves to their creator.

* * *

In a sudden vision I stand within a room of gold and cream. . . There are sunken baths, and standing around these pools of cool water are men in loose, white garments. They are happy, their faces beaming, eyes alight. . . The picture fades, and I stand a moment, reluctant to part with such feelings of serenity, harmony and brotherhood. . . .

The main building - "the sanctuary" - of Evenstone, was enclosed on three sides by the courtyard in the rear. Its face was graced with a covered walkway that was intersected with seven arches, each arch capped with a point and a small cross - the middle arch being higher than the others. The cedar pillars that held up the roof over this walkway were rough-hewn - to remind them of the cross. Inside, the atrium with its sunken baths was always cool and marvelously reviving. This sanctuary was the residence of the unmarried brothers only.

Behind the courtyard of the sanctuary, were the houses of the married couples and families. Each of these houses was part of an orderly design by the Disciple, being part of a row of three. The houses on each end of each row had shed roofs slanting to the outer side, whereas the middle house had a higher, gabled roof, so that the three in their row presented a pleasing symmetry of line. These rows were continued as Evenstone's population grew.

As years went by, they converted others of this country to Christianity and those from their own country traveled there to join them. Although they were loved and blessed and permitted to run free in the courtyard, children were not allowed in the room for prayer and worship until they were of age. Marriage was allowed but not greatly encouraged, not only because they believed it was a distraction to spiritual thought, but also because they believed the second coming of Christ was imminent.

So firm was their belief that Christ would soon come again that they built a watch-tower where they took turns in watching over the sky, night and day. They reminded themselves often; spending time in contemplation as they waited for this blessed event. They vowed they would not be "the virgin caught without a lighted lamp," as Christ had said. Once, the brother who was on watch in the tower fell asleep and when he awoke, no one was about. It was so quiet and still in the quarters below him that he thought Christ may have come while he slept and that all the others had gone from the earth to heaven - leaving him alone! Struck with fear and guilt for falling asleep at his watch, he raced down the small spiral stairs so hastily that he tripped on his sandals and fell the rest of the way down. He was not greatly injured, but it was laughed about for years, and thereafter he was often called "the hasty virgin."

It is true that the Disciple did not believe that Christ would come again in that manner, but he also believed that the focus on the coming of Christ, whatever physical form it took, would be good for his flock, so he encouraged this.

Some of their members were adept with medical cures and prayers, and received tithes - meat, wild herbs and such - from others who lived in that country who had asked for their help. The foremost of these healers was Hannah. She was old and her face was a mask of wrinkles, but her black eyes were very alive. She was a Christian Jew and the mother of the Preacher who had been the Disciple's friend and mentor. When the Preacher had died in prison, the Greek had taken Hannah into his own home. He called her "mother" out of respect, but he did indeed care for her as if she were his own mother. Now, at Evenstone, she was valued for her healing hands and the medicines she made from herbs and oils.

There were, also, those farmers who plowed the fields, reaped the harvest, stored it, and raised geese and other livestock. Others were scribes, who - with quills made from goose feathers - copied the books of the disciples, other spiritual writings and the records of the sanctuary, onto scrolls that were kept in carved stone boxes. Then there were the carpenters and masons who had labored so carefully and so long, and the Roman who had come to work there. It was he who had designed the conduit system of water supply from their central spring and fountain. . . Then, when the work was done, he had decided to stay; for the attraction of Evenstone was very strong.

Everyone at Evenstone had taken a vow of simplicity, in order to live as Jesus had lived, and the emphasis was placed on developing the beautiful soul within, rather than the outer image. Therefore, they had no silver or gold vessels, for they shunned that which was purely for material value, yet the craftsmen among them made carvings that were both useful and decorative. These carvings from wood and bone (and even their vessels of clay) were fine works of art. This did not seem a paradox to the Disciple; who worshipped the God of beauty.

Evenstone had cost little - because they had used whatever materials were available - yet it was very beautiful due to the talent of the designer and the craftsmanship of the workers and because of that very simplicity that allowed it to blend with the land. They were pleased with the work of their hands, which, in their thoughts, they offered up to God.

The Corinthians were a joyful group and content. At the end of their workday, they always refreshed their bodies with baths. They soaked, each in private contemplation, sipping a drink brewed with herbs. (This was not considered a luxury. The Disciple believed in keeping the physical body in good condition and comfortable so that one might be a better worker for God.) After their baths, they would exchange their rough, homespun garments for the long, white tunics they wore while at rest. Then they felt clean, physically and spiritually. While they broke bread together, they would recite the written word, and debate their interpretations. This fellowship among the brothers was one of the things that made Evenstone such a pleasant place in which to live.

* * *

The Crown (cont.)
The Refugee

It is night. A full moon comes and goes behind scudding clouds. It is presently hiding itself. Someone is breathing heavily, hoarsely, gasping - that is the only sound I hear. . . Then out of the dark the dim figure of a boy materializes. He is racing along a path - oh, so carefully silent . . . taking advantage of the darkness while it lasts.

Then I see that at some distance behind him there is a light, swinging to and fro. . He looks back and I feel his frustration . . . It is always still coming, relentless, this accursed light, seemingly unattached to anyone or anything. . . Each time he looks behind him, it is still pursuing him, always behind him, never stopping, no matter how many evasive moves he has made in his route. A sliver of the moon shows itself beyond the cloud's edge . . . and once again he slips silently from the path to crouch in the bushes on the slope below. . These are thorn bushes and their cruel points dig into him as he sits trembling in the thick of them - his knees are drawn up; his arms wrapped around his bare legs — as he tries to make himself as small as possible. (This is not as difficult as it might have been, had he not been so thin from being hungry all his life.) He is panting quietly; struggling to catch his breath and trying not to cry. The many puncture wounds from these accursed thorn bushes are making his whole body sting like it is on fire and the rivulets of blood trickling from them gives his skin a queer, striped appearance in the light cast by the treacherous moon. He is trying to think coherently, but a great chill of monstrous fear runs up his body, numbing his brain and overwhelming him with nausea. Silently, the vomit, that foul bile of fear, runs down his skinny knees to mingle with the blood from his wounds. The face of the child, pressed against his knees, is innocence tormented; the head elongated, pitiful. The nape of his neck, so thin, yet so sweetly childish, is a place made for a mother's kiss — yet he has never experienced such a pleasure.

Behind him on the path, the lamp comes nearer, only now dark figures are revealed trudging along behind it. Quickly, while the moon still gives its light, the boy scans the horizon - and there to the right of the path - what does he see but a miracle from Heaven! (He denies it could be a delusion.) Bathed in moonlight is a stone fortress, or perhaps it is a temple, he knows not, but there it stands on a plateau above the wasteland surrounding it. Instantly his miserable little body is shot through with hope, and he is revived. He does not waste a moment. Quickly, while the moon still illuminates the landscape, he studies the dark terrain which lies between himself and his salvation . . . Then, amazingly (yet it seems appropriate for such a miracle), a shaft of moonlight falls just beyond where he crouches in the thicket - illuminating a direct, unobstructed path to that sanctuary. Awed, he stares as both path and sanctuary seem to grow brighter, beckoning him. He is not one to question salvation. He leaps to his feet, and not pausing to see if he is being followed, nor waiting for the moon to be covered with clouds again, he flies along that path, aiming as straight as the swallow for its cliff-side home.

(Later, he could not even remember racing along the path toward his destiny, but only the moment when he had stood there at the alcove within the garden wall.) His straw blond hair stood up in little unthrifty tufts, his blue eyes were watery, the whole of his thin body covered with dirt and blood. Suddenly overcome with weakness and trembling, his knees started to give way just as his hands groped for the doorway. Then, someone who had been standing there just within the opened gate reached out and drew him in. . . . Thin, strong arms gathered him up. He had the impression she had been waiting there for him - as though she had known he was coming - had even expected him. He sighed and gave himself up to the old woman, for her touch and voice were that of a friend.

What happened after that was like bits and pieces of a dream to the boy. He was aware of the presence of other people - all looking somehow alike. They looked at him with calm, curious eyes and asked questions of the woman who had drawn him into the safety of the sanctuary. There were wonderful, soothing sensations - of being bathed and of balm being applied to his wounds, then being laid to rest on a straw mattress. And woven through all this were the soft, comforting words spoken in a language that was strange to him, but the meaning of which he understood nonetheless. "All is well," she said as her hands stroked his body. . . "Rest, rest. . . All is well."

Absolute peace, comfort and pure delight swept his soul and soothed his body like a cool spring of divine, healing, delicious water. Refreshed beyond measure, the boy sighed and slept. It seemed his body did not even touch the mattress, but floated above it in ethereal delight, free of aches and pains. . . In fact, his body seemed to have no feeling at all - only his spirit seemed conscious. His rest was unbroken and his only thought was that he had arrived, at last, on the other side. At last he was free from the horror and starvation he had experienced on the wrong side of the wall.

* * *

It was a curious thing, but no one ever came to Evenstone to ask for the boy to be returned to them. The brothers waited in expectation and in readiness with their refusal, but it had been unnecessary to explain their pledge of asylum, for strangely, no one ever came.

The old woman who had waited for him was Hannah. When he was once again conscious, he had seen her sitting by his bed (although he had been aware all along of her healing hands, touching and soothing him). She had worn a white robe, as they all did when they were in the sanctuary. This, he realized, was why he had thought they all looked alike. He smiled at the first sight of her ancient and wrinkled face. He could not remember seeing it before, but he had felt and loved the essence of Hannah from the time they had met at the gate.

When the boy was well enough, the Disciple plied him with questions. The Greek knew several languages, but the boy knew the Roman tongue for he was the bastard son of a Roman soldier. He did not know, he said, where his father had gone, and his mother was dead. He willingly told the Disciple how he had been enslaved, but then his large dark eyes rolled and hid themselves beneath his eyelids. He did not dare confess that he had stolen bread to appease his hunger, for he feared he would be made to leave.

Thereafter, the boy followed the Disciple around, eager to help in any way he could, to repay for all they had given him. He had heard of gods, and heaven, and a place of perdition. Now as he followed the Disciple through his day's work, he learned new things and readily adopted them all - so open had he flung his heart's door. (He believed any religion these people had must be right and good, for were they not so good, so loving? Was not this place a refuge of delight?)

As for the Disciple, the boy's eyes were so eager, so guileless, that his heart was moved. He knew that whatever the boy had been wanted for, he could not have been guilty of any great crime. Soon, he even began to regard the boy as a son and each rejoiced in the other.

* * *

At times, the boy would ramble over the countryside, looking for such things as wild herbs and mushrooms which gave their meals some variety. On one of these rambles his eye was caught by a flash of color - some pretty crystals in an outcropping of broken rock. They glittered in the sun and charmed him with their beauty. As he pried them out and examined them on his palm, his first thought was how the Disciple, that lover of beauty, would like them.

Always, he yearned to bring his benefactor some gift worthy of his goodness, and now an idea occurred tom him. In the inner room of the sanctuary was a bas-relief carving in dark wood, of Christ. The Christ figure, rather than being carved in an upright position, was shown bending over with his arms outstretched to little figures below him, while suspended above the Christ figure there was an ornately carved crown. The Disciple had explained that the crown had awaited Jesus in heaven, while he was on earth helping others to learn the way to join him there. The boy had stared at the crown and was disappointed, for it was only dull, brown wood, and was not, in his opinion, worthy of the son of God, about whom he was learning. Now as he gazed at the glittering stones, he imagined how they could make the crown shine with color. . . For every crown, he thought, needed jewels.

He worked with eagerness, for he had a purpose. The work of shaping and smoothing the stones was very difficult, for he had only the crudest tools; a hollow abrasive rock in which he turned the face of each stone, abrading its surface until it was relatively smooth, and a substance that he got from the edge of a stream, to polish them until their clear colors could be seen. The backs of the stones were left rough, but crudely pointed to fit into the wooden crown. Secretly, he visited the inner room to measure for the stones until he thought they were the right size. Finally, after two whole years of painstaking work, he had them ready. Late in the night, he gouged the wood and inserted the stones. He could hardly sleep at all that night, for thinking of the wonderful surprise that was in store for the Disciple, and how pleased they all would be.

(This boy had never experienced love before, and now he was surrounded by it from all who lived there. He eagerly gathered it in, stored it up, pleasured in it - but it had become so great a thing inside him that it had become a burden. It needed to be given out again, so that he might have relief from it. He was young and simple. To give intangible love was not enough for him - he must give something that could be seen, or held in the hands. He had not yet learned that love is seen in the eyes and heard in the voice of the one who loves, and felt in the heart by the one who is loved, and that these spiritual gifts were greater than all the material ones that one human could give to another.)

The next morning (in the merciless light of day) the effect of the jewels in the crown on the discerning eye of the Disciple was not the same as it had been on the uneducated boy. How horrible it was to him! Those crude gouges in the beautiful carved wood! The dead, opaque look of the stones forced into that dark setting! He was revolted - this fastidious man. His mouth dropped open in disbelief. His face flushed with the rising heat of anger, he turned to look at the boy with scolding words ready on his tongue (Yes, in spite of all his "discipline!"). But when his flashing eyes fell on his "son," he saw him standing there with such a light of love glowing in his eyes. . Waiting - expecting . . . what? What was it that he was expecting? His approval, of course, his love! The Disciple's anger faded into confusion . . . That face! So innocent, so tender. . . Ah, well! And so, his heart turned over and the steam went out of him.

Still, it was hard! His eyes were drawn again to the destruction of the fine carving. His irritation turned to grief; it was all he could do to look at it and not shudder! He thought, "It ruins the perfection of Evenstone - of all I have worked for!" And, as soon as that thought made its appearance, the quiet voice within whispered; prodding him to pay attention to what had just come into his mind. So, he caught the thought and examined it. Then he felt uneasy. What sin did it imply? Pride! Too proud of this edifice of his own creation? Was this a lesson meant for him?

No! No! His heart cried out even as he studied the thing . . . Ugly! Horrible! An insult to God! (Then the small voice whispered again: This innocent boy - insulting God? How could something done with no motive in mind but that of Love be an insult to God?) He struggled with the truth of this revelation, as he stared at the monstrosity. It nauseated him. His hands itched to tear it out, to smooth the ruptured wood and cast aside the offending stones. He could not bear to tolerate ugliness in the name of Love. (Yet, which was the greater - beauty or Love? Wasn't beauty an expression of, or the servant of, Love?) He was totally confused for the first time since he had become a convert. He had been so sure of himself - yet now he had the distinct impression that he had somehow gone wrong . . had somehow missed something very important.

Though his mind was in turmoil, he was aware of the boy waiting beside him (so good - so tenderhearted . . and so wrong!). He, himself could have gilded and bejeweled Evenstone if he had thought it was the way . . yet the boy had not come far in his lessons yet. He didn't understand.

The boy knew something had gone wrong. Yearningly scanning the face of his mentor, he had become restless and uneasy from what he had seen there. The Disciple, who had detected his mood, laid aside that which was in his mind, to be taken up later - in quiet meditation. Composing his features, he turned again to the boy. Choosing his words carefully (for he was ruthlessly honest by nature), he thanked him for his gift – for this gesture of love (and perhaps, whispered the voice, for a difficult, but precious lesson?). He added that he knew he had worked very hard - then he embraced him in the way of the Christian brothers. The boy was so moved he was almost in tears and could not speak for the constriction of his throat. The Disciple left him to master himself and hurried away. He was off to find solitude where he could plumb the secret bottom of his own soul - to seek and rip out that dark imperfection which had lain there undetected until a moment ago.

The crown continued to be a source of self-sacrifice for the Disciple for some months to come. At first, each time he went to the inner room he would avert his eyes and tell himself Love was above all. He told himself he had become so obsessed by building a sanctuary of such beauty, so perfect in every way, that he had forgotten that its primary purpose was to serve God, and therefore to help man; who was, himself, imperfect.

Later, he would force himself to look at it. Repulsed, he would stare and cringe, and discipline himself to contemplate Love - the Love of God which forgave all the imperfections of man. And who was he, but just such an imperfect creature? This crude barbarism before him - this mixture of beauty and ruin - now seemed a mocking symbol of himself. He was ashamed. Smug and proud, he had gloried in his own creation and lost sight of his true purpose. This small thing - this act of a child - had kicked the props out from under him and left him lying, wondering, in the dust. So, faced with this flaw in the building of his inner self, he tore it out and began building anew.

Then something happened which distracted him, and all the others living at Evenstone.

The Crown (cont.)
Man Trap

I see a man in a deep pit, tangled up somehow with rope and branches. It comes to me that this is a "man trap" and is the work of those who are called the "Phoenicians," who deal in slaves. They are marauders and nomads who dwell farther inland, and prey near the coast on the poor and unsuspecting, the ones they steal to sell to others as laborers.

Several men on horseback ride up and peer down into the pit. They are a dark-haired race; much smaller in build and stature, than the man in the pit. Their horses are also smaller than modern horses, and have furry, padded-looking hooves. In their clothing, they seem to have a preference for stripes woven of various colors. Each man wears a cloth wrapped around his loins in such a way that it has the appearance of short, puffy, pants. They are bare-legged with sandals on their feet and wear cylindrical shaped hats trimmed with various small objects and feathers. Altogether, they are a gaudy, exotic-looking band.

They raised the man from the pit and examined him. They were impressed by his size as he lay stretched out upon the ground. Using the lances they carried to prod him, they forced him to turn over (for he could not stand) and shook their heads. They didn't speak English and although he knew a little of other languages, their speech was strange to him. Like glittering ants with a prized large beetle, the gaudy band struggled together until they had succeeded in propping him against the trunk of a tree. He could feel the bark digging into the bare flesh of his back, but no longer cared. He no longer cared, even if they killed him, so long as they were quick about it. Although he was much taller than they, and larger-boned, he was very thin. His rib cage stood out from his emaciated body. His eyes were sunken in their sockets. Some of them examined him minutely,

bending quite near his face to stare into his eyes. He noticed their breath -
for it was different, too, though not unpleasant . . . as though they ate some
herb unknown to him. The way they stood and strode about indicated
arrogance, as if they were all little emperors. They gabbled to each other,
and positioning themselves in his face once more, they waved and pointed
in such a way that he realized they wanted to know from whence he had
come. He pointed seaward, weakly sketching pictures in the air with his
hands: waves . . . sails . . . and the keel of a ship. He grasped his belly and
pointed to his mouth. They nodded. They understood quite well, now. He
was a starving sailor, who had left his vessel when it had come landward,
desperate to find food. They wanted to know if there were others who had
escaped from the vessel. He didn't know where the others were, nor if they
had made it to shore, so he pretended not to understand.

One of them gave him something to drink. He yearned for pure water,
and this was pungently sweet, yet he found it marvelously reviving - so
much so that he could soon stand alone. While some of them stayed with
him, others split off from the party and rode up and down the shore, looking for more foreign sailors like him. They found a dead man floating
face down in the water a little distance out, and debris from what they
conjectured might have been an abandoned ship, yet nothing more. They
wheeled their horses around and rode back to join the others. Soon they
were on their way to camp with their captive, leading him along at the end
of a rope. They rode at a slow and easy pace, though this was not mercy on
their part. (He was no good to them dead; though they thought it quite
likely he would die anyway.)

The Captive, staggering along the best he could in his weakened state,
thought them peculiar. He observed that their movements and those of
their little horses, were quicker than those of his people of the isles (of Britain), and other (European) people he had known before. Their spare horses

were loaded with what he assumed was booty, so that there wasn't one for him to ride unless they threw some of this aside - which, knowing the kind of men they were - he knew they would never do.

Fortunately for him, their destination was not far away - an arrangement of tents within a grove of trees, and only temporary, for they would dismantle it and carry it with them when they returned to the land from which they had come. As they approached, another man rode out of the camp to meet them. They halted as he drew up beside them and the Captive, though tired and ill from laboring in the dust to keep up with the riders, focused on this man. Since the group seemed suddenly wary; their attitude subservient, he judged the newcomer to be their chief.

They dismounted, and from their packs they brought out and showed their chief a sampling of the loot they had brought. At first, the Captive thought he must be affected by his illness and could not believe what he saw, for the newcomer was a strange figure for a commander of men. Whereas his men were a slim and small-boned race, this man was stocky, his face was broad, square and ugly, the nose flattened, the lips wide and thick. His black marble eyes could be observed only as a malicious glint that slid covertly between slit lids as he looked from the loot his men displayed to the captured man, and back again. His strange appearance was heightened by his costume. He wore arm and ankle bands of cropped ostrich feathers. Wrapped around each of his wrists were metal strands that crossed in a figure 8 over the backs of his hands, the second loop over the middle two fingers. Where the strands met on the back of the hands there was set a jewel - blue on the right hand, red on the left.

His habit, when he was excited (which he was now when he saw what his men had brought him) was to flex his hands - tightening and relaxing these strands so that the jewels winked on the backs of his ugly, blunt hands. His version of their headgear was higher than that of the others, so that he wouldn't appear so short - for the shocking thing was that he was a dwarf. He sat astride his horse like an ungainly lump. His stirrups had been especially made for him; the straps shortened to accommodate his stubby legs and feet. His eyes sharpened whenever he stared at the bowed but towering figure of the prisoner at the rear of the procession. As they rode on together into camp, he was far more impressed than he let on, his gaze often straying to the prisoner straggling behind.

Once arrived, the Captive was shoved to the ground. There he lay in the shelter of the trees, shivering from exhaustion and trying to catch his breath. All around him was the noise of unharnessing and unpacking, the stamping of horses and cries of welcome from the others in the camp as the tribesmen went about their business.

The chief, however, had not taken his eyes off the prisoner. He slid from his mare onto a mounting block and with a shambling, afflicted gait he went to bend over his prostrate trophy. He stared into the face of the big stranger, and their eyes met with a shock. . . The dwarf's pupils dilated suddenly into inky orbs. The blue eyes of the prisoner grew pale with alarm as he wondered what this fellow might have in store for him. Just as the Captive's soul shrank from that of the heathen chief, the dwarf's spirit leapt forward eagerly, as if to consume him.

Even in his prone position under the trees (and starved as he was) the Captive still appeared - to the dwarf - like a giant. His slow wit began to spin the prospect of having such a one as his own slave. . . Ah! The power of it! This idea brought such a surge of blood into his face that it made his ears tingle. With his will of iron that carried all before him, he vowed in that instant, that this man would live. He couldn't take his eyes from the prisoner, but walked up and down the length of him where he lay fainting on the ground, gloating over the immensity of his prize. His eyes sparkled;

his heart bounded joyfully (for he was woefully bent in his heart and mind by the curse of his size).

The others leapt to obey him and soon the Captive was laid upon a pallet to accommodate his length and comfort. After the women had managed to get some mare's milk into him, the poor man fell into a deep sleep, only awakening when one of the women bade him drink their concoction of broth and herbs. Throughout the day and evening, men, women and children came to stare down at the sleeping stranger, speculating as to his race and marveling at his size.

It was early dawn of the second day before the Captive became wide awake. He was instantly alarmed - trying to remember what had gone before and where he was. All was quiet. He turned his head, surveying his surroundings. A few drab-dressed women stood around the campfire, preparing food. He remembered the pit, and then the small, dark men like bejeweled ants in their gossamer clothes, who had swarmed over him and carried him here to this camp in the shady grove.

He tried to sit up but he was still too weak. A little damsel, who had seen he was awake, came and stood by his side, her large black liquid eyes staring solemnly into his own pale blue ones. She spoke not a word, but surprised him a great deal, for she laid her tiny hand on his large, hairy arm and leaned forward to stare deliberately, piercingly, into his eyes. Her eyes were trying to tell him something. He was confused and alarmed. What did she mean? The whole camp was stirring then. Somewhere, a voice called and then the damsel scampered off, to disappear somewhere among the tangle of tents.

Two tribesmen came and looked down at him. He remembered them from the raiding party, but now they were clothed in flowing, fine silk robes and sandals. Apparently they would not be riding soon, he thought, or they would be dressed as they had been before. They seemed pleased by the look of him and grunted to one another in satisfaction before they moved away. He examined himself, and found that he lay on a soft pallet, propped up on fine, soft pillows. . and wonder of wonders! He had been bathed, so he was both clean and comfortable. His amazement quickly became suspicion. What did these people plan to do with him? Even before the question was fully formed, he groaned, for he knew the answer: They were only making him well so that he could be sold as a slave.

Soon, a woman came and offered him a bowl of something that looked like curds and whey, and a cake of thin, flat bread. She offered, with nervous gestures, to feed him. She was a little afraid of him, even in his weakened state, so when he grumbled and waved her away, she quickly laid the food by his side and scurried off. He looked at it for a while, puzzling in his mind what to do. If he refused food, he would soon die and would be free of the specter of slavery, which was sometimes worse than death. But he knew there were some lucky ones who were treated well and, if they were wise and industrious, were even allowed to earn money to buy their own freedom. Besides, he reasoned, he needed to be strong to escape from these little men if he found the opportunity. So he comforted himself with that shred of hope and hungrily reached out for the strange-looking stuff. He ate slowly, but even then it was difficult going, for it had been a long time since his belly had had to deal with solid food.

For the next few days, he ate and rested; watched and listened. A hunting party came and went out a few times during this period. Once, they returned with several wild-eyed, terrified men and a woman with a child. These new captives were all on foot and tied together with ropes held by the riders, who roughly dragged them to the edge of the camp. There they were kept tethered and treated like beasts, their meager food actually thrown at them. The Captive could see them from where he lay so comfortably bedded and fed. He was shocked and puzzled by the way they

were treated, while he was given soft bedding and good food. Sometimes
the eyes of the other prisoners would flicker toward him in curiosity, but
mainly they stared at nothing, their eyes dull. Later they were taken away
and he never knew what became of them, for he never saw them again.

From the time he was able to rise from his pallet, they had watched
him – yet, so far, he had not been shackled. He had decided he could not
hope to outrun them until he was fully well and strong again, so he willingly worked toward attaining that goal, eating, sleeping and exercising
his weak and flaccid limbs - peacefully biding his time. For a while, as he
walked around the camp, flexing his limbs, the men would watch him in
fascination, but later they grew accustomed to his large presence and paid
little attention.

Their strange chief often observed him, but never up close. The Captive
would feel his gaze upon him (so intense was his stare) and turning toward
it, he would find him standing some distance away within the clutter of
tents. Sometimes he would appear to be discussing him with one of the
others, but then he would turn away without coming near. As the chief
spied on him, so the Captive covertly studied the chief. Although he had
seen several dwarfs in his lifetime, he thought this one's appearance was
bizarre. He also seemed different - possibly because he was a ruler of a sort.
He had never seen a dwarf in any position other than a very menial one, or
treated as a pet. It was obvious that this dwarf was ashamed of his size, for
when he wanted to address his men as a group; an ornately-carved box was
brought out and ceremoniously placed for him to stand on. Thus elevated,
he could look out over their heads and they would be forced to look up to
him. (The Captive was greatly amused by this, but wisely kept his humor
hidden.)

Within a few weeks, the band was ready to leave the grove. Mounted
on their little shaggy-footed horses, they dragged behind them litters piled

high with all their belongings and plunder. The Captive, who was also mounted on a pony, would have worried for the animal if he hadn't lost so much of his usual weight. As it was, his legs reached far past the belly of the beast; his feet nearly dragging on the ground. The tribesmen laughed at the sight of him. All of them wore loose robes over their other clothes, and had given him a makeshift article that passed for the same. He didn't understand why they were dressed in this manner until they arrived at the desert. Then he understood – for it protected them from blowing sand and scorching sun. The Captive had never seen such a place before and was glad when, by late afternoon, the landscape changed abruptly to grassy plains and scattered groves of trees. Here they found water and camped for the night. All the while, the Captive had been trying desperately to mark the direction they took, so that when he escaped, he could return to the sea.

The chief, who had had his prisoner riding just behind him, would glance back now and then, as if to reassure himself that he was there, but in truth, he was gloating. He had never had such a prize before and he was fascinated by him. The Captive, in turn, was intrigued with the dwarf - his actions and appearance continued to amaze him. He stared at the back of the chief as they rode and wondered about him. The dwarf's torso was not abnormally short. On horseback, and wearing the long caftan that more than covered his legs, he looked much like an ordinary tribesman. However, this illusion was destroyed when they reached their destination and the dwarf was helped to dismount. Sliding from the saddle, he became most awkwardly entangled in the long folds of his robe. Struggling, red-faced, to free himself, he clawed at his men to save himself from falling. They yelped in pain, and their chief became a ludicrous figure - even comical - once more. The Captive turned away to hide his face.

At the end of their journey the Captive discovered that their homeland - a grassy plain at the foot of a range of blue hills - was still nothing but

a tent village. Tents were not proper homes, in the Captive's opinion. He
had expected dwellings of wood or stone. There were some rough wooden
structures at the outer edge of the cluster of tents, but they were only for
the livestock. Yet in this setting, they lived very well. (Later, he discovered
that they would not build anything that would keep them there, although
this had been their home for some years. They must be ready to move
quickly, in case the Romans should rouse themselves and come again, to
punish them for their pillaging.)

The Captive continued to improve in the following weeks. He ate and
rested; waiting for the first opportunity to escape. Even now, he was never
bound, though he could always feel dark eyes upon him. He soon became
aware which ones had been selected to watch him. In any case, they didn't
seem very worried. And why should they be, he thought sourly, their village was far removed from any other and he could hardly outrun them all.
He abandoned the idea of stealing a horse, for he doubted if one of their
little horses could support his present weight for any distance, and certainly
it would not be able to keep to its usual speed.

In the meantime, he wandered around the village - savoring its strangeness. Instead of many tents, each in its own space, there were simply coverings between the people and the sky - all huddled cheek by jowl. Where
one tent pole ended another began, so that it seemed to be one gigantic
canopy of animal skins stretched from pole to tree to pole. This arrangement did little more than keep out the sun and occasional rain. Sometimes
carpets were rolled down, forming sides to the shelters in the evenings, giving a minimum of privacy, but it also prevented cooling breezes. The Captive was revolted by this way they had of mingling and herding together
so tightly. His was a private nature, and he found their way suffocating,
especially since it was unnecessary, with land as far as the eye could see to
make use of. The women cooked together at one great fire, and they all ate

together. It was as if they never got enough of each other, he thought in disgust, and wondered if there were not many family disagreements.

He was not an ignorant man. Since he had set out on his travels in his early youth, he had learned a good deal. Yet, he had never seen a race quite like this, and so he watched and marveled over them. They stole from others in the land, and enslaved them, with no conscience. Their clothing, woven through with gold strands, also seemed strange to him - so rich-looking for scavenging people who dwelt in a wilderness. They glittered in the evening firelight, where they remained after the meal to converse. The Captive joined this circle for he was anxious to learn more of their tongue. Often a piper would play, and when his searching notes came together in a tune of the sort they liked, they would cease their talk and listen. Once a tribesman rose from his seat by the fire and sensuously stretched himself, raising his arms above his head. He had straight black hair and his brown face reflected the warm, orange glow of firelight. His eyes glittered as he clapped his hands together, and he grinned widely - his teeth gleaming white within his black beard. This set off a tingle of excitement around the fire. The other men clapped and called to him, and as the music of the pipe increased in volume, they leapt to their feet and joined him in the dance. He liked music, but this is not what he was used to. The dance was slow, sinuous, the dancers swaying, contorting.

It was the first time he was ever repelled by music and merry-making.

He was used to rough behavior among sea-faring men and of coarse-natured people in all the places he had traveled, but the behavior of these people puzzled him, for they did not seem coarse in some of their ways. They were refined enough in their everyday manners. Their bodies and clothing were clean, which was more than he could say for his own country's lower class. When they relieved themselves, they had the niceness to squat in the area outside the tents, at the animal pens. Still, they were crude in their sexual behavior and treated their women with casual disdain, though he assumed that some truly loved their wives. Since the sides of their dwellings were rolled up during warm days, there was no privacy, and acts that should have been kept private, were exposed for all to see. He had noticed that some, especially the younger couples, seemed to desire more privacy and he had seen some fond expressions and secretive, tender gestures between them.

The women - who were the real workers within the camp - were subdued, for they were kept humbled by their men. If they fell behind in their work or were disobedient, they were deliberately and publicly humiliated. To his great disgust, he found that the most barbaric custom of this tribe was to punish their women by sodomy. This was considered the ultimate punishment and abasement for any woman's misbehavior - it was to teach them to be subservient to the men. All of the women were horrified by the possibility of it happening to them. It humiliated them by making them appear as copulating beasts, their masters astride them. The shame that accompanied this punishment lasted for days, even months. During this time, the humbled woman was unable to look into another's face, and kept her eyes to the ground as she did her chores. Because of this and the other, lesser, punishments - all inflicted upon them before the eyes of all the others of the tribe - the women were very reserved, serving their gaudily dressed men in silence and with downcast eyes; trembling lest they made a mistake.

It was even the women's task to bathe their men - as though they were great gentlemen. A tribesman would sit on a low stool (seemingly nonchalant - although his nudity was exposed to everyone passing through if they cared to look) while his patient woman sluiced him down with buckets of water that she had laboriously carried from the spring.

He was moved for the plight of the women and was sad for the little dark-eyed damsel who was born into this tribe. She still kept watch over him, and brought him extra food - delicacies, like sweetmeats - and no one seemed to mind that she did so.

* * *

Mirola' had loved the Captive when they first brought him into the camp. She did not find him strange at all, but felt she had always known him. It was as though he had finally come home after a long absence - as though she had been waiting, and when she saw his face she said to her-self – "Ah! There he is!" She was one of those who had helped to bathe and clothe him while he had been unconscious. When the women had stripped him of his rags his privates had been exposed and there was a tittering and blushing among the younger two. The older woman snapped at them, say-ing bitterly that all men were alike in what they did with their appendages, and there was nothing marvelous about any of them.

Mirola', although she had seen much for her age, had been ashamed for the man lying there exposed without his knowledge of it. She had a deep distrust of men - even her father seemed despicable to her by this time of her life. But, somehow in spite of this she continued to love the Captive as time went on. The old woman (who noticed how she stroked his face when he was sleeping, how she lingered there beside his pallet), cautioned her, for Mirola' was promised to a tribesman. But Mirola' denied that she wanted a mate at all, and tried to explain her "familiar" kind of liking for the Captive. Then the old woman said that perhaps Mirola's soul had known his soul in another time on the earth. The girl had heard of this - that the soul lived to be reborn again and again, and was attracted to those it had known before. She mused over this, but found it difficult to imagine herself as anyone else, and she only knew the Captive as he was then. She loved him, but there was nothing in it of sexual love.

As for the Captive, well, he thought her a dear child, for she brought a little sweetness into his time of imprisonment. She tried to teach him her name, but his tongue stumbled over it. The language puzzled him - it was truly foreign to his ears. A few of their words, however, were similar to the Hispanic and Roman, and gestures filled the gap. Soon, he had divined that the damsel was betrothed to a man - one of the coarser ones, he thought, when she had pointed him out. He was not particularly surprised that she was promised at her young age (which he guessed to be nine or ten years) but he was appalled to learn that the ceremony would actually take place in the near future (for it seemed they were only waiting for a certain time of the moon and season, according to the stars). He scanned the poor child's body, formless under the shift she wore. She didn't even have breasts, yet. It was a great wrong, he thought, and he chafed against his inability to do anything about it (for he was of a race that always protected their women and children).

What was worse, the middle-aged widower to whom the damsel was betrothed was spending his waiting time by lusting over the child, fondling her on his lap, "to prepare her," the shocked Captive was given to understand. It made him miserable to see the child at those times when the man had trapped her and pulled her down onto his lap. She would sit limply, her head hanging down, as the barbarian's hand parted her legs and explored her childish, virgin parts. When he would laugh and let her go, she would slide off his lap and run away into the meadow. There, among wildflowers, flowed a clear stream where she could wash and wash. Then, the "bridegroom" would go off to sate his lust with one or another of the women of the place. It did not matter if the woman he picked was another's wife, for they were expected to share on such needy occasions. Only once had the Captive seen a husband rebel against the use of his wife in such a way. There had been a confrontation between the angry husband, the randy man and the tribal leaders, including the dwarf. He did not know what had been said, but afterward, the husband left for the hills. The next day, the Captive had seen him quietly squatting by the fire, with a face like a stone and pain in his eyes. He was a young husband and the Captive believed he cherished his wife in secret. He had begun to realize that any tribesman who showed such love for his wife was considered a weakling.

Time went by and he recovered his strength and flesh, the Captive was relieved to find that he was not to be sold into slavery. But slowly, it was borne in upon him that he was, in fact, already a slave and that his master was the dwarf himself. The chief was kind to him at first; the work he was given to do was slight. His food and clothing were as good as that of the tribe. But when he had gained complete recovery, things subtly changed in a way he did not at first understand.

He had kept his auburn hair cut very short and brushed back with grease while he had been aboard ship, for he hated the sting of it when the wind whipped long strands into his eyes and obscured his vision. Now, it had grown long, but he kept it clean and groomed. His body was heavy with flesh again, and he rejoiced in the feeling of renewed strength that flowed through him. His shoulders were naturally broad, for he had worked on sailing ships since his tender youth and had taken his turn at the oars when the wind was still. He was now a dangerous-looking presence.

The stunted, tree trunk of a man had, at first, been pleased with his "giant." He would think; was not this great man in his power, to do with as he would? Was he not his slave? But as the Captive regained his strength and put on muscle, it could be seen that he was not only large, but a handsome figure - with hair that shone in the sun like bright gold. The dwarf spent more and more time silently staring at his prize. He was both dazzled and irritated by the look of him. It was not right, he thought - the fellow seemed more like a chief, or even a king, than a slave. He became discomfited by his own comparison between the towering height and phy- sique of his slave and that of his own self . . . for although he might roar and threaten his tribe into subservience, he knew he was still a disfigured lump - so low to the earth that the dust from his own shuffling footfalls could rise up and leave him coughing and covered with shame.

Even as his giant slave became more helpful to him, the dwarf became more bitter and dissatisfied. The slave had great strength and was able to lift the heaviest tent poles, alone, and with ease. Usually it took two of their men to do so. While his slave performed such tasks that showed his strength and rippling muscle, the dwarf would stand and watch with a sour expression. His men - being naturally idle when they did not ride out to loot the countryside - were greatly entertained by the slave and admired this show of strength. . . This aggravated their leader all the more.

The Captive - who knew human nature - had by this time discovered the dwarf's weaknesses. He took care, therefore, to be very accommodating. He would wait on his "master" with reserve and grace, always taking care of the appearances. When the dwarf's handicap made him awkward, he would quickly act so that it would appear that it was himself who had been the awkward one, or he would take care that the incident went unnoticed by the others and would appear not to notice it, himself. This did not help matters. The dwarf, being very shrewd (for he too knew the cunning ways of men), suspected his motives and resented him all the more for his con- descension. His slave was much too presumptuous, he thought. He needed to be humbled.

At first, the acts of humiliation were petty ones. Angrily, the dwarf would kick over the slave's cup of wine, and berate him in his strange tongue. He threw the stew at him, and then demanded he serve him more. Gradually, these acts increased in severity and frequency along with the dwarf's perverse pleasure. He set him to hard, unnecessary work and ordered him to tasks that required him to lift more weight than was possible for any one man, then he would call the whole tribe to watch his failure. When the Captive had strained for a while to no avail, the dwarf, standing on his box, would laugh with superior scorn and his loyal tribe would mimic his derision. Once, when told to hoist and move a laden pony, he shocked them all by doing it. The gasps of the tribe changed to excited gabbling and admiration. Not until he saw the dwarf's fury did the Captive realize his mistake - until then, it had never occurred to him that he should sham weakness. It was also then that he realized he could never please his "master."

The lightest job given the Captive, but the one he found most burdensome was, (as he thought of it) "to always be carrying that accursed box for that freak of nature to stand upon, so that he might feel tall." That, however, was soon to change.

One day the dwarf, studying his personal slave with his great (and, he thought, most unfair) height and the wide breadth of shoulders that could carry such loads, conceived a grand notion. From that time, the box was no longer needed, for the dwarf rode the shoulders of his slave as though he were a two-legged horse. When he had risen in the morning and had broken his fast, he would summon his man-beast to squat upon the carpet where he would climb upon him, to straddle his neck. Roughly, he would wind around his stubby fingers that auburn hair (that he had demanded be braided that he might better keep his grip upon the poor man's head). In this way they went about the camp, sun-up to sundown, except for times for food and defecation. This novel occupation gave the dwarf great joy, and for awhile it satisfied his craving for dominance over the giant. It was a great spectacle to the others in the camp, and most of the men relished the scene, for they were masters of derision.

As for the Captive, it was this treatment that finally made him angry. For one thing, the dwarf was not as clean as the others, and an odor came from his privates as he straddled his neck. This stench - so near his nose - made him ill. He came to dread this part the most. Day after day being treated like a pack animal by the twisted man became more intolerable. Squat down, stand up, squat down, stand up, parade around for all to see and mock. . . and all the while his hair was practically torn from his head from the continual yanking this way and that in those thick ugly hands with the incongruous jewels gleaming on them. Sometimes he caught the damsel's eyes upon him and the glances of women - yes, they felt compassion for him, but what could they do?

Eventually, the novelty of the spectacle waned and then the dwarf became, once more, dissatisfied. Even this was no longer enough. He would dig his heels into the great chest of his slave until the Captive was bruised. He beat upon the golden head in frustration when the slave did not move the right way, or at the right speed, and would grab him under his chin, snatching his head up and back and forth, this way and that - as though to direct him where he wanted to go, but it was really, (as they both knew) just to abuse him. The stink and dirt of the dwarf's hands upon his face just under his nose, the scratches from the filthy fingernails, galled the Captive further.

As usual, as the dwarf's dissatisfaction grew, the Captive's humiliation was increased. He was urinated on, while the dwarf laughed. He was kicked, and had his privates exposed to the camp at large, as all the men screamed in ridicule. The flame of the Captive's fury, which showed in his face and eyes during this latter degradation, made his master gasp with delight and it might have been that which triggered his most evil thought - that which was to be the final injury.

The sodomy was committed in full view of any who were willing to watch. Children were taken away by the women, who hid themselves behind the tents and trees. Mirola' was crying and vomiting beside the stream. The Captive, who suspected too late what was going to happen, fought against the men who tied him and forced him down until he was straddled over the felled trunk of a tree. The bark of the log tore into the tender skin of his naked belly, and this is what he focused his attention on, so that he could block out the other disgusting thing that was happening to him. Sailors had done this sort of thing to each other, and he had seen such things, but never, he had vowed, would it ever happen to him, for he would have slain the man who had tried and would not have flinched about it. Now, unbelievably, it was happening and there was nothing he could do to stop it. So, he removed himself the only way he could, and dreamed of pleasant scenes he had seen in the islands of the sea, the greenness of the shallows overlapping pure, white sands. . . He was *there*, he was not *here*.

When it was over, he was left alone in his tent. For awhile, he just lay there but he became aware of women, and the damsel who had come in with basins of water and sweetish, pungent smelling ointment. They gestured to him that it was for bathing, and then silently they withdrew and stealthily made their way back to their tents before their men could discover that they had aided the slave who had been disgraced by their chief.

The Captive didn't know it at the time, but the feeling of the tribe toward their chief was changing. Some of the men had never liked him, yet, because he was fierce and had led them into many successful forays from which they had become rich with other people's goods they had accepted him. They thought the behavior of their chief had become ridiculous since he had gotten the slave, and they were becoming weary of it. It rankled them to think they had a leader who was a foolish man. Now, they were beginning to see him as he really was - an ugly, strange, little man - an embarrassment. They said to each other that his mind was eaten up with the slave and was not on the leadership of the tribe. Some of the women were not without influence with their husbands, and whispered softly in their men's ears. Eventually, many were strongly moved against the dwarf, wanting to be rid of either one or the other - their "leader" or the slave.

* * *

It was very early morning. The dwarf, who had noticed signs of rebellion and sought to re-exert his power again, had taken most of the men and gone on another looting expedition. The Captive had decided this was the time. He would not let such a thing happen to him again. He waited until the tribesmen were well out of range and for the others who were left in camp to settle down. There were three healthy men left behind, whom he would have to outrun. Suddenly, there was a flurry of excitement in the camp. A young boy came and said he had found a honey tree in the woods. This was not a common occurrence, and sweets were much relished by the tribe.

(Unknown to the Captive, others were also plotting his escape. The act was played out so, with the honey as bait.) It was Mirola's suggestion that they should take along the slave to help with the gathering. After all, she said to the men, he was only a slave, and why should they risk being stung? They grinned and agreed, for the wild bees were vicious stingers, and it was a job that had to be done carefully. They went along to watch and keep an eye, half-heartedly, on the slave. (Although the chief would be angry with them if the slave ran away, they fervently wished he would.)

As they followed the boy to the honey tree, the Captive's heart was racing; his mind was busy. This was his chance. He wished he knew more of the terrain and remembered the way back to the sea, but he had been very weak at that time and, since it had been months ago, he doubted his memory.

When the tree was found again, the boy climbed it while the others waited below. Mirola' had given the Captive to wear an enveloping garment rubbed with bee repellent herbs. She also had changed her usual shift for this kind of covering. The two of them stood under the tree, holding a cloth by its four corners, to catch the honeycomb, which the boy would drop down to them. Then the long-legged Captive was supposed to gather up the corners of the cloth and run with it back to the camp. It was to be hoped that he outran the bees. However, Mirola and the boy had planned for him to throw the comb and swarming bees down into the cloth. Then, she and the slave would toss it onto the tribesmen. The Captive, in his ignorance, had noticed that Mirola' moved closer to his side, brushing his thigh – but he only thought perhaps she was afraid of the fierce bees.

The grinning tribesmen had retreated and waited some yards away, intent on the lad in the tree. The small risk made this adventure fun for them. They thought the boy was in the worst predicament and would surely be covered with stings for some days, but he would be rewarded for his trouble with a large piece of the comb. He carried a cloth sack to cover himself after he had taken the honey and dropped it down, for he would then sit very still upon the branch, covered with the cloth which smelled of the herb that the bees did not like. Then, after the angry insects had settled down again, he would climb down from the tree and he, too, would return to camp.

When the boy was up in the tree and straddled on the limb from which he could reach into the honeyed recess, he glanced down at the damsel, who nudged the Captive again, a message in her dark eyes. He was slow to respond. Just when he began to have an idea of what she meant, something unexpected happened, suddenly and violently. The boy had taken things into his own hands. He had rudely snatched the comb full of swarming bees and larvae and thrown it - not into the cloth held by the Captive and Mirola', but directly onto the tribesmen. They howled and the air was alive with angry bees. Mirola trod upon the Captive's foot and pushed him. Yet, even as he tensed to run, his grateful eyes were caught by hers. She looked so desperate – so alone. Into his mind flashed the memory of her on her "betrothed's" lap.

Soon, he was running through the woods, the girl clinging to his back like a barnacle, her arms wrapped around his neck.

He followed his instincts. From the sea he had come, so to the sea he must return, to find a friendly ship anchored there. He did not think of going inland, for he did not know that land and most certainly had no desire to stay in this country. She seemed to know the way he wanted and would slap his chest and point to indicate when he should change directions. He was grateful and glad he'd brought her. Small trees with low, switching limbs whipped them thoroughly, but he continued without pause. When the raiding party had returned and learned of their escape, they would follow on horseback and they knew this land like the backs of their hands.

After some time of running, he suddenly burst from the woods and into a clearing before he could stop himself. His long legs carried them, stumbling, over a clay ridge and then down into a low place - damp and muddy. He soon realized it was a dried-up riverbed. When he paused to rest and survey this terrain, Mirola' slid from his back and went to some thick rushes fringing the edge of this depression. Digging at the base of them, she gathered some stalks. From within her robe she slipped a blade and, with it, showed him how they could be peeled, exposing the white, tender core at the bottom. She bit off a little of this and gave him a little to taste. He thought the stuff was bland but she was bent on gathering some and since it was moist, he could see it would be good to carry along. As they worked at this, he glanced down the length of the riverbed where it disappeared into a meadow, and spied - far across on the horizon - what appeared to be a village or fortress of some sort, standing upon a plateau. His heart rose within him as he stood still, wondering what it might be.

The damsel, seeing where he looked, ran in front of him, shaking her hands at him, motioning him back toward the woods. She made motions of dire meaning, seeming to say that those who dwelt there would either slay or enslave them. He still hesitated, dreaming toward that citadel, for he had been thinking of the unlikelihood of finding a ship waiting at the seaside, just at the time when they arrived. They would be very lucky to find one within days, and the dwarf would surely find them before then. It could even be a matter of months before a ship was seen, and even if they eluded the dwarf for so long a time, what would happen to the damsel? She would never be allowed on a ship, unless she were to go as a slave.

He soothingly patted her arm. Indicating his light hair and skin, his height, and using the words she seemed to understand, he pointed to the habitation across the plain - his question clear upon his face. She hesitated, uneasily looking from him (whom she trusted) to that place she seemed to dread. Then, with a puzzled expression she nodded, reluctantly, (as though she did not like it or had not thought of it) admitting that the ones who lived there were indeed, like himself. Still, her fear returned and she snatched at his clothes, holding his arm as she beseeched him in her alien tongue, not to go there. He was tempted anyway, for he had heard there were Christian sanctuaries in this country, and knew there were Roman settlements here, also. But, her eyes were larger than ever and terror shone in their depths. So, he was persuaded to return to their route to the sea, to try their luck there first.

They found springs of water when they had gone some miles farther, but they had nothing to carry it in. He was hungry from running through miles of rough terrain. The damsel then surprised him by lifting her robe. Underneath she wore another garment, looped up and tied at her waist with a braided cord so that it formed a pocket. In this, she had secreted a little food - as much as she could take without being noticed. (This was when he realized she had hoped all along that he would take her with him.)

Unfortunately, it was a meager ration - some dried fruit, a bit of unleavened bread - that they quickly devoured. Afterward, when the girl bent over the spring to drink, she cried out and collapsed on the ground. When he rolled her over onto her back, she clasped her stomach and raised her legs in agony. He laid his large hand on her belly. It was swollen and hot to the touch. Her face and throat were also hot. She was sick, no doubt of it. He considered what to do. He helped her wet herself down with the cool water —after that, she smiled brightly and acted as though she felt better. He doubted that was true, but they had to move on.

About mid-afternoon, they heard voices and movement in the woods along the path, and prostrated themselves in the shade of a copse. From there they watched the approach of three men - an old man leading an ass, and two young men with him. The ass was loaded with sacks whose contents he could not ascertain, but which he fervently hoped was food. The men talked idly as they tramped along. He strained his ears to hear their language, for he could see they were not the dwarf's tribesmen and had the look of those farmers from his own land. He started to rise from hiding, but the damsel held him back. Tears running down her cheeks, she silently implored him, yet even as she did so, she was forced to stretch herself out on the ground in order to ease the pressure in her belly which caused her such pain. This decided him. He motioned to her that she should stay hidden and quiet, while he would see if they had food, then he would return to her.

He circled the trees and appeared before the men on the path. That startled them, for they had not seen or heard him coming, and the sun was at his back, making a halo around his frighteningly large form. They gasped and were about to draw their knives. He waved his hands in the air to show himself a peaceful man and tried the Roman tongue, whereupon they calmed themselves and sheathed their weapons. Once they had gotten over their shock, they were avidly curious about him. So he quickly told them how he had been captured and kept in slavery by the heathen tribe. This made them intensely angry. The old man spat upon the ground and launched himself into such a tirade against the looters and despoilers who roamed the land that the Captive began to think he would never be quiet long enough for him to ask for food.

They didn't have any food to spare, for they were journeying to their home in the fastness of the blue mountains. He told them of the shipwreck and of his destination - the seacoast - where he hoped to find and hail, another vessel. The old man shook his head, (and the Captive's heart sank) then told him that the only safe harbor was a good forty miles away, to the East and over rough terrain. The old man was toothless, and chewed his gums as he ruminated on the situation. But his son interrupted his sire's rambling conversation to tell the Captive about a sanctuary. When he eagerly described it and its location, the Captive recognized this as the place he had been tempted by. Then both farmers were pleased and relieved that the problem was thus solved. Yes, they said, the sanctuary would be the best place for the Captive, for they were Christians there. They did not turn anyone away and would protect him from harm.

* * *

The Disciple had been dreaming of lost sheep. In the dream, he felt he must go to find them. It seemed important to him, and he remembered it well when he awoke. It continued to bother him all the day. So, when the Evenstone shepherd went to fetch the flock from their place of grazing, he stopped him, and said he would go instead. That is how it happened that when the weary Captive stumbled his way across the plain toward the sanctuary, carrying the sick and sleeping damsel in his arms, he saw a figure walking out to meet them.

Hannah was once more called upon for her skill, and prayers were uplifted to God as they laid their hands on the sick child. Later, Mirola' awakened to the shock of cool water on her skin. She was in the bath, where Hannah held her. At first, her eyes grew large with alarm, but the water was so refreshing and something about the face of the old woman calmed her. So she gave herself into Hannah's care. Through the following days while she became well again she took on the serenity of Evenstone and was at peace. The Christians welcomed her among them. Though she could have lived with a family in the outer quarters, she chose to stay with Hannah - and within sight of her Captive.

The Captive and the Disciple talked for long hours. It was a pleasure to both of them, for the Captive knew much of the news in other lands, and the Disciple was a learned man who explained much about the races of people in this land where they had settled. The Disciple was disgusted by the stories the Captive had to tell of wickedness among the tribes people. Although he had given these two - the giant man and the little heathen girl - sanctuary, he was troubled by the fact that the little maid was one of that race who were becoming more encroaching; more daring, and therefore might cause trouble for his people. And the strength of the Roman armies was much weaker now, and less feared.

* * *

The Crown (cont.)
and the Jewels

I see a man . . . . a jewel merchant. He buys stones in this land and sells them across the sea, in other lands around the Mediterranean. I see him seated on a carpet inside a tent . . . Someone brings him jewels to inspect. They are displayed on a cloth with padding underneath, so that they will not roll off. The gems are clustered in the center of the cloth, like a beautiful flower - they glow in shades of yellow, red and blue. They are not really smooth stones, but polished enough to appraise the colors.

After he has inspected the stones, he draws up the corners of the dark cloth and making a bag of it, secures the top with a double ring closure. Then he places the bag under his robe. He does not dress like the dwarf's tribesmen. He wears a long tunic and over that a robe, belted at his waist. When traveling, his headdress is a length of cloth - half of it wrapped around his head and secured in the back, where the remaining end of it is allowed to drape over the nape of his neck. He is obviously a man who spends much time in the sun, for the skin of his face is thin and brown, stretched tight over high cheekbones . . . and the forks of those deep wrinkles at the corners of his eyes extend far down his face, past the jaw line. But it is a patrician face - set with grey eyes. His long hair is the same grey, and of a fine texture.

When he travels, he has bodyguards - for they may be attacked at any time by those who know what he carries. First, they will try to out-run them, for they have fine, fast horses, but if they cannot, they will fight.

I see one of his mounted bodyguards racing along, leaning forward in the saddle, his clothing curling in the wind of his passage. He is quite a spectacle, a dramatic subject for the artist's brush. . . He holds the reins in both hands, but between his teeth is his long curved knife, ready to his hand. In the event that one of their pursuers comes alongside him, He will gather the reins in one hand, and seize the hilt of his knife. Then the thieves will soon see their error and will soon leave them alone. This man's naturally dark beard has been bleached by the sun to a fiery red, and

*his eyes are a warm red brown. He is called "Red Beard" and is known and feared
by many thieves, some of whom bear the marks of his wicked knife.*

At Evenstone, the new refugees had settled in. Although he now understood the lesson, the Disciple was still offended by the carving – to him,
the carved crown was flawed and made ugly by the ill placed stones. But,
although he had prayed for guidance, he couldn't think of a way to correct
this without greater sin.

One evening, the jewel merchant and his men halted in their travel
to ask for food and a bed at the sanctuary, where none were turned away
hungry. He had visited before. The people there were kind and since he
loved beautiful things, he was always interested in the place. He had great
respect for their Christian leader, who could conceive and build such a place
in this wilderness. When he and his men arrived, a tall man whom he had
not noticed before was at work raising a beam for a grape arbor. He saw his
naked back first, with the sweat trickling down it - All the workers were
stripped to the waist for it was still hot, even this late in the day. When the
tall man had secured his burden and turned around, the merchant knew
he had not seen his face before. Perhaps a new convert, he thought. . . a big
Roman, probably.

As they all broke bread together, the talk was friendly but although the
tall man sat with them, no explanation was given for his appearance among
them and the merchant's manners forbade that he ask outright. After the
meal, when his men found their pallets, he strolled through the sanctuary - admiring, as always, the craftsmanship. This time he was brought up
abruptly by a most peculiar change - so unexpected because it was ugly
- the jewels so crudely set in the crown.

He waited until morning to ask his host about it, but the Disciple
made little of it, as though he were ashamed. The puzzled merchant could

easily believe that such a thing would grate on the fastidious Christian, but
why, then, was it done? Drawn once more to the chapel, he examined the
stones more closely in the light of morning. When he had assured himself
as to what they were, he was even more intrigued. Although some were
flawed, among them were some very large and very valuable gems. He was
excited by this discovery, for the hunt for such treasure was the spice of his
life, but he had an obligation to his host - to make sure he was informed
of their value. So, he sought him out again and with excellent manners,
explained his concern. The Disciple listened, sighed, and inviting him to
sit with him in the garden, he related the story of the boy and how he had
set the stones.

The merchant was amused, by the attitudes of both - the boy and the
Disciple, who was now worried about the material value of the gems. He
knew that these particular Christians shunned the amassing of wealth, but
he did not understand the distinction. Evenstone and its buildings were
beautiful, the carvings and ornamentation were a delight. The place was
a marvel of ingenuity in the layout of its gardens and water courses. So
surely the place itself was valuable, he pointed out to the Disciple. "What
is a stone?" he asked. "Evenstone is made of stones. Just because men place
more value on some than others, what is the difference, really?" Also, he
reasoned with his troubled host, wasn't the ornamentation of the crown just
the work of the boy's hands, just as Evenstone, as a whole, was the work of
all of them? His argument gave the Disciple another lesson to study.

The merchant truly sympathized about the crudity of the setting,
and returned to the carving to explore it further. Running his forefin-
ger over the rough edges of the wood which surrounded the stones, he
thought about it and finally suggested that the situation could be rem-
edied by smoothly cutting the holes, then setting ivory cups within to
hold the stones. The jewels could be reshaped and refined so that they

would be more translucent and their colors would glow against the white of the ivory.

The Disciple brought in the boy to hear what the merchant had to say. It went well, and he was pleased to see how the boy was not hurt, but was eager to learn how to improve the crown. The merchant, who enjoyed making money, had a selfish motive too, because he wanted the boy to find more such stones for him. So he spent some time explaining the assessment of jewels and the polishing and setting of them. The boy, who was attracted by the beauty of the stones and wanted to enhance that beauty, was very interested. In short, they were all three very pleased with the visit and the boy looked forward to the merchant's return, when he would bring the ivory to make the settings.

* * *

The Jewel merchant and his body guards were maneuvering their horses down a slippery slope which led from the hills to the sea, when they were caught off guard by the dwarf and his men. Red Beard cried out a warning and brandished his wicked curved blade, but as they wheeled their mounts around to retreat, they found they were surrounded. The dwarf had many men, armed with lances. The merchant's men saw they were trapped and although Red Beard and the others would have fought valiantly, the merchant surrendered. It was not the first time they had been robbed, but it was a bitter thing for the merchant just the same, for he was carrying some fine stones and a customer across the sea was waiting for them.

To the merchant's surprise, the dwarf did not get on with it immediately, but asked them an odd question. He wanted to know if they had seen a large man . . . light of skin - a foreigner. At first he didn't understand, for he had seen no such traveler on his way. But the dwarf was persistent, and the tribesmen prodded him with their lances, to awaken his memory. Then he thought of the large man who had spoken but little, at the Christians' table. Shrewdly, he bargained for the information. If they would release him and his men with their main possessions, he would tell them what he knew.

* * *

Even while the dwarf and his men besieged Evenstone, the blood of the Jewel merchant and the great Red Beard watered the roots of the wild flowers that grew in the meadow at the base of the hills. The other guards, being more cowardly, had managed to escape in the commotion.

All of those within the houses outside Evenstone's walls had sought safety within the sanctuary and the courtyard. They huddled together, praying silently, as they listened to the exchange between the Disciple in the watchtower and the barbarians outside. Mirola and the boy sought out the strength of Hannah, and stayed by her side. The dwarf was angry and wanted his slave and the girl returned. The Disciple, who understood their language, spoke calmly, but he did not dare to open the gate, for then they might have stormed in and slaughtered them all.

When the Disciple came down to speak to his people, he was grave. It would not be difficult for the tribesmen to scale the walls, nor to loot the outer houses. Yet, they could not give up the girl and man to be treated as they would certainly be. They had always promised sanctuary to the lost and alone, and they would give it. He thought of a ransom for these robbers, but Evenstone had nothing which would be valued by the heathen - they would be blind to its beauty and would simply trample it underfoot. There was no gold or silver, few Roman coins, and their small flock of sheep outside they would certainly take, anyway. The sight of the tribes-people had disgusted him, they were like jackdaws with their finery and jewels, parading their stolen loot with pride . . . And then he thought of the jewels in the crown.

As the boy stood before the carving, looking at the dark stones and the little figures reaching toward the bending Son of God, the Disciple explained the carving to him and as he did so, the boy understood – that those riches valued by men were not important to God. As Christ had said, "silver and gold, have I none, yet such as I have, I give unto you." The real jewels in the heavenly crown of Christ were all those souls who were saved by his sacrifice. Now, the Disciple said, they could sacrifice those jewels (which were only stones) for the lives and souls of the man and the girl. The boy's tender heart was greatly moved, and he ran to fetch the chisel so that they could remove the stones.

The offer was made, and accepted. The dwarf was not really so courageous as to destroy the place - since it had the blessing of the Romans - and besides, the jewels dazzled him. These, with the ones he had taken from the merchant, would swell his treasure and increase his prestige. As for his men, they were weary to the point of rebellion. There was no heart in them to fight the men of Evenstone, for they didn't want the slave returned to them, nor did they think the girl was important. As long as she and the slave had been paid for, their pride was appeased. And so the affair ended with relief all around, though the depth and quality of satisfaction may have differed between the parties concerned.

As for the crown - the rough, gaping holes (even larger now) that had held the jewels were left just as they were, for as long as Evenstone stood. It served as a constant reminder that the most beautiful things cannot be seen with human eyes and that, of all beautiful things, LOVE is, by far, the greatest.

* * *

Dear Richard

Well, I don't know what to make of this one. Obviously it seems further back in time. I don't have any ties to anything in this story that I can think of. Well, on second thought, I have always loved horses and when I "saw" the wild horses moving harmoniously, in unison, in waves through the grass, it was truly sensational for me – made my spine tingle. Nothing else, though.

I can't say for sure where they were. Land masses were not as they are now. It was confusing, different, and I felt disoriented. However, I had a strong feeling that the "wild land of the horses" was at least a portion of what is now North America. Yes, I confirmed that prehistoric horse bones have been found here in the USA; also I know there were cliff dwellings of this type, so I suppose it is possible that this could have happened. But I am trying not to care anymore about whether it "really happened." In fact, I am beginning to question the truth about what we see and hear in the world. There is something false about the whole thing. I know when we are little babies the world scares us with its oddness. Maybe, as some say, it is all an illusion. So perhaps some of this book is factual "history," and some of it isn't. I don't know.

Tell me Richard, do you think life experience on earth is a projection of mind from the still point of the present into the past and future? If so, can we relive our past from the present moment and change it, to make it right? Has everything already happened? Are we rewriting history?

Anyway, here's the last story. I had a couple of others but will not publish them.

The Lure

They call him by a word meaning "bald one" because he is the son of the bald man, though he himself is not bald. Whenever he has just sharpened his knife blade, and while it still has the keenest edge, he trims his abundant black hair and beard. This is not because of vanity, but because it must be kept shorn so that it will not be a nuisance to him in the wilds where he hunts. His hair is seldom seen, for he wears a soft leather hat — a tight-fitting, dome-shaped article that protects him from the elements and while flying past tree limbs on his tearing rides.

His homeland is temperate, with ice only in the higher elevations. Their habitation within this land is a sunlit valley sheltered by great brooding mountains and plateaus. It is a good place, their valley, because there is ample green grass for the horses which they capture and breed, and have improved in size. Yet, he is a man torn between two lands - his homeland, and that other land he loves - the wild land - the land where they hunt the wild horses.

While he is in the wild land, he can look toward the setting sun, and feel secure in the knowledge that his home lies in that direction. He delights in the hunt, and the adventures he has in that land satisfy a great need within him. Back home he has a woman and children. They dwell within the protection of his wife's people while he is away. She and his home are one in his mind - both represent comfort and safety to him. When he returns to the village in the valley, he lays down his weapon and hunting snares and takes up yeoman's tools. There his life becomes tame again as he teaches his young sons to do simple things. While he is home, he is sated for awhile - relieved of his urges by his wife, and full of the food prepared by her. But after some time - when he is well rested again and the seasons change, he will begin dreaming of that other place. The thought of it makes his heart race. His eyes gleam as his mind envisions the glory of it. Even though he knows it also means danger and deprivation, he is irresistibly drawn. He cannot help himself. When this urge overtakes him, he will make preparations, and - deaf to the complaints of his wife - he will leave his comfortable fireside and go. The nearer he comes to that shore — to that wild, wonderful land of horses - the more exhilarated he becomes.

Bald was the leader of a band of horse-hunters. Every few years they would leave their homeland to travel to the far country. Bald had made his first such journey when he was only a beardless boy. The trip was always tedious, but it was worth the trouble, for they all profited by the trade of the horses that they captured there, and had tamed. At one point along the way, they would make crude boats, then, after they had passed the two places where they would use them to get themselves, their horses and gear across, they would leave them behind. Hiding them the best they could in brush and reeds, they would hope they would still be there when they returned. If they were not, they would have to stay there until they could build more, along with the rafts on which they would carry the captured horses. The boats were rowed or poled, as necessity dictated, and the rafts were towed behind them.

At the time of his forty-first year, he had readied himself for another such hunting expedition. During the winter months, they and their wives had been busy preparing the dried meat, vegetable roots and cakes of grain for them to eat when there was no fresh thing to be had. Then, one morning, Bald could smell spring in the air. The soil was beginning to warm early. The ice was breaking over the high places. . . It was time, he said, and they made haste.

There were always some men left behind with the women, children, and the old people. It was left to them to plant and gather the harvest in the meantime. When the hunters returned, they would bring, besides the horses, choice furs and deerskins for the women and toys they had carved in their idle hours for the children. This was done to appease those whose tiresome complaints always followed them on the trail eastward, taking the edge off their great adventure.

His wife did not understand his need for adventure and she was blind to the beauty he saw in earthly things. She was not beautiful, but he had not expected to be blessed with a beautiful wife. She had a round face, pale blue eyes, a short nose and her blonde hair was dull, as she was herself. Like all her people, she was stout and sturdy. They were the conquerors, and had not forgotten it. Bald was often exasperated with them, because they were stern; with no humor. His people (who were more recent immigrants to her land) were different - both in appearance and in their ways. His people, his father, had come over the mountains in the harshness of winter, thirsty and tired. Humbly they had come, ready to do the bidding of these unbending, stolid people who had cut off their routes to water. They had almost all died out now. He had found it was good to be away, sometimes, from his wife's people.

Everyone and everything in the village was astir with excitement when the hunting party made their departure. Bald, breathing deeply, felt full and happy, looking forward to whatever lay ahead. Then his little daughter, her legs hampered by the heavy wrappings which protected her against the raw wind sweeping down from the mountains, stumped her way over to him and clung to his legs, looking up at him with large blue eyes. Then somehow, it did not feel right that he should be so happy to go. She would yearn for him, he knew. That was the only thing that dampened his spirits when he bid his land and people farewell, and her little round face framed in red-gold hair would haunt his mind for that first part of their journey. But then, when the trials of their journey began, he would give his attention to those.

He had told her he would come again, and would bring her a pretty fur to keep her warm. He did not know he would never see her face again.

* * *

Not only does he have a passion for the hunt, but for the horses, themselves. He is filled with delight by the sight of a flock feeding on the plain. These horses are a small, compact breed - shaggy ponies with long tails. It is their wild nature that has charmed him so, for they are like no tame beasts, nor like any other creature on earth. From a high place, he can watch them, fascinated, for hours. They seem to be guided by something unseen and unheard by man, something from outside themselves, which each one of the flock hears, or feel - for they are always joined in a kind of rhythm. Even when they sport and frisk about, their frolic does not seem random but rather like a synchronized dance. Digging in their hooves, they make sharp turns effortlessly, wheeling and twisting. Their movements are quick and fluid . . . manes tossing and tails flashing. With those sharp hooves, they beat upon the ground in that particular rhythm to which they are attuned. He listens to that staccato beat . . . amazed by the music in it. He watches as they sweep the valley floor, the waving blades of grass, in turn, becoming part of the rhythm by their passage. Even as they run at high speed, they do not part from this rhythm, but willingly, gracefully, manifest that spirit which moves them. They are the willing instruments, that which moves them is the conductor. They flow over the plain - like the wind, which suddenly blows, then ebbs, blows and ebbs, sinuously sighing and circling . . . then gusts yearningly forward again. They are "the birds of the grass," he thinks, because as the flocks of the air turn and wheel freely yet as one being in the sky, so do these horses move upon the earth. There was a magic in this that he wanted to understand.

But then he and his men must interfere and cause a crude departure in that lovely rhythm. Then all is chaos, as the little ponies whirl and start with shock. Then, they have lost the rhythm, and they rear and kick and churn the grass . . . . eyes rolling, nostrils flaring - indignant that men should come and ruin their peace. If Bald and his men are lucky, the animals will not injure themselves or their captors. If they cannot tame a horse enough before they return home, then they must leave it behind. But they are skilled with horses, so this is rare.

When they survey a herd from the high land above, they ride quietly up to the place, then storm into the valley and surround the herd. He chooses the stallion that is their leader and relishes the confrontation, the cunning moves of the horse. They use ropes - those they have made for themselves on winter nights at home. Sometimes they use a length of rope with elongated metal weights on each end, which, when thrown at the animals legs, will make him halt until they ride swiftly in to bridle him. This is risky, and they must get to him soon, or the horse will injure himself.

Bald has devised a method that is more subtle, and more sure. I see him dragging something over the ground. This device is a bladder containing sex lure; urine from a mare in breeding time. (A stallion's eyes dilate, his nostrils flare and his soft muzzle quivers as he smells the scent. Then the horse whickers and looks around, seeking the unseen mare. He acts dazed and slow-witted. Bald, watching out of scent range, is amused by this.) In this way the men can attract the lead stallion and his herd into the enclosed place they have selected. When the stallion is within the one opening, they secure it, rolling boulders into it, so that he cannot escape. Sometimes, though, the horse outsmarts them and escapes. When this happens, the other men may curse, but Bald only laughs, his eyes alight with pleasure in the game.

The Lure (cont.)
Deep in the Wild Land

One day, Bald had left his men and gone off on his own, on foot. He was following the course of a river through deeply forested terrain, scouting for horses and game. He had made his way into unfamiliar and rough woods above the stream, seeking a rise of land from which he might see over the river into any valley which might exist below. The forest where he wandered was ferned and lushly overgrown - unlike the woods of his homeland. He was always freshly amazed at the monstrous size of the trees - for nothing grew like that from where he came. He had walked for some time, circling around impassable areas, trying to follow the route of the river, which he knew was there somewhere below him although he could no longer see it. He had not intended to come so far, but he was not very concerned. He could find his way back.

He was straining his ears for the sound of the water, when he heard, at some distance away, a high, singing-sighing sound, at some distance away. It sounded like a keening wind, but the day was still. He stopped, and wondered - and then warily, slowly, made his way toward it. His hand on his knife hilt, he trod softly, trying to make no noise as he made his way through the landscape of tangled brush and overgrown vines. All the time he was following the sound. When it stopped, he stopped, and when it began again he once more made his way toward its source.

As he drew nearer, he knew for certain that it was not the river, waterfall, or wind, and he was greatly puzzled about what sort of animal living in this country would make such a queer noise. At the same time, he was caught up in this new adventure; excited, and curious. Head down, carefully watching his feet, he continued through the thick woods. He knew he was almost upon it, when he was surprised by bright sunlight and raised

THE LURE   389

his head to see an unexpected opening in the wooded screen before him. Just at that time, the noise (which had been silent for a little time) suddenly shrieked to life with such velocity, and sounded so near, that he sprang forward in haste (a great mistake for a careful hunter), slid over rocks covered with wet leaves and vines that rolled underfoot, and fell heavily over the edge of a deep ravine, his arms flailing outward in a vain attempt to catch hold of a branch or vine to stop his fall.

Later, when he regained his wits, all was quiet. He lay there in the bottom of the steep abyss - partly saved by the brush growing in the bottom. First, he cursed his carelessness, then he assessed the damage. There was a numbing, tingling pain in his left leg and hip, his elbow was bleeding, and his left arm would not move. He stirred, trying to get some relief from the rocks and brush that were digging into him. He straightened his legs, and since he saw that he could move both of them and no flesh was torn, he was relieved.

When he could stand, he cradled his helpless left arm, (which was losing its numbness and beginning to pain him) and stumbled around that prison in which he found himself. The sides of the ravine were slippery rocks, covered with mud and wet moss and plants. The bottom of the place was sandy and was marked with water trails, so he knew that at times water ran rapidly through here. There was something more, which made the hair upon his neck stand up, so aware was he of danger. He could see signs of frantic disturbance within the ravine. There were wallowed out places at the base of the walls that scuffling, human feet had made, and clumps of mud and leaves lying on the ground where it had been skinned from the slippery, now-exposed rocks. Someone had been trying to climb out - unsuccessfully, it appeared. He was still here. Warily, Bald quickly turned his attention to a narrow recess formed by this land fissure; that side so thickly overgrown with brush that he could not see what was behind it.

The brush in that part of the ravine was wickedly thick and thorny, but he could see that it had been disturbed, for there were broken limbs. Whoever was in there was a desperate creature - and Bald knew that a desperate, caged man or animal could be dangerous indeed. And here he was, handicapped by his fall. He paused, knowing it would be foolhardy to crash his way into the overgrowth and find an armed enemy waiting behind it. Yet, Bald was not a man to wait for danger to come to him, and he had to find a way out. He flexed his left arm. It was stronger now, although still painful. He unsheathed his knife and automatically tested its blade, and then cautiously, he pressed into the thicket, slashing at the tangle with his knife.

He soon found a barrier ahead. It was an overhanging rock ledge, just at his eye level. Uneasily, and with his knife ready, he squatted down to see under it. To his surprise, beneath the ledge in a sort of small cave, was a small boy. They stared at each other and Bald relaxed, for this child was no threat to him. The boy's eyes were dark, as was his hair, and his skin was pale. He was squatting, his knees drawn up under his chin - just a small, frightened chick of a boy. Then there was a noise and Bald was quickly on guard again, as the boy's eyes flicked to where the saplings beyond the ledge rattled and shook. Once more, Bald heard the sound that he had followed - that keening noise, which now sounded much more like a human being. "Perhaps another child," he thought. He started to rise to his feet, but the boy became upset at his movement, skittering around under the ledge in a frantic way.

Bald couldn't know it, but he was a frightening, alien sight to the boy, who had never seen such a man as he looked, nor dressed as he was. The face that Bald made (although he intended it to be pleasant and calming) shocked the boy to the core. The smile disappeared into the recesses of a black mustache and beard, while his broad cheeks stretched across and upward, making a mass of wrinkles below his blue eyes. The hunter's face was fierce and shaped by many years of wind and sun. The black brows were wiry and bristling below the strange cap which fit his skull so well that at first the boy had thought it was his skull, until he saw the tendrils of black hair sticking out from behind the man's ears. Bald remained silent, but made (what he thought were) soothing gestures to reassure the boy that he meant him no harm. Then rising, he followed the noises and the vibration coming from that thicket of branches - his mind busy with his thoughts. His tension had dissipated, for now, he knew well what this was - these children had fallen into the same trap, and one had hung himself up in the thicket, trying to escape. Well, perhaps that was the only way to get out. . . He would see.

He was in sympathy for the children, for it was a struggle to make a way through the thicket, even for him - a thick, meaty man of full age, and used to a life in the wild. (His mind ignored his present weakness, the pain from the fall. He was still a mighty man.) It was an extraordinary kind of scrubby growth, for when the seed fell into this gorge, they sent up narrow, leafless sprigs that twisted and entwined themselves and leaning their spindly frames upon the rocks, they levered upward, stubbornly determined to reach the sunlight above. Protected from the wind and cold within the walls of the gorge, they also grew abnormally thick - battling each other for what little space there was.

The wiry branches were cruelly frustrating, for they hampered every move of an arm or leg, forcing him to stop often and cut away the wood. Even as he did so, other limbs tore at his stout clothing. Even his snug-fitting hat, which had remained on his head during his fall and had remained in its place through many wild rides and battles, was loosed so that he had to stop and pull it down again. When he had worked his way through the maze to the spot where the noises emanated, he wrenched aside the last branches that impeded his way and twisting his frame, peered upward toward the source of the sounds.

Then, his mouth fell open with his surprise, for it was not a boy in this thicket, but a woman, and from the look of it, she was bound within the weave of the torturous limbs, as surely as the best trap could have done. Some of it was her own doing, he supposed, as he surveyed the situation, since she had twisted this way and that and in trying to escape the loops which bound her, she had, instead, become more surely ensnared. The vines and branches girded her torso and when she struggled to free herself by moving one of those restrictions, another branch, connected to the first, would throttle her. As he puzzled over this odd situation, deciding which were the best limbs and vines to cut in order to free her, she stopped her writhing and twisted her head to look down on him. Her brown hair curtained her face, but he could see the dark of her eyes, and then, as they registered her fear - the whites of them. (No doubt she was not used to civilized men, he thought.)

She rattled the branches in a fresh frenzy, and he thought of Ampligole, the leader of a tribe of wild men in this part of the land. This woman must be one of his people, he thought. If he freed her, she would surely run to Ampligole and tell him of their presence. That wouldn't do. They had been taking horses that Ampligole claimed as his own, for he was unfair and claimed rights to everything in this land. So, Bald rested a moment, leaning back against the wall of saplings, as he thought and considered the woman in her cage. Then there was a rustle at his feet and he glanced down to find the boy standing there. He was small and frail and strangely pale, he thought, to be one of Ampligole's tribe. Well, anyway, he had to find his own way out of here and, until then, he would return this boy's mother to him. Later, he would decide what to do with them.

"Quiet!" he called loudly to the woman. "You will get your boy in a froth." He knew she would not know what he said, but it had the desired effect, anyway. She was still as he whittled at the branches that held her prisoner. While he worked he wondered how long she had been like this. Finally, he reached up where the limbs clasped her waist, and grasped her clothing, holding her fast to keep her from falling when he pulled her free. Her waist was thin, and felt warm - in fact, the heat caused by her exertions came off her like steam. When the last limb fell and she dangled from his hand, she reached out to lay her hands on him to steady herself. As she did so, she looked him in the face. . . and he looked fully, for the first time, into hers.

A strange feeling came over him as he looked at her. He was caught by surprise. He didn't have time to understand it, but it was almost like fear. It was only a fleeting moment, though it seemed a long time that they looked at each other - and her with that stern look on her face - those piercing dark eyes. For a moment he thought he would strangle, from the fullness in his chest. He was aware only of silence, perfect stillness, as he was nailed to the moment. But then she moved a little and he had to rouse himself to set her down on the ground, and then when he had done so, he was appalled to find that his hands were trembling. But, he asked himself, couldn't even a man like himself be overcome with such a fall as he had made, and the labor after it? She trod upon his feet when they stood, since there was not room in the thicket stumps and hewn limbs for them both to stand upright. He backed up and staggered against the brush. He felt awkward . . It was odd and he hated that feeling.

She pushed her way around him and took the boy back into the little cave. There she sat shaking and panting like a wild animal, the boy huddled against her. Bald came and squatted before the opening, looking at them for a moment. Her hair was dark brown - wavy and full. It made a thick screen around her head and shoulders. She tossed it back from her eyes like a horse does its mane, and stared back at him. Although she was tired and probably in need of food and water, her face said she was not afraid of him. She even dared him with her eyes. That shocked him. Abruptly, he drew back and stood upright.

Still in an odd haze of distraction and puzzlement, he made his way back to the open area of the ravine. There, he forced his mind to practical matters and looked around. He soon found there would be no exit within the clearing, and he would be a fool to try. The only way out would be to get a footing on the slippery wall of the ravine, by using the saplings and vines as support to climb upward, just as the woman had tried.

The woman . . . His thoughts reeled back to her - that strange, dark-eyed woman, squatting in the cave. Why had she hated him with her eyes? He felt suddenly sad.

He caught himself wandering aimlessly about, no longer strong and decisive, his thinking muddled. A sudden tiredness overwhelmed him. He thought his fall must have been worse than he had thought. Gathering his wits, he decided he needed rest . . . . Yes, he would rest a little while before he went back to work some way out. Stumbling, he made his way back into the tangle from which he had come. It was easier now, of course, since he had cleared a narrow way through to the cave.

When he got to the cave, he found the woman and boy were outside. Evidently they had been searching again, for another way out. When she saw him, she pressed herself against the wet rocks. He wondered if the rocks were always wet, or whether they might yet scramble out during dry weather. He asked her that, indicating the wetness, pointing toward the sun with the question. She shook her head, and made a stretching gesture with her hands which he took to mean it would be a long time before that happened, and she showed him the water marks in the ground which he had noticed earlier. Her face was tense. The flood might come through here if it rained. Again, he considered her - wishing she spoke his language and wondering where she lived. Whose woman was she? But he knew no way to ask that by signs.

He bent and entered the little cave. Once in, he could stand upright and look around. There were no comforts of home here, so they could not have been in there long - existing on what little this place could offer in food, and with no fresh water that he could see. He found a dry place and lay down - avoiding his left side where the pain was throbbing now. He did not remove his pack, even to sleep – not in the wild country. He only shifted it around his waist from the back to his right side. His knives were safe in their sheaths, one in his shirt and the one at his waist, both near to hand. When she of the dark eyes came in again, he observed her through slitted eyes. Stealthily, she squatted down near the opening, obscuring what little light there was. When she saw he was only resting, she relaxed. The boy came and sat down beside her, laying his head in her lap. It was quiet except for the gentle rustling of leaves and she sat there, soothingly strok- ing the boy's hair. Bald, feigning sleep, saw she was no longer a vixen, but was capable of tenderness. It was peaceful. Their dark figures were haloed by the dim light from outside. He fell asleep.

As though a bad spirit had come to disturb his sleep, he woke with a start. She was bending over him, her arms raised, his large knife in her hand, the blade glimmering in the pale light. Her upper lip was twitching. The boy was standing behind her, trembling and ashen-faced. This much he saw before he lunged forward, butting his head into her middle, as he would have done to any enemy who crept up on him while he was sleeping. Not thinking of her being a woman, he did not spare her, but knocked the breath out of her. Still, even though she was in a swoon and trying to

breathe, he had to pry her fingers from the knife-hilt. He admired her spirit -
she was no weak female.

It was when he forced the knife from her hand, that he saw the marks
on her arms and wrists. He sat beside her as she struggled for breath, holding her arms so that he could examine them. Burns and scars from being
bound. So - then he understood why she acted this way against him - she
had been once been a captive of Ampligole and he knew what happened to
captive women there. They were tied spread-legged and arms tied, and the
men came at them again and again. He had heard some had died from it.
Then they would cut the stiff bodies loose and would roll them off across
the ground and away from their campfire, discarded like bones from a meal.
If the women lived, they sometimes kept them as slaves. Then they would
move on to their next prey in another village, or they would return to their
homes where their own women waited.

He had thought she didn't look like them. She had to be from a different people. He hoped she had escaped before they had done their worst.
From the looks of her arms, she had endured this treatment more than
once, but not very recently, for the scars were old and faint. He pondered
this, wondering what her story was - if she had been kept captive for a
long time, or had been released, to have been captured again. As he held
her arms, he became aware that she was breathing raggedly, her dark eyes
staring, boring into his mind, as though she knew what he was thinking.
He thought she was odd, even eerie, yet she fascinated him. He pointed to
her arms. "Ampligole?" he asked. Her eyes widened with surprise, and then
she nodded.

When she saw the disgust on his face, a glad singing went through
her tense body, as though doors had opened in her being and a sweet
breeze blew through. It was all right. He was not such a man as the others. He was as different as he looked. Then, the sudden relaxing of her

nerves and body were too much, so that tears welled up in her eyes, and her chin trembled.

He was amazed. It was so unexpected. The change from fierce fighting woman to sweet, trembling female now wounded his heart. She had been hurt and needed protection, that was all. Impulsively, he lifted the wrist he held and caressed her scars with his cheek and lips. Then it was her turn to be amazed - as he was himself - by what he had done. Her face broke into gentleness, the hardness gone. He filled his eyes with her . . . and there came upon him such a powerful, hot fullness throughout his body that he thought he would burst. Never had he felt such a strong desire for a woman. He was startled, and caution came down with a snap. He knew that he could not stay close to her, because the urge was too strong to do to her what the others had done. He was confused and then, ashamed. He would have had her, if she had been some other woman, but she had been hurt by men and now, he could see, she trusted him as her protector. Yet, in his temptation, he yearned over her. He would not hurt her - he would be gentle with her. When he thought about how he would be with her, it took all his strength to tear himself away. He rose from the ground and stepped back. Then he saw that the boy was watching them.

Bald had forgotten his existence and now he resented his presence.

Abruptly, he went out of the cave, concentrating his thoughts on finding a way out of their prison. Yet, as he chopped his way along the sides of the crevasse looking for a foothold, now he knew there was no danger of her running to Ampligole.

Finally, he found what he was looking for - rough outcroppings of stone where he could move upward and then, perhaps he could also brace his back against the thick woven branches to support himself. First, with the aid of broken branches, he scraped the outcroppings, the best that he could, of the slippery mud and ferns. When he turned, she was there, watching him sharply through a veil of branches. That fierce look was back on her face again. He smiled and gestured to the wall before him. She did not move, nor did she soften toward him, but merely watched. He wondered what to do with them. She needed his protection, he felt this strongly, yet he didn't want to take them back to his band because he would be expected to share her, and they had been away from women for a long time. Yet, he didn't want to leave them, either. The conflict in his mind hampered his efforts to ascend the wall. Distractedly, he slowly scrabbled his way along a lower level - twigs and vines breaking when he tested them. For some reason he did not understand, he was not eager to ascend and dallied, but when he looked down and caught a look of scorn on her face, he stirred himself. Sharpening his dulled wits, he easily propelled himself up and over the edge, grabbing at vines and limbs to bring himself over the final space and up and over the sloping rim.

Once up, he looked about and found a heavy vine, which he hung over the side to her. Because of the projecting ledge, he could not at first see where they were below and had to lean out and over the treacherous side to beckon to her to send the boy up. But she was already working her way up the vine, the boy clinging to her back! He was alarmed, for the weight of the boy would unbalance her, pulling her backward. He shouted down to her: "Wait!" he said, "Wait!". . . .And she looked up. . . .

Ah! Too late he realized he shouldn't have called to her, because when she leaned back at that sharp angle to look up over the ledge at him, the boy slid from her back and onto the rocks below. From where he stood, Bald could not see him land, but he heard most clearly the crack of the little skull as it struck the rocks. He shuddered, and could not move for a moment. Then he heard her wail. It was an awful sound. It tore through his inside like a knife. He sat back on the cold ground staring blindly into the trees. His guilt covering him like a cloak, he listened to the pitiful sounds from below: scrabbling, snuffling and weeping. For the first time, he was a coward. He made no move, but stayed where he was, his face in his hands.

After some time, the setting of the sun roused him, and he paced up and down the rim of the ravine, careful not to fall in again, looking for a way down. He could see that it would not be wise to go down the way he had come up. He called out to her at intervals, but she made no sound except for the weeping which had grown faint. He could not see into the thickness, to tell what she was doing. "Is the boy dead?" he called in his distress, knowing she did not understand what he said, and knowing the boy was surely dead. Still she did not make any answer, nor did she come up. Finally, when the woods grew dark, he checked the vine that it was still secure, then settled himself nearby. He unpacked his deerskin, wrapped himself in it and waited like a coward for the morning.

By now, his men would be wondering where he was, he thought. They might track him, or might not, depending on where they had got to and what they were doing. Thinking it over, he doubted they would find him, since he had strayed far from where he had intended. Well, he knew where they would be, and he could find them when he wanted.

* * *

At sun up, she surprises him again. Rushing from behind the trees, she flails at him with a stick, beating him with all her strength, whipping him for the loss of her son. He bears with it for a while, for his heart is full of sadness for her. He weeps inside for this woman. He cannot get near enough to stop her, for her arms are long and she is like an eagle, beating him with her wings. Finally, he lunges at her and grabs her legs, turning her upside down to disarm her. She drops her stick, but continues to fight, twisting and kicking, trying to bite his legs, even growling. The skirt she wears falls downward, so that her legs and private parts are exposed. Suddenly, she becomes aware of this circumstance, and stops, frozen in shock, for she realizes another danger, now. He feels her body go limp. He is also shocked, but aroused, but with this arousal there is a thread of the sympathy and remorse he had felt before this little incident had made his blood rise.

He takes her, there in the leaves, but first, he lies quietly beside her, his leg holding hers to the ground. Holding her wrists with his left hand, he strokes her face with his free hand. Gently caressing her he says all the sweet words he knows, hoping she understands their sound. She knows what is coming, but she is exhausted and weak with the weakness of a woman who desperately needs the support of a man. At first, she was sick with the thought of the thing that he would do, but then she sees tears standing in his eyes from the fullness of his emotion. This extraordinary thing surprises her into gentleness and weeping.

Finally, she holds him as he holds her. It is both sweet and sad, and so deeply felt that it was more than a physical mating. It was the sealing of the union of these two souls which was to last them all their earth time, and perhaps even beyond.

She grieved all the day, but she stayed with him, always keeping him within her sight while she gathered the herbs that she shared with him. He was surprised by her knowledge of these things. He, himself, had always relied on whatever meat could be found and certain berries they had learned would not poison them. He and his men did not know a great deal about the vegetation of this land. At first he thought she existed entirely on the herbs, but then she willingly took the partridge he had trapped and roasted for her, and seemed to relish it.

He lingered near the river in a temporary camp. He bathed himself, as did she. She treated his arm and they rested and comforted each other. He unpacked his bag and sharpened his tools as she foraged. It was a deep quiet except for the noises of birds and other animals that lived in these woods. There was such a wealth of game that food was never a problem.

As he rested and lingered with her, he thought of his home; the tameness of life there. His wife and her family were of the ruling tribe and it was a custom of those people to make a test of those mates who had been separated from their spouses, by using the crossed sticks. To do this, two sticks were laid - one atop the other - in a cross. Then the husband stepped over the sticks - if the top stick rolled from its place, then they all knew the man had been unfaithful to his mate. Bald was disgusted by this "test," for he had seen it lie. One of his men had been persuaded to take it after one of these expeditions and was, he knew, quite innocent of any such thing - yet, the "test" had spoken otherwise. He was also indignant that such a thing would be asked of a man. It stripped him of the respect due to a man, and made him weak before the tribe. He, himself, had refused to take the test and spoke the reason why. They would not force him, for they knew he would leave them if they tried such a thing. He was of value to them, since he was a strong man; a good leader of hunting men. For this reason, they had left him alone.

The next day, he was still no nearer to his camp, for he could not leave the woman. If she had held a leash, she could not have led him more surely. She was beautiful in his eyes. Her ways charmed him; her body was graceful, her breasts sweet. He could not leave. Yet, how could he stay? So in his indecision, he tarried with her, though they did not stay in one place long. He knew he was turning away from the direction where his men would be waiting, letting her lead him, gently, softly, where she wanted to go.

He made snares and traps, baiting them with whatever could be found, or with a bit of the grain cakes he kept in his forage bag. He was nearly out of what he had brought on his person and knew he would have to return to camp, soon. But he would not. Not yet.

The Lure (cont.)
The Bear

His leg is gashed and dangling from a wound just below the hip. It is an awful sight and I think his body can't possibly ever be right again. She nurses him loyally, and she has a great store of knowledge with herbs and rituals. She places a sharp stick in the ground, point upward, in the center of their camping place to attract healing energy. While he is unconscious, she sews the flesh together. Probing with her fingers she has seen that the large blood vessel is still in one piece - pulsing, but not torn.

Through the days they are camped there, she has to cauterize the wound more than once. He wants to die. She gives him pain-killing root, but not enough of it, for his thinking, and he quarrels with her in his agony, thinking she is mean.

She relents sometimes, but later, when he is recovering, she adamantly refuses to dig or prepare the root, nor will she tell him what it is.

The bear had just been lying there - making no sound at all and he had not detected her scent since the wind was blowing the wrong way. They had come right up upon her before they were aware of her presence. Then, she stirred a little and turned her head around to look at them. They froze. Then, making a great effort, the she-bear raised herself, staggering a little, as though her legs were weak. Bald pushed at the woman behind him to make her run, and this flutter of movement goaded the sick bear into action. Mustering all her remaining strength and roaring with her last breath, she reared upward and lunged at him. The thought passed through him, even as he prepared to meet her claws: What a pity it was - that the bear should expend her last bit of strength to attack him, who meant her no harm, and that he now had to fight her and perhaps die, too. Then, she was on top of him, her great weight upon his arm and chest, felling him to the ground, his knife, useless. He defended himself by kicking at her. She sunk her great claws and stinking teeth into his groin, at the thigh. He shuddered as he heard the tearing of his own flesh. But with his arm free once more, he plunged his long knife again and again into her belly, finally pulling the knife upward to disembowel her. With this final thrust, she stiffened and rolled to the side, her eyes already glazing . . . her breath slowing to nothing. He lay there stunned, a slight breeze fanning his sweating face - then the searing pain started. He braced himself to rise up and survey his injury, but already thinking, this then, was how fate had decided he should die: wounded by a sick bear in the wild country.

As he struggled to rise, the woman was there with him, pushing him down again. He did not have to look at his wound. Her face was blanched and distorted from the sight of him. He waved her away, to let him die in peace. It was strange, he thought as he lay there, that for all the searing pain, he could also feel the slight prickle in the broken flesh from the dry leaves of the forest floor. Such a small thing to feel, while this greater thing was going on. . . . The breeze was cooler, now, and he began to shake. The woman was doing something. He did not know what.

Nor did he know anything further for several days. After that, he awoke - to find they were still in the same area, nearer the water. The bear, not too distant, was beginning to stink and that was what woke him. He did not know how long he had lain there. At first, he was surprised that he was not yet dead, and then he despaired, thinking now he would still have to die, and would have to prepare himself to meet it all over again.

She saw his eyes were open - that he was awake and knowing, so she came to him and knelt down beside him. Her brows were like straight, black wings of ravens, he thought, as her face hung above his. She looked stern, yet she was not like his wife, for she was giving and feeling. His heart swelled with the love he felt for this woman and his eyes filled with tears brought on by that, and by his weakness. She sat back on her heels, relieved, and smiled softly. She examined his eyes, felt his face with her hands, and the smile widened to a grin. Then she nodded and hurried away, to return with some brew, which she made him swallow. He was thinking now. How long had it been? He signed and asked her. How many days? And she gave him the sign for two days and two nights - today being the third day. Mentally, he assessed his body - there was a numbness in his right side, and the feeling of a stick plunged through his joint at the thigh. He struggled to raise his head, so that he might see what it was, and she came to him, raising him in her arms.

He was appalled by what he saw. His clothing was in rags, the wound was a great, swollen mass covered with wet leaves. His leg was discolored and swollen as though about to burst - yet it was all in one piece, and no blood was running. He lifted the leaves to look at the wound, and could hardly believe what he saw . . . She had taken a bone needle and the entrails or the skin of some animal and had stitched him up as neatly as a torn blanket. The stitches looked black against his mottled skin, puckered tightly by the swelling. He lay back in despair, his eyes rolling up to meet hers. He saw loving compassion there - such as he had never before seen in anyone's eyes – and it was for him. This impressed him so that he forgot what it was that he had wanted to ask, and so he was silent.

Ah, well, he would see. This might be a slow and painful death, and he would not thank her for saving him to suffer through it, but she had tried her best, and he was moved that she had worked so hard to save him.

She watched over him when he slept again - knowing what his thoughts were as if they were her own. They were of one mind. She was not sure she had been right to save him, but she had wanted so much to keep him. He was a strong man, so she had told herself that he would live and walk again. Stitching the torn meat of his thigh together had taken all her knowledge and skill. It was backward from the rendering of meat from game. She had tried to think of it that way while she pieced it together again. She had detached her thoughts from him as a man, her man. She was sewing back together a joint of meat and sinew – a familiar thing. She doubted that he would ever be the same, for she had never seen such a wound. Still, the large blood vessel was whole, so perhaps. . . They would see. Now that he was conscious, she worried about the bouts of pain to come. If she could help him through that - but then, perhaps the wound would not heal, anyway. . . Then he would have to go through the process of death all over again. But she had learned to be defiant under the worst circumstances. She would make him well, she was determined and her faith was great.

Fiercely, she worked over him in the following days, and supplied their needs of food by gathering what she could find while he was sleeping. It was not easy, because she limited herself to foraging within hearing range of him. She could not leave him alone and exposed to wild animals. She had burned the carcass of the bear, little by little, building a fire upon it. She had not saved the meat, because first, it was foul, because the bear had been sick and even if she had taken a chance, the man would be unable to eat such for some time to come. Then, too, she had to keep a fire going to warn off scavenging animals from the helpless man, and for preparing the herbs and cauterizing the wound.

The first time, when the woman showed him what she intended to do, he was unwilling, for he was so very sick and feverish. "Let me die!" he bellowed. But she spat the word at him; "No!" He was startled and wondered if she had known his language, all along. He could tell from her ferocity, that she would not let him die, no matter how much he might wish it. Silent then, he watched her make her preparations. She gave him a green twig to bite on, so that he would not break his teeth when the pain hit him. She used a length of sapwood of some kind, wrapped in leaves that

smelled aromatic when she roasted it in the fire. He did not see the sense
in this, since for all he could see, the leaves were completely burned away
by the time the tip of the wood became a suitably red-hot ember to sear
his puckering flesh. Before she touched him with it, she threw on the fire
some other leaves and twigs, which cast up a strange-smelling steam. She
had dragged him toward the fire so that he could breathe deeply from this
steam. It soon made him groggy, but still, when she descended with her
brand, it was all he could do not to scream.

In later days, it became necessary to lance and burn the wound again,
and after that, again, for it festered from within from poison and would
not heal. When she would descend on him with her fiery brand, he would
scream at her to leave him alone; that she was a fiend, and that she should
let him die. The image of her at these times was burned into his mind and
memory. Her face was so severe, the black eyes brilliant with concentration,
her lips pressed into a thin, tight line. He thought, in his hysteria, that she
was enjoying the torture - and the idea shocked him. As his wound festered,
so did he, for it galled him that he should be so helpless, so completely in
the care and power of the woman. It was strange, but he began to hate her,
even as he loved her.

There was little to do in his conscious hours but watch her, and this
is what he did. His life focused on her now. He watched her comings and
goings, her work of preparing food and medicine. For awhile, when the
pain was so very bad, she used some leaves that she would be very secretive
about. Coming back to the camp, she would take them out, furtively, so
that he did not get a good look at them. Then she would arrange a com-
plicated apparatus to steam the leaves, so that they would sweat, and she
would dose him with the liquid from this immediately, for it did not keep
well. He was grateful for the relief it gave him, and his bad temper was
eased along with his misery.

As time went on, they began to understand each other better and she was rapidly learning his words. She was called, she said, "Lee-ah." The sound of it was foreign to him, but he liked it. He lay there rolling the two syllables around on his tongue, and would call her to him, just to see her come within view. And she would love him with her look, her face soft. She had woven mats and must have rolled him on his side to place them under him, and had covered them with a cloth from his pack. He didn't remember this and hadn't noticed the mats beneath him for some days. He wondered how she had accomplished it, and how she had managed to find food within such a small area. She could take care of herself and him too, he thought.

Sometimes he would beg her for more of the soothing liquid, but she would say no - making him understand that it would be bad for him to have too much. Yet, how he yearned for it, because it was such a peaceful escape. After a dose of it, he would lie dreaming under the tree, watching the leaves and birds in the wind, and the relief was wonderful. He yearned for it all the time. . . But she would not give it to him, except at those times when she had burned out the wound or at other times, when the pain had worn him out, and he needed rest. Never more than once every three days. He learned to count the days, and freely expressed his pain and misery on the third day. At the same time, he was ashamed. Not such a great man, now, just a whining wretch, he thought, and this made him angry at himself, and sometimes at her. It seemed she was in such control of him, his jailer, and he greatly resented her at the same time that he depended on her for his every need.

He could not even relieve himself without her help. She had been careful to give him liquids only for many days, and green herbage after, but eventually his bowel had to be emptied, and the pain and ludicrous maneuvers it took to permit this to take place embarrassed him to such an extent that he could not look her in the face for several days afterward.

Once, he screamed at her, abusing her in his language, words she did not know - yet she understood. Later, when the pain had subsided to a bearable level, he was sorry, and turned his head to look for her. She was curled up on her side beneath a tree. She was silent, but he knew she was weeping. He could not comfort her, since he was still flat on his back, the only position he could bear for long. He looked at her from beneath his lashes and wondered why she did not leave him. Why did she stay on and bear all the anguish he heaped upon her? He knew he would have died a miserable death without her. So, through all these trying days, this was the way of it: He would regret having been hard with her, but then when the pain came on again, he would be that way, again. He did not understand himself. Still, she had stayed with him faithfully. When he was an angry beast, she would soothe him. Using the herb to dose him, she would cast some leaves upon the fire, fanning the smoke toward his nostrils. When he was easier, she would stroke his face, or just sit beside him, her hand upon his breast. All these things together, made the pain bearable.

She had placed a pointed stick in the center of their camp when he had been wounded, to attract healing power from all around them, he understood her to say. It had a shining metal tip, which she had apparently taken from that sack she had always had on her. It seemed she had many odd but useful things stored in that sack. Now, he noticed that she had added certain smooth rocks from the river, spacing them a distance away from the stick, and forming a rough circle around it. She would move the rocks sometimes, and added others of different sizes to the pattern. He couldn't figure it out, but it caught his interest when he was feeling better and not so distracted by pain. As he recuperated, he watched her more closely. She observed the stars at night, and then, sometimes muttering to herself, she would make those small changes to the stones. Once, she stood looking upward to the sky, holding her arms straight out from her sides, and she held this position for such a long time that he was uneasy, wondering if she was a wolf-woman, after all.

Finally the time came when he was able to sit up. The swelling was nearly gone and his leg had lost most of the strange color. He was weak from the fight with death, and from having little of the kind of food which gave strength. She was like a mother bird, combing the woods for something to feed her chick. Once, she had caught a rabbit in her snare, and she was so proud of it. She skinned it before him, and cooked it carefully over the fire. He saw her steal glances at him to see if he was enjoying the aroma of the roasting meat, and there was such sweetness and joy in her eyes. That was when the last bitter dregs of the hatred he had felt for her melted away, and he loved her again, with his whole heart. After this, he started regaining his strength, and she was free to wander farther away from him on her foraging and trapping, leaving him to guard himself.

While she was away from camp, he would test his strength and exercise his leg. He was unwilling for her to see his weakness, but once she observed him from the trees, as he took trembling and wavering steps. Her heart loved him so, her arms ached to hold him, to give him support, to heal him . . . but he was a proud man. So she kept still, and watched him in secret from the woods, and when he stumbled and groaned with anguish she turned her face against the tree's rough bark and wept for him.

She had bullied him all the time he had lain wounded. Now, he was nearly well again and could turn the tables. She thought there was still a thin layer of bitterness against her, under his skin. He was no longer angry, and was truly grateful that she had made him well, yet whenever she became what he considered dominating, that bitterness would raise its head again, and although he wondered at himself, he would be a little hard to her. She understood this better than he did. She had witnessed him at his lowest point. Always he had been a proud man, conscious of his masculine attributes. He had been the courageous leader, the protector, the defender and great hunter. Then, he had been stripped of that, reduced to a weak, whining rag of a man, and she had taken his place and done, not only what a good man would have done, but much more - for what man would have gone to so much trouble to save another?

Soon, he was able to limp about and prepare the game she brought from her snares. Even this was a bit galling, because, although he and his men prepared all the food when they were on their hunts, when they were with their women, it was always the woman's job. It irritated him that she seemed to enjoy being the provider - "the strong hunter," he would think. But then, he was ashamed that he had these thoughts. His heart knew it was wrong, but his mind seemed to have been damaged like his leg, so that he was scarred inside and out.

One day while he was feeling sorry for himself he realized he had not once tried to ask her about the boy. They had managed to communicate fairly well. If words did not suffice they drew pictures in the dirt with a stick. He had learned the words for "Man" and "woman" in her language by this process. Now he drew a small "man" and asked her by signs and words, about her boy, about her man by whom she had borne the child. He had given little thought to the latter and now when it had occurred to him he was shaken with it – for he would be loathe to give her up.

She was so troubled by this that he wished he hadn't asked, but she told him, with quavering voice and violent drawings. It was quite a story she told with that dirty stick. All the violence she had endured came out with the stabbing of her stick into the ground, the weeping and anguish that accompanied the story. He understood it very well. Afterward, while he held her to him until she was still, he was ashamed of himself for his smallness, his anger and his failing to see her as wounded as deeply as he. She had been repeatedly raped by disgusting men and kept as a slave. She had borne a boy child of their despicable kind, against her will. Yet, when she had managed to escape she had taken the boy with her. Each time she had looked at the child, he must have reminded her of pain, yet she took him with her. He knew nothing of sin, he only knew her as "mother." Surely there had been no one else who loved him.

For a long time after that, Bald considered this thing. He believed she had been torn in two by the child. She had been a dutiful mother and she was naturally loving, but the boy had also been the source of great pain to her, because he was a remnant of the despised tribe of Ampligole. He wondered if, when the boy had fallen and died, she had felt relief and then guilt, and then, well she had probably hated herself as well as him, for having caused the fall. And he understood, and his heart was moved for her conflict must have been great indeed. He marveled at the situation, the story, and at her strength.

There was, however, no man of her tribe waiting for her, no man who claimed her. No one to come out to slay him if he went home with her. And she wanted to leave, to go home again. He could understand that too, and would delay her no longer, now that he was able to carry himself along. He detested their campsite by then and was glad to leave those dark, sick memories behind.

Resting frequently, they slowly edged along, always going south, he noticed. (He took little interest in it, for he had no say in the matter. Having given her the reins during his illness, he left it that way.) She seemed to know where she was going and after some days, at the time of the new moon, her eagerness began to show. The landscape was familiar to her. He was very tired, but his leg had been improving more rapidly since they were traveling. Sometimes the pain was a nasty, tearing thing, but he said nothing about it, and was proud of that. She was good, always - too good. Coming to him to see if he needed anything, she goaded him unintentionally since he was reminded that he was nothing, and she was so strong, so able. "Why do I feel this way?" he wondered. He knew it was not just, but he still could not tear it completely from his thoughts.

They tramped through woods and bog, crossing river and streams with difficulty. Finally, they came to a beautiful meadow-land, and he raised his head to smell the air, much as a horse would do, and it was this kind of country that the horses loved. Yet, he did not remember this particular bit of country from their horse hunting days. The wind rippled the grass, bringing to his nostrils that pleasant, musky scent of good herbage. He knew there would be horses here, sooner or later. He was excited, and ignored his leg as he struggled through the grass. She was excited too, and, catching his attention, she pointed toward a rise beyond, sheltered by trees. He understood the word she said from the soft sound it made in her mouth and from the look on her face. It was universal, no matter what the language. It was *"Home..."*

When they reached the beginning of the hill, he knew by the scent, that men were there among the trees. Then, he saw them coming toward them. He started back and drew his long knife, but Leeah restrained his arm, holding it warmly and gladly. These were her people. He supposed they had not seen year in years, not since she had been taken away. They probably hadn't known about the boy. It was apparent that they were glad to see her, although they looked at him warily as they came forward. Bald was uneasy, and Leeah had to tug at him to draw him along with her. They were dark-haired people, he noted - the men short and stocky, the women comely enough. . . All were older than Leeah. Bald wondered how they had known he and Leeah were coming. Had they been watching them? How?

They studied him as he did them, while Leeah talked to them. He was embarrassed when she gestured to his lame leg, but what she said evidently impressed them, for they made much of him after it, so that he felt like the hero of a homecoming, rather than a scorned weakling.

He finally saw their dwellings, when they came out of the trees. The great high bluff was broken-faced and in the cleft were holes - at least, that's what he thought at first. As they came nearer, and he scanned those high ledges above them, he could see the holes were the openings to dwellings. The dwellings were carved into the rock of the ledges and added on to with other rock. There were more people up there, many people, watching their approach. What a fortress! He was awed by the security of such a place, for he could see no way an enemy could scale the cliff. Then he wondered how the tribes people themselves could reach their dwellings from below. But, as they stood at the base of the cliff, those above threw a ladder of rope and lumber over the side and his thought was answered.

When he would have tried to follow them up the ladder (even though he did not think he would be able to do so), one of the men stopped him. They shouted at those above and another apparatus was thrown over - a kind of platform hoisted by another rope. It was pulled over a wheel at the top level, and they had him seat himself on this. Then, he was raised up the cliff with such swiftness, that it startled him at first, though he was grinning when he reached the top.

The Lure (cont.)
The New Life

She is dancing for him. . . It seems not so much a dance as it is a movement that tells a story. He has never seen anything like it. She poses and moves very gracefully, her body carefully drawing fluid lines in the air. She is sketching out a story from the distant past. At first she is proud and strong, and makes drawing gestures from skyward to below, as though she is pulling strength down from there. Then she is humbled and greatly distressed, finally, grieving, she kneels low to the ground . . . Her hair is thrown forward. It lies spread upon the ground, like a fallen bird . . . and that is the end of the dance. Then, she is smiling expectantly at him, and seems pleased and confident that she has explained something to him . . . He smiles, but inwardly he is ashamed, for he does not understand.

Bald was a curious man and the dwellings and customs of his woman's people excited his interest. They were clever, and he admired cleverness. Among their works were terraced gardens built into the ledges. The job of filling these with soil from below near the stream had been hard labor, he knew, but they were now fertile and provided the herbage they needed. Water was stored in covered earthen jars in the coolness of the caves. He found that the dwellings were remarkably cool inside in contrast to the heat of the sun outside. He saw that they were kept clean-swept, and that no birds were allowed to nest within those parts that were their dwellings. Bird droppings from the cliff sides were scraped away and added to the gardens. He saw that they could survive even under siege for some time.

As the days went by, he became very content with his fate. He had made a surprising recovery. There was a little stiffness in the joint, and some pain in bad weather, but nothing more. The tribesmen were good to him. The dwelling he and Leeah lived in was secure and dry. Most of all, he loved the view from the heights - the ring of hills in the distance and the meadow in front of them where the wild horses came to eat the lush grass. Leeah would come to sit beside him on the ledge overlooking the valley, and together they would watch the horses below or the birds wheeling in the air. She was very loving to him as though she did not remember the hard times before she had brought him here. Stroking his face tenderly, she would teach him their words, drawing pictures in the earth to show him their meaning.

Their language was difficult, and at first, he did not think he would ever learn it well, for their words consisted of rapid, stuttering sounds - eh-eh-eh-eh-eh- with different pitches. "Sounds like an insect makes," he thought, and their sentences often ended with an emphatic, clicking sound. They were patient with him, though, and slowed their speech, spacing out the individual words, so that he could learn them. They learned some of his words, also, for they were very interested in what he could tell them of the ways of his land and his people. As he understood them better, he was deeply impressed with them, for they were very wise and quick to learn. He had the feeling that they had knowledge, secrets perhaps, that he was ignorant of.

There was a man among their tribe who, unlike the others, had star-tling blue eyes. His skin was dusky brown from the sun, and he was tall and thin - except for his belly, which Bald thought was soft-looking - per-haps because he did not do as much of the labor as the others. For this reason, Bald was, at first, of the opinion that this tribesman was a lesser man and he secretly disdained him, but seeing that the others esteemed him, he watched to see why this was. He observed that this man, whom they called Cheelak, laughed a lot and said funny things that made all the others laugh - and Bald thought perhaps it was for this happy reason alone that he was a valuable member of their tribe. However, it was not long before he discovered that Cheelak was the seer of their tribe. Bald watched him at those times when he became entranced. Sometimes, Cheelak would lie flat upon the floor of the ledge, where he could see the sky and clouds and then "his spirit would fly away," as Leeah said, to join with the "Spirit of All." In this state, he was able to warn them of things to come - things they should prepare for. Bald studied Cheelak and his sayings intently. It seemed to him that Cheelak could detect changes in the weave of things — a dent in the whole, a bump in the rhythmic wave that activated all living things on earth.

One early morning, Bald saw Cheelak standing on the ledge with his arms outstretched, facing the misty valley beyond. There was no one there, yet he was speaking. His voice was like nothing Bald had ever heard – it was more vibrant than usual, and there was the sound of running waters within his voice. He felt uneasy after he had come upon Cheelak like this and he sought out Leeah and asked her what it was that the man had been saying. She told him it was a song of gratitude to the Creator for the earth; their dwelling place.

Bald adapted well to their community, and was pleased that he could make himself useful in the ways that he was able, such as tanning leather and making boots and showing them ways of weaponry which were new to them. They, in turn, showed him their inventions and drew for him a map on a rock, aligned to the sun, which showed him their location and of the homelands of Ampligole and other people of that land. He was surprised to find that other groups of people lived here in this land. He and his men had thought this country was the hunting ground of only Ampligole's lit-tle band and his related kind. They were different - Leeah's people - but he liked them for it. They were like him in some ways, yet not at all like his tribe back in the homeland. He never told them of his wife and children in his homeland, and they did not ask. He knew Cheelak knew. Cheelak knew all about him and his past. He could tell from the light in those blue eyes when he looked at him. Yet there was a pleased affirmation in the seer's look – as though he had always expected him and now he was glad that he had come home.

After Bald had been with them for some time and was accepted as the husband of Leeah, they began to show him some of their secrets. They had ground a powder which, when applied over their skins, made them glow in the dark of night. They would show themselves at the cave entrances at the times when those others, the heathen, watched, thinking to rob or destroy them. It was an eerie thing, to see ghost men walking the ledges of the cliffs, and even Bald - though he was close at hand and knew the reason - was disturbed at first. But they all laughed afterward, for it was a good joke on the wild men, who would howl and run away. They had another powder that would explode when lit with fire, making a great burst of flame, stink and noise. Both were tools to daunt their enemy, and were very seldom used. Then, there was the third thing - the thing that made Bald a changed man.

It was the reason that Ampligole's people called them "Bird-men." When he had first learned that they were called this, he had thought it was because they lived in the cliff-side, but it was more than that. He was puzzled when they showed him the large wings and tails, made with strong, light wooden pieces and bound together with the dyed, corded bands they made. His bewilderment changed to amazement when they showed him how they could suspend themselves from these wings - sailing out from the ledges above into the valley below. The tail, he saw, was in three pieces, and could be adjusted to suit the wind. They would wait for just the right wind to support them and knew the variances of it, so that they moved with the bending of the breeze. This was only for sport, but it was also one of the things that unnerved Ampligole's men so that they were left unmolested. But it was more than all that to Bald.

The first time they fitted him into the wings, he was frightened, but they had worked with him to show how it was done and he was launched from a safe place. How to explain the thrill of his first short flight? How to explain the joy of moving freely, unhampered by his lame leg - sailing like a bird? He could hardly wait to come up again, so that he might fly out and downward once more - and again and again! He was able to stay in the air longer each time that he "flew." The wings excited him more than anyone could have expected. Leeah and her people had thought - because of his lameness - that it would be an easier way for him to descend the cliff, but it was more than that. It was the fulfillment of a great need. It was ecstasy, for Bald. During those flights, his spirit was united with that of the wild horses, the birds, and the soul of this wild land. He thought this must be what Cheelak felt, when he was one with "the Spirit of All." He was one with it all, now . . and his heart rejoiced in that feeling of belonging, of unity, of completeness.

Cheelak, watching from his ledge, sees that the man, healed in mind, is growing in spirit. He admires the outsider's force and energy – what Cheelak expresses as his "bloom." One day when he is alone with Bald, he offers to teach him their way. But this was a secret way, not given to anyone unless he was ready. What did Bald learn? I cannot tell of the many unspeakable moments in his time. I can only say that Bald learned to fly inwardly as well. He was truly unbound in spirit, not shackled by his lame leg, his scarred body.

The tribe had not been interested in taming horses for riding, but Bald made them see that it could be useful. An enclosure was made in the pasture below, for the few mounts he had tamed and which they used for hunting. The wild herds were safe from him, now, although they still thrilled him as he watched their coming and going - tossing their manes and drumming their hooves. Sometimes the sounds of neighing and hoof beats were caught and carried on the wind to where he worked on the cliffs above, and he would raise his head, pausing in his work to listen, and would smile. When he was fully recovered, he went out hunting again, but only for meat. Even with his limp, he was still a good hunter, and the tribe relied on him. Because their needs were simple, there were idle hours, too - time spent in conversation and quiet contemplation.

There were other tribes, too. And occasionally there were bands of armed traders who brought packs of woven cloth and metal tools. They traded for special stones and powders with magic properties. Once Bald recognized a fancy woven belt of a pattern that was only made in his old valley, smoothing it with his fingers, he thought of that time, but not with yearning.

In later years as he sat by his fireside, he sometimes wondered about the band of men he had led, and if they had looked for him. It was extraordinary, he thought, that they had not found him in all that time when he lay wounded. Sometimes, he thought of his first wife in the old country, but he could no longer remember her face clearly. The passing remembrance of her did not make him feel ashamed, since he knew she would have been well cared for. She was safe in the protection of her family. The only time he felt a stab of regret was when his daughter's face came to mind.

In the beginning, he had considered the rightness of returning to his own land, but - even had he been convinced that it was the good thing to do, he could not have left the woman he loved. He was once more a man, because of her. The leg was a little stiff, but it did not prevent his straddling a horse and riding with the men, to bring back to their women the meat they needed. To ride the meadows was glorious and he never tired of it, nor did he ever tire of her, his woman, Leeah.

She was a proper woman - not over-bold toward her man, at least, never within the sight of the others. She still scraped his nerves sometimes, but he would not be alive without her and now he could not go on living without her. Before - when he had come and gone home again to his own land - it would be in the expectation of more honor and good trade for the horses and furs they brought. But life was tame there after the exhilarating wildness of this country and the life of the village had been fraught with hindrances to curb the spirit. Here, he was free to ride with the horses he loved, to roam where he might - even to soar like a bird over the land! His love also, was free.... no sternness inhibited it, no conventions restricted it. Here, he did not need to build up wealth - his children by Leeah were his legacy. They looked to him with honor. He needed no other riches. It was not as comfortable a life, perhaps, but it made up for that in adventure and the many sensations that fed his spirit.

It amused him to think of his woman as his lure, and he, the captured horse. As the horse could not resist the lure, neither could he. A most willing captive was he, for here he had found great freedom. His woman loved him with a depth that had not been possible for his first wife. When he came to her at day's end, her presence was the cool spring from which he, her thirsty captive, drank - and, Ah! How he loved her!

* * *

Dear Richard,

I was surprised you wanted to discuss that bit I wrote you about projection from the present into the past and future. Yes, it would imply then, that there is one who projects and he who is projected. Two of us. The silent projector, of whom we are seldom aware, is the divine us (God's Son). The projected is his "creation." You might call this the puppet and the puppeteer. I personally do not like this term because when I think of the misery we go through, I want to scream at the puppeteer, that faceless, silent, seemingly sadistic being; "*What are you doing? What is wrong with you?*" But THAT, Richard must be the crux of the matter. There *is* something wrong with the puppeteer! The one who is pulling our strings has either fallen asleep or his mind is sick. Can we wake him up? Are these "the lost" that Jesus came to save? Not the man incarnate, but the unconscious puppeteer?

And which of the two is the greater, the puppet or the puppeteer? Surely the puppet, being solely a product of the puppeteer, to whom it owes its existence, is of little importance. The puppeteer is the greater. The projected is only an idea of the projector. The animator is the owner of the animation.

Because of "stories" I have seen recently, together with my studies of great spiritual teachings and prayer, I have this theory. Our very ancient ancestors not only knew the origin of mankind, but they were still in the process of "the fall," being partially conscious on that higher level of being, and perhaps not yet fully "solid" in the three dimensional realm. These divine sons projected matter, played with it and ultimately became it, at which time they lost their memory of who they really were. Now we are creatures of the creature, for the material us - enslaved by matter, encased in body - has become us, rather than it being our projection, a puppet to our will. Our real self is asleep and doesn't know how to wake up. Spiritual teachers, such as Jesus, incarnated to save the fallen sons of God from this enslavement and the guilt caused by our separation from God. Karma is no longer necessary. Blood sacrifice and suffering is not the way to light. Acceptance of the way back home is the answer. The way is forgiveness and love, thereby detaching from the material world.

The consciousness of divine man can only be reached from this worldly state – illusion though it may be. Because this is where we think we are. We don't remember that we are still with God and projecting from afar, asleep at the wheel. We are asleep there, but at least partially awake here. Our consciousness, limited as it may be, is here with our projection. Therefore here is where we must be informed and enlightened. Here is where we awaken from the illusion. Here is where time ends and eternity begins.

I have this recurring vision. I see a hard metal object made up of pieces like a jigsaw puzzle. It is very ornate and an awesome, artistic thing to see, but solid, dense and dark. It is vibrating. Then I see cracks form between the pieces and glimmering light behind. As the separation between the pieces widens and vibration continues, blinding white shafts of light burst through. I think this must be what is happening now. I think mankind is waking up, and the density of matter is becoming perceived differently. The light is bursting through.

Oh, by the way, I have this additional little story that I am sending on to you, though I doubt we should include it in the collection that you have sent on to the publisher. It came while I had been in a great deal of physical pain and contemplating risky surgery. As you know, my garden is my oasis and I was spending a good deal of time out there in silent meditation.

It seemed to remind me of another garden, another place. Then this came. However, it didn't come complete. It didn't finish for a long time, as a matter of fact. I think I had to have a breakthrough, had to learn more before I could understand the truth of it. Even now, I feel a little like a heretic offering it to you to read. (I still have not entirely rid myself of the fear of revealing my spiritual beliefs and being perceived as against the religious establishment.)

I will tell you that the experiences I had in my own garden were worth all the pain I was experiencing. I have not had such peaceful wonders since that time under my arbor. There was a Christ-like Presence there. I would be sitting quietly in the shade under my roses and there would come a kind of expectancy in the still atmosphere, a stall in time. Then, I would sense a presence. He seemed to enter through the gate at the end of the arbor, and roses would suddenly, quietly, shatter, scattering their petals along His path. Colors that I saw there were far greater than I have ever perceived before - intense, glowing from within. (The artist in me gloried in that!) A peace that I cannot describe was there at those times. I was carefully still, so as not to disturb the preciousness of those moments.

Now, since the surgeries, I am glad for the relief from pain, but Ah, how I miss those moments!

The Gardener

It was quiet in my garden. The only sounds were the birds, the rustling of lizards and the faint grinding of the sand between my sandals and the paving stones. It was early morning and all was still bedewed; the spider's web a jeweled net fit for the hair of a goddess. I snipped herbs while they were still fresh and cool, my mind at peace. The garden was my consolation for having to live in that alien land.   My husband is an emissary, a merchant whose livelihood required him to live there for a time. My place was with him, but I did not like it in that country. He was good to me though, and allowed me everything I desired that was within his means. He was an agent for goods of craftsmen who made beautiful colored glass and chased metal wares - containers and ornaments fit for kings, and indeed, they were purchased by the nobility and the rich. I was proud of his connection with this business, since it brought those of power and money to our home and they were always in awe of the beautiful objects he brokered. I, too, loved the look of the jewel-colored glass when the light shone through it. Even those glass stones that mocked genuine gems and were set in jewelry were indeed quite lovely, and the workmanship was famous throughout the world.

I called it "my" garden. In fact we were allowed to stay in that house and on that land as guests of the Sanhedrin, who were in fact, its owners. This was an honor endowed to any who served the purpose of pleasing the wealthy Jews and the Roman rulers there. We were allowed to remain as long as we had business of supplying them with their desires spun or blown into glass. Many wanted their own designs manifested into reality and it took some time to send the orders and have them completed to the buyers' specifications. We had the best artisans in Egypt at our command. My husband is Greek, a student of the Philosophers, I am Egyptian. I am an educated woman.

We had been in that place for three years.

I began to be aware of noise beyond my garden wall – the sound of a number of people approaching from the road to the east. I detested crowds. This garden was my oasis of peace and I resented any encroachment upon its privacy. Here I was protected from the barbarians.

Judging by the sounds beyond, they seemed to be halting at my gate. Then – through the aperture in the gate - I could see that it was the man they called "The Master" with his friends. I was alarmed. He attracted such a mob of people. Would they come in? Politeness demanded that I not turn them away. Would they trample my garden underfoot? But no, he left them at the gate and came in alone. Those beyond the wall passed on.

I sighed and tried to calm my irritation. I faced him where he stood there on the garden path, the gate behind framing his tall figure. There was a sudden silence within my garden walls, as though all its creatures drew in their breath and held it, just as I held mine. His eyes (such eyes!) did not just look at me, did not just meet my glance, but looked into me as though he read my soul - and that inward entity – my soul – fell backward and bowed down, so that I was faint and falling. . . But then, as quickly as it had bowed, it leapt upward in a strange kind of ecstasy. It filled my heart so that it beat upon my breastbone as though a bird battered there, seeking to escape through my throat. I stood trembling, the herbs I had cut falling from my hand.

"Sister," he said gently, "I need a place to rest. May I tarry here awhile?" Then all those tight, small feelings of a little while ago flew away and I could not give him welcome enough. I wanted to rush to him – indeed, my heart bounded forward, though I remained where I was. I dipped and bowed, gesturing to my favorite seat in the garden.

When I looked around me everything that had seemed near perfection a moment ago was now not good enough. "Please Master, take your ease, read, whatever is your pleasure. I will see that you are not disturbed. May I bring you a drink of water with herbs, to refresh you?" He smiled and consented and I fled from his presence.

Shaking with eagerness, I went at once into the cool shaded portico, to my jar of precious scented water that I had begun a month ago for a special occasion. A thread of wonder passed through my mind as I did this. I watched myself go through the motions as though my body was that of a stranger. The sense of living in the present moment was strong upon me, so that each small thing stood out with a kind of crackling reality in the alternating sunlight and shade – the solidity and whiteness of my fingers, the earthy clay texture of the lid of the pottery jar as I raised it and examined the glistening, cool water within. I sniffed - the fragrance was perfect. With my dipper of cedar wood, I filled a clean cup with this sparkling liquid. A small flower floated on the surface. I gazed at it. It seemed appropriate. I wiped the moisture from the cup's surface and took it out to him.

His head was turned from me. The birds were singing beautifully, thrillingly – the little ones feeding at his very feet. I thought, "I will not disturb him," so I placed the drink at his side and went softly away.

At first, I stood gazing out at him from the corridor, but then I was touched by the feeling that this was not right. It seemed as though he were looking at me, although his back was turned - his figure quiet, at peace. Perhaps he felt my presence. I would not spy on him. He would have his quiet meditation – that he might pray to his God (for that is why he came). My heart swelled protectively. Poor man! Always mobbed by the crowds. Let him have his peace. I would see that this place would always be his whenever he chose. So then, I went into my house and left him alone.

And so it was each time he came. Later, I could feel him come – could sense his presence and, if I were in the house, I would go and look out to see where he was. He walked softly, touching the flowers, breathing in the essence of the green and growing herbs, the cedar, and the olive. It pleased me that he enjoyed my garden as much as I. He did not need to speak, for I would bring him water and disappear so that he might have silence. He would sit awhile, his mind elsewhere. Later when I looked again, he would be gone. I did nothing in the garden those times when he was there. Sometimes he would find me and bless me with his eyes, his smile, with words of kindness. Later on, I learned from him things that illuminated my mind and gladdened my spirit.

I would have brought him wine – the finest from abroad – but he preferred the water. We spoke of simple joys. I spoke little, for I was timid. He spoke little but his few words were important ones. He did not waste his speech on trivialities. The things I marveled about – the intricate form and color of flower petals, the spider web bedewed with the finest of earth's jewels, the preciousness of a cup of pure and sparkling water – he, too, loved these gifts.

His presence uplifted me. When he had gone, I would go and walk where he had gone. I would sit where he had sat – stroking with my hands the seat where he had talked to his God. I had found that if I went straight away to this seat, there would be a strange, palpitating energy hovering there. Here I was relieved of my tiredness, and would rise from it invigorated. It was as though he left behind him some of his presence, to bless me.

Later, I realized it was the Spirit of his God lingering in my garden and his God became my God. I had always loved my garden and had worked to make it a place of ultimate peace and joy. But now it seemed to lack something vital until he came. Only then did I feel it was complete.

Later, when my husband had enquired about him, we discovered that we had heard about him before. In his youth he had been in our country and he was talked about widely.

My husband respected him greatly and we invited him to our home to teach us his way to God. We had invited others, merchants from our country, and he, the Master, would have the servants included. So, we all sat and marveled at his teaching, his wisdom. Here was an enlightened one as we had heard of but never seen. We felt greatly honored that this would happen in our lifetime. Our visitors went away full of wonder and repeated his teaching everywhere, telling those in Egypt of him, how he had returned to his country and was changing ideas everywhere, and bringing light into men's minds.

* * *

It was the time of sacrifice in the city. Out of curiosity I had gone out to shop in the market and see what these people did on this day. It was very busy, for farmers who lived outside the city were bringing in lambs and other things to sell. The noises and smells were different also. It was dustier than usual and everywhere there was the bleating of lambs - then a clink, clink, clink noise that I couldn't identify. When I followed the sound I discovered it was a metalworker hammering out a basin. There were others too, doing the same. Evidently there was a demand for these at this time for their ceremony. Crowing cocks were penned and covered so that they would remain in the dark, for it was considered very bad luck, somehow, for them to crow during this time. One such cockerel sitting in the gloom of a blanketed cage dared one brave gurgle as I was passing. "OOOH, shh, shh," gasped the flurried vendor, as he reached in and grabbed his flapping fowl by the beak. It was all very interesting, but it soon turned overly warm and I returned to the cool of my garden and house.

It was late but not yet dark. I had been sitting outside sewing, but I laid it aside. There was a sudden calm – a stillness in the garden. Then, He came – My Lord, the Master. He came through the gate and when he passed by, the flowers shed their petals at his feet. I watched Him come. . . Joy rose within me as always when He came, yet this time something followed closely and fell upon that joy; something heavy. I sat still. I did not understand.

He came and stood over me where I sat. Several of his disciples followed him with shambling, uncertain steps. They seemed lost. Before when I had seen them they had been so sure of themselves. Did they sense this strangeness that I was feeling? He had never carried this sad burdened atmosphere before. "I seek solitude in your garden" – I knew what he meant. I said nothing but hurried to lock the gate, my heart filled with a sudden rush of heat in my desire to protect him from the mob that followed him everywhere. (How foolish I was!)

He left his men behind and went on into the grotto to pray. There was water there. A quiet pool, with very faint music from its flow. I had been pleased with it. It had taken time and trial to adjust the flow, to correct the depth, until it had lost its too-strident splashing. Finally, I had achieved this level of faint melodic sound. I was comforted that he went there now. He went most quietly and unhurried. Why then did I have this feeling he was being pursued? There was no one else – yet I felt something there – in the air behind him, over him. As I stared I seemed to see it for a moment – a dark mist following his bright one.

He laid himself upon the ground and seemed to be in conflict. I had never seen him that way. He had always been joyful, at peace, very loving to all, so that we warmed ourselves by his presence. He was the one who gave us such perfect ease and comfort. I scurried away inside my house, filled with great fear. I was sick and vomited into a basin, washed my face and stared into the gloom for an answer.

When dusk set in, I raised myself and went out to see if they were still there. I could see his bent figure in the gloom. He rose and went to his disciples and wakened them. He was standing there, quiet, seemingly at peace again. I was relieved. But, just then I heard a tumult outside the garden gate. The barbarians were demanding entry, making a great banging and shouting. Angry and disturbed, I went and unlocked the gate. I didn't care what they wanted, I only wanted them gone.

My husband opened the door to our house. He is, I think, of elegant appearance – a slim figure, small boned, refined. He spoke with great courtesy and restraint to the officials, for he always worried that he must keep good relations with the Jews and the Romans, with whom he did business. I didn't know what he was saying to them, but he showed them his credentials of service and took one of them inside where he talked with him and offered him money. But they, the Jews, were enraged and not to be deterred from their purpose. They had come for the Master! I felt so weak, powerless, small, and ashamed. I could not protect him from the mob and the soldiers of the government.

They led him by us, roughly. There was so much noise - protesting and shouting, and I was shaking, weak, wanting this to be over and for them to go away. It was hard for me to see through those meshed and struggling figures, so much taller than I. Inside I was protesting loudly, "NO, NO, NO! and my heart within me fell over in pain, yet I said nothing. No words came from my mouth, nor did it seem possible that they could. I stood mute while they all surged forth out of my garden, bursting loudly from the gate like a torrent of water from a broken dam. They took their noise and violence with them.

I stood alone in the emptiness; the flowers trampled underfoot, the night birds silenced. The only sound was my pounding heart; the only movement the shaking of my hands - yet the air seemed to vibrate still. I heard them as they moved farther away. Then, on the other side of the wall there were other noises - running feet and voices - voices raised to question what was happening, exhilarated angry voices; protesting, meekly questioning voices. Just beyond the gate I could hear hushed, serious voices between two who were just hearing the news.

I had wanted quiet; peace. Well, I had quiet now, but he was gone. There was no peace. What would they do to him? Why did they hate him so? I went inside. I did not let the servant light a lamp, but sat in the dark for a long time. My husband came and said to me words I did not later remember, but I knew he had gone to see what was happening in the Roman court.

Later, I heard what they had done, what atrocities they had executed upon this man with his higher knowledge, who had never harmed anyone, who had brought joy and peace to all who knew him. I was filled with flame and fury, pleading with my husband to leave this land, to avenge the Master in some way, for I wanted to heap punishment upon these people - barbarians who possessed no wisdom, no heart. I raged and wept and wished horrible recompense upon all concerned – and secretly, not the least of them was myself – coward that I had been. It did no good to ask (as my husband had told me) what I could have done to prevent it. I could not have done so, nor could my husband have done anything at that time to prevent it. None of this assuaged my guilt. I knew that I had been a coward not to protest, not to be indignant, and not to cry out against this wickedness that had been done to a great teacher. It would not have stopped them, no. But I would not have had this guilt upon my soul from saying nothing at all, from cringing within, repelled, by that violence. Because the event had made my self-centered life so unpleasant, I had only wanted them to be gone.

How many days did I grieve, sitting in my garden, weeping until exhausted? I don't remember, but finally, the flood quieted and that quiet inner presence, that small voice he told me of, came to me. It quietly reminded me of the lessons he had taught me. It gave me peace and consoled me. I wondered, at first, if the presence was the Master, but I realized this voice had been with me all along, but I had not acknowledged Him. This stranger had been waiting to refresh me with His water, His spirit. But he was not truly a stranger to me. He was that which I had always known was there in all life - the flowers, the birds, and in me. All in One – as the Master had said, One in All – united, a Loving Spirit, not seen by our eyes, but perceived by those who sought Love with love. I said to myself the words he had taught me, "My heart in God and God in my heart," and I sought that perfect stillness and sat as the Master had. With a quiet mind and an open heart, I sought this Spirit, and allowed myself to be filled with this Presence. I finally knew peace at these times.

My husband had heard, he said, a rumor that the teacher had come to life again and walked the streets. The officials said his followers had stolen his body to make it appear that he had risen from the dead. I knew he had done many miracles while he had been alive. I didn't know if he could resurrect his body and I wondered why he would. He had told me that the body was nothing; that the inner man never really died, but merely passed on into another place of the living. This was according to the teaching of my country and I understood it. If this was true, then he had gone to join his "Father," the Spirit of All, the one to whom we must all return.

So, why would he want his body again? Why would he want to suffer more? And did he suffer? He knew the way. He did not have to suffer. So why did they say he had? With all my heart I rebelled from the idea that he had died a miserable death. He had not taught misery and death – only life and freedom. I didn't know the truth of it. I only knew that in return for a drink of water and a quiet place to pray, he had left me the greatest gift imaginable, and I had not been able to give anything to him in his time of need.

A few days later, I went into the garden with my shears and a basin, to cut blooms for the mother of the Master, and for my own house. I was startled, for there was a man standing there, his back to me. His hair waved gently in a slight breeze, and I had a strange feeling he was looking at me, although his back was turned. I was afraid, but then he turned and it was the Master. I dropped the shears and the basin clattered onto the stone walk. I stood there and cried, sobbing and gasping, and He came and comforted me. His arm felt firm and real, his breath upon my hair was real enough. I backed away from him to see his wounds, his body, as it must be.

He seemed different, though. He was thinner, yet refined, less virile but stronger. I knew of masters who had left their bodies and later taken them up again. I assumed this was what he had done.

It is not for me to say what he revealed to us, my husband and me. But I was given a task from him that cured my pain of not being able to help him when he had needed us. He gave me a writing of his, and gave us instructions for its care. He had written five of these documents and I was given one to store away cleverly, into a safe place, until the time was right for it to be found. Only the Father knew this time but it would be found then. The other writings were to be given to other people who were traveling to other countries and these also would be entombed in various ways in order to stand the test of time and the rigors of the fluctuations of the earth.

How can I say the gratitude I felt then? I had been able to redeem myself. Somehow he had known that I needed his redemption above all things. To be forgiven and to be entrusted with something this important to him was joy beyond measure.

And I did as I was instructed.

Has the world found it yet?